LOVE IS ALL: VOLUME 7

XIO AXELROD   LEE BLAIR   SKYLAR M. CATES

A.D. ELLIS   GABBI GREY   PIPER MALONE

CHANTAL MER   RL MERRILL

SUSAN SCOTT SHELLEY   SOPHIA SOAMES

CONTENTS

HOLD ON FOREVER
SUSAN SCOTT SHELLEY

OUR FIRST LOVE
CHANTAL MER

FALLEN
XIO AXELROD

THE MAIDEN AND THE CRONE
R.L. MERRILL

THE REUNION
SOPHIA SOAMES

PIPE DREAMS
LEE BLAIR

OUR NEXT CHAPTER
A.D. ELLIS

THE EXCEPTION
SKYLAR M. CATES

FOREWORD

Six years ago, I launched a passion project called Love Is All, a queer romance anthology that raises funds for organizations that support LGBTQIA+ rights. This year, as we prepare to celebrate Volume 7, I'm so grateful for all of the authors who have participated and all the readers who have supported the cause.

I had so much fun designing the cover which celebrates this year's theme, for me: Hope and Healing. Something we all need right now.

Thank you for supporting Love Is All. Happy reading!

Don't forget to vote.

~Xio

THE BOYFRIEND ARRANGEMENT

GABBI GREY

ABOUT THE BOYFRIEND ARRANGEMENT

Felix

I should be on top of the world. I'm renovating my first real home, creating a safe place to bring Josette, my best friend and the woman I've been pledged to marry since we were infants. I'm about to have it all—a wife, then kids, and a settled life. So why is my stomach in knots, and why am I having very inappropriate thoughts about her older brother?

Jacob

My sister Josette is marrying her childhood sweetheart, and I'm busy renovating their new house. I should be thrilled for my sister. And I am. Truly. But there's always been something special about Felix, and lately, when I catch him looking at me, I can't help wondering what it would be like if this was *our* dream coming true.

This 25k novella is a best friend's brother gay romance with a shy elementary school teacher, a brawny contractor, and a wrong dream turned right.

CHAPTER
ONE

FELIX

I could pinpoint the exact day I realized I didn't love the woman I was intended to marry.

Josette Fogal was objectively one of the most beautiful women I'd ever met. Long blonde hair, sky-blue eyes, willowy figure, and a broad, serene smile.

From our early childhood, strangers remarked on how beautiful she was.

At age four, a scouting agent spotted her on a trip to Vancouver, and soon she was modelling and acting.

She hated all of it.

But I was the only one she told—and she swore me to secrecy.

I kept that promise until the day she turned sixteen. She was up for a major role on a new television series, and she was so afraid she'd get it that she'd made herself ill.

I gathered our mothers and told them.

See, our mothers were best friends. And they'd married best friends. Then my older brother Wally and Josette's older brother Jacob were born within days of each other. To finish off the fairytale, Josie was born three weeks after me.

At our joint christening, our mothers set a pledge that we'd marry.

A marriage pact, of sorts.

Made before we'd been a month old.

Something our mothers clung to.

Anyway, I told them Josette didn't want to act or model.

When confronted, she finally admitted the truth.

From that day on, our mothers started planning our wedding.

And for nine years, I'd managed to hold them at bay.

I eyed the derelict cabin in the woods as Josette stood next to me.

Well, a big cabin with three bedrooms, three bathrooms, and a massive great room. Just...it'd fallen into disrepair over the past five years since its owner died and the family fought over the property in court. So I'd been able to snap it up for a steal.

Naturally, it helped that I got control of my inheritance a week ago. Sucked that my dad died when I was fifteen, but my older brother Wally got his money when he turned twenty-five, and I got mine on that birthday as well.

Josette held out her hands as if framing a photograph. "It's charming."

I snickered. Of the two of us, she was always the optimist. "I could've tried for something in better shape, but the cost would've been much higher." I toed the gravel. "Jacob said he'd do the renovations for me. At cost."

Josette's gaze flew to mine. "My brother?" She sputtered. "Really?"

"Family and friend discount."

Her eyes narrowed.

I tried to keep from blushing, but the heat crept into my cheeks.

She laughed. "Oh, well, isn't this interesting? Cousin Bradford needed a bathroom renovation, and I think my darling brother charged a premium."

Despite myself, I joined her in laughter. "Your cousin Bradford is a stuck-up, good-for-nothing asshole. He was lucky your brother agreed to do the work at all."

She tapped her index finger to her lips. "True. I think Jacob was his third contractor."

"See? Jacob's a good guy."

I was forever defending him to Josette, who only saw an oafish, overly protective older brother who was forever meddling. I saw love.

She felt he was overbearing.

I wished someone would look out for me the way he did for her.

Oh, I loved my brother, Wally. But...he didn't notice me most of the time. He was a guy's guy. Stereotypical Canadian man—hockey-playing, beer-drinking, dart-throwing dude who enjoyed watching a game on television.

I said stereotypical because I knew just as many women like that. As well as many, many, many men who weren't like that. But when outsiders pictured Canadians, they thought of guys like my brother.

Guys like Josette's brother, Jacob.

As I looked at Josette, a profound realization struck.

I'm not in love with you.

Not the way a husband should love a wife.

This probably should've occurred to me before my twenty-fifth birthday, but I'd been sliding through life waiting for my inheritance. I'd graduated from university with a teaching degree, and taught French Immersion at Cedar Street Elementary in Mission City, British Columbia. I'd lived at home while building a little nest egg to pay for renovations and decorations of the house I'd acquire when I turned twenty-five.

I hadn't known it'd be *this* house, but I'd kept my eye on listings for years, so I had some idea. Josette and I had discussed this day hundreds of times.

Given our mothers had grown up in abject poverty, having secure futures for their children was critical. Josette and Jacob's parents helped them save money, but Wally and I were taken care of by my father's life insurance policy that provided an annuity for our mother and a lump-sum payment for both Wally and me.

Wally had taken his money and bought landscaping equipment. He'd started his own business three years ago, and now the company was a growing concern. In turn, he'd partnered with an arborist, and the two often bid for larger projects.

I liked August the arborist. Oh, and his employee, Julian. Two yummy men. Who'd recently hooked up and were now engaged.

A lot of the guys I knew were doing that. Or it felt like they were.

Which made me kind of envious, even though I didn't have anything to be jealous of. I had Josette. Now we had a house.

Everything was perfect.

Except it wasn't.

Still, we headed up the gravel driveway to the wood A-frame cabin in the woods. Well, ten acres of mostly woodland with a creek running through the back of the property. Far more rural than the identical houses we'd grown up in near the center of town.

The sturdy porch wrapped around the front of the house, and I could envision sitting on a rocker and waiting for guests to arrive.

Well, Josette's guests.

I wasn't really enamored of people.

An introvert, my mother had explained.

As she had explained that Josette, Jacob, and Wally were all extroverts—they loved being around people. Derived their energy from those interactions.

On the other hand, I'd tolerate people long enough to do whatever social obligation was required, then I'd squirrel myself away for as long as I could.

Kids were the exception to that rule. I could spend an entire day in the classroom and feel energized and contented.

Okay, but then I'd come home and crash.

I jiggled the key in the lock until the door gave way.

We'd been in here precisely once. Which meant, theoretically, we knew how bad it was.

Except we hadn't. The previous owner had been a geriatric hoarder with about sixty years' worth of…junk. I'd tried to look for antiques, but hadn't found anything. When the woman's family agreed to empty the place out, we took them up on that offer.

Now, as I looked around the cavernous space, I winced. "It almost looked better with all the…stuff."

"Nonsense." Josette stepped into the great room and executed a pirouette. "Oh, Felix, all this space. A clean slate. Think of all the things we can do."

"Well, you're the one with a design background." I eyed the thick layer of dust on the window. "You know you're free to do whatever you want. Within reason," I added quickly. We'd discussed a budget, but I'd paid attention while we watched all those renovation shows. I knew how often things ran over.

She swore they did that for dramatic effect.

I wasn't convinced.

"Okay, we're having a party on Saturday."

"What?" I couldn't possibly have heard her correctly. Today was Monday. She thought we'd have everything ready to entertain in five days? Generally, she was an optimistic soul. I hadn't thought her delusional.

"Wrecking party." Her blue eyes glinted with amusement. "We'll get Jacob to organize what needs to be done, and then we're inviting all our friends. We demo the inside and then have a barbecue and beer party." She eyed me. "Okay, light on the booze. But maybe a bonfire?"

"There are bears in these woods."

She scowled. "I know that. They're not going to come join the party, Felix. We just have to make certain we clean up afterward. Oh, and we need to get that industrial bear-proof compost thing. Wally wants us to have plenty of compost he can use when he does the landscaping."

"Uh..." I scratched my head. "My brother's doing the landscaping?"

"Of course."

"I thought we were going for the *natural* look."

She arched an eyebrow and sighed. "You still have to have a front lawn. And August is coming by to do an assessment of all the trees on the property. Wouldn't do to have one fall over during a storm and hit the house."

Given the house had been standing for more than seventy years, I had doubts about that happening. That being said, I'd hate for a tree to take out my investment. My forever home. "Right. When's he coming by?"

"Friday. You're going to invite him to the party."

My eyebrows shot up. "Oh, I am, am I? What makes you think he'll want to come?"

"Because you're going to bat your eyelashes, promise a good time, and he'll feel compelled."

"Are you suggesting I offer him…" I flushed. "Because, Josette—"

"God no." She laughed. "Invite Julian as well. Tell them it's a family thing."

"Uh… Again, work with me here…they aren't family."

"No, but Julian comes from a big one, and he'll get it. I think we went to school with one of his cousins. Oh, I should invite her as well." Even as she said the words, she pulled out her cell phone and started doing something. She was always doing something with her phone.

I often forgot mine at home.

After looking around longingly, I moved into the kitchen and pulled the paperwork out of my messenger bag.

This place was all mine.

And when Josette and I married, it'd become hers as well.

I should buy a ring or something.

Because that's what good fiancés did, right?

Except we'd never gone on a date. Never kissed. Never made out. Never had sex. And I told myself we hadn't done those things because we were saving ourselves for marriage.

Yeah, right, keep telling yourself that.

Okay, I could admit I didn't feel an attraction to the woman I considered my best friend. But did that matter? We'd build a life based on mutual affection and matching goals in life.

I wanted to be a teacher and a father.

She wanted to be an interior designer and a mother.

Those were compatible dreams.

Yet just the idea of going to bed with her left me cold.

Get over yourself. It'll be fine.

But didn't she deserve more? Didn't she deserve passion? A great love affair?

More than just a small-town teacher who volunteered at the local animal shelter on weekends.

Mission City was a stone's throw from Vancouver. She should be living in the metropolitan city with bigwig clients and grand projects. Not piddling around this mid-century cabin that was in desperate need of help.

She's a grown woman. She can make her own decisions.

Except...shouldn't I talk to her about it? Before I propose?

I didn't have an appropriate answer for that.

Josette grabbed my hands. "Oh, Felix, this is going to be stunning."

As much as I wanted to believe her, I couldn't replicate her enthusiasm. Oh well, perhaps I'd get in the spirit during the party.

CHAPTER
TWO

JACOB

My sister knew how to throw a party.

And somehow, in the process, wrangle twenty-two of our closest friends and family to help.

Our parents, Linda and Wayne, our aunt Bertha and Uncle Keller, and their three kids. Fortunately, cousin Bradford stayed away.

Asshole.

Wally and Felix, of course, and their mom, Christie.

August and Julian from the arborist company.

Isaac, the harbormaster, and Ben, an elementary school teacher who worked with Felix. Actually, Felix had probably asked them. Or Josie had. I was never sure about these things.

My sister'd also seen fit to invite my on-again, off-again girlfriend Izzie. Would've been nice if Josette had asked, seeing as Izzie and I were currently off. Still, Izzie had come with her friend Vanna who was always down for a good time. Demolition while wearing inch-long fingernails and three-inch heels probably wasn't happening.

My crew had also shown up voluntarily.

Darah, my electrician, oversaw the demo of the walls.

Agatha, my plumber, supervised the removal of old fixtures.

Niall, my general construction guy, monitored the removal of flooring.

And Curtis, my drywall guy, made certain everything removed wound up in the right bin.

Truthfully, almost nothing could be recycled, and that broke my heart. I hated adding to the landfill. That being said, my job as a contractor meant overseeing plenty of trips to that place.

I eyed Felix's neighbor, Seth, heading up the driveway wearing a tool belt.

Neighbor was a relative term—the RCMP officer's property was a good half-mile down the road. Still, he'd spotted us and offered to help since today was a day off for him.

I figured having a member of the Royal Canadian Mounted Police in our mix would keep the afterparty tame.

The cop was gorgeous—six feet, blond hair, hazel eyes, and muscular frame.

I wasn't the only one who noticed, as Izzie attached herself to him immediately.

Poor guy. Should I warn him? Nah, he seems like an adult.

Plus, maybe they'd make a good match. God knew Izzie and I didn't.

A nudge to my shoulder pulled me from my reverie.

"He's pretty cute."

I turned to find Julian, with his dark-auburn hair and soft-brown eyes. "Who?"

"The guy who just arrived. The one your ex is fawning over."

"She's not fawning."

Except she kind of was.

"He's a neighbor from down the road. Seth…something. An RCMP officer."

Julian sighed. "Well, he can arrest me anytime."

I bumped him. "I'm pretty sure he's straight, and aren't you in a committed relationship?"

"I'm allowed to look." He pressed a hand to his chest. "August isn't a jealous man."

"And if he looked?"

Julian's eyes narrowed.

I guffawed. "Oh God, you're so transparent. When's the wedding?"

"Early fall. August wanted to wait a year after his sister's passing. I thought we might honor her final wishes that he be happy, but he wanted to be respectful. Whatever, we're practically living together."

"Practically?"

"Well, he's got a nicer house, I think, but he loves spending time at my place. I've suggested he rent his place out and move in with me." Julian glanced at the gorgeous Black man examining a tree near the house. "We're fiancés, right? That would mean living together isn't a sin."

August had the cutest butt. But I was pretty sure pointing that out to Julian wouldn't earn me brownie points, and since he was the guy who'd trim and fell any trees August deemed needing to come down, I'd keep my mouth shut.

Plus, I wasn't really out to my family. Oh, Josette had inklings I was bi, but she kept that to herself. I wasn't sure how my parents would react, anyway. My mother went on and on about how Josie and I needed to marry, buy homes, and settle down. Not necessarily in that order. Knowing Mom had grown up in poverty and using that knowledge to excuse her pushiness proved trying at times.

I didn't have the inheritance that Wally and Felix received. And, given the choice between having the money or my dad, I'd pick my having Dad around every time.

Wally and Felix stood off to one side as Wally pointed at part of the porch.

Huh.

I hadn't noticed the sagging. In my notes, I had it as sturdy. I added it to the monumental list of things that needed to be fixed.

My mother kept hinting she wanted everything finished so Felix and Josette could marry in late August.

Seriously? The height of summer in British Columbia? In the middle of wildfire season, when we might be blanketed by smoke? Better during autumn. Like around Thanksgiving. The second Monday in October. Cooler. Slight chance of rain. If they kept the wedding small enough, they could do it in the great room of the house.

But no. Mom and Christie wanted a huge wedding with all the frou-frou stuff.

Josie seemed to be on board.

Felix? I couldn't get a read on him. I couldn't ever get a read on him. He seemed excited enough about the house, trepidatious about the repairs and all the people traipsing through, and generally a cheerful guy. He loved his job—I knew that much. He loved his mother and brother—although he didn't always seem to understand them.

Nor they him.

Felix was a gentle soul. Quiet and introspective. Loving and kind. No one ever got left behind when he was around. Even as children, he'd always ensure everyone got their fair share.

Wally wasn't a bully or anything like that…just not as considerate. More like a bull in a china shop.

Yet he did the most meticulous landscaping with precision and care. Almost in contradiction to the rough-and-tumble sports guy he was. He loved his rec hockey, but he'd also played football and lacrosse in high school.

Felix, to the best of my recollection, had never played any sport.

Wait…no, he'd been a figure skater before his dad died.

I wracked my brain, but couldn't remember why he'd stopped. Grief? Money?

Nope, wouldn't come to me.

But he'd been good. I remembered that much.

Julian nudged me again. "August is waving us over."

All those inner ruminations had me no closer to understanding my best friend's younger brother, but I dutifully followed Julian over to his fiancé. "What's up?"

August pointed to a tree. "That one's in really rough shape. I think a strong wind will fell it. Frankly, I'm not sure how it's still standing."

I winced. "How much?"

He met my gaze. "There are a dozen or so other trees that'll require trimming. I can give you a discount—"

I held up my hand. "That's not fair."

"Well, Wally gives me good referrals, and Josette promised to look over my house and make some recommendations on updating the décor."

Julian tilted his head. "Really?"

"Well, if I'm going to rent it out, it should—"

His sentence was cut off midstream as Julian tackled him and engulfed him in a bear hug. "Oh my God, that's so awesome. You're moving in with me. Finally."

I smiled at my friend's enthusiasm.

While he'd been out of the closet for practically his whole life, August had only emerged when his sister passed. Word filtered around Mission City, as it often did, when he'd come out. Some speculation passed through the rumor mill questioning if the two men had been together beforehand, but I knew August had decided to come out and had proclaimed his affection for his employee around the same time.

They'd been inseparable ever since.

I cleared my throat. "Okay, so, a discount?"

Julian vibrated happiness. His grin was so infectious. "I'll happily volunteer my time. Like, as a wedding gift."

"Uh, I didn't realize you were that close to my sister and Felix." I also wasn't aware their impending nuptials were common knowledge. Although I supposed since they'd been thrust together since before they could sit up unaided, most people probably knew about this promise.

August offered a more-measured enthusiasm. "I'll offer up my services as well. Wally's a good business associate."

More connections. Sometimes I marvelled at how small Mission City felt even though the population recently hit forty-thousand. We clung to the small-town moniker. Close enough to Vancouver to be useful, but far enough we were still a distinctive community.

I eyed the trees. "Well, why don't you share the good news with Felix and Josette? Not that the tree needs to come down," I quickly amended. "But that you're willing to donate the work as a wedding present."

"Their wedding is in what, two months?"

"Yeah." I removed my hat, wiped my brow, then plopped it back on. "God, I hope this heat has dissipated by then."

August slapped me on the back. "You keep wishing that. The rest of us will plan accordingly." He eyed the backyard.

The grass went back about thirty feet before the wilderness began.

Pretty damn rustic.

"They thinking of holding the ceremony here?" August looked around. "The tree canopy would be decent if you have it in late afternoon."

"Yeah, but the bugs." Julian shivered.

Both had valid points. "I'd thought maybe inside."

"The house doesn't have AC, right?"

"We're installing it."

August clapped me on the back. "You're a good brother."

"Yeah. The house has good ventilation, so they'll only need to run it on super-hot days. We're also installing solar panels on the roof and geothermal heating."

Julian whistled. "I'm not even going to ask what that all costs."

I was grateful he didn't.

Felix thought I was doing this at cost.

I wasn't. I was footing a decent part of the bill myself. I wanted my sister and her new husband to have the very best. They were making this a forever home. I intended to make it the best house possible.

"Hey, Jacob." Darah waved out one of the guest bedroom windows.

A bedroom that would be perfect for a child.

My niece or nephew.

I waved back. "On my way."

With a quick nod to August and Julian, I headed inside.

CHAPTER
THREE

FELIX

Having a police officer attend our demolition party ensured all the people planning to drive stayed sober and those for whom that didn't apply didn't overindulge.

For which I'd be forever grateful.

Josette cozied up next to me in a matching lounge chair as we sat around the firepit. We'd had an unusually wet spring, so fire bans hadn't come into play yet. But they would. They always did. And the world would be set ablaze again. Well, at least my province would.

As Josie took my hand, I tried to meet her smile. "Today we accomplished a lot."

Her blue eyes sparkled. "That we did. Jacob says if they push hard, the renovations will be done in a few weeks."

He'd said the same thing to me while shifting from foot to foot. Either his toe had been itchy or he had some doubts.

"I have one more week of school, and then I'm off for the summer." I glanced up at the starry sky—the stars I could never see from our house in downtown Mission City. "I don't know how much help I can be, but I'll be here every day."

"You and Jacob can have some bonding time."

I nearly choked on the mouthful of sparkling mineral water I'd just drunk. I cleared my throat. "What makes you think Jacob and I need *bonding time*? We've known each other our entire lives."

"Yes, but not as future in-laws. Not as the two most important men in my life."

She had a point.

Didn't make me any less uncomfortable. More peopling. More interactions. More…stuff.

"He and his crew are doing the bathroom remodel first, right? For the master bathroom? So that we don't have to bring a portapotty out." Josette considered.

"Yeah." Another expense and, frankly, gross. "Once he gets that done, I can camp out here as well."

She scrunched her nose. "You worried about thieves?"

"Building supplies do get stolen." I rubbed my arms, wishing I'd brought a sweater. "More that I want to get used to being out here. I've lived in town my entire life." My ulterior motive, though, was to start cutting the apron strings sooner rather than later.

Wally moved out when he graduated from college with a certificate in landscape architecture. He'd gone to work for a great firm until he came into his inheritance, then he'd been able to buy his own equipment and start his own business.

His old boss had wished him well, encouraging Wally to take the bigger properties outside of Mission City. Richer, more demanding clients.

Pains in the ass as far as I could figure, based on Wally's whining, but the money was damn good.

He'd recently moved from a rental apartment to his own townhouse with a down-payment he'd diligently saved to go with the remainder of his inheritance that he hadn't yet spent.

I, on the other hand, still lived with Mom.

She didn't want me to move out, and although she was here today, she wasn't happy about this.

Linda, Josette and Jacob's mother, was dropping broad hints that Mom would happily move out here to keep me company. That she'd sell her house in the city, and I could build her a cabin on the property. She'd be able to come and babysit the grandkids while I taught and Josie decorated.

Jesus.

I loved my mom. Desperately. I admired the way she picked herself up after Dad died and had striven to make the best life she could for us. How she'd encouraged us to follow our dreams and gave us money to help pay for post-secondary education. Money she could barely afford. Her annuity was helpful, but was meant for her, not to take care of us as well.

Dad hadn't been supposed to die.

Young. Vital. Healthy. Then cancer struck and he was gone within a month.

If not for the strategic life insurance policy they'd taken out when Wally was born, we would've been in dire straits.

Josette squeezed my hand.

I blinked.

"Where'd you go, Felix? You seem to be wandering off more than usual." She smiled. "And that's saying something."

Ah, yes. Felix with his head in the clouds. Felix who forgets everything. Felix who manages to get to work every day, but anything else seems beyond him.

I was accustomed to the not-so-thinly veiled criticisms.

"I'm fine, Josie." I looked around. Our friends had paired off where appropriate and were mingling with others as well.

Izzie and Vanna were gone.

I was kind of annoyed with myself for being pleased with that.

Bertha and Keller had taken their brood home after dinner.

Only Darah remained, of Jacob's crew. She and Wally were deep in conversation about something.

August and Julian sat close to Ben and Isaac, conversing about something animatedly.

Well, Ben and Julian were animated.

I found Isaac to be a quieter man. More contemplative. Apparently he used to be a lightkeeper out in Tofino. He'd once explained how that was solitary work. How he'd go weeks or months without genuine and deep interactions. Then he met Ben and, despite his love of the ocean, he'd come inland. His work as a harbormaster in Mission City on the Fraser River kept him close enough to the water that he got his fill.

Oh, and he and Ben took every opportunity to head to the west side of Vancouver Island and the ocean. In fact, they were headed there for a week of hiking when school ended.

Isaac caught my eye and raised his beer.

We often shared a little laugh over Ben's enthusiasm versus our... quietness. The man was a solid and positive presence in Ben's life. As husbands, they made a good match.

Ben, like me, was still young. We both wanted children but also agreed waiting until we were at least in our late twenties made sense.

The couple lived in an apartment in Mission City and were saving for their own place. Tough to do with real estate prices what they were.

Again, I marvelled at my house. I shouldn't have been able to afford it.

Jacob should be charging me more for the renovations.

But I pushed aside those thoughts and clung to Josette. "You're happy, right?"

Her smile faltered just a touch. "Why do you ask?"

"Well, just because you said you wanted a wedding in the woods when you were five years old, doesn't mean you want to live in them when you're twenty-five."

She laughed. "We're not exactly living *in the woods*. We'll have indoor plumbing, Felix." She gazed at the house. "It's everything I could've asked for. It's you."

"And you," I quickly added.

"And me," she agreed, although more slowly.

I wasn't convinced.

Still, when the party broke up, I accepted the congratulations from everyone.

And noticed how Jacob and Seth kept talking long after everyone had left except Josie and me.

"What do you think is so fascinating?" Josie grinned. "Do you think they might be forming a *friendship*?"

No missing the emphasis. Jacob was a lover of all people, but I hadn't gotten a vibe from the cop that he might be gay. "Don't meddle, Josette."

She placed a hand on her chest dramatically. "Moi?"

"Yes, you." I scowled. "You're way too much in Jacob's business."

She pursed her lips. "I want him to find the happiness we have."

"He's got a thriving business, dates regularly, plays rec hockey, and has close friends. Oh, and a meddling sister. What else could a guy want?"

I compared Jacob's life to mine. How could I not? I had a job I loved and the woman I was supposed to love. I had a few close friends like Ben and Isaac, so that counted for something. But I didn't play sports or, obviously, date regularly.

Twenty-five years old and still a virgin.

Josie stroked my cheek. "Soon, okay, love?"

Does she mean sex, moving in together, or marriage?

And why did all three leave me cold?

I saw the last of the revelers off. Well, helpers who stuck around for a barbecue. We'd completely gutted the place.

Jacob and his team were ready to go Monday morning.

Josette had all the design stuff organized and was ready to tackle the house after that.

I had a week of school and then the entire summer break to settle in and organize the wedding.

Well, I wasn't organizing the wedding. But Josette insisted I have some part in the planning.

She'd shown me her wedding gown.

I'd asked if that didn't violate some kind of bride/groom superstition thing, and she said no.

Whatever.

The gown she chose surprised me. Instead of poofy and princessy, she'd chosen sleek and elegant. Instead of virginal white, she opted for a champagne color. All clingy and sexy. Appropriate for a wedding in the woods? I wasn't certain, but whatever made her happy.

Honestly.

Josette talked about our wedding all the time. She had a scrapbook where she planned out her dream wedding. She even cut pictures out of what it was going to be like—the seating, the ribbons, the flowers, the location. In the past week, since I'd taken possession of the house, she'd been out to snap pictures of the backyard. Making calculations of where everything would go, I assumed.

Her scrapbook was something else. Way more than I'd ever put into it.

She had one for the house as well. Ironically, that one she didn't share with me. She wanted me to be surprised, or so she maintained. Since I was helping with the renovations—including the painting—I wasn't entirely certain how that'd work.

I turned off the last of the lights, locked the house, and headed to my car using the light of the moon.

To my surprise, Jacob leaned against it, clearly waiting for me.

"Uh, h-hey." *Did I just stammer that?* Didn't make sense, since I'd known the guy my entire life, but I suddenly felt shy.

"Hey."

"So…did you and Seth get along?" *Didn't you just tell Josette this was none of your business?*

Despite the shadows, I caught a glint of perfect white teeth. "He's a cool guy. It'll be good to have a cop just down the road. He didn't bring his husky, MacKenzie, but I said if he dropped by during construction, he might consider it. You know I love dogs. We'll have to be careful of nails and stuff, but I always am."

I knew this about him. Safety was always *the* top priority.

"Hopefully I'll be here. You know I love dogs as well."

"But your mom's allergic, right? That's why you never had one growing up?"

I winced. "And the responsibility. I swore I'd take care of him or her, but Mom was adamant she didn't want the trouble—especially after Dad died."

"Ouch." He pointed to the house. "But you can get your own dog now, right?"

"And leave them home alone all day?"

Jacob laughed. "Plenty of dogs stay home alone all day. There are ways to acclimatize the dog. I can like, send you an article or six."

I eyed him. "Why would you have them?"

"Because I considered doing it myself. But, as a single guy who works long hours, it didn't seem fair. Teachers have regular schedules, right? And I can build you a dog run, if you'd like."

"I, uh, will have to talk to Josette."

He frowned. "Yeah, I guess so. If she does her fancy designs with sculptures and artwork and frou-frou couches, you might have a problem."

"You think she'll do that?" Panic seized me. I saw this place as rustic and rural. Sure, some of the mansions up here were fancy and frou-frou, but many were just comfortable homes. I'd been looking at real estate listings for almost ten years—I'd seen a good portion of the houses up here.

Jacob cocked his head. "She hasn't consulted you on the designs?"

I shook my head. "She wants me to be surprised."

He whistled. "Well, okay, then. I think you're nuts if you're going along with it."

I put my hands on my hips. "It's her house as well. If she wants—" I scrambled for the right words but could only repeat what'd been said before. "—frou-frou and fancy, then that's what she'll get."

"You're more accommodating than I would be." He eyed the house. "You don't even have a man cave."

"A what?" I wrinkled my nose.

"A room where you can hang out with the guys. Play video games. Watch sports."

I shuddered. "I don't do those things. You know that."

He winced. "Sorry." He took a deep breath. "Master bedroom, two guest bedrooms—"

"Kids' bedrooms."

"—and three bathrooms." He frowned. "Not a lot of privacy."

"Why would I need it? Plenty of families have much less. Three bathrooms is a luxury. And the master bedroom is on one side of the loft while the kids' bedrooms are on the other."

"Josie tell you what you're having?"

I looked at him, startled. *What? Who'd have thought? Hey. No. Is he implying?*

He chuckled. "Well, she's got everything planned out. I figured she'd have that organized as well." He pushed off my car. "Gotta go. I'll be here first thing Monday morning. I know you're working, but feel free to drop by at any point."

"I'll be able to help—"

He grasped my hands, running his roughened, callused thumbs along my pristine, soft fingers.

Little tingles went up and down my spine, and my body stirred. My breath caught.

"Soft hands." His teeth glinted in his smile. "We'll find something easy for you to do."

I didn't want easy. I wanted to be one of his best helpers.

Still, when he released my hands, an odd bereft feeling settled over me.

Aside from Josette stroking my cheek this evening, when was the last time I'd been touched? Mom and Wally weren't big on showing affection.

And in a romantic sense?

Never.

But he's not touching you in a romantic sense. He's proving you're not fit for hard labor.

So true.

Then why do I want more? Why am I imagining him kissing me? Holding me? Telling me everything will be okay?

He nodded, made his way over to his pickup truck, and within a few moments was pulling out of the driveway.

I followed, but much later.

CHAPTER
FOUR

JACOB

The first day of construction always got my juices revving. I was always ready to tackle everything all at once, even though that wasn't realistic. Still, with my crew all there at seven a.m., the possibilities felt endless.

Darah tackled the electrical work in the master bathroom while Agatha and Niall took delivery of the bathroom fixtures for all three.

Felix hadn't wanted to do all three at once, but I explained it made sense to do the entire remodel in one go. So they wouldn't forever be fixing things. All three of the old toilets had issues, and I'd been happy to consign them to the rubbish heap.

As I eyed the steel, antique clawfoot tub Josie had acquired, I was kind of glad I'd hired a few extra laborers to help out. Jay and Kris were guys I'd hired before, while Gina was new to the crew. And, after about half an hour, I acknowledged she was as strong as she'd claimed. Of course, she did volunteer firefighting out of House Three up near where we were, so she'd be able to lug around about a hundred pounds worth of equipment. She also kept her cell phone close to hand in case she got a call. With the higher temperatures came dryer conditions, and structure fires became critical to put out in case sparks got into the dry underbrush or parched trees.

She eyed the tub. "Well, okay, then."

"Flooring first," Niall pointed out.

Gina turned at the sound of a truck pulling into the driveway. Her eyes lit when she realized more supplies were arriving. She did a little happy dance and headed down to meet the driver.

Niall slapped me on the back. "She's a keeper."

Eight hours later, I had to agree. Gina earned her pay and then some. So did all my crew. We worked like demons on the bathroom and, after a few problems, the entire thing was done.

I patted her on the back as we stood, as a group, on the front porch.

Kris eyed the drooping porch. "I should probably do that tomorrow."

"Yeah, we should do a quick safety survey in the morning. I did it before, but I missed that, and now I'm worried what else I might've missed." I wiped my damp forehead with my sleeve. "Okay, let's call it a day."

"Don't have to tell me twice." Gina bounded down the stairs and headed along the long driveway to where she'd parked her car on the road.

Darah nudged me, then took off as well.

The rest of the crew followed. Mine was the only vehicle in the parking area of the house because we'd had deliveries arriving all day.

Even with eight of us, this would be a tight project to finish on time. I'd cleared the decks, though, and this was the only thing we had to work on.

As Agatha drove off in her van—the last straggler—Felix's car appeared, and he drove up the driveway.

More sweat dripped down my face.

Ah, fuck it.

The workday was over, so I yanked my T-shirt over my head then stuck my face in the stinky thing so I could wipe the sweat off my face. Fuck, was it ever hot. Even up here in the mountains where we might've expected a bit of respite, we got none. Just brutal, unrelenting heat.

Felix stopped at the edge of the walkway and stared at me.

More specifically, he stared at my bare chest.

Like…huh?

He'd seen me virtually, or even completely, naked hundreds of times. My family had a swimming pool, for crying out loud. Yet he was looking at me…in a weird way.

I glanced down at my chest, trying to discern if something was amiss. Alas, just my abs that weren't quite as washboard as I'd wish, a bit too much chest hair for my liking, and no tan because Mom drilled into us how bad the sun was. Even at twenty-eight, I listened to my mother, and if that meant sunscreen, then it was a small price to pay to keep her happy.

What's he staring at?

I just wasn't certain. "You want to come see the work we've done today?"

Slowly, he nodded. "Uh, sure."

Holding his gaze for just another moment, I nodded then gestured to the cabin doorway.

He followed me in.

"Watch your step." He was smart enough to know that, but I said that to everyone stepping into my construction zone. He didn't need a hard hat, but he probably should be wearing boots instead of his shiny loafers. *I'll tell him that later.*

I gingerly led him up the stairs. We'd stripped the carpet off and pulled up all the carpenter nails. "The stairs will be one of the last things we do."

"Makes sense. You're still hauling things up and down."

I chuckled, thinking of that bloody bathtub. Well, both—the one we'd carried up and the one we'd removed and thrown away. "In here."

We'd made our way across the empty master bedroom and into the master bath.

Felix gasped.

I grinned. "Yeah, pretty cool, eh?"

"It's…" He faltered at the doorway.

"It's okay to come in. Everything's set and working."

We'd busted our balls to get it done. Well, butts, since half my team didn't have balls. Still…we'd worked so fricking hard to get this done.

"I can't believe you did it."

"Truthfully, I can't either. My crew—" I swallowed the lump in my throat, feeling an unaccustomed emotion. Beyond the normal gratitude I felt for my people. "They really like you and Josie. They want it done properly and quickly. I mean, we never dawdle on jobs, but…" I pointed. "Now, the bathtub's not hooked up, and the shower's not finished, but by tomorrow night everything will be perfect."

"Right. No showers or baths." He cut me a sly grin. "I think I can manage one day."

"Don't you swim at the leisure center some mornings?"

He offered a shy smile. "I didn't realize you knew that. Yeah, a couple of mornings a week. I was planning to go tomorrow."

How I'd known that random fact, I couldn't remember. In fact, I suspected I knew a lot on minutiae about my future brother-in-law that would fill a small part of my brain. "Well, I should be going."

"Oh." He held up his finger and retreated to his car. Within a moment, he headed back with a pizza box in his hands. "You like Canadian, right? Mushrooms, pepperoni…" He wrinkled his nose.

"You don't like Canadian?"

"No, I can't remember the other ingredient."

"I think bacon is the one you've forgotten. Although each pizzeria does it a little differently." I pointed to the box. "But they are the best in town."

A look of relief crossed his face, and he let out a little puff of air. "Yeah, I thought I remembered you saying that." He indicated his backpack with his chin. "Sodas. I considered getting beer—"

"Soda is perfect." I relieved him of the pizza box, and we walked inside.

Sawdust covered just about every surface, as Niall had cut some wood today that we'd used to shore up some areas that needed extra reinforcement. Again, I wished Felix had bought something newer, but his budget wouldn't have stretched that far. Not if he wanted to live in the country, which he obviously did.

He eyed the place. "Uh, maybe we should sit on the porch?"

I grinned. "Good idea."

We headed back outside, and within a few moments, we'd plopped onto the step, distributed pizza and sodas, and were chowing down.

Oh, he'd remembered my favorite was fizzy lemonade.

What a sweetheart.

Which is why he's the perfect guy for your sister—considerate, gentle, and kind.

As we ate, Felix tried to tuck his mushrooms onto a napkin.

"You don't like mushrooms?"

He flushed.

"Then why did you order a Canadian pizza? Or didn't at least ask for half without mushrooms..." *Because he was being considerate, gentle, and kind.*

He winced. "I forgot. Well, I remembered you liked Canadian, but I forgot they put mushrooms on it until I saw it, and..." He shrugged.

"I'll eat them." No sense wasting good fungi.

After a moment, he handed over his napkin.

I took it gratefully, indelicately shoving them all in my mouth.

He offered up his current slice which had several.

"Uh, I'm not going to touch your pizza. As it is, I didn't really clean my hands." I'd washed them but not scrubbed them yet. I hadn't handled anything toxic or bacteria-carrying, so I wasn't worried.

He caught his lower lip in his teeth.

I grinned. "You can feed them to me."

His eyes widened. Then, after a moment, they narrowed. "That feels like a trick of some kind."

"Never." Even as I said the word, I flashed to all the pranks I'd pulled over the years on various friends. As well as on family, such as Josie.

But never on Felix.

Had I always known? How sensitive he was? How easily he might be hurt? Even before his dad died, he'd been a quiet and introverted guy. So unlike Wally, Josie, and me. We were all loud, boisterous, and mischief-makers.

I reconsidered. Josie tempered that impetuousness when she was around Felix.

And, if I was honest, so did I.

Wally was the only one who didn't seem cognizant of his younger brother's delicate nature.

Slowly, Felix pulled a mushroom off his pizza.

I opened my mouth and angled myself so he could drop it in.

He did.

Our gazes met.

He giggled and pointed to my chin.

"What...?" I swiped. "Oh, cheese."

"You want the others?"

"I want everything you're willing to give me."

Even as I said the words, the misinterpretation opportunities popped into my head. *Sexual innuendo? Really?*

And yet clearly Felix didn't see it that way. He gathered the remaining pieces of mushroom—less than a mouthful—and offered them to me.

Guileless deep-brown eyes stared at me as I took the mushrooms into my mouth. Slowly, I closed said mouth and chewed mechanically.

What the actual fuck, dude? Are you crushing on your sister's fiancé?

That shook me out of the trance. "I should get going."

"You haven't finished your drink."

"It's in a bottle, so I can just take it with me." I eyed the sky with the slowly setting sun. "You going to be all right out here by yourself?"

"I've got a tent, an air horn, and bear spray."

I didn't like the sound of any of that. "Not a lot of help with coyotes." Or determined bears, for that matter. "Are you sure you don't want to come home with me? I've got a spare bedroom…"

"The insurance company says someone has to be on the grounds for the homeowner's policy to be valid. Plus, I'd hate to have someone come along and steal everything."

I wasn't positive about the insurance, but yeah, getting everything stolen would suck. Of course for someone to know there was stuff to steal, they would've had to be scoping out the property and, this far from town, that wasn't really a thing.

After securing the cap to my soda, I rose.

Felix leapt up as well. "Here, take the leftover pizza."

All of one slice. We'd devoured it. Well, I'd eaten five slices, and he'd eaten two. I comforted myself that he'd bought a medium so the slices were smaller, but the rest of me admitted I was starving and hadn't been forward looking to going home alone and whipping up something to eat.

Probably would've done drive-thru.

Yeah, but that *cost* money, and I was trying to *save* money. "You sure you don't want it?"

He glanced at the woods. "Better to not tempt fate. I've got a chocolate bar if I get peckish."

I almost laughed at the word *peckish*. Partly because it was just so Felix and partly because I thought of the word pecker, which got my cock perking up and taking notice. Oh, that might also have been because of the super cute guy sitting next to me. "You'll be okay?"

He nodded, meeting my gaze. "Yeah, I'll be fine. Don't worry about me."

Yet, even as I drove back down the long, winding driveway, I knew I would.

CHAPTER
FIVE

FELIX

The end of the school year always made me melancholy.

Saying farewell to my students as they headed off to their summer break.

Saying goodbye to my fellow teachers as they scattered in many directions.

Saying adios to the administrators who held the place together.

Most of all, I disliked the idea of being rootless for two months. I'd applied for a school in the next town over that ran classes all year long with several weeks-long breaks scattered throughout the year. I hadn't been accepted, but Cedar Street Elementary school had been happy to snap me up.

I'd landed where I was meant to be.

"Hey, Mr. Stevenson."

Angus Braun, my favorite student, waved. Yeah, I wasn't supposed to have favorites. But with kids like Angus, that adage proved difficult.

"Hey, Angus." The young boy's deep-brown eyes spoke of a soulfulness few his age held. His mother died when he was five, and then his father when Angus had been all of eight.

The handsome man who stood next to him was his uncle, Stanley. Both Stanley and his husband Justin were very involved in Angus's education.

With my pupil being so bright, I'd chosen to give him extra work to keep his mind occupied.

Angus ate it up.

Stanley extended his hand. His brown eyes matched Angus's, but his dark-brown hair was liberally peppered with serious amounts of gray. He held a young girl, maybe five years old, in his arms.

"This is Opal." Angus pointed. "She's my sister."

"Uh..." Stanley frowned. "Well, sort of..."

I arched an eyebrow. None of my business, but the guy looked a little confounded.

"We're fostering her."

"Like, forever." Angus put his hands on his hips. "That makes her my sister."

Articulate, even at ten. He was my brightest student in the fifth-grade class.

Stanley cleared his throat.

"Angus, why don't you make sure your desk is cleared out?" I offered a smile.

He glanced between the two of us. "I get it. No-kids discussion." He pointed off to the corner. "I want to play with Kylie, anyway."

"Yes, that's great." Stanley indicated the young girl at the other end of the playground. "Oh, and isn't that Adam there as well?"

"Yep." Angus started to stalk off.

"Take Opal with you."

Where I expected my student to complain, he waited patiently while Stanley set the young girl down.

He grabbed her hand and headed off to join the group of kids.

I turned to Stanley.

"Opal's mother has...problems. We thought she was getting help, but she wasn't. And now she's taken off, and there's a warrant for her arrest."

"Ouch."

"Yeah. And we're trying to figure out how much to tell Angus. I mean, my husband's a counsellor who's getting his PhD in child psychology, and he works at Healing Horses Ranch with another child psychologist—"

"Adam's mom?"

"Yeah, Denise Lang." He rubbed his forehead. "Angus loves Opal. Considers her a sister. But social services might take her away." He sighed yet again. "Or they might not."

"Whatever you need me to do, just let me know." I wasn't certain how I could help—especially since Angus wasn't going to be in my class anymore.

"I think...I just needed to tell someone else, you know? All our friends are invested. They all think we should just adopt Opal, but it's not that simple."

"And this is breaking your heart." I might not know the man well, but even I could see the strain and pain.

"Yeah. That." He ran his hand over his short hair. "Oh, and we're going to be neighbors, and—"

"What?" I gaped. Like mouth dropping open.

"You bought the old Graman property, right?"

"Uh, yeah..."

"Well, your house is next to Maddox and Ravi's." He cleared his throat. "Maddox might be my ex, but we don't talk about that."

Uh, awkward. "Okay..."

"We live a couple of properties down. About half a mile. Angus bikes between the two houses, so he'll be riding in front of your house. I just wanted you to know so you wouldn't be surprised."

"How did you find out?" I squinted.

"Well, your realtor is Cadence Crawford. Cadence helped me buy my property, and we're kind of friends and, well, you know..."

A lot of trailing sentences in this discussion. "I guess there isn't really realtor/client privilege."

Stanley's eyes widened. "I didn't mean for him to get in trouble."

I offered an impish grin. "No worries. Especially now that Angus isn't in my class anymore. Point out my property and let him know he's welcome anytime. As long as he tells someone where he's going," I added.

"He's got a cell phone and instructions on how often to keep in touch." Stanley shook his head. "They grow up so damn fast."

"Yeah. This is my second year teaching. In a couple of years, those first kids will be off to high school."

Stanley snickered. "You're young, Mr. Stevenson."

"Please, call me Felix."

"Yeah, I can do that. And it's Stanley."

Since I'd been calling him that in my mind this entire time, it didn't require much of a mindset shift. See? Letting go of this school year already.

A cry from the group of kids caught our attention.

Before I could register anything, Stanley sprinted away. For a guy who was almost fifty, he moved fast.

I followed at a more sedate pace since he was already at the kids' side.

He swept Opal up into his arms.

"Is she okay?" Angus's brow furrowed. "She tripped." He caught my gaze. "Honestly, we didn't push her."

"I'm sure you didn't." Stanley brushed her hair from her face.

Adam and Kylie looked just as bewildered.

"Papa," Opal wailed, wrapping her arms around Stanley's neck.

My heart took a knock. I wanted that. A kid of my own.

And I couldn't fathom the uncertainty Justin and Stanley faced with Opal's future up in the air. How would I cope if I cared that deeply for a child who might be taken away at any moment?

Well, as long as Josette and I were able to have children of our own, I wouldn't have to face the uncertainty that foster parents faced. And although Stanley was Angus's uncle, he and Justin had adopted the boy, offering all the protection they could.

Oh, Opal had scraped her knee. Didn't look too bad, but looks could be deceiving. "Would you like me to get the first aid kit?"

Stanley shook his head, pressing another kiss to Opal's temple. "We should be heading home. I'll take care of it there." He smiled at Angus. "Everything's going to be okay. Say goodbye to Mr. Stevenson."

Angus turned to me. "Goodbye, Mr. Stevenson."

A lump caught in my throat. "Goodbye, Angus. You can always talk to me, okay? Even if I'm not your teacher."

"Yeah, I know that." Angus gazed up at Stanley. "Just like I can always talk to my dad."

Stanley blinked.

I hadn't realized, although I probably should have, that Angus referred to his uncle as his *dad*. Likely it wouldn't have registered until I had the two before me.

"Papa, home." Little imperious Opal.

"Yes, darling, home."

Angus scooped up his abandoned backpack, and the family headed out.

That. That's what I want. Teaching kids was great, but I wanted some of my own. And I assumed Josette did as well. Although I probably should check with her on that assumption.

An hour later, as I pulled into my driveway, my heart sank when I spotted her car.

Jesus, she's your fiancée, you should be excited. And I was…to a certain extent. I was also tired and looking forward to having a burger with Jacob. Every night this week, I'd brought home fast food, and we'd sat on the porch and eaten together while I'd recounted my adventures of that day and he'd give me an update on the renovations.

Truthfully, I was in awe. Josette liked to watch renovation shows with me, and those projects always took weeks or even months.

Jacob maintained my needs were simple, and that's why he'd be done at the end of next week.

That felt fanciful but, as of tomorrow, the master bedroom would be finished, and I'd be sleeping in the bed instead of in the tent.

I hadn't told anyone of my irrational bear fear.

Well…not irrational. Just because there hadn't been a bear attack in years didn't mean they wouldn't take a swipe at me, given half a chance.

"Felix." Josette waved from the porch where she stood next to Jacob.

The front lawn and street were empty of vehicles save Jacob's pickup truck, so obviously his crew had knocked off for the day.

Feeling like an idiot, I carried the bag of food along with the drink tray, with just two drinks, up the steps to the front porch.

Jacob caught my eye and gave me the *what can we do about her, she's my sister* look that I now realized he'd been giving me for years.

A warning?

"Oh, you brought dinner." Josette nabbed the bag and opened it. "Two big burgers and onion rings?" She wrinkled her nose.

Jacob snatched the bag from her. "Felix brought that for me. He's taking you out to dinner."

I blinked. "Uh, yeah. Stavros's?" At least I wouldn't need reservations at the best Greek restaurant in Cedar Valley.

Josette put her hands on her hips.

Jacob rescued the drink tray I was about to drop.

"But I wanted to go over the decorating with the two of you." She offered a little pout that was, frankly, adorable.

I could never refuse her anything.

"We can stow the burgers and onion rings in the fridge." I eyed Jacob. "Then we can do the interior decorating stuff, and then the three of us can go to Stavros's." The restaurant wasn't all that romantic, so the three of us hanging there wouldn't be too weird.

No, not weird at all.

Oh God.

Why did I feel like Josette was the third wheel? Because I'd looked forward to being alone with Jacob?

Quite possibly.

Quite probably.

And that was all kinds of wrong.

CHAPTER
SIX

JACOB

As I looked over Josie's swatches, a feeling of unease settled over me. I couldn't pinpoint the exact reason. Except this wasn't what I'd expected. Josie was a frilly girl. And sure, she decorated for her clients' aesthetics and not her own, but I expected…more white, flowers, and pink.

I wasn't going to speak up, though. Josie knew what she was doing. And her bold color palettes looked spectacular. The master bedroom had dark colors like navy blue, hunter green, royal purple, and deep burgundy. The bathrooms were gray, light blue, and an oatmeal that shouldn't have worked, but did. Even the shower curtains were devoid of frill.

This was the opposite of her apartment.

When she showed us the dark gray for the living room, I had to speak up. "Josie, this seems…dark."

She grinned. "With the amount of sun this room gets, it'll pop. And even on dreary days, the paint will reflect in the lamplight."

"Okay." I wasn't sure what any of that meant. "But…you're going to do floral accents, right? For the cushions and drapes?"

"Oh, drapes." She squealed. "I've ordered slatted blinds for all the windows, but I want blackout drapes for all the bedrooms. Despite the canopy of the forest, all but the north windows are going to get plenty of light. Don't want the little ones waking up before they have to."

Ah, the Josie I expected. Making little comments about the kids they were going to have. They only had two spare bedrooms, but I could easily build an extension. She'd once said she wanted ten. I had my doubts, but they'd need to get going on that pretty quickly, unless they planned to adopt.

Come to think of it, I wasn't certain how many kids Felix wanted. I just sort of figured he'd go along with whatever Josie wanted. We all just sort of went along with what she wanted.

When she pointed out the dark cabinets and slate-gray backsplash in the kitchen, I had to speak up. "Really, Josie?"

She spun to me.

"Where are the flowers? The frilly? The lace?"

Felix also looked at Josie, his brow furrowing in that cute way it did when he was also super confused.

Josie smiled. "That's not the style for this house." She waved her arms. "This is a cabin in the woods, not a condo in the city. If you want flowers, you can do that in accents." She turned to Felix. "Are you not happy with these choices? Because we can totally change things up."

Felix looked helplessly between the two of us. "Uh, no, I think these are great selections." His gaze locked on mine. "I think Jacob's worried that you're taking my likes into consideration, but not your own."

She eyed the two of us. "I know what I'm doing. Unless you're unhappy…"

"No." Felix scratched his forehead. "I'm really happy. This is exactly what I would've chosen."

I could see that. Sand, forest, and mountains were all represented in the colors. The earthy feel suited their nature paradise. Maybe I shouldn't have said anything. Except it'd be a pain to change everything around once they'd settled in and Josie had second thoughts.

"Okay." She hugged her design binder to her chest. "Dinner at Stavros's. My treat."

Felix frowned, again catching my gaze. "That's generous, but—"

"No buts. I aced an interview and I want to celebrate."

"That's great." He grinned but, to my surprise, didn't touch Josie. No hug, no kiss, no physical interaction of any kind. Come to think of it, for engaged people, they sure didn't show a lot of affection. *They're not engaged, and maybe they're not demonstrative.* Okay, they hadn't exchanged rings, but we all knew the wedding would come soon after this house was ready. And Felix often came across as a little shy, but Josie was boisterous. She often hugged me, Wally, and anyone else in her vicinity. So why not Felix?

None of your fucking business.

After Felix locked the house, we all got into our separate vehicles and headed to downtown Mission City.

Luckily, we nabbed the last three spots in Stavros's parking lot.

I arrived at the host's station first and requested a table for three.

They had a booth available and, within moments, the three of us slid in.

Before we'd even opened our menus, our server arrived to take our drink orders. Felix chose soda, Josette opted for water with lemon, and I indulged in beer. Only one since I was driving.

I sat across from the happy couple and gave them surreptitious glances as I decided on a couple of gyros. Felix would have gyros, and Josie would have a Greek salad with a side of bread. We were nothing if not predictable.

After the server had returned with our drinks, taken our food order, and removed our menus, I offered a smile. "So, Felix...sleeping in a proper bed."

He blushed.

Which was kind of adorable.

"Yeah, thanks for that. Not that I minded the bears for company, but I like the idea of not having to keep the bear spray close at hand."

Josie giggled. "You know, you'll have to figure out some way to make it safe for when the kids want sleepovers outside."

Felix frowned. "Kids?"

"The gaggle of kids you're going to have." She patted down her hair. "I don't know if a fence is feasible. And you'll need a system to contain the dogs."

"Dogs?"

He appeared mildly distressed, with a furrow in his brow.

"Well, of course you're going to have dogs. All kids need dogs. Don't worry, you'll figure out how to handle it."

Wait. Not once had she said *we*.

I nearly called her out on it, but tonight didn't feel like the time or place. "So, what interview did you nail?"

As I'd hoped, that launched her into a long discussion about some opportunity that at once felt specific, but also felt weirdly vague. I assumed the job would be in Vancouver and was about to seek clarification of that when our food arrived.

During the meal, Felix told us about an interaction with a parent. Something about maybe not being able to keep a foster child the man and his partner had cared for. I also figured out Felix's favorite student just lived down the road and, now that Felix was no longer the boy's teacher, that he could interact more freely with the kid.

I was definitely glad Felix would get to know some of his neighbors. And having the cop down the road wouldn't go amiss either.

"Okay, I have to go." Josie leapt up, quite unexpectedly. She pressed a kiss to my cheek, squeezed Felix's hand, then headed to the host stand. Presumedly to pay.

"Well…" Felix eyed me. "She seems really happy."

"I think she is. She loves her fashion-design work."

He scratched his stubble that was barely visible. "Right. Well, I'm going to head out."

For a moment, I thought he was going to kiss me on the cheek. But he didn't. Instead, he nodded and then beat a hasty retreat.

That was weird.

I contemplated eating dessert, but didn't want to do so alone. In a moment of inspiration, I texted Julian. Immediately, an invitation arrived.

After ensuring Josie had paid the bill, I hopped into my car and headed over to Julian and August's home.

August had finally agreed to move into Julian's place. Josie had updated and decorated his old home, and now he rented it out.

In some ways this felt slow because they'd been together for months now. In other ways it felt fast because August had said he was going to wait for a year after his sister's passing. Ironically, although I'd always seen Julian as the impulsive one, now that he'd decided to move, August had taken the reins in getting them settled properly in Julian's house. Or maybe I shouldn't have been surprised—August was a take-charge kind of guy. Hence running his own arborist business for years.

In a moment of odd candor, he'd also admitted his sister died suddenly, leaving him over a billion dollars from some app she'd designed, and that he'd started a charitable foundation in her name. He'd found a woman to run it, apparently someone very competent, and he took a hands-off approach, just reading the reports and making decisions when pressed to do so.

As I drove into the suburb where Julian lived, my brain kept swirling. Every time I tried to push Josie and Felix out of my mind, they wormed their way back in.

Well, mostly Felix.

I grinned when I pulled up to the house and found both August and Julian sitting on their front porch, gazing out over the setting sun. I exited the car and walked over to them. "Too late for a visit?"

Julian leapt up, strode over to me, embraced me, then slapped me on the back. "Never too late for friends."

August rose, a bit slower. "Can I get you a drink? We're just having hot chocolates."

I gazed around, acting dumbfounded. "Dudes, it's the beginning of summer. Did you not sweat all day?"

Julian slung his arm around my neck.

Of course, I had to hunch a bit, given he was shorter than me.

"Nights are still cooler." He grinned. "Hot chocolate? We could always add some rum?"

"You have rum?"

He gazed upward. "Well, no…"

"Then I'll happily stick to the hot chocolate."

"Great, I'll get it." He indicated his seat. "Keep my fiancé company for me, eh?"

I plopped and sighed.

August smiled. "You just come to hang or are you going to talk about what's really going on?"

"Uh…" I chewed my lower lip. "I just came to shoot the shit."

"And maybe talk about the night of the party."

I hadn't seen the men since then. "I honestly don't know what you're talking about."

Julian popped out of the house, handed me the mug of hot chocolate, then sat on the steps, looking incredibly relaxed in a distressed Vancouver Whitecaps T-shirt and cargo shorts. August, on the other hand, wore khaki pants and a button-down shirt.

I eyed him. "You work as an arborist."

He snickered. "Yes, I do. Except when I'm expected to attend meetings with the woman running my sister's foundation. Some kind of board meeting where I was expected to put in an appearance."

"You must miss your sister."

He blinked. "Yeah, I do. I really do. But days like today, where I see how much good her money's doing for the community, I feel like she's here in spirit. Giving me a boost and reminding me why putting on a shirt for a few hours isn't the worst thing in the world."

I couldn't fathom it. As much of a pain as Josie was, I couldn't imagine my life without her.

Julian squeezed his husband's ankle. An oddly intimate gesture. "Nia's here in spirit. Now, you." I glanced at me. "You solve your love-life problem yet?"

"Uh…" Again with the inability to be articulate.

August chuckled, "Julian, I don't think he realizes."

Julian snickered. "How his future brother-in-law kept staring him at the renovation party and during the bonfire? Or how our friend here kept staring back? Poor Izzie was completely ignored."

Now it was my turn to snicker. "I didn't ignore Izzie. She kept hitting on that cop."

"Seth," August supplied.

"Right." I sipped the warm goodness. "And Felix was staring at Josie—"

"Bullshit." Julian coughed the word out. Then gave me the most unrepentant grin I'd ever seen.

"He's right." August sipped whatever was in his mug.

My friend didn't drink, so it was likely hot chocolate as well, as they'd said.

"I think your Felix might have a crush on you."

"He's not *my* Felix."

August and Julian exchanged a long look that I struggled to interpret.

Then August laid his hand on mine. "I think we need to have a serious talk."

An hour later, I took off for home, even more confused than when I'd arrived.

CHAPTER
SEVEN

FELIX

I glanced at my co-worker Nita, as we sat on the patio at Starbucks, and cocked my head.

She grinned. "What?"

"Huh. Your brother Kade is gay."

"Duh."

"Your best friend Tanner is gay."

"Double duh."

"But they've never dated?"

She shivered with a wince. "No. Although I love them both, some guys just aren't meant to hook up, even if they might be compatible."

"Compatible?"

"Don't make me say it."

"Oh." Realization dawned. "So one likes—"

"Yes."

"And the other prefers—"

"Oh my God, yes, and since I don't want to think about my brother and gay sex, maybe we should move along to another topic?"

I laughed. "Nita, you brought it up."

"Because you keep talking about your future brother-in-law, and I keep wondering if you get that."

My laughter died. "He's my contractor. At the moment, I'm spending more time with him than Josette. But that's about to change. We've set a date for the wedding."

Nita eyed me. "You know, we've worked together for quite some time now."

"With Ben. I know. We all started about the same time."

"And I'm a plainspoken woman."

Duh, as she would say. "I appreciate that about you." And I did. When I was struggling in my chosen vocation, I often turned to Ben and Nita because they'd give it to me plain. And they were both around my age. We were the youngest teachers in the school. The newest. The greenest.

She took a deep breath, sipped her iced coffee, and regarded me. "I've met someone. And I haven't told anyone. Not even Tanner. Which is proving interesting since we share a house together. I mean, he knows I go out on dates with guys, but he doesn't know who."

"Okay. Would there be some objection?" I couldn't fathom where she was going with this.

She shrugged. "I don't know. Honestly, I don't. I mean, my parents wouldn't care. Neither would Kade nor Tanner. But his family…"

I wanted to ask more, but didn't want to rock the boat. I was working on the assumption that Nita's heritage was an issue. She was white, like me. Some families didn't want interracial marriages. To me, that was all kinds of wrong. It also wasn't incumbent on me to change the world. I could do my part, though, by teaching my children tolerance and love. I grasped Nita's hand. "I'm sorry you're going through this."

"It might not last, anyway."

Yet I heard the catch in her voice. She cleared it. "We're here to talk about you."

"And the wedding? I'm hoping you'll attend. Ben and Isaac have already said yes."

"Felix?"

I nodded.

"Do you realize you never talk about Josette?"

I stifled my knee-jerk argument and took a moment to let her words sink in. I replayed all the times I'd spoken to her over the last few months. School, the house, my car, the state of the education system in Canada, and British Columbia in particular, universal healthcare and — "Huh."

"Right. I mean, she's the woman you're going to marry. And I'm not saying that you're not entitled to keep your life private. Like I have," she added quickly.

"But I…" I almost said *love*, but I knew that would be a lie. "I care for Josie deeply. We're meant to get married."

"Do you love her, Felix?"

I scrunched my nose. "What's love, anyway? My mom loved my dad, and he died. We make the best with what we have."

"Does she love you?"

"Uh…" I closed my eyes, replaying the past few encounters with Josie. Hell, the past twenty-five years. When we were kids, she used to hug me and tell me that she loved me. That'd stopped when we hit grade five or so. I couldn't remember why, but I was certain there must've been an excellent reason. "Well, I assume so."

"You know what they say about assumptions."

"Well, sure. If you want to get all authoritative on me."

She snickered. "Felix, you're a great guy."

I eyed her. "Yeah?"

"But sometimes you don't see what's in front of you."

"Is it safe to assume you're going to elaborate?"

"Only that you spend more time checking out Isaac's ass than you do looking at my breasts."

I choked on my lemonade. After sputtering a bit, I wiped my hand across my mouth and then swiped it across my khaki pants. A little too warm for the weather, but we were meeting fairly early. I'd change later. And, why she'd suggested meeting this early, when we didn't have to get up for school, was something I probably should have questioned. I blinked back the tears. "I don't look at any woman's breasts—"

"That's my point."

"Because it would be rude. Good Lord, Nita, my mother taught me to respect women."

"Do you even know the size of Josette's breasts?"

"I cannot believe you just asked me that. I don't know sizes—"

"Large, medium, or small?"

A strangled sound escaped my throat.

"Well, mine are medium."

Despite my best intentions, I glanced. She wore a T-shirt that molded to her...breasts. "Uh..." I wracked my brain to picture Josette. We'd gone swimming a couple of months ago. Had I noticed her figure at all? "She's...slender. And short. Like, way shorter than Jacob."

"Right." Nita sipped her drink. "Josette has high, firm, and small breasts."

How am I supposed to respond to that?

"Isaac has a nice round ass."

This time, I didn't sputter. "Isaac and Ben *are married*. I would never look at a married man."

"But you'd look at a single one? Because I have to say that Cadence Crawford is an attractive man."

"My realtor?" I frowned. "He's gay?"

Nita snickered. "Yes, he's gay. Although I keep wondering if he's seeing someone on the sly because I haven't seen him out on a date for more than a year. Heck, maybe even two."

"Maybe the guy's discreet."

She clearly considered. "Yeah...no. He likes guys. A lot. Dated a couple losers, saw a few nice ones, but never went for long without being with someone."

"And you figure he's seeing someone."

"Yep."

"Okay, then why did you bring him up?"

"Oh, have you met Septimus Knight? He's an architect."

"And?" I was struggling.

"He's gay."

I blinked. "I'm still not understanding."

"Heck, your future brother-in-law is bi."

This, at least, I knew. "I'm marrying Josette."

"But you're…"

I waited.

"Oh, Felix, I love you. You know that, right?"

"Sure."

"But I think you're a little gay. Or a lot gay. And I'm not outing you or anything like that. We never have to talk about it again. But I'm worried that you're marrying Josette out of some kind of obligation and that you're not really thinking about this clearly. You both deserve happiness. You also need to be honest with her. I mean, have you folks even…you know…"

"No." I shushed her. "Don't say stuff like that."

"I didn't *say* anything." She sat a little straighter. "I implied it. And if you can't say *fuck*—"

"Oh my God, you did not just say that."

"Say what?"

Nita and I both turned to find a newcomer approaching. I recognized him instantly. As I should. Since he was my dentist. And as much as I would've called him Dr. Johns, he was adamant he was just *Cam* when I wasn't in the torture chair.

Sorry, dental chair.

While I smiled, Nita grinned. "Just in time."

Cam arched an eyebrow. "For what?"

"I was telling—"

"Nita."

She kept right on going. "—Felix here that sex is an important part of marriage, and—"

This time, Cam cleared his throat. With his dark skin, I couldn't tell if he was blushing. But he was clearly uncomfortable. "Are you certain…" He glanced around. "Okay, at least there aren't any kids."

Nita snickered. "Teacher's instincts. I *always* know when there are children around."

Since I had the same instinct, I didn't call bullshit.

"I'm saying Felix should reconsider his plan to marry Josette."

Cam gazed at me as Nita's words settled. "I didn't realize you and Josette were engaged. I mean, I'm not exactly plugged into the gossip network—"

Nita snorted.

Both of us gazed at her.

"Oh, please. Your receptionist is Kyla, and we all know she's the biggest gossip in town."

"Dental office manager."

Nita snorted again.

Cameron glared. "What?"

"She's a glorified receptionist. Now, I'd never say anything to put someone down—"

This time, I snickered.

And she glared at me. "But Kyla went to school with us, and I'm amazed she figured out how to type."

"That's cruel." I whispered the words.

She rolled her eyes. "She'd say the same damn thing. Those thumbs get quite a workout."

Cam cleared his throat. "Yes, she does spend an inordinate amount of time on her phone. But the billing's done correctly and patients like her."

Nita said, "I wonder why," so only I could hear.

I was going to assume that had something to do with Kyla's looks. Not that I'd ever really noticed. Which was maybe the point Nita was making...

Cam eyed me. "What's Nita nagging you about?" He asked his question in the nicest tone possible. He wasn't ragging on Nita for nagging me. Which was sweet of him.

"I'm suggesting that he might not be ready for marriage to Josette." Nita gazed at me with an intense stare. "That he might not ever be ready for marriage to a woman." Then she looked at Cam. "You know what I mean."

His eyes went wide. "Uh, I have no idea what you mean."

Quick on that denial.

"Like with Kade." She nudged his arm. "I love my brother, but I'm not sure he's the marrying kind."

"He might meet the right man," Cam argued.

"As long as it's not Tanner." Nita winced. "Like I said, I love my brother. He's not a *forever* kind of guy. Tanner is." She eyed me. "You are too—with the right person. I'm sorry, but that person's not Josette."

Cam excused himself so he could go grab a coffee before heading into the office. As he expressed his regrets at not being able to stay—which I questioned the sincerity of—I took advantage and slipped away.

Only as I was driving out of the parking lot, did I realize I didn't have the coffee I'd meant to grab to take back to Jacob. I got into the line for Tim Horton's drive-thru and ordered an extra-large coffee for him—double, double, of course. I ordered a large for myself since I'd dumped my half-drunk cup of lemonade in the garbage in my haste to get away from Nita. Then I ordered a mix of a dozen donuts so I could take it to the construction crew. Within just a few minutes, I was off again, this time heading back into the hills.

As I drove north, I parsed Nita's words. Clearly, she thought I was gay.

Well, I wasn't.

Because I hadn't had gay sex. Hadn't even kissed a man.

I winced. Yeah. But if one of the kids in sixth grade told me they were gay, even though they'd never acted on it physically, would I tell them they weren't gay? That they had to wait to have sex with someone of the same gender to know for sure?

Of course not. One could be gay without having gay sex. And, frankly, gay sex didn't weird me out like it did for some guys.

Also, I hadn't kissed a woman either. Not Josette or any other female-identifying person.

And why is that?

Because I'm marrying Josette.

So maybe shouldn't you, I dunno, kiss Josette?

Oh, shut up.

Yet as my car ate up the miles, I kept circling in my mind. What if Nita was right? I wasn't afraid of being gay. I just had thought of myself as more asexual. I didn't really think of anyone *that* way. I guess I assumed, when the time came, that I'd find a way to make it work with Josette. Clearly this entire situation was a bigger problem than I'd imagined.

And I had no idea how to solve it.

CHAPTER
EIGHT

JACOB

Felix's arrival this morning bearing both the nectar of the Gods—coffee
—and a pile of donuts, had me thinking all kinds of thoughts about
him. Not sexual, of course, but of stuff like how generous he was. How
he always thought of others.

How, to the best of my knowledge, he'd never made a move on my
sister.

After our impromptu snacks, Felix tackled painting the master
bedroom while Darah fixed the wiring in the kitchen, Agatha fixed the
plumbing in the downstairs bathroom, Curtis did the drywall in the
laundry room, and the rest of my crew—including myself—tackled the
flooring for the upstairs.

We stopped for lunch, discussed appliances and whether the
Vancouver Canucks had any possible chance of making the Stanley
Cup next season, and then we got back to work.

In the afternoon, Gina worked with the HVAC guy to install everything needed so the house would have air conditioning with the heat
pump. Seventy-some-odd years ago, when it'd been built, that hadn't
been a thing. Today? With climate change? British Columbia often

baked during the summer. Even the northern parts were seeing hotter days. Down here, near Vancouver, there had been many temperature records broken over the past few summers. Scientists weren't predicting we'd get cooler, or even go back to normal, so Felix needed his house to have air conditioning. And tomorrow we had a guy drilling a three-hundred-and-fifty-foot well in the back yard. The current one was too shallow and often ran dry in the hottest summer months.

And Josie. How could I forget my sister and her impossibly long showers? We were also installing hot water on demand so they'd never run out.

"Hey, boss, it's quitting time."

I glanced up from where I'd been laying the laminate floor to find Niall, Curtis, Agatha, Kris, and Gina all staring at me from the bedroom door. I surveyed the room, ensuring I hadn't somehow screwed up. I hadn't. "Yeah, sure. Thanks for today."

"Felix got the master bedroom painted. Looks pretty good." Gina yanked on her ponytail.

"He should be able to do this room tomorrow."

"Wouldn't it have been better to get him to paint before you put the flooring down?" Curtis snickered.

"Possibly." More like probably, but we were plowing through this reno with breakneck speed. "Thanks. We'll see you later."

Kris saluted, then led my crew down the stairs. That was a job for tomorrow as well.

I rose, removed my kneepads, and went in search of Felix.

As predicted, the bedroom was done, and the soft, muted gray looked amazing.

Felix sat in the center of the room, flipping through Josie's design book.

"Hey, what's up?"

He glanced up at me. "I don't know. Something feels...off."

Feeling awkward as hell, I decided to sit across from him. "Talk to me."

After a moment, he flipped to a page near the back, and spun the book to face me. I frowned. "I don't get it." An arch of flowers was backdropped by a forest. In the foreground, what was clearly a minis-ter, and a groom stood. "Okay, so this is how she envisions her wedding."

"Okay, but wouldn't you think, I don't know, that the bride would be in the picture?"

"Well, you'd think. But isn't there some superstition about the groom seeing the dress before the wedding?"

Felix snickered. "You see Josette as a traditionalist?"

I cocked my head. "In some respects, yes. Like I believe she believes in 'til death do us part." I rubbed my nose, a little itchy from the plaster dust. "I think she'll make a brilliant wife. Just like I think you'll make a great husband."

Another snicker.

Annoyance rose within me and my chest tightened. "You don't think you'll make a great husband? You're kind, compassionate, and caring. You defend the weak and stand up to bullies. You protect those around you. Finally, you've seen the darker side of life, and yet you still have a positive attitude. It takes courage to keep going after a tragedy—"

Felix closed the book, moved it to the side, turned back to me...and lunged.

I caught him, because he was a lightweight, but momentum had us crashing to the ground. I didn't hit my head, but that was sheer luck. Before I could ask what was going on, Felix's mouth descended on mine. I could've stopped him, of course. Could've made a joke. Or even forcefully pushed him off. I didn't, of course.

Because I wanted him apparently as much as he wanted me. I opened my mouth to welcome his tongue. He grasped my hair in his fists while I adjusted our bodies so they aligned. So I could feel his hard cock pressing against my own burgeoning erection. Okay, so at least I knew he could get it up. I'd sort of started to worry because he never appeared physical with Josie. As he continued to tug my hair and frot against me, I had no doubts left. I grabbed his perfect ass to hold him in place as I canted my hips so I could push up against him.

He pulled away, but only enough so he could meet my gaze. "Please, I need..."

I waited, but he didn't finish the sentence. Which was, for me, the deciding factor. If he couldn't articulate what he wanted, I certainly wasn't going to try to give him something that might not be what he intended. Very slowly, I eased him off me.

He made a sound low in his throat.

A moan? A whine? A whimper? Although I was uncertain, I wasn't going to seek clarity either. *This is so very wrong.* I pushed him off me. Maybe with a touch more strength than I should have as he plopped onto the floor.

This time, he didn't make a sound.

I rose, standing over him and pointing. "You're gay, and you're going to marry my sister anyway? You're going to break her heart." The words lanced through me. I'd do anything to shield my sister. She drove me nuts and brought out every protective instinct within me. Usually at the same time.

Felix scrambled to his feet. "No. But she's planned our life out for twenty years. If I don't go through with the wedding, that will break her heart. And what about our moms? What are they going to feel? I will just marry Josette and pretend everything is fine. We'll have kids, and she'll be happy, and so will I."

Anger roiled through me. Against my better judgment, I stepped into Felix's space. Without warning, I snagged his erect cock and squeezed.

None too gently.

He whimpered.

I gazed into his dark eyes. "You ever get hard like this for my sister? You ever want to take her to bed and ravish her? Or, fucking hell, even just make sweet love to her? Hell, Felix, have you ever kissed her?"

He didn't answer. He didn't need to. The answer was written right across his features. No, he hadn't done any of those things. Nor had he ever felt the urge to. That was plain as day.

I removed my hand from his cock.

He pressed a hand to his chest. "I want to love her. Hell, I do love her. Just…not in *that* way. I've never…" His cheeks flushed scarlet.

Oh for fuck's sake. "You've never gotten hard for anyone, have you?"

The shaking of his head was accompanied by a purely miserable expression of pain. He blinked repeatedly.

"And it just had to be me." Said more to myself, yet he nodded. I sighed. "What are we going to do about it?"

"Nothing." He held out his hands as if trying to placate me.

It wasn't working.

"I'm going to marry Josette. We're going to build a life here. We're going to raise a family and grow old. Our mothers will visit all the time and be happy grandmothers. They'll forget about the pain of their childhoods because we'll make them so happy."

"And how, precisely, do you intend to get Josie pregnant if you can't even get it up for her?" I'd thought his coloring couldn't go more scarlet. I'd been wrong. Puce was apparently a thing.

"Uh…"

I waved my hand impatiently.

"Like…drugs…"

I arched an eyebrow. "You're twenty-five years old, and you're going to ask Dr. Raymond for boner drugs?" Our doctor was in his mid-forties and, although pretty progressive, would likely struggle with this one. *You need to stop this.* And yet, I wouldn't. Far more people would be hurt if Josie and Felix didn't go through with the marriage. Both took their vows seriously. They'd make a family. Somehow. And that wasn't any of my business. "Well, I'll be back tomorrow to finish off the flooring in the spare room."

"I was going to paint it tonight."

Offer to help. "Yeah, great. Well, see you later." Before I did something stupid—like offering to show him how things should really be between two people who were attracted to each other, I bolted.

An hour later, as Wally and I battled for supremacy in ball hockey on the street, I knew I'd made the wrong choice.

"Jesus, Fogal, get your head out of your ass and play properly. You're unfocused." He leaned on his stick. "Or does some girl have your attention?" He tapped the ball on both sides, never letting it roll away.

"Uh..."

"Oh, like that is it?"

"Well..."

Wally eyed me. "Okay, it's a guy, isn't it? You're always more intense when you're seeing a guy. Which, as you know, is so not my thing. But each to his own. If you want to have some guy stick his dick up—"

I cleared my throat.

"Right, or you stick your dick—"

I coughed.

Finally, Wally glanced behind himself. He waved. "Hey, Ma, how's it going?"

Christie waved back. "You boys want some lemonade?"

Since I lived in a condo and Wally lived in a townhouse, we had to come to his mom's place when we wanted to play hockey on the streets. Somehow, playing in the schoolyard didn't feel the same. Quintessentially Canadian meant playing in the road and dragging the net to the side when a car drove by. Christie lived on a cul-de-sac, so we hardly encountered any cars.

"Only if it's got vodka," Wally shot back. "Jacob's got girl troubles." He grinned. "Oh, sorry, boy troubles."

I advanced on him and without warning, bodychecked him. Then I got the ball and shot it into the net. Finally, I glanced up to meet Christie's gaze. "Not this time, Mrs. Stevenson, but thank you. I need to be getting home. Early up, you know?"

"Your mom says you're doing a great job on the renovation, that's very kind of you."

Instead of responding, I merely nodded, then grabbed one of the nets.

Wally sighed and grabbed the other.

Only when I lay in my bed that night, did I admit the truth.

I wanted Felix.

Had for years and years. When he'd hit puberty, late, I'd finally noticed him in *that* way. But I'd shelved those thoughts. He was my best friend's younger brother. He was practically engaged to my sister, although they were just fourteen at the time.

Years of suppressing those desires hadn't yielded any great results. I'd dated any number of men and women. But none had ever been *right*. Now I knew why.

None had ever been Felix.

His sexual aggression today had come out of left field. We'd been talking about the fact Josie's wedding picture didn't show the bride, and the next thing I knew, he'd been on top of me. And it'd felt so fucking good. In fact, I probably could've taken him right there and then. With little to no persuading necessary on my part. For all my bravado when I talked to Wally, I took sex seriously. Aside from keeping a packet of lube and a condom in my wallet, I also didn't fuck just anyone. I might not be overly picky, but I also rarely did it on the first date. I liked getting to know a person—their quirks, their interests, their dreams.

You know all that about Felix.

Goddamnit, that was so fucking true. In fact, before today, I'd have said I knew Felix as well as I knew Wally or Josie. He was an open book. I had the answer key.

Or so I'd thought. Now, though, I knew nothing.

And that scared the shit out of me.

Because, here in the dark, I could admit what I'd suppressed for years.

I was in love with Felix.

CHAPTER
NINE

FELIX

As I sat on my bed, I reflected over the last month.

Renovations finished? Check.

Decorations completed? Check.

Wedding date set? Check.

My heightened state of stress had my stomach continuously in knots. I'd assumed Josette would want an extended engagement period. She didn't. Heck, I couldn't even pinpoint the moment we'd agreed on a wedding date. She just told me to show up on the first Saturday of August. My tuxedo sat on a hanger in the closet. With all my other clothes. Today was the last Sunday in July. The day of our engagement party.

Josie had yet to move her things into the house. Something about superstition…I thought…? Everything just seemed to pass me by these days. Wally had insisted we go out for a bachelor party last night. When Ben, my teaching friend, found me in the bathroom throwing up, he and Isaac, his husband, shepherded me home. Wally, Jacob, and the other guys had stayed at the Springs Brew Pub to, apparently, close the place down. Meanwhile, Ben coaxed me into bed and Isaac made some kind of special tea with ginger to calm my stomach.

I'm having an engagement party today. Except that hadn't really sunk in. I'd spent the last month getting the house organized, but Josie kept me away from wedding-planning stuff. I probably should've cared. But I hadn't.

A knock on the bedroom door caught me by surprise. I rarely closed the door since I was the only one living here, but probably Ben and Isaac had done it before they'd left. And my front door was likely unlocked as well, although that wasn't much of a concern in these parts. "Uh, come in."

The door opened slowly, and a blonde head popped around the corner.

My breath caught until I realized Josette had come.

And my stomach clenched when I acknowledged, if only to myself, that I'd really hoped it was going to be the other Fogal.

One month. Of longing, pining, and knowing it would never happen. One month of wishing I could be the man Josie needed, while knowing I should be backing out of this arrangement. Thirty days of struggling over the fact that not only was I gay—that'd been pretty obvious in retrospect—but that I was in love with my fiancée's older brother. That hadn't been so clear in my mind until the moment I'd landed on top of him, after admittedly tackling him, and knowing—in my gut—that I was meant to be with him.

Josette blinked several times. "You're not okay, are you?"

I managed to push off the bed. "I'm fine. The party's not for a couple of hours, right?" I glanced at the clock radio. Had I messed up the time?

"You're right, it's not for a bit." She bit her lower lip.

My stomach twisted. Did she know? Had she figured out how I felt? How I wanted Jacob and not her?

"We need to talk." She tucked a lock of hair behind her ear.

"Right." And because breaking down into tears wasn't an option, I stepped toward her.

She held up her hand.

I halted.

"What I have to say…it's going to hurt you, Felix, and I'm more sorry than I can say about that."

My mind raced. How could *she* hurt *me*? I was the one who wasn't in love with her. I loved her—with all my heart—but I wasn't in love with her. Not remotely like what I felt for Jacob, and wasn't that just a kick to the balls? More effective of a libido killer than summarily being pushed off someone while you were finally enjoying an erection brought on by them. We'd spent the last month pretending it'd never happened.

I'd never forget, though.

Her obvious distress pulled me from my own spiraling thoughts. "It's okay if you hurt me. I'm a big boy. I just hate seeing you like this."

More biting of her lower lip. "I'm leaving."

"Okay." My mind raced. "But you'll be back for the wedding, right?"

She motioned her hand in a so-so gesture. Her blonde hair swung lightly around her heart-achingly beautiful face. "No, Felix, I'm going for good. Well, not forever. I don't think. Although I can't be certain. So…maybe…?"

"Josette, what's going on?"

"I sent my portfolio to a count in Europe. Swear to God, an actual count."

Okay, that sounded fishier than hell, but I didn't stop her.

"And he liked my work. So much he's invited me to his castle in Romania, and I'm going to redesign the interior."

I arched an eyebrow. "I'm pretty sure there isn't nobility left in Romania." I didn't actually know this, but my gut told me this was a ruse. A quick internet search, though, would clear everything else up.

"Well, it isn't actually a title, at this point. But his family's owned the castle for hundreds of years, and it used to be entitled."

"Okay." I waved my hand. "Let's say this is legit—"

"I have a contract."

"That I hope you showed a lawyer."

"I did. My friend Susan's dad is a corporate lawyer. He looked it over and then talked to someone really important in Europe. The deposit has already been put into my account."

What the hell is going on? I couldn't wrap my mind around it. "So you're just jetting off to Europe? To be with some old dude and to make his castle look spiffy?"

She blinked. "I thought you believed in my talent."

I snagged her hand. "Of course I do. You know I do." I gestured around the room, attempting to encompass the entire house. "I love what you've done here, Josie. You made this old derelict place into a home."

Well, you and Jacob.

Wrong thought.

I took a deep breath. "So this Romania thing is legit?"

She nodded. Then opened her mouth, almost spoke, then closed it again.

"Just say it, Josette. Better I know now than find out later."

"Well, uh…" She winced. "He's not exactly old."

I arched an eyebrow.

"He's about Jacob's age."

So just a handful of years older than us. "Are you attracted to him?"

She blushed pink. "Of course not. That would be wildly inappropriate."

More inappropriate than her flying to Europe and staying with this guy while she decorated his house? I couldn't wrap my mind around this.

"Okay. So we'll put off the engagement. If you're not back by—"

"I'm not marrying you, Felix."

My stomach dropped out, a feeling of dread overtaking me. "We promised our mothers."

She blinked. "I know." She scrubbed her face. "Okay, so maybe I can turn him down. Or…like you said…come back after I'm done. You'd be willing to wait?"

In that instant, I knew. I saw both her life and mine clearly—our futures—and the worlds didn't intersect. She wasn't meant for small-town living in a rustic cabin with me. I wasn't meant to pine over her and wait for her to come home. I drew in a deep breath and let it out slowly. "I'd wait, Josette. But that's not really what you want. You might not stay in Europe, but we both know your talents would be wasted in Mission City. You're destined for greater things—and I think we both need to acknowledge that."

She blinked, as if bringing me into focus. "You're relieved."

Now I winced. "Never doubt that I love you, okay? But I love you like a best friend. Not as a man should love a woman. Not as a husband would love his wife. I'd have done right by you. Never question that, okay? Yet…you're right." Possibly the hardest words I'd ever uttered.

"Oh, Felix."

She held her arms open, and I stepped into her embrace. Like coming home. Like I felt when my mom or Aunt Linda held me. Protected and treasured.

Eventually, I pulled back. I smiled as I swiped at her tears.

She bit her lower lip. Then she ventured to speak. "What would you do if I moved away?"

"Uh…"

"Be honest, Felix." Her blue eyes held a wariness.

Go for it. "There's a guy…"

She nodded as if she'd expected this response. As if she'd known I was gay. Might that be part of why she was headed to Europe? Because she'd known we were never going to be compatible?

"I didn't know I was gay. Or that I am gay. Or that I might be gay."

After a moment, she pressed a finger to my lips. "I have to say I'm not surprised."

"Because we haven't made out?"

She smiled kindly. "Because you've never looked at me that way. And I appreciate you would've married me and we would've had kids and life would've been amazing, but that's not what we were destined for."

"Is this count going to treat you right? Like the precious and wonderful person you are?"

"Of course."

Yet I caught a flicker of uncertainty in those blue orbs. She wasn't one-hundred percent certain. But she was going anyway.

She grabbed my hand. "So there's a guy?"

I winced. "Well, I tried to, um…"

"And he rejected you?" She squeezed tightly.

"Possibly because I was engaged to you." Past tense. We were no longer obliged to each other. Didn't mean Jacob would come running over here and proclaim his undying love to me. But I was allowed to dream…right?

She blinked. Several times. Not as in trying to keep herself from crying, but as in trying to bring something into focus. "Jacob?" Her voice might've gone a little high on her brother's name.

Heat raced up my chest and into my cheeks.

"And he rejected you." Now she sounded pissed.

"In fairness to him, he's your brother. He knew the date was pretty much set."

"How long ago?"

"Like…a month?"

She again squeezed my hand, this time, painfully. "You are two of the most stubborn, pigheaded—"

"Hey." I needed to stop her. I didn't mind being called those things —because I could be—but I didn't want to hear her criticizing her own brother.

The man you love.

Well, yeah, that was true.

She tapped her toes. "So, if not for our moms, and their obsession with us getting married, would you be sitting here considering marrying me?"

I closed my eyes. "Probably not."

"And if Jacob were here right now, asking you to be with him, would you?"

"He won't."

"Not the question, Felix."

A choked laugh escaped me. "Would I turn him down if he asked me to go out with him? Absolutely not. Will he ever do it? Absolutely not. Josette, he made his feelings crystal clear."

"Because he was being my stubborn older brother."

Given I had a stubborn older brother, I couldn't argue that Jacob was as bad as Wally.

"Okay, I want you to stay here."

"Why? Don't we have an engagement party?"

"I'm going to call it off."

Relief like I'd never known rushed through me. "Okay." Then guilt beset me. "Shouldn't I, you know, help or something?" Like, be there to support her? Let everyone know I was happy for her.

She shook her head. "Leave this to me."

That didn't sit right with me, but I'd leave the decision up to her. My entire life, I'd been deferring to her. Why stop now?

She pulled me in for a hug.

We were close in size, and she felt right in my arms. As a friend. As a confidante. As someone I'd always care for, but never love romantically.

After she'd left, I flopped onto my bed, then curled into a little ball. The great debate of whether or not to turn off my phone didn't even materialize as I slipped into the sleep that had eluded me for the past month.

CHAPTER
TEN

JACOB

As I stood on Felix's doorstep, my stomach twisted.

The last hour had been close to insanity.

The next few minutes were likely to be the most consequential of my life.

With Josie's words in my mind, I knocked on the door.

Nothing.

Knocked again.

Nothing.

Pounded.

I had raised my arm again when the door flew open.

Felix, hair mussed and a little disheveled, stood before me. Before I could evaluate the wisdom of my actions, I pushed into the house. Then I hauled him into a massive hug. He felt small in my arms, reminding me of the difference in our sizes.

The sound of high heels clacking on the porch was all the warning I got before the door closed.

Slowly, Felix pulled back.

I gazed into his eyes, but found them only a little hazy. Not red, as I'd first imagined.

We turned, together, to face Josie.

I eyed my sister. "Okay, you said he needed me."

"He does." She pointed to Felix. "Tell him."

Before me, Felix turned a bright shade of scarlet.

"Look around the house, guys."

Together, with my arm still supporting Felix, we did a slow survey of the great room with the living area as well as the kitchen and dining room. Everything was exactly as she'd said it should be—right down to the placement of the throw pillows and wool blanket she said was for cold, rainy days.

"Uh, Josette, I'm confused." Felix huffed.

It always startled me when he used her full name. He always did, while I only ever did it when she pissed me off. Which was admittedly less and less over the years.

My sister sighed. "I designed it for you."

Felix pressed a hand to his chest. "Right. For us."

"Yes."

"So I'm—"

"You and your future partner. And yeah, until today, I wasn't positive it'd be my brother. I mean, you've barely got your head out of your ass while Jacob's is still firmly planted—"

"Josette." Apparently she could still piss me off. More because of her implication Felix had done anything wrong. I never worried about myself. I wasn't the sensitive one. I drew in a deep breath. "You and Felix aren't getting married."

"Nope."

"You designed this house for Felix and me?"

"See, I know you're a little slow, but you get there eventually."

I chose to ignore the barb. "And so now, what, you expect Felix and I to…?" I couldn't finish the sentence. Because over the past month, all I'd thought about was how I wanted to *fill in the blank* with Felix. Kiss? Fuck? Marry? But it'd all been out of reach, so I hadn't gone there. Like, at all.

So you tell yourself.

"I'm moving to Romania in just over a week. I'll be here for the wedding." She held my gaze. "Go for it, big brother." Then she walked away. Right out the door, down the porch, to her little green sedan, and off. Likely heading back into town.

My head hurt. Slowly I pulled away from Felix, who I'd still been supporting with my hand against his lower back. I shut the front door, then leaned against it. "So, you two aren't getting married?"

"Nope." Felix blinked those huge dark-brown eyes several times. Like he couldn't quite believe what had just happened either.

"And Josie's not brokenhearted about it?"

"Nope." He shrugged. "Like she said, she's off to some castle in Romania. Which I think sounds a little suspicious, and I hope you're planning to do some due diligence to follow up on this count guy before she actually flies to Europe."

My head spun. I'd do what he suggested. At the moment, though, I had a more pressing issue. "And you're not brokenhearted about it?"

"Nope." Not a flicker of disappointment in his gaze. Aside from still looking a little sleep rumpled—had he been taking a nap? —he appeared completely unconcerned. But he'd had longer to absorb this, since Josie had come here first.

"Right. But our mothers are still expecting a wedding?" As much as I'd worried about Felix's feelings, our mothers' hearts were right up there in my concern.

"Yep."

We just stared at each other as the moment hung in time.

I cleared my throat. "You do have a cheerful house. It's very big."

"Yep." His monosyllabic answers gave nothing away.

"You still want to get married in the middle of the woods?"

"Yep."

Slowly, ever so slowly, I saw my life before me. It didn't scare me. In fact, I wasn't certain anything had ever felt so right. Again I cleared my throat. "Will you be upset if I ask your brother to be best man? I mean, he can be best man for both of us, can't he?"

"Are you proposing to me?"

No hint of his feelings about this. If he hadn't jumped me a month ago, I doubted I'd even be saying these things. Still… "Maybe. Do you want to be proposed to?"

Felix shrugged. "I don't think I actually ever proposed to Josette. Everyone just thought we were getting married. So, uh, do you mind if I do the proposing instead?"

"I fucking well don't care, as long as you fucking well get on with it so we can get to the kissing part."

"Oh. Okay."

To my shock, he got down on one knee. I towered over him but the surprise overrode most of the discomfort.

Most.

"Jacob, will you marry me in the woods with your sister as maid of honor and my brother as best man and our two mothers crying copious amounts of tears? And then will you live with me in this cabin. Together? And have kids?"

This time, I blinked. And not so much from confusion—although that was part of it—but because I was holding back tears. Everything I'd ever wanted but hadn't known I wanted, was before me. I knelt to join him.

He rolled his eyes.

"Yes. To all of it. I didn't think I could have those things, but I say *yes.*" I winked, "Okay. Can we kiss now?"

"Oh my God, yes, please."

I rose, gently guiding him up with me. When we were upright, I cupped his cheek and drew him close. Where I expected his eyes to drift shut and for us to enjoy a nice, languorous kiss, he wrapped his arms around my neck, grabbed my hair, and yanked me down to him.

He plundered my mouth with his tongue, demanding in a way I would never have predicted. He thrust against me in a way that pretty much assured me he hadn't done this before.

In response, I placed my hands on his hips to hold him steady.

A low moan came from his throat. He pulled back, gazing up at me. "I want you. I thought you wanted me, too."

"I did. I do." I drew in a breath. "But last time, we were wrong to do anything—"

He ducked his head. "I said I was sorry."

"And I know you were. But we could've really hurt my sister. Neither of us knew she had this planned." I swept my arm to encompass the room. "It's a lot to take in."

"Yeah, I suppose." He eased his hand from around my neck and started to pull away.

"Hey, I didn't mean it like that." I snagged his hands and pulled them to my chest. "I'm just saying..." I hesitated. "Tell me if I'm wrong, but you don't seem very experienced."

He pinkened.

"Yeah, okay. So there's nothing wrong with taking things slow."

He blinked big brown eyes up at me. "What if I'm no good?"

My heart broke a little. "First, I won't be comparing you—"

"Well, that's good." Just a touch of sarcasm.

I smiled. "We have to do things our own way." I drew my finger down his smooth skin. How had I never seen him this way? Or had this attraction always been simmering just below the surface? I grasped his cheeks in my hand and drew him into a kiss.

This time, I did the plundering. I thrust my tongue into his mouth, searching out the recesses. Slowly, he eased himself against me. This time, I didn't try to hold him away.

Capitulation.

And, as he brushed his erection against mine, I knew. Not just the physical—although that was pretty awesome—but that this was the way things were supposed to unfold. He'd always been destined to marry a Fogal. I just had to make certain *I* was the Fogal he chose. I also had to hope he felt the same way.

I cupped his ass.

"Please, Jacob." He pulled away from the kiss to nuzzle my neck. "I need to know."

Which pretty much confirmed what I'd known—not only had he never done anything with Josie, he'd never done anything with anyone else. My mind screamed *slow down* while my cock demanded *now, now, now.* We had to land somewhere in the middle. I'd have to figure out what to do.

In turn, I bent my knees so I could nuzzle his neck.

He arched it back, giving me full exposure.

I'd never before wanted to claim in this primal way. I held back, though, deciding with my last functioning brain cell that sending him into the world with a hickey might not be the brightest choice.

His hand trailed down my chest and lower still. It stalled around my waist.

Ah. I snagged his wrist and gently guided him lower.

He curled his fingers around my denim-clad erection and squeezed.

I saw stars. And reveled in the headiness of knowing he'd never done this with anyone before. "Can I suck you?"

"Is that, like, a blow job?" The dark brown of his irises were nearly invisible with the blown pupils.

"Uh, yeah, that would be a blow job."

He dragged his lower lip through his teeth. After a long moment of holding my gaze, he nodded.

I kissed him again. Long and sweet. All the while, I meandered my hand down his chest, past his abdomen, and to the button on his jeans.

More time passed before he nodded.

Taking that for the assent it clearly was, I unbuttoned his jeans, then drew the zipper down. Good thing I was dexterous, seeing as I did it with one hand. The other still grasped his hair. I slid my hand under his boxer briefs so I could get my skin against his.

He sucked in a breath. "Cold."

I laughed. "You don't seem to mind."

"Uh, no." He pressed into my fingers. "The callouses are so sexy."

Not something I'd ever heard before, but I liked the playful side of Felix that I didn't see very often. *Have to bring that out more often.* I met his gaze. "I'm going to give you your very first blow job."

Then I dropped to my knees.

CHAPTER
ELEVEN

FELIX

My first thought was to worry about Jacob's knees against the hard laminate floor.

My second thought was that I'd never done this before.

My third thought was worrying about reciprocating and whether I'd be able to manage.

My final thought, as he took me into his mouth, was that thinking was highly overrated.

The warmth and wetness of his mouth against my cock sent shivers up and down my spine. The suction he created when he hollowed his cheeks stimulated my senses. I swayed a little, placing my hand on his head for balance. I caressed his soft long hair with shaky fingers. In my mind, I'd idly wondered over the years about blow jobs. And could never envision Josette giving me one. Maybe that should've been my first clue.

Except I hadn't envisioned Jacob giving me one either.

Now, though, I saw my life flash before my eyes. Not what had passed, but what was to come. With a certainty I felt to the marrow of my bones, I knew we'd make this work.

And not just because he gave amazing head.

My balls drew up in a manner I recognized. "I'm coming."

Barely a croak, but as he doubled down and sucked harder, I interpreted that as permission to come. And I did. Spectacularly. Hard. With tingles racing through my body.

Eventually, when I truly had nothing left to give, he pulled off me. My limp dick didn't like the chilled air hitting it, but that thought was lost when he rose, snagged the back of my neck, and drew me in for a soul-searing, teeth-clashing, tongues-duelling kiss.

I tasted something odd. Oh, right, my cum. Something I'd never tasted before. I'd been idly curious, but was now glad I'd waited. Another first I could share with him.

Boldly, as the kiss lingered, I drew my hand down his chest. When I got to the button on his jeans, I undid it.

He pressed his hand to mine. He pulled back and met my gaze. "You don't have to do anything."

I pretended to pout. "So you get all the fun?"

"Uh, well I guess that's one way to look at it."

He guided my hand, so I tugged down his zipper.

Then he coaxed my hand under the fabric of his boxer briefs.

I'd held a cock before—my own—but I'd never caressed another man's. I marvelled at the drop of precum. Fisted his dick in my hand and gently squeezed.

Breath hissed from his lungs. "Yeah, that."

"May I..." I meant to ask about reciprocating with a blow job, but he snagged my hand and guided me to jerk him off. In the back of my mind, I worried about friction burn, but his movement suggested he was far beyond caring.

A few tugs later, he spurted over my hand and roared a release.

My cock stirred. I did that. To him. And something told me this was just the beginning. Thinking of all the things he could do to me, and all the things I could do to him, brought tears to my eyes.

I was twenty-five and had missed all of this.

Except sharing it with someone I wasn't in love with would've been wrong. Obviously, I needed a connection. I needed someone I truly loved.

Huh.

Okay.

Yeah.

I loved Jacob Fogal. And somehow I needed to tell him before—

His phone rang. He met my gaze. "They can wait."

"It might be important. After all, my engagement party was supposed to start in…" I glanced at the clock. "Twenty-three minutes?" My scrambled brain couldn't figure it out.

He wiped his hand on his T-shirt and grabbed his phone from his back pocket. He winced before swiping. "Hey, Josie." A pause. "Sure, I can put you on speaker."

In no way did he look pleased about this and, I suspected, if it had been any other day, he would've refused.

"Hey, Felix."

"Hi—" I cleared my throat after the croak. "Hey, Josette."

"Right. So, I hope you got your jollies off."

I coughed.

She giggled. "Yeah, I figured. Don't forget the party starts in twenty. I can hold off the hordes for a bit. At least shower and change so you don't show up smelling like spunk—"

"Jesus, Josie." Jacob winced.

Another laugh. "Yeah, that's what I thought. I know you keep a spare pair of underwear in your glove box. Shower and be here in… forty minutes?"

The drive would take eighteen…

"Okay, Josette." I hit the end call button. "Like holy shit. You grab your underwear, and I'll get the shower going."

"Separately. You better be out by the time I get there. You don't need to wash your hair."

He was right, of course. I dashed upstairs while he headed out to his car.

Miraculously, we arrived at their parents' house only eight minutes later than his sister had demanded. He parked his truck on the side of the road, almost a block away, because the street was full of vehicles. Yet we didn't get out.

After a moment, he snagged my hand. "This is going to change everything."

"I know."

"Is this really what you want? Because it's not too late to back out."

I gazed into his ocean-blue eyes. "Are you having second thoughts?"

"Fuck no. I mean, when I woke up today, I didn't think I'd be getting engaged to my sister's fiancé."

A laugh escaped my chest.

He kissed my knuckles. "But I also have zero regrets."

"Then, let's go." And with more bravado than I felt, I leaned over and gave him another of those toe-curling kisses.

We exited the truck, headed into his parents' house, and chaos ensued. But a good chaos. The kind where everyone pretended they'd known this was going to happen all along. The kind where our moms embraced us with hugs and tears. The kind where Wally took me aside and asked if this was really what I wanted and where Jacob's dad, not so quietly, gave him the lecture about how to be a good husband.

Several hours later, Jacob drove me home.

In silence.

Because, really, what was there to say?

We didn't make out, as I'd hoped. Instead, Jacob gave me a peck on the lips and a promise we'd *make up for it* next weekend. After the wedding.

That promise, along with the panic over my upcoming nuptials, kept me prowling my house the entire week. Although I spoke to Jacob every night, we didn't actually manage to see each other. I couldn't decide if this was some nefarious plan to give me blue balls, or if, as he said, he was busy finishing off a project so he could take time off with me after our wedding.

I believed him when he said that. Because Jacob didn't lie to me. Hadn't ever, really. Despite the fact I kept questioning his love for me, deep inside, I knew he wouldn't lie about that either. He was a good man. Despite Josette's machinations, if he hadn't wanted to tie himself to me for the rest of his life, then he wouldn't have. He'd have found a way to let me down gently.

Instead, each night, he talked about our future. About the trees we were going to plant. About the garden he wanted to build for me. One the deer couldn't get into. About the kids we were going to have.

Oh, and the dog. I wasn't allowed to forget the dog. We had plans, once we were home from our honeymoon, to visit the animal shelter. And we'd keep visiting until we found the perfect companion. Or two, Jacob said. Because we worked all day, the pooches would need company.

I should've been overwhelmed. Everything was happening so damn fast. Except everything also felt so damn right.

Saturday morning dawned bright, with pink streaking across the sky and puffy white clouds meandering along. The meteorologist predicted sunny skies with only a hint of wind. Given how tightly Josette and our mothers had tied down the arch, I didn't figure the thing was going anywhere.

Jacob had built it, of course, weeks ago. Thinking he'd be standing off to the side while watching his sister marry me. Instead, he'd be front and center with Wally by his side and Josette by me.

Somehow, the champagne-colored silk gown she'd chosen was appropriate for a maid of honor. Not really suited for a bride at all.

More proof that had never been her plan.

A knock sounded on my bedroom door. "Come in." I continued to struggle with my tie.

Wally stepped behind me.

Our gazes caught in the mirror.

"Turn around."

I did, pinkening a little that I couldn't even tie a bow tie.

In mere moments, Wally had it straight. "Mom and Christie are holding court downstairs. You should probably consider coming down, though."

I bit my lower lip. "Is Jacob here yet?"

Wally snickered. "Josie's decided it's bad luck for you to see each other before he walks down the aisle. I don't understand this whole walking down the aisle thing myself."

"When you meet the right woman, you'll want her to walk down the aisle to meet you as well. To pledge herself to you."

"You're worried he's not going to show."

"Of course not." *Yes. So that.* "He said he'd be here. Jacob's never let me down. Plus, I think Josette would kill him—given how much work she's put into this."

My brother chuckled. "Yeah. And I'd probably kill him too. For breaking your heart." He feathered my hair. "You really want this?"

"Yeah, I do."

He eyed me. "I suspected you were gay. Or maybe bi, since it seemed like you and Josie were going to tie the knot. And I'd have supported you," he quickly assured me. "Just like I'm supporting you now. You being gay doesn't bother me. Jacob being gay doesn't bother me either. Kind of wish I'd known, though."

"You never said homophobic things, Wally, if that's what you're worried about."

The look of relief on his face, including the little smile, assured me I'd nailed his discomfort.

"Look, I probably should've known I was gay. Just...I never really felt physically attracted to anyone. I thought something was wrong with me—"

Wally cleared his throat. "But you and..."

"Yeah."

"So you're..."

"Yeah." Heat crept into my cheeks. "Well, not entirely—"

He held up his hand. "Yeah, that's all I need to know. I wouldn't want to know about you and Josie any more than about you and Jacob. You're my younger brother. We used to take baths together." He punched me lightly in the arm. "And look at us now."

I tilted my head. "You'll meet someone."

"Yeah. Maybe. In time." He didn't look convinced, and today wasn't the time for this discussion.

I made a note to have it later.

Laughter filtered up from the backyard.

"I think I'm ready."

Wally straightened my jacket lapels—which I was quite certain didn't need straightening—and grinned. "Yeah, I think you are."

About thirty people mingled in my backyard, many holding drinks.

The day promised to be pretty hot. Good thing Josette had planned a midday ceremony. I'd be able to shed my jacket soon after the photos were taken.

Mom was the first to embrace me.

I cleared my throat. "Thanks for holding down the fort."

"We figured you needed time." She pointed to Christie, who was trying to wrangle Opal, our flower girl.

Justin and Stanley's daughter was just the cutest thing ever.

Angus just grinned. He had infinite patience for the little girl.

Justin was conversing with Nita and Tanner while Stanley was deep in conversation with Ronald, Jacob's father.

August and Julian stood off to one side, examining a tree.

Ben and Isaac held hands and gazed intently at each other.

Other friends filled in the spaces, including Jacob's crew—looking all spiffy and presentable—as well as Aunt Bertha, Uncle Keller, and three of their kids. Oh, phew. Cousin Bradford was nowhere to be seen.

Josette appeared by my side. "The officiant is ready." Her blue eyes sparkled. "Are you?"

I stood a little taller. "Yeah, I am."

She pressed her lips to my cheek. "Great. I'll get Opal settled, you stand by the arch, and your groom will be joining you in mere moments."

Okay, this shit's getting real.

CHAPTER
TWELVE

JACOB

Opal made it down the aisle. She didn't drop any of the rose petals Josie had meticulously organized. Basically, the little girl sprinted to Angus, who waited for her.

Our friends and family cheered.

She appeared startled.

Stanley snagged her up and cooed, avoiding a potential meltdown.

Felix stood under the arch with our officiant, the inappropriately named Lolita.

Josette stood beside him, looking beautiful in her dress.

Wally stood on the other side, imploring me with his gaze to get a move on. Yeah, he was looking forward to the barbecue lunch we'd organized.

Mom linked her arm through mine. "Ready, darling?"

I met her gaze. "Yeah." Then I looked over at my father. "Thanks for this." Not just for their financial contribution. But for their flexibility and welcoming of Felix to our family—and not into the role everyone assumed he'd take. Yes, he'd be their son-in-law. Just married to a different child.

Dad slapped me on the back. "Yeah, well, let's get on with this."

Because he likely was thinking of a cold beer he could drink. The day's heat was all-encompassing, and as soon as we'd finished with the photos, I suspected everyone would be shucking their jackets. Too bad we didn't have a pool.

Huh. Something to consider in the future.

I walked with my parents down the wide aisle, keeping my gaze trained on Felix.

He grinned. No hesitation. No questioning. During all of our conversations over the last week, his certainty had been clear.

As we recited our vows, my hands shook. Not because of fear or trepidation, but because of uncontrollable happiness. We'd discussed starting our family in a couple of years. I wanted us settled first. Felix teaching, me continuing to build my business, a couple of dogs—

"I do." Felix grinned.

After the officiant said something, I added, "I do." Technically we should've had a rehearsal, but the woman had been flexible. Had spoken to both of us separately. Had taken our assurances we were, in fact, very much in love. Even if we'd barely been engaged a week.

She declared us to be married partners.

I stepped forward, wrapped my arm around Felix's waist, and dipped him backward, sealing my lips to his. His *oh* of surprised turned to a giggle as I kissed him senseless.

Applause reached us as we righted. I snagged Felix's hand and held it aloft in the *yeah, we just did that thing* universal gesture. More applause followed as we made our way back down the aisle.

Josie and Wally followed us, with Stanley carrying Opal and Justin holding Angus's hand as they trailed behind.

Chaos ensued. Somehow, the photographer got everyone wrangled into a group shot, then pulled different people aside. Parents. Siblings. Parents and Siblings. A few romantic poses as well as a few goofy ones. We were just like that.

Getting everyone out the door at the end of the night was easier than I imagined. Of course, Josie and Wally whispering in everyone's ears how Felix and I couldn't wait to go to bed caused a few laughs and winks.

Jesus.

Well, Wally would go back to work on Monday after driving Josie to the airport so she could fly to Romania.

Felix and I planned a honeymoon at home—everyone promising they'd give us the week. We'd stocked up on provisions and were ready to go.

We shut the door after giving our parents one final hug goodbye.

Felix leaned against the door and offered a shy smile. "Okay, so we survived."

I ran my hand up and down his biceps, covered in the cotton button-down he continued to wear, although he'd rolled up the sleeves at some point. He also had grass stains from when he was down on the ground playing with Opal and Angus. I would've thought the boy too old for games, but he truly adored his sister and so had gotten on the ground.

Stanley merely smiled at Opal's messy dress and Angus's dirty knees.

My heart expanded at the thought of doing that with our kids. Maybe at Wally's wedding. If my best friend ever married, that was.

"What's the smile for?"

"Honestly?"

Felix nodded. Of course he nodded. He'd never want me to be anything other than brutally honest.

"I was thinking about our kids playing at Wally's wedding."

His eyes went comically wide.

"But I'm getting ahead—"

He launched himself at me, crashing his mouth into mine.

I caught him, of course, because he was slight in comparison to my bulk. In a heartbeat, I bent at the waist, put my shoulder against his stomach, and hauled him over my shoulder.

"Oof. What do you think you're doing?" Might've been a touch of righteous indignation in there.

"Carrying you to our marriage bed. Where I've wanted to get you since I built the damn thing." Which was the truth, I'd realized, at some point this week. I'd never imagined him sharing it with Josie—

ick—but with myself. Thinking of all the things I'd do to him. With him. That we'd do to each other.

"Jacob, you're going to hurt yourself."

I laughed and slapped his ass. "Piddly thing like you? You're a lightweight."

"I think I'm supposed to resent that comment."

"Well, don't. You're sturdy. A good size. The perfect size for me."

He stilled his squirming as I carried him up the stairs. I could've tried bridal style, but that likely would've been too challenging. Carrying him like this put added pressure on my knees, but I'd be fine.

"Perfect size?" He might've squeaked that.

I caressed his ass. "We haven't talked preferences. I've done it both ways—and liked it both ways—so I'm totally open. Whatever you want, sweetheart. Or we can take it slow and just do suck and jerk—"

"What?" Yeah, he definitely squeaked that.

"I suck you and you jerk me. Or I jerk you and you suck me. Or we both suck each other. Or we both jerk—"

"I get the picture." He stroked my back, fingering the waistband of my jeans. "I've spent the entire week imagining..."

We entered our bedroom. Oh, I'd carried him over the threshold. Cute. Something to tell Josie. Slowly, I eased him to his feet, and held him steady when he swayed from the head rush of having been upside down.

His cheeks were bright red. *Should I have done that to him?*

In a moment, though, he recovered. And offered me the widest grin.

"You said something about imagining...?"

"First, we get naked, then you show me all that I've been missing. I've got quite a few years to make up for."

I wanted to ask why me? Why now? What had changed since all those other men and women he'd met, especially in university, who hadn't caught his eye?

You don't need to know. It's not important.

No, it really wasn't. He was here. Now. With me. In our bed. I unbuttoned my shirt as he did the same. He stilled, though, when I yanked my shirt off. I cocked an eyebrow.

He cleared his throat. "Don't think I didn't notice before. But I wasn't allowed to look."

I undid my belt, unbuttoned my pants, drew the zipper down, then yanked everything off.

Except my socks were still on which made me appear weird, but Felix's gaze made everything worthwhile. "You can always look, okay? I'm yours. No one else's."

"I'm adamantly against objectification." He scratched his stubble.

"And I don't want you objectifying anyone but me." I advanced on him.

He held his ground.

I unbuttoned his shirt and pulled it away from his body. Then I repeated all the things I'd done to myself and, as he stepped out of his pants and underwear, his erect cock bobbed.

Matching my own hard-on, of course.

Keeping my gaze on his, I swiped my thumb along his slit.

He hissed, pressing his cock into my fingers.

The temptation to get him off right there was strong, but I wanted him in bed. "Do you need to piss?"

"Nope. Did that earlier." He looked quite pleased with himself.

As had I. Planning was important with these things. Which meant... "I went to the clinic earlier this week. Dr. McCauley called. I'm clean."

He blushed. "And I've never—"

I crashed my mouth to his. I'd never bedded a virgin before—man or woman. The thought terrified and aroused at the same time. I'd be the one to teach him...everything.

He snagged my shaft and squeezed experimentally.

"Yeah, like that." I gazed down at him.

And he looked up at me, his pupils blown in the low light of the lamps. "Will you do me? Fuck me, I mean."

"I'll make love to you." He needed to know this was different for me. This wasn't about getting my rocks off. This was about initiating him into pleasure like he'd never known. This was about ensuring he wanted to do this over and over and over.

He pulled his lower lip through his teeth. "Yeah. That."

"Great. So we don't need condoms and... Crap."

He winked. Actually winked. "Lube's under the pillow."

I grabbed the comforter and the top sheet, yanking them down.

A lot of yanking going on. Ah well, more proof of my enthusiasm.

Felix slid onto the bed and positioned himself in the middle. Then he pulled a bottle of lube from under the pillow. He handed it to me. "I don't..." He swallowed. "I haven't..."

Yeah, I got it. I was used to guys who knew their prostates or, if that wasn't their jam, knew how to use their dicks to find mine. I smiled. "I'm going to ask you to relax, even though that's going to be tough. I'm going to ask you to trust me, even though—"

"That's an easy one." He smiled. "Yeah, that's an easy one."

"Okay. Pull your legs apart for me, okay? Can you do that?"

He rolled his eyes. "Duh."

Part of me was about to quip about gay porn, but I decided that would be inappropriate.

As he spread his thighs, and gave me a view of his hole, my cock swelled. *Patience.* Yeah, right. Still, I coated my fingers and held his gaze as I ran my finger around his rim.

He nodded.

Slowly, I sank one finger in.

His mouth opened.

Watching his every reaction, I wiggled that finger, eventually adding a second.

"Uh..."

"Yes, sweetheart?"

"Is this...oh, sweet Jesus."

I grinned as I gently prodded his spongy spot. "That would be your prostate. We can have an anatomy lesson later—"

"Please, Jacob. I mean, I'd prefer not to beg, but I totally will if you'll just—"

I removed my finger, leaned over, and pressed a quick kiss to his lips. "You'll never have to beg." I pretended to consider. "Well, unless I'm edging you."

"Now, please." His eyes were wild with passion.

Grinning, I rocked back on my heels. I coated my cock in lube and lined myself up.

He nodded.

Slowly, millimeter by millimeter, I slid in. Watching my beloved's face, I caught every nuance. The twinge of pain as I breached him. The wonder as I pressed home. The love as he arched up to accept more of me.

"I love you." I whispered the words with reverence. I'd never said them to anyone before. And he needed to know that. But those words could wait.

He strained his neck to kiss me, all the while pressing on my ass.

I dove in for the kiss, even as I slowly moved in him.

His breath caught.

Then I did what I was damn good at—I made love to him. Only this wasn't like the other men and women I'd been with before. This was my Felix. And with each thrust, I increased the intensity of our intimacy. Needing to chase the orgasm, but also needing him to come first, I snagged his cock in my hand. The thing was rock hard, and it took only a few quick tugs before he came, spilling his cum over my fingers and against my belly.

That was all I needed. Him contracting around me sent me into the stratosphere of pleasure and, within another heartbeat, I came. My entire body went rigid as I rode the waves of pleasure.

He pulled me down for yet another kiss.

Huh, he seemed to like this kissing thing. Was getting better at it as well. We needed more practice, of course.

As he ended the kiss, I eased my weight on him, slowly sliding my limp dick from him.

Grinning, he wrapped his arms around me. "All mine."

"All yours."

Later we could wipe ourselves down. Later we could pull up the sheet as the ceiling fan's light breeze wicked away the heat. Later we could discuss the future and all the things we wanted to do together.

Right now, though, we could just settle into our love. "I love you." I repeated the words when I wasn't making love to him because he needed to know that sex wasn't part of the equation.

"I love you too, Jacob. I think I always have and I know I always will."

With a sense of security, I tucked my face into his neck and breathed his scent in. I'd never tire of him.

Best life ever.

EPILOGUE

FELIX

Pounding at the front door woke me.

"Too early," Jacob grumbled. "Saturday morning, no less."

The sun hadn't crested the horizon yet, but that meant little this close to Christmas. Dawn always felt elusive.

The pounding continued.

Cujo, our teacup poodle started barking her ferocious little head off. Sparky, the shepherd-cross, bolted for the bathroom and hid in the shower stall.

Par for the course.

"My fault for locking the doors." I petted Cujo.

"Have to keep the bears out." He pulled the pillow over his head. My husband was not a morning person.

I tossed off the covers and wrapped my dressing gown around me. I opened Jacob's arms and shoved Cujo into them.

Instantly, she calmed.

I could do nothing about Sparky, but I'd reassure her later. Finally, I stepped into my eminently practical slippers, then headed to the stairs.

The pounding continued.

Open the door? Yell? Perhaps check the peephole? I found those notoriously challenging and didn't want to—

"Felix and Jacob, you assholes, wake the fuck up."

Well, that explained a lot. I raced to the door, flipped the lock, and opened the front door.

The bright motion-sensor lights from the porch illuminated one very wet woman with stringy dark-blonde hair, a soaked overcoat, and flashing blue eyes.

I gazed behind her. "How did you...?"

"I don't want to talk about it." She picked up her rolling suitcase and shoved it at me.

Obligingly, I put it to the side and opened the door wide for her.

She stomped in, her muddy boots leaving a mess on my welcome mat.

Behind her, I shut the front door, quickly scanning to see if I might spot another car or some other explanation of how she'd wound up more than seven miles from town on a rainy Saturday morning.

Nothing.

I locked the door, even though I knew a bear couldn't operate the handle, and I held out my hand. "Let me take your coat?"

Her glare faltered.

Giving her my warmest smile, I tried again. "Josette, we weren't expecting you." I tried again. "Uh, how are you?"

"Pregnant." She deadpanned as she removed her coat and flung it at me. "And furious. Now get me some decaf coffee. And if a certain gentleman who looks like he could be Romanian royalty arrives, I'm not here. Got it?"

I got it.

Hours later, as a drier Josette slept in the guest bedroom, Jacob and I cuddled on the couch with Cujo on my lap and Sparky at our feet.

"I hate to ask if she can stay."

I glared at my husband. "As if I'd ever consider turning her away. She might be your sister, but she's also my best friend. She can stay as long as she needs."

"That might get...intrusive."

I chuckled. "Oh, I can guarantee that. But I also know we're built of stronger stuff. And if she's still here when the baby arrives, then we'll set up the nursery for her."

Jacob nuzzled my neck. "I thought that would be for our babies."

As I kissed his cheek, I smiled. "In good time. We agreed to wait a couple more years."

He groused. "I'm not getting any younger."

I laughed. "Oh yeah, old man." I met his intense gaze. "We can plan for sooner, if you really want. I just wanted to give us time to settle into being married."

His smile lit me from the inside. "I was settled the day we said our vows. This is forever, Felix, okay?"

"Okay." I glanced toward the stairs. "I promise once we get Josette settled, then we can talk about expanding our family."

"Yeah?"

"Yeah."

"I love you."

He said the words all the time, and I believed him to be sincere, but they still took my breath away every time. "In a forever kind of way?"

"In a *thank God you didn't marry my sister* kind of way."

We laughed.

Then he pulled me onto his lap, drew my lips down to his, and kissed me soundly.

Yeah, we'd be okay. Whatever came next, we'd handle it.

Together.

Forever.

ABOUT GABBI GREY

USA Today Bestselling author Gabbi Grey lives in beautiful British Columbia where her fur baby chin-poo keeps her safe from the nasty neighborhood squirrels. Working for the government by day, she spends her early mornings writing contemporary, gay, sweet, and dark erotic BDSM romances. While she firmly believes in happy endings, she also believes in making her characters suffer before finding their true love. She also writes m/f romances as Gabbi Black and Gabbi Powell.

Interested in knowing more about Gabbi?

Sign up for her newsletter
Follow her on Bookbub
Follow her on Instagram

Interested in Justin and Stanley's love story? Check out *Stanley Christmas Redemption* *here:* https://books2read.com/u/mV86x2

f facebook.com/authorgabbigrey

⊙ instagram.com/authorgabbigrey

THE GAMER AND HIS SIDE QUEST

PIPER MALONE

The Gamer and His Side Quest

By Piper Malone

ABOUT THE GAMER AND HIS SIDE QUEST

Bram Ridley's responsibilities as the marketing intern for video game design phenom, Oliver Kent, were clear: create dazzling promo for Oliver's popular games, engage followers and share sweet images of his boss and celebrity girlfriend, Isley Berns, and keep his massive crush on Oliver a secret. When Oliver is chosen to receive a prestigious gaming award, Bram creates media to showcase Oliver's crowning achievement, then resigns. His unrequited heartache overshadows the fear of unemployment and Bram needs to forget Oliver's quiver-inducing smile.

When Bram left, Oliver instantly felt the loss. He missed their conversations, brainstorming sessions, and Bram's striking hazel eyes. Despite the public image, Oliver and Isely's romance was game over. Oliver's quiet infatuation with Bram didn't help.

Hours before the award ceremony, Bram is called to support Oliver on the red carpet. As the media enjoys Bram and Oliver's playful reunion, the relationship between Oliver and Isley suffers a fatal blow. To navigate the upheaval, Isley proposes a distraction: share that their relationship is open and Bram is Oliver's boyfriend. It's temporary—like a gamer's side quest—and perfect because the chemistry between Oliver and Bram is obvious…to everyone.

Bram is reluctant to tease his crush, but Oliver is ready to play. Oliver quietly booked a luxury island getaway to celebrate his success, which is the ideal location for their side quest. White sands, crystal blue waters, and Oliver are temptations Bram cannot resist. But as they enjoy their private escape, their fake romance begins to feel very real.

CHAPTER
ONE

BRAM

On a scale of one to all *the paper cuts, how awful will it be to watch the live stream of the Games for All annual gala?*

Bram knew that supporting Oliver Kent, his former internship supervisor, would be professionally respectful. Maybe even fun. Oliver was to receive GFA's prestigious Gamer of the Year award. Bram would watch the live stream from the comfort of his apartment, where no one could see him moon, drool, or squeeze out a tear over Oliver Kent, the man he could never have.

With the pre-awards streaming on his TV, Bram changed into proper gala-watching attire—sweatpants and the well-worn T-shirt he'd won on the first day of freshman orientation—and prepared for an elegant meal of King Ramen, Special #2 and the best bottle of prosecco he could afford as an almost-graduated grad student with no job.

Oliver's skill set for creating cozy video games that millions of people across demographic strata loved was astonishing. When Bram was hired as a social media marketing intern to support the launch of *Otter's River Cleanup*, he could hardly believe his luck.

What grad student wouldn't want a paid internship to promote a video game in which an adorable otter swam through oceans, rivers, and lakes cleaning up water-clogging refuse and shipping it to the recycling center? It was a great way for children to learn about environmentalism without it being scary. Great for people who loved cleaning things up, and organizing bottles, cans, and jars into piles based on color, size, or recycling number. Bonus: a portion of all proceeds went to nonprofits whose mission was to clean waterways. Double bonus: Otter was adorable.

The success of *Otter's River Cleanup,* and that Oliver Kent was as kind and charismatic as he was handsome, had landed him the coveted award. Bram was proud of *Otter's* success and humbled by Oliver's efforts to ensure Bram's name was front and center for the online marketing. While Oliver was a genius with game design, he was not savvy with social media. Months had been dedicated to curating *Otter's* launch to draw a wider audience.

All of it had fanned the yearslong crush Bram held for the prince of ethically minded cozy gaming. His proximity to Oliver, watching him develop games, taking part in live streams, and sharing their joint passion for sports had done nothing to dampen Bram's feelings.

Weeks of facials, modified exercise and diet routines, and finding the most classically dramatic ensemble imaginable were ingrained into Bram's mind. Bram had also spent months planning, developing, and delivering Oliver's content in preparation for tonight's award ceremony. He'd spent endless hours engaging Oliver's fans and followers and a fair amount of time coaching Oliver on creating live content, but mostly helping Oliver choose the best-looking hoodie for the day. Thankfully, it didn't take Bram long to coax Oliver from hot, cozy gamer into lethally handsome guy next door, wearing a white T-shirt and rocking warm-chestnut hair that possessed a natural tussle.

Bram's daily snippets of living in the haze of an Oliver Kent dream fantasy had come to a screeching halt two weeks ago. He'd been filming one of Oliver's pre-gala workouts, which was more exciting than he'd predicted. Listening to Oliver's gut-wrenchingly humble speech afterward edged Bram closer to dumping his deepest feelings, which Bram was sure Oliver didn't want to hear.

When Bram accompanied Oliver to a suit fitting, he knew his time was up. The slim fit of the dress shirt slipped along the lean line of his waist as Oliver shrugged into a jacket that made his striking blue eyes glow. The tailor's brisk measurement of Oliver's inseam forced Bram to choke back a spike of jealousy, and he resolved to exit his internship two weeks early.

His tasks were done, so he professionally resigned, and it was over. All of it. The internship. Bram's daily mantra: Don't stare at Oliver's mouth. Lingering curiosities about Oliver's ongoing relationship with Isley Berns, an influencer with so many followers she might as well have been a deity.

What wasn't over was how Bram still felt the sting of it all.

When Oliver started dating Isely, their online engagement skyrocketed. Bram's role at the helm of Oliver's social media was to fold Isely into content. He'd ground his teeth at the weekly posts designed to connect with Oliver's gaming community and tease Isley's followers.

Isley had a history of loving and leaving her partners, using her heartbreak as a foundation for influencing her followers. Breakup with a lifestyle guru? Pitch your own personal meditation journal. Fall out with a footballer? Plink out a ballad about heartbreak on your acoustic guitar, then share your shock as your fans demand you receive studio time to record your emotional retching. Oliver ticked all of Isley's boxes: handsome, charismatic, and popular, with an effortlessly chill vibe … and he was a self-made millionaire.

Bram wasn't a fan of Isley. He also knew he was irrationally salty about their whirlwind romance. Even though he'd followed Isley's socials as a necessity of the job, he had yet to unfollow her. He itched to tap that button with the gusto of a lover scorned.

He didn't want to watch Isley Berns primp for the Games for All gala. He didn't want to wonder what it would be like to hear Oliver's speech live, in real time. Since he was home, alone, unemployed, and wondering if now was the time to adopt a cat, he wasted no more time in calling up his favorite restaurant and order the only thing that could soothe him. Ramen.

Bram had settled into the couch and shoveled a pile of delicious noodles into his mouth, only to nearly choke when his phone rang. Bram swallowed and took a breath. On Thursday evenings, his neighbors, Con and Rosa, went to their weekly ballroom soiree (Rosa's word, not Bram's). They dressed for their events like royalty: Rosa wore shimmering dresses, Con was dapper in tailored suits. They always called to share when they were going to play music and practice for their next competition. According to Con, the people who'd vacated Bram's apartment hadn't enjoyed dancing, music, or people.

A quick scoot off the couch for his phone had him stumbling, especially when a name he never expected to see again illuminated the screen.

"Margaret?"

"R-ram?" Oliver's assistant was the walking embodiment of a cracked whip. She'd box till you bled, then kick you into next week. Somehow, you thanked her for all of it. Now she sounded like all the plagues had hit her at once. "Han you 'ear me?"

"Margaret? Are you okay?"

On the other end of the phone, Bram heard rustling, some mumbled protests, then a centering sigh.

"Hello, Bram. It's Lucy." Margaret's nanny and personal assistant sounded bright and filled with sunshine.

When Lucy had come to the office, she'd hovered in the background and never engaged the staff working with Oliver. Bram had marveled at her Mary Poppins-like style. She had all the stuff Margaret, and Margaret's children, needed on hand and at a moment's notice.

"Hey, Lucy. Is she okay?"

"She is not." The words were punched, as if Lucy was informing Bram and also reprimanding Margaret. "The twins were sick last week, so we've all had a turn of this nastiness. Margaret looks as terrible as she sounds." Lucy paused. "She's writing me a note ... She says you need to go tonight."

Bram blinked and made a swiping grab at the bottle of prosecco. "I need to do what?"

"Sa hala!" he heard Margaret rasp out on the other end of the phone, then clear her throat. "Go to the gala."

Go to the gala and watch Oliver and Isley look lovely and effortless? "I can't. I'm not connected with Oliver anymore. He signed off on my paperwork."

"Hold on. She's got a tablet. Let's wait while she types." Lucy sounded like a Zen master, or as calm as someone could be who regularly managed twins and Margaret. "Click the speaker button and it will read what you wrote," she coached.

A tinny robotic voice filtered over the line. "Listen to me right now, Bram. You need to go tonight and act as Kent Technologies support for Oliver. He's going to give his speech and someone from the company should be there. I can't because I'm birthing an alien right now, or I would. You're the only one who knows what he's been doing. You've been with him every day for months."

Despite the low, robotic voice, Bram could hear Margaret's voice punching out the words. "I have nothing to wear."

The droning robot was back. "Find something. With the clear understanding that no one will look at you."

Ouch. "Only you could make AI throw shade, Margaret."

"I'll pay you."

Bram stared at his phone. He needed the money. Resumes he'd posted everywhere over the past two weeks had landed him nothing. "Per hour or for the entire night?"

"Whatever it takes to make it worth your time."

Even with the possibility of cushioning his threadbare account, Bram hesitated. "I'm not sure that stepping in for you is the best idea."

"I told him I was calling you," Margaret's robot voice jerked out.

Bram felt a familiar tug in his chest. "Oh?"

"He sounded relieved." Margaret's nails clacked against the tablet. "Please don't make him accept this award without one of us there. He's built this company by himself. From nothing. Oliver deserves to have his team watch him in person."

Bram pushed out a long breath and searched the ceiling. "If I look like shit, I do not want any comments from you. Agreed?"

"No promises," her robot voice bit out. "It's black-tie. The limo will pick you up in forty-five minutes."

Ten minutes later, with every imaginable piece of his college wardrobe on the floor, Bram was furious with himself.

"How the hell did my closet turn into a mess?" he snarled. "Oh yeah, living on a zero-clothing budget for six years while I worked my way through college and grad school." He sank into the pile, silently praying it would consume him, and that the sleek limo with Oliver in it would only wait the longest five minutes of Bram's life before pulling away.

Bram mentally prepared to call Margaret and tell her he couldn't do it when he heard brass instruments bleeding through the walls; a moment later, the sound of feet moving in rhythm with the horns.

"Con!" Bram yelled as he scampered out of the mass of jeans and ill-fitting business attire he'd pilfered from the second-hand closet at his college's career center.

Before Bram's door closed with a heavy thud he was knocking on Con and Rosa's. They supplied him with food, hugs when he felt like every choice he'd made was a mistake, and reassurances that every-thing—no matter the circumstance—would eventually be okay.

Con opened the door with Rosa behind him, both looking skeptical. "Bram, what's wrong?"

Bram looked Con up and down. They had similar builds, even if Con was a little broader in the chest. It was a long shot, but it might work.

"I need to go to a black-tie gala in thirty minutes and I have nothing to wear."

Con blinked, then a debonair smile took over his entire face. "My boy, you came to the right place."

CHAPTER
TWO

OLIVER

Tonight is no different from a live stream.

During a live stream, Oliver could touch his hair, or face, or pants without fearing for his life. Kimmy, his stylist, gave zero cares about Oliver's nerves. *"Do not,"* she bit out, *"touch your hair!"* Then she air-kissed his cheeks like she hadn't tried to shank him with her tone.

Like a child, he sat on his hands and waited for Bram to emerge from the concrete monstrosity that marked the address Maggie had given their driver. Did Bram really live in a place with no green space? Bram seemed like a man who enjoyed being outside. He had always encouraged outdoor photo opportunities and talked about his weekend hiking adventures.

Oliver's visual scan of the apartment building halted when the front double doors burst open, and Bram, flanked by an elderly couple, rushed down the steps. Relief swept over Oliver and he scooted across the bench seat in the back of the limo as the driver opened the door. The early December air gusted into his lungs as he sucked in a breath. Bram, always classically dressed, stalled in front of him, wearing sleek dark-gray trousers paired with a crisp white button-down and accented with a brightly colored floral tie.

"Kimmy didn't take your request for a sophisticated athleisure look seriously?" Bram asked as his entourage helped him shrug into a hunter-green, crushed-velvet suit coat.

Bram was handsome. His smile was infectious. The deep hazel of Bram's eyes, framed by long dark lashes, always triggered Oliver's pulse. The green fabric of his coat made Bram's eyes pop, and made Oliver trip over his thoughts.

"Kimmy promised death if I touched my hair." The lame response was slathered in Oliver's near drooling over Bram.

"Don't test her. You look great." Bram's gaze skimmed Oliver before he stepped aside to reveal the couple who'd ushered him outside. "Oliver, this is Con and Rosa. They graciously agreed to style me this evening."

Oliver barely got a word of thanks into the world before receiving hugs from Con and Rosa, both unnervingly strong for older adults.

"We were so happy to help our Bram *suit up*!" Con beamed with pride.

"We can't seem to agree if tonight's event is a *gal-uh* or a *gay-la*. What do you think, Oliver? Does it matter?" Rosa shrugged and waved the words away. "It doesn't matter. Here, get together for a picture."

"A picture?" Oliver asked Bram as Con shoved them together so they were shoulder to shoulder.

Rosa pulled a phone from her pocket and held it up. "Look at these handsome men! Everyone say, *gal-uh*!"

"It's *gay-la*, Rosa," Con teased with a raspy laugh. "Don't wear your coats while you're driving," he said. "Have fun, and call us if you need a ride home." The driver cleared his throat, earning a suspicious look from Con. "We're here for you if you need us," he whispered before stepping back and wrapping an arm around Rosa. "Have a good night, boys!"

"Have fun! We love you!" Rosa called.

Both of them waited on the steps until the limo turned down the street and out of sight.

"You live next to that energy all the time?" Oliver felt the warm love of Con and Rosa settle over him.

"Yep." Bram huffed out a laugh. "When Margaret called me, I was elbow-deep in a bowl of ramen and had nothing to wear."

"King Ramen, Special #2?" Oliver asked. It was Bram's favorite.

"There is no other," he confirmed. "Con and Rosa are ballroom dancers. From time to time they host classes at the local senior center, but they still compete regularly."

"Wow. You live next door to ballroom legends who have serious style. And I thought a single home tucked away on acres of land was the dream."

Bram tilted his head in consideration. "Both have their benefits. Not to change the subject, but let's figure out what I'm supposed to be doing tonight. Did you talk to Margaret at all?"

"Lucy called me first and translated for Maggie." Oliver knew Margaret despised when he shortened her name, but when she couldn't launch a full counterattack it was fun to poke the bear. He'd pay for it when she felt better. "She comes to these events to network and look for ways to expand my brand. In all honesty, if you stay close and feed me updates on local game stats, I'm happy."

"Is Isley meeting you there?" Oliver could hear the dip in Bram's voice. He was Business Bram, firm and distant. Oliver wanted the fun, sports-loving friend he'd missed since Bram's abrupt departure two weeks ago.

"She'll be there. There's some exclusive interview she's doing with the new brand she signed with."

Oliver shook his head. Isley had been busy with this new venture; he didn't even know what the company was. They needed time together that wasn't infused with phones, or business deals, or other people. He was hungry for some connection.

"I'm sure I'll get a text when it's all over. I planned a surprise trip for her after the event, so eventually she'll come around."

"Good." Bram looked as unconvinced as he sounded. "I can take pictures for your socials tonight." He looked out the window for a moment, before his gaze landed on Oliver. "I'll also give you whatever stat updates you want."

Oliver breathed a sigh of relief. "You're the best."

"Based on this award you're getting tonight, I think you're the best."

Oliver knew the Gamer of the Year award was an honor, but he always felt more comfortable behind his computer. He could design and build a cozy video game. Be ruthless in online gaming competitions. He could lobby for environmental causes he loved. Standing in front of a crowd and accepting an award felt strange. "Let me get through this speech tonight, then we'll see how I rank."

Bram shrugged. "It's not about the speech. You could get up there, say thank you, and exit. This award is about everything that led up to the speech. You've done amazing things for the gaming community. You've inspired people to follow their dreams. Helped people be honest about who they are as human beings. You've shared your know-how in workshops and held live training courses. The ways you've given back to the community through gaming events and fundraising alone are more than enough to earn this achievement. All of it paved the way for tonight. You've done amazing work. You deserve this."

Oliver nodded as he swallowed the knot in his throat. He had voiced his insecurity about receiving the GFA award since its announcement to Maggie. It was imposter syndrome. Wondering if all his hard work had actually paid off. The fear that everything he was told as a teen—that there was no way he could make a living by gaming—was true.

His concerns were dismissed. Maggie told him to embrace the moment. Nothing else mattered because now he had the accolade.

"I didn't think about it like that," he mumbled.

Bram shifted to face him. "Think about it this way: you can have a stellar team and not make it to the championship game. If your team does make it to the championship game, there is no guarantee that you'll win. It's the season that counts. Every accomplishment along the way leads you to the next round. Tonight is your championship game. You're giving the speech. The audience is receiving. Just like when you do a live stream. There are no guarantees. You need to play the game."

Oliver's chest felt tight as warmth erupted throughout his body. "Bram ..."

"Can you do that?" Bram's voice was firm as his eyes flickered to the line of people swarming the event center. His lean frame jostled as the limo came to a stop. "Can you play the game?"

Damn. He missed Bram so much. "Yeah," he said with a rasp. "I can do that."

"Good." A moment later, their driver was beside the door. Bram collected their suit coats, gently handing Oliver his. "It's go time."

CHAPTER
THREE

BRAM

Bram listened to the rushed instructions from an event coordinator that was more clipboard-and-comm-devices than a welcome wagon as they were funneled from the limo to the red carpet.

Oliver was to stop at specific spots to allow for photographers to shoot him from every angle. Then he had three two-minute interviews with different influencers. Oliver would wrap up the red-carpet walk with a three-minute conversation with the youth who'd won the GFA Teen Gamer award, given to an adolescent who embodied the values of the gaming community and shared them with their neighborhood, school, or religious organizations.

Bram could keep all of that in order. Easy-peasy.

From the start, Bram logged into Oliver's socials. When Oliver engaged the throngs of gamers, fans, and paparazzi watching the red carpet, waving and giving a dazzling smile, Bram knew time was of the essence. He started a live stream, following at a measured distance, capturing his former boss's statuesque form draped in a tux tailored so expertly it should have been illegal, earning likes, hearts, and a bevy of fire and eggplant emojis within minutes.

Oliver moved to the first photo stop and posed as he had been trained. Bram quickly added hashtags and responded to comments before tucking his phone away. As Oliver moved to the next station, Bram followed, but hovered next to the line of coordinators rattling orders into headsets. When Oliver unbuttoned his suit coat, holding the side wide for photographers to capture, Bram's mouth fell open.

Oliver's coat was lined with a dizzying pattern of images from *Otter's River Cleanup*. Otter's smiling face. The recycling symbol. The trademark bottles. Even Otter's handy garbage-snatching net. The crowd went wild. Photographers couldn't get enough. The catcalls at Oliver's reveal might have called actual cats.

Bram was in awe. Handsome was only the exterior. Oliver was brilliant in a lot of ways. This was one of them. Bram breathed a sigh of gratitude. He'd had months with this man, and now he had one more night of fun.

Stepping back to grab a few more pictures, he barely dodged a woman barreling toward him with obvious purpose. Bram gasped as she grabbed his arm. "I have him," she said into her headset.

"I-I think you have me confused with someone else." Bram tried to pull away, but she held firm.

"Nope. You're with Oliver."

"I'm not *with* Oliver. I'm his assistant for the evening."

"You arrived with him, so you're with him. People are talking about the hottie in hunter green. Get out there."

"The, wha—" His protests were lost as she shoved him onto the red carpet and in Oliver's general direction.

"What the hell was that?" Oliver asked through a camera-ready grin when Bram settled next to him.

"She said they—the internet—saw me and they want me to walk the carpet with you." Bram schooled his features, hoping he looked confident.

Oliver turned to him with a smile Bram knew was forced. "Thank you," he said. "This is terrifying."

Bram tipped his chin, giving Oliver a quick wink. "I'm here to run defense." He felt a tug in his chest at Oliver's relieved expression. Bram held his fist up for Oliver to bump. "Let's have a pose off. Winner buys the loser ramen."

Oliver tapped his knuckles against Bram's. A flash of bold confidence seemed to chase away his nerves. "You're going to regret that bet."

Bram followed Oliver to the next photo stop, where the attendant introduced both of them against the whirling shouts of their names from fans.

"Bram, who are you wearing?"

"This"—Bram ran the lapel made of lush crushed velvet between his thumb and index finger—"is from a vintage collection, exclusively procured from designers Con & Rosa." He pushed every ounce of sexy swagger in his arsenal toward the camera as he turned, posed, and engaged the crowd.

Beside him, Oliver cursed. "And I lost."

Bram watched Oliver navigate the crowd at the gala's plated dinner. He charmed their companions and prompted shy attendants to share their favorite game expansions. Bram knew Oliver was wrestling with his nerves even as he appeared calm and collected.

A fellow gamer and designer leaned into the table at a lull in the conversation and set her sights on Oliver. "While your friend is a lovely addition to dinner, we were hoping for a visit from a certain someone this evening."

Oliver laughed and pulled his phone from his trouser pocket, glancing at the screen. "From her last text, Isley is running late. That was an hour ago. Let's hope she arrives in time for dessert."

Bram's thoughts screeched to a halt. Isley had been tagged at the gala in several posts throughout the evening.

"Are you okay if I step away for a few minutes?" he whispered to Oliver. At his nod, Bram excused himself from the table.

Bram ducked into a hallway and scanned his phone. Isley had been tagged fifteen minutes before on the red carpet. *Where the hell are you?* Bram whispered to himself. He was happy to support Oliver, but as much as Bram had more than friendly feelings for his former boss, he wasn't Oliver's partner. Isley should be the one to show up as part of Oliver's team and offer support as he prepared to accept the GFA award.

This was part of the reason Bram wasn't a fan. When things worked for Isely, everything was great. When they didn't ... Well, Isely found a way to make things work for her.

Bram set off down the hallway, hoping to intercept Isley, give her a piece of his mind now that he was no longer an intern, and get her settled next to Oliver. Bram could go home, change out of Con's pants, reheat his Special #2, and cry over the brief life he had as Oliver Kent's plus-one at a black-tie gala.

The walkways of the GFA gala were simple black fabric panels designed to herd the masses from one location to another. Most of the attendees were two courses into a four-course culinary delight, but Bram was doing his best not to appear like a weirdo asking if anyone knew where he could find Isley Berns—for Oliver Kent, of course.

A few helpful coordinators later, Bram turned down a hallway that was so sparsely lit he had to use his phone to illuminate the path. A few steps into the darkness, Bram paused at a rustling behind him. Or around him? He couldn't quite make out the exact location, but the icy shiver that leaked down his spine and into his limbs propelled him forward. Bram was never one for ghost stories, haunted houses, or horror movies. He liked warm and cuddly. The hallway he was wandering down felt icy and stabby.

He breathed through the irrational thought and took another step, only to hear an equally terrifying sound.

The seductive laughter of Isley Berns.

Not the laughter Isley exuded when she was gaming with Oliver. It was a tease. A giggle that sounded heated and sensual, followed by an inaudible conversation that held Isley's hushed tone.

Bram blinked. Oliver was eating dinner at the other end of the stabby hallway. He would have sent a text if he was going to take time away with Isley, right?

As Bram was ready to text Oliver—awkwardly, and just to make sure—Bram heard a second voice. A deep, rumbling voice.

Then an unmistakable moan of Isley enjoying ... herself?

What. The. Hell?

A gasp of pleasure bloomed behind the makeshift wall moments before Bram could make sense of it all.

Pounding footsteps barreled down on Bram. The flashlight on his phone illuminated the passing rush of a man wearing a T-shirt with the logo of a million-dollar tabloid syndicate emblazoned on his back. In his hand, a camera.

Without thinking, Bram followed the cameraman. Margaret would skewer Bram within an inch of his life if a private moment between Isley and Oliver was exposed. Bram needed a positive recommendation from Margaret to get a job offer, and he would not let the decision to engage in an exhibitionist fantasy at a very classy, highly televised gala, where one of the public humpers was to receive one of the highest honors in the gaming community, undermine his job prospects.

The paparazzi had the jump, but Bram did the only thing he could. He called Oliver.

"Bram? Are you okay?" Oliver asked quietly.

Bram tucked himself into a corner, covering his mouth and the phone with his hand. "Whatever you're doing, stop. Pap are on to you."

"What are you talking about?" Oliver sounded genuinely confused.

"What are *you* talking about?" Bram pulled back from the corner and glanced down the hall. "Where are you?"

"At the table." Bram could hear Oliver excuse himself. "Where are you?"

"I-I don't know." Bram watched as the paparazzi shoved his camera between the black sheets of the makeshift wall with too much force.

The curtain ripped from its weak frame, revealing Isley Berns in a sparkling dress that would have barely covered her rear end if it hadn't been up around her waist. Her breast spilled from the top of her dress. With her was a man Bram didn't initially recognize because his face was nestled between her thighs.

Isley shrieked.

The man disengaged.

The man who wasn't Oliver.

"Bram," Oliver said with a force that indicated Bram hadn't responded the first time. "Is that Isley?"

"Oh, shit." Bram stumbled back as Isley howled her outrage at the paparazzi, who continued to film as she pulled her skirt down and readjusted her bustline. The guy—a clan gamer known as Wombat—looked like a caged animal searching for the easiest escape route.

Isley attempted to scamper after Wombat, twisting her ankle as her thin, spiky heel slipped on the parquet flooring. When she caught her balance her gaze locked on Bram, eyes flaring in horror.

"Wait!" she screamed as Bram gained traction and ran as fast as Con's dress shoes would allow.

CHAPTER
FOUR

OLIVER

"As we craft worlds that support exploration and acceptance, we must use our platforms to extend those values to our own communities. Encourage your followers to meet up and join in-person gaming groups. We have heard too often about the fear and worry associated with building new relationships, but we have already constructed the foundation. We are gamers, but we are also a community of vibrant, eclectic human beings who share a bond. Squad up. Join a group. Plan an event. Share your tips and tricks. Be a community beyond the screen and build your own dynamic world. Thank you for this award. Please know that I share it with all of you." Oliver held up the golden game controller and looked over the crowd. The smiles were blinding, the applause was overwhelming, but the only thing Oliver could focus on was Bram.

Moments before Oliver walked on stage, Bram had returned looking harried.

"Give me your phone before you go up there." It hadn't been a question. Bram's hand opened to receive the device, then his fingers curled to hurry Oliver up. "People watching the live stream will text you. This is no time to be distracted." Bram shoved the phone in his pocket and nailed Oliver with a confident smile. "You know the game plan. Go get 'em."

It was enough to propel Oliver forward. Now, at the end of it all, with his fingers shaking from the adrenaline rush, he wanted off the stage and away from the spotlight.

"Need a break?" Bram asked too quickly. "How about some down-time in the limo?"

"What?" Oliver wanted some quiet, but he didn't need a time-out. "Let's see where Isley is at. I'm sure she'll want a few pictures for her story."

"Ah." Bram rubbed the back of his neck. "Oliver, I need to tell you—"

"Do you have my phone? Let me text her and then we can grab a drink. I'm over being stressed about this evening."

"I can't do that." Bram's words came in a rush as his gaze bounced around the room.

"Is something wrong? Is the Special #2 not sitting well?" Oliver finally felt centered and relaxed. The speech was over. He was hanging out with Bram. All he had to do was get some face time with Isley and his night would be complete.

"Now is not the time to besmirch Special #2—"

Oliver snorted. "Besmirch."

"I think we should leave." Bram sounded serious.

"Bram, find a bathroom far away and take care of business." Oliver understood the need for privacy in delicate moments, but this was a bit much.

"I do not need the bathroom," Bram said through ground teeth. "I need to talk to you."

"Phone." Oliver leveled a serious glare when Bram shook his head. "Phone, or I will tell Maggie that you didn't take the best possible care of me."

Oliver knew it was the right threat when Bram's cheeks puffed wide and he dug into his pocket.

Bram laid the phone on his palm, his fingers curling around his hand and holding it tight. "I need you to know that whatever you see, I know you can work through it."

"Ease up, man. The hard part of the evening is over." Bram looked unconvinced, then resigned, as his touch trailed away, leaving the phone.

For a moment, Oliver felt the urge to connect their hands again. He wanted to tangle his fingers with Bram's and pull him close.

When the home screen of Oliver's phone lit up, he could barely see the cover art—the plucky otter who encouraged players to clean up waterways by putting trash in the trash can, then commandeering a recycling center to make sure all the plastics were sorted. Otter's sweet smile was smothered in notifications.

He'd been tagged in over a dozen social media posts. He had a pile of text messages, the latest one from a fellow live streamer: *I am here for you. But first, I knew it!*

"What the hell is going on?" Oliver scrolled through the notifications until he saw a headline.

Isley Berns Caught with Her Skirt … Up. Click to Watch.

Oliver felt a slithering in his gut.

His brain knew he shouldn't do it.

"Do not open that link," Bram warned.

His finger pressed the little arrow.

It was only thirty seconds. The longest, most embarrassing thirty seconds of his life. Not only had he been cheated on, it had been publicly revealed. With Isley's very naked rear end, and one of her breasts, exposed for all the world to consume.

His stomach rolled. "I don't …"

"When I left, I tried to find her. I didn't know the camera guy was following me." Bram shifted, then wrapped an arm around Oliver's shoulders as he stared at the phone.

A blinding flash made everything too dark. "Oliver! Do you have anything to say about Isley's out-of-relationship romp? Is your relationship open? Is that why you both brought dates to the event tonight?"

"No comment," Bram said firmly as he hedged Oliver backstage.

"What the fuck?" Oliver's brain was spinning, his legs bumping against Bram's as they moved through the hall.

This was his night. His achievements were being celebrated on a grand scale. He had a faux-gold controller in the shape of a gaming system he never played. And she was banging some dude. No, not some dude. Wombat. A fellow gamer Oliver had worked with, played with, and competed against for years.

He'd planned a romantic vacation. He'd made sure everything was picture perfect … literally. For Isley, everything was for the camera. The private bungalow. Their meals. Even their excursions. All of it was for her to take pictures and share them with the world. For her to gain more popularity and enchant her followers.

Now it was her no-carb, non-dairy, three-hour-yoga-sessions-fit ass going viral for cheating when it should have been their dream getaway.

Oliver felt his entire body vibrate.

"She never saw my speech, did she?" It might have been selfish, but he needed to know.

"No." Bram's reply was devoid of any remorse.

Isley Berns was a mirage. An image that reflected what people wanted, but never what he needed.

"Bram." His throat felt tight, his vision now blurry. "I can't be here."

"Then we're gone."

CHAPTER
FIVE

BRAM

Bram's eyes burned from the light illuminating the back of the limo. Oliver watched the video a nauseating number of times.

Then he dove into reading some of the gossip blogs before spelunking in the bowels of the comments. Bram let him go for a few minutes before demanding he hand over the device.

"It won't do any good right now." Bram slid to the limo's tiny liquor station and lifted the bottle of whiskey toward Oliver.

"That will do." His voice was resigned.

"I'm sorry," Bram said as he handed Oliver the drink.

"For what happened? Or for not filling this glass to the brim."

"Yes." Bram lifted his glass to Oliver before taking a sip. He swallowed down the amber liquor, enjoying the warm burn. "Did you have any idea?"

Oliver snorted, his gaze fixed on his glass. "None," he mumbled before tossing back the rest of his drink. He handed the empty glass to Bram. "Again."

"One more," Bram said reluctantly. "We might have a designated driver, but drowning sorrows now will earn you a headache tomorrow."

"Thanks, Dad. Pour one for you, too. I want to drop you off sloppy and watch you pretend to be sober for Con and Rosa."

"Well"—Bram tipped his head as he splashed whiskey into their glasses—"joke's on you. They'd want to join the party. When I came home from my last day at work, they had shots ready for me."

"I need them to adopt me."

"After tonight, I think they already have."

"Good." Oliver lifted his glass again. "To new grandparents and good whis—"

A knock at the window caused both their drinks to slosh over the rim.

"Do not open the door." Bram rushed forward as Oliver leaned toward the window. When his face came precariously close to the glass, Bram punched his thigh.

"Ow." Oliver rubbed his leg. "Unnecessary," he hissed.

The intercom crackling to life sent even more whiskey splashing onto the floor of the limo. "Shit," Bram muttered as he dabbed liquor off Con's pants.

"Sir"—the limo driver's deep voice came over the intercom—"Miss Berns is outside and is requesting to speak to you."

Oliver's endless blue eyes hardened to icy orbs, his mouth firming as if to hold back the slew of words he hadn't said yet.

Bram inhaled, the oaky liquor failing to stabilize his heartbeat. "You don't have to talk to her," he whispered.

Oliver looked at the door, then at Bram. "I think I need to," he whispered back.

Fingernails tapped on the window with an annoyed staccato. "I can hear you talking. Open the door."

Bram had heard Isley irritated before. Her sharp retorts and willingness to engage in internet-based drama was how she'd gained her early following. Bram had witnessed arguments between Isley and Oliver, but they were awkward. Never angry.

Isley was upset.

"Oliver!" Isley's voice cut through the glass. "Let me in, *now*."

Oliver seemed to wrestle with his thoughts as he looked at the opposite door, then closed his eyes. His lips pursed and the tiniest shake of his head made a rogue flop of his hair bounce.

He leaned over and popped the door, forcing Isley to open it wide before entering.

"There." Oliver pointed to the bench opposite Bram when she attempted to sit next to him.

Isley schooled her shock as she settled. "You can give us some privacy, Bram. Thank you," she said, issuing her command and its acceptance.

"He's staying right here." Oliver's voice dropped the air of the cozy limo to frigid temps.

"This is a private matter." Isley seemed to do her best to sound bossy and contrite.

"Oh? *This* is a private matter." He scoffed a nasty laugh. "Thank you for clarifying that *this* is a private matter and not you publicly fucking another man while I'm receiving a career-highlight award." Oliver tossed back the rest of his drink. "What the hell, Izzy?"

Her shrug was both irritated and dismissive. "Can I have a drink?"

"No." Bram wasn't one to be disrespectful, but Isley had been in the limo for less than five minutes. Oliver was seething, and she appeared to think this was her domain.

"Bram, I'm not even sure why you're here tonight. I barely tolerated you while you worked for Oliver."

"Funny, I was going to say the same thing."

"Enough pleasantries, Izzy." Oliver focused on his drink. "We're done."

"Oh, no." Isley chuckled. "I'm not squandering years of overhauling my brand because of this."

"Then maybe you should have saved your sexy stuff for a place with locked doors." Bram slapped a hand over his mouth. The muffled "sorry" was directed at Oliver. Isley could kiss his Con & Rosa vintage-clad ass.

"Everyone knows that we've had transparent relationships. You are openly bi, and people have caught us canoodling in public."

"Kissing, while fully dressed, is canoodling, Izzy. He was face down in your crotch. Totally different." Oliver rested his arms on the back of the bench seat. "Why are you here?"

"I'm here to offer a way out of this that saves both of us."

"He has zero reasons to save you. This was you, and no one else." Bram had tried, but he couldn't keep quiet. She had disregarded Oliver's work, his heart, and their relationship, and she wanted to make a deal?

"The only reason I'm tolerating your presence right now is because you're going to help us."

"Us, as in you two?" Bram settled into his seat. "Oliver? Yes. You? Not a chance."

"Oh, I think you will." For the first time since Isley entered the limo, she turned to face Bram. "I've watched you admire him for months. I suspected you had a thing for Oliver. A crush, maybe? An infatuation? I'm sure it's part of what sparked you to apply to intern with his company. Tonight's showing made it clear to me, and the world, that you have a hopeless crush on him. It's plastered all over the internet."

Bram's tongue felt sticky. Denying Isley's claim meant denying Oliver, and way too much of that had gone on for one evening.

"That's enough, Isely." Oliver's voice was bitter. "What do you want?"

A low *huh* pushed from her before she focused on Oliver. "There is speculation that we"—she ticked her finger between herself and Oliver—"have opened our relationship and that this event is the debut of our new partners. The world knows you've always had a thing for blonds."

"Wombat can be your new partner." Oliver leaned forward slightly. "Again, we're done."

"Sure, we could spin that angle. If you're willing to risk it."

"There's no risk. You cheated."

"And people will look for a reason why." Isley paused, watching him closely. "Oliver, you're a good guy. You create amazing products and have a gaming legacy that others would die for. But there is also a wholesome vibe to you. One that presents as caring and genuine.

Despite your affections, you couldn't keep one of the most popular women in pop culture today satisfied." Oliver's snort of disbelief didn't slow her. "So she went out and found another man."

Bram was ready for Isley to leave. "That's beyond crass, even for you."

"Maybe." She lifted an elegant shoulder. "Think about it, Oliver. Our fans will always wonder where you were lacking." Isley's smile was pitying. "I know your needs aren't satisfied with me. I think you know that things between us have been growing distant."

"I did know that," he replied. "Things between us have been challenging, but I planned a trip for us. An opportunity for us to reconnect."

"Where?" Her instantaneous perkiness made Bram cringe.

"A private island in the Indian Ocean."

Isley blinked rapidly. "The Maldives?"

"Yes." Oliver's tone was calm and distant, but the news shook Isley.

"And now?"

Oliver shrugged. "According to your well-designed plan, I'm going there with my new boyfriend."

"We can figure it out." Isley looked slightly panicked, but Bram had had enough.

"I need to be clear about something." He was thrilled to watch Isley flinch when he reentered the conversation. "Am I supposed to be Oliver's boyfriend right now?"

Isley nodded and swallowed. "That's the plan. You two are an item until this blows over."

It was a terrible idea. Bram knew he was lousy at hiding his feelings. His mother always knew when he was lying, crushing on someone, or trying to be sneaky. Even as Isley confronted Bram's transparency, she paid no attention to Oliver's obvious discomfort with her suggestion. Even if his former boss wasn't interested in pretending to cuddle up with him, Bram could help smooth this epic shit show by creating a social media campaign to help Oliver survive.

Bram cleared his throat. "Well, then, there's only one thing to do."

He leaned across the limo, his arm brushing Oliver's knee, and popped the door handle. Cool air rushed into the limo as the door swung open.

"Get out. You've ruined our evening and overstayed your welcome." Bram gestured for her to move. "We have a plane to catch."

CHAPTER
SIX

OLIVER

Bram refused to return Oliver's phone until they landed in the Maldives, so he was forced to watch Bram manage the clusterfuck fallout.

As their driver navigated clogged streets, Bram tapped at his phone like his life depended on it, brows knit, issuing a final swipe with a satisfied flourish. It was adorable.

Equally sweet had been his conversation with Con and Rosa. Bram let them know that he would be away for a few days and asked if they could pack a bag for him. He walked them through his apartment for his clothing and passport. Con refused to have a courier service deliver the bag and agreed to drop it at the airport.

When Bram asked them to water his plants and bring in his mail, they had demanded to speak with both of them. They'd seen what happened and offered their heartfelt regrets to Oliver, with several blush-inducing compliments that made Bram squirm in his seat.

At the airport, Bram asked the driver to meet the person dropping off the order he'd quickly purchased on his favorite delivery app. Bram handed Oliver a bag containing two gaming magazines, jalapeño kettle chips, gummy fish, and two hydrating face masks before grabbing the duffle bag of clothing Con had dropped off.

"Two face masks?" he asked Bram as they walked up the steps of the jet.

"After everything I've seen tonight," he replied, landing with a weary flop in a wide plush recliner, "I need a little self-care, too." Bram settled then began rummaging through his bag. "Give me a minute here. I want to make sure I have enough clothing since I can't wear this suit for the next week."

Oliver didn't think before he blurted out, "Where we're going, you don't need to wear a lot."

"Sunscreen?" Bram managed after the slightest flinch. He sighed at Oliver's nod and set his phone down. "We need to discuss how to present this to your followers."

Oliver extended his seat to a full recline. "Business already?"

"I think it will help us"—Bram paused as the flight attendant scurried by—"sell this."

Oliver rolled to his side, propped on his elbow. "Sell what? We're friends. We're on vacation. Let's have a good time. Post some pictures of both of us in swim trunks looking sexy and sun-kissed and that will be enough."

Bram leaned back, his long legs crossing at his ankles. He looked party-boy sexy. His hair was a little wild from running his fingers through it. The top buttons of his shirt were undone, revealing the smooth skin just under the dip of his throat. Oliver caught himself staring as he teased the question: *Does Bram taste as good as he smells?*

Isley was too close to revealing one of the stumbling blocks in their relationship. When they'd discussed what he wanted, what he craved, Isley listened and said she was open to exploration. They tried, but the experience was never satisfying. Something was missing.

When Oliver was alone, he chased his unmet longing with his own hands. Touch and sensation that sparked vivid fantasies about Bram.

"Oliver?" Bram's voice pulled Oliver back into awareness.

The flight attendant was standing a few feet away with an expectant look on their face. "We're ready if you are, sir. Can I get you a drink before takeoff?"

"Water," Oliver said with a rasp before pointing to Bram.

"The same, please," Bram said. "Can you stay with me for a few minutes while we talk about this before you zoom off into outer space or wherever you just were?"

Oliver sat up. "Sure. Yes." He nodded to the flight attendant and turned to Bram. "What do you have in mind?"

"I don't think we should play up our alleged coupledom."

Oliver nearly choked on his water.

"I'm worried it might be too soon. It might spark more questions about why Isley did what she did."

"We're going to deny that we're dating?" Oliver tried not to sound as disappointed as he felt.

"No. She's already posted the ruse. Some people are calling bull-shit. Others are loving your new relationship status."

"You mean *our* relationship status?"

A sweet rosy color filled Bram's cheeks. "They think we're cute."

"Because we are. If we aren't going to enjoy everyone loving on us—"

"Not everyone is loving us."

"—what's your plan?"

Bram inhaled, and a sly look accompanied a deviously sexy grin. "Let's think of this as a side quest. We'll wander off the beaten path, engage in a few adventures that we'll share with your followers. We don't have to confirm or deny a relationship status. It will be my job to make you look delicious. Let your followers draw their own conclusions about our status, and make sure Isley Berns regrets the day she decided Oliver Kent wasn't her man."

CHAPTER
SEVEN

BRAM

Bram soaked in every delightful moment of the smooth flight to Male Velana International Airport, until he realized their bags were being loaded onto a small seaplane.

He stopped in his tracks, Oliver slamming into him from behind. "What the hell, Bram?"

Bram could only shake his head. With a bubbling sensation, saliva and the taste of gummy fish filled his mouth at the sight.

"No way," he squeaked out.

Oliver looked sweetly concerned. "Did our state-of-the-art hybrid flight pamper you too much?"

"That thing is a flying tuna can." Bram hoped Oliver didn't hear his voice shaking.

"That tuna can is going to take you to a caviar location." Oliver bodychecked Bram, jostling him forward. Still hesitant, Bram absorbed most of the hit.

Oliver hooked his arm around his shoulders, his mouth dipping close to Bram's ear. "C'mon. I'll be next to you the entire time."

Oliver must have felt the shiver that resulted from the lightning bolt of lust that struck Bram's body because he chuckled as he tugged him forward.

Bram was exhausted. Still shaken from the night's events. He felt grimy in Con's suit, which needed to be professionally cleaned. Hopefully Con and Rosa had grabbed something clean from the pile of clothing he'd left before attending the gala.

But planning all the ways he was going to post images of Oliver to his socials had Bram's body thrumming with excitement.

None of that would matter if they fell out of the sky on their way to a private resort meant for lovers.

Side questers.

Friends who might be enjoying benefits, but who also might just be friends adventuring.

Bram wanted benefits. With Oliver. Badly.

He'd thought he could face-mask-and-meditate away the edge that had gripped him with a near-constant hard-on since he kicked Isley out of the limo.

But no. Her suggestion had him by the balls.

Bram watched Oliver engage the pilot, confirm their destination, then followed him into the tiny cabin.

"It's a twenty-five minute flight. We're up, and then we're down." Oliver looked too happy for just being publicly dumped.

"How are you so awake?"

Oliver shrugged. "I love traveling and exploring unknown places."

"I'm exhausted."

Bram felt pressure on his thigh, his muscle jumping at the firm touch of Oliver's hand. "It's been a wild night." Oliver's fingers kneaded his leg, the warm touch causing Bram to melt in his seat. A knowing grunt shook him back into the present moment.

"We'll have some dinner and relax tonight. We both deserve to rest. Tomorrow, we can take it easy or explore."

Before Bram could protest, the seaplane sputtered to life. Bram set a pair of clunky headphones over his ears and offered up a hopeful prayer to all the good, supportive, and loving beings in the universe who might help keep their plane aloft, then closed his eyes.

He should have known that Oliver would spare no expense for Isley. Bram only dared a peek as the plane descended toward a single island in the middle of the expansive ocean, the turquoise-blue water lapping against pristine white sand.

"Oliver. Is that where we're staying?" Bram yelled over the churn of the plane engine.

"Yeah." His smile was dazzling. "The pictures don't do it justice."

"You rented an entire island!"

"Bram, I'm the GFA Gamer of the Year," he said without arrogance. "I work hard and I like to play hard." Oliver leaned over to whisper, as if the pilot could hear them. "I won't lie; this was for her." Bram nodded in understanding. "However," Oliver continued, "I'm psyched you're with me because I knew I'd be snorkeling and boating by myself if she were here."

"Really?" Bram's frame bounced as the plane hit turbulence. "She wouldn't do any of those things with you?"

Oliver considered the question. "If she could lounge and take a stellar photo, sure. Izzy never went fishing with me. Snorkeling was okay, but she never wanted to boat or jet ski."

Bram nodded. "We'll do all that stuff, and I'll take great pictures of you."

"I know what your plan is, but let's just enjoy it, okay? Not everything needs to be documented for the world." Oliver looked past Bram. "Good. We're here."

Bram blinked in disbelief as the staff started pulling luggage from the plane, which now idled in shallow water.

"How the hell did I miss that?"

"Rocketing across the ocean in a flying tuna can?" Oliver said, deadpan, before flashing a devastatingly handsome smile. "I guess I'm just that captivating."

"Easy with that ego, Golden Gamer." Bram unbuckled his safety belt and set his headphones on the seat. "If your head is that big when we go snorkeling, you'll sink. I'll be forced to leave you to the reef and then how will I ever get that well-deserved job recommendation from Margaret?"

"Geez! We need to call Maggie!" Oliver's eyes darted around the plane, as if she was going to spring from the cargo hold and demand an explanation for what the hell had happened.

"*We* are not calling Margaret. *You* are calling Margaret. *I* am taking a shower."

"Are you really going to leave me alone while she yells?"

"By now, she's seen everything. Con and Rosa know what happened. Margaret felt a shift in the force and immediately logged on. If anything, I'm sure she's happy you maintained yourself in the moment. Her tone might be elevated but she will yell into your pain, not at your pain."

"Stay with me." Oliver's fingers teased at Bram's. "As my fake boyfriend, please support me while my pain is yelled into."

Bram widened his fingers to accept Oliver's palm against his. "I thought we agreed we were side questing."

"As my partner in adventure, you should be by my side when I face fierce adversaries." Oliver's thumb rubbed against Bram's. "You can have a shower. I'll call Maggie. Then I want to have dinner with you."

Bram swallowed down the thundering pulse that shook his throat. "Fine. I'm going to clock how quickly she can type her rage. Now, let's go check this place out."

"Okay," Oliver said, agreeing too easily.

Bram didn't protest when Oliver didn't let go of his hand as they walked down the short exit ramp and into the most luxurious bungalow he had ever laid eyes on.

CHAPTER
EIGHT

OLIVER

Maggie was a ballbuster normally, but damn, she was a mama bear when shit hit the fan.

"I can't believe she did that to you," she seethed, her voice raspy but stronger than before. "Are you okay? I'm glad you took the trip. I know you were planning on taking it with her, but I think it's good for you to reset."

"Yeah." Oliver glanced across the open concept bungalow and breathed in the sweet smell of the ocean. "It's good to be here. We're going to take advantage of—"

"Wait, who is *we*?"

"Bram is with me." Oliver's gaze drifted across the bungalow to the closed door of the bedroom suite. When he heard Maggie's sigh of judgment filter over the line, he rolled his eyes. "It's fine, Maggie."

"It's not, Oliver. He was your intern for months. A paid intern at that. I understand Isley is trying to save face by saying you two have already split—"

"That's not what she's saying. She's pitching that we're in an open relationship."

"Why can't she just break up with you?"

"Because somehow that would be less brutal? It's bad enough that my girlfriend, on the eve of my whisking her away to a romantic getaway, bones a guy who is my gaming rival. To make matters worse, she somehow manipulated me into agreeing to pretend to date Bram."

"Does Bram know that?"

"He was there for the conversation."

"What did he say?"

Oliver drifted to the deck when he heard Bram moving around the suite. "He said we should focus on me and not on us. He thinks he can make us look believable without splashing us all over social media." Maggie was quiet for a moment too long. "Are you still there?"

She cleared her throat. "Are you okay with this? An open relationship?"

"No. Izzy and I are done."

"Are you and Bram on?"

"Izzy confronted him about having a crush on me."

"And that you glow like you've had a million energy drinks when he's around," Maggie drawled.

Bram's movement through the bungalow sounded close, triggering Oliver's swift walk down the pier to the beach.

"Excuse me?" he snapped.

Maggie scoffed. "Oliver, he left and you veered into Frown Town. Population, your sad ass."

"Not accurate."

Maggie choked on a hoarse cough. "Yes," she wheezed. "Just be careful with each other. You just suffered a nasty relationship curveball and he, well, he's a gem. Do not break his heart."

"What if he breaks my heart?"

"I think if you gave him that privilege, he'd hold it close for life." Oliver didn't have time to consider Maggie's insight before she banged left into Cringeville without a signal. "You have condoms, right?"

Before Oliver could answer, Bram materialized beside him. "Hey." His tone was gentle, his hair deliciously damp from the shower. A simple shirt and cotton shorts made him look relaxed. *Unbutton your shirt*, he mouthed as he held up his phone.

"Oliver? Did I kill you?" Maggie asked with a squawk.

"Uh, no ...," he mumbled as he held his phone between his ear and shoulder. He fumbled with two tiny disks before Bram's warm hands brushed up against his to pull the buttons free. A whimper died in his throat when Bram's fingers ruffled his hair.

"We have discussed the merits of safe sex, Oliver. I don't care if Isley was on the shot. I don't care if you're tested regularly. Condoms are an added layer—"

"Bram is here to take some thirst traps, Maggie, so ...."

Keep talking, Bram prompted as he tugged on the hem, allowing his shirt to billow in the breeze.

He was going to die of embarrassment-fueled lust. Maggie and Bram would only have themselves to blame for their tragic loss.

"Okay, so did you watch my speech?" Oliver tried desperately to create a relaxed posture so that Bram could get a worthy photo.

"I just texted the on-island infirmary. They confirmed that a box of condoms is in the bathroom of the main sleeping quarters."

"I think it went well also," Oliver chirped through a forced smile. His chest burned with the agony of having a parental-level sex talk while the man he yearned for knelt down in front of him. Bram on his knees at Oliver's feet ... An image that would haunt him for life.

"For the record, you deserve a little fun. Even if you aren't boyfriends, you can have some hot sex."

"Sounds great," he said too loudly. "I'll call you in a few days. Bye!" Maggie started to protest but Oliver ended the call and took a stabilizing breath before clapping his hands. "What do we want for dinner?"

CHAPTER
NINE

BRAM

Pouring over images of Oliver looking professional and focused, the gleaming Indian Ocean winking behind him, was easy. He needed to focus on something other than their luxurious accommodations. The private bungalow held treasure upon treasure—gleaming teak floors, plush white furniture, bathrooms that put swanky spas to shame, and the largest, sexiest bed Bram had ever laid eyes on.

It was simple in its design. Four sturdy posts framed a lush mattress draped with delicate linen. It exuded relaxation, and offered a space for the dirtiest of deeds known to man.

Bram had stared at it too long.

Then he'd hid under the deluge from the waterfall shower and prayed for his brain to stop envisioning Oliver tangled in the rumpled sheets.

"See one you like?" Oliver asked from behind the kitchen island as he picked over a selection of fruit. "Mmm." The sound of satisfaction sent prickles down Bram's spine. "I love pineapple," Oliver said without realizing Bram was moments from drooling.

Bram cleared his throat and hoped his body would calm down. "There are a bunch, actually. I can send them to you for approval."

"No need." Oliver loaded a plate of fruit and sauntered over. He straddled the bench Bram sat on, his knees nearly bracketing Bram's hips. "Show me what you got."

They weren't touching, but Bram could feel his close presence. "I like these." He pointed to three images for Oliver's approval. "We can post all three and ask people to vote on their favorite. Or we can just share one and say you've arrived."

"We've arrived." Oliver popped a plump strawberry into his mouth. "What are people saying?"

It had been Bram's job to make sure Oliver's comments section was positive and engaged followers, who he enjoyed talking to. They had read Isley's post together on the plane but hadn't talked about her claim that they were dating.

Bram inhaled. "As usual, there are haters." He shrugged. "If you weren't going to hell for being bi, your ticket is now punched for dating a man."

"I think we're hotties, but we're not going to hell." Oliver smiled as he bit into a tempting sliver of mango. Bram watched his lips as he enjoyed the firm fruit for a moment too long. "Tell me the good stuff."

The haters' posts were always present, but the posts of love and support for them outshined any bigoted garbage. "It seems like, despite the abrupt shift in relationship status, people are open to you and Isley being open."

"Good. Why aren't you in the image with me? We have to go along with this."

"My job is to make you look happy."

"Happy in my new open relationship?"

"Yes," Bram confirmed.

"Which includes you … but doesn't?"

"Correct."

"That won't help our cause."

He sagged in his seat. "Oliver, it's a lie."

"Bram," Oliver said, volleying his name like an admonishment. "Pictures say a thousand words. Let the images tell the tale."

That was the problem. Bram had gone into marketing and social media because choosing a career path as a teacher, police officer, politician, or spy required a specific skill set, which included mastering a poker face.

According to Isley, Bram's crush on Oliver was visible to the world. If he was in the pictures with Oliver, his affection for him would be tattooed on the internet long after their ruse was done.

Yet they would resurface every time Oliver dated someone or the gossip circuit was hungry for the handsome bisexual gamer/philanthropist who ate fresh pineapple like a lion enjoying the kill.

Bram watched Oliver's teeth bisect the sweet yellow flesh, juice trickling over his dusky-pink lip before his tongue swiped it away.

"How—" The word cracked in Bram's throat. "How should we go about making us look like a couple?"

Oliver set down his fork, turning his full attention to Bram. He edged closer, his wide knees hugging Bram's thigh. "Was what she said true?"

Bram's gaze traced the wide fall of Oliver's quads. "Help me with that one." He inhaled and met Oliver's gaze. "She said a lot of things."

Oliver's tongue played along his teeth. "About you."

"That she never cared for me? Yes, that's true. You knew that."

The knowing tilt of his head passed as agreement. "That was her issue, but I'm not talking about that." Oliver paused. "What she said about the way you look at me."

The once-comfortable bench felt like a seat of needles. "You looked handsome last night," he admitted with a cautious laugh. The chuckle died in his throat with Oliver's devilish grin. "Every night. You look handsome all the time."

Oliver's fingers toyed with the edge of a cotton napkin. "She was jealous of you." His voice was so light it could have been the breeze.

"Me?"

Oliver nodded. "I talked about you. I might have mentioned your … aptitudes. More than she would have liked."

Bram suddenly felt the weight of the evening: the whirlwind red carpet; Isley's exposed body, now burned in his memory; the suggestion that he was Oliver's lover; the flight he'd barely registered because he was in damage-control mode; Oliver's long limbs first sprawled in the limo and draped in expensive formal wear, and now—clad in a breezy linen—inches from Bram's body. They were close enough for Bram to snuggle against Oliver's chest and feel him inhale. "I post to your social media." His mouth felt dry. "I do nothing but show off the amazing things you do."

Oliver hummed. "And you do that very well." They sat for a moment, listening to the calming lap of the ocean. "What's on the itinerary for tomorrow?"

Yes. That's what he needed. A job. "A hike in the morning and scuba diving in the afternoon. Sounds like a perfect opportunity to show off my aptitudes."

Bram didn't want to feel the electric bolt of lust when he caught Oliver looking at him with unmasked amusement. "I can't wait."

He needed five minutes to breathe air that didn't smell like Oliver, or fresh fruit, or the clean ocean breeze. This trip might only be five days, but he would reimagine this moment for the rest of his life. "Since there is only the main suite, I can stay out here." Bram gestured loosely to the couch that could easily fit ten bodies. "It's big enough for an orgy," he said with a snort.

Oliver's jaw rolled. "Maybe you could test that theory on another day. I think you should stay in the main suite."

"You're going to sleep on the orgy couch?"

"Not tonight."

"You're going to stay in the main suite? With me?"

"Yes." Oliver stood, his body skating by Bram's. "C'mon, it's been a long day."

Bram watched Oliver's broad frame fade as he moved down the darkened hallway then disappeared into the bedroom.

He should have spent more time in the shower.

CHAPTER
TEN

OLIVER

When Oliver had planned the rigorous hike around the island, it was designed as a solo trip. Taking on the physical challenges of the terrain was a time for personal reflection and goal planning. With Bram by his side, enjoying the athletic challenge of it all, the adventure now bloomed with life. They were sweaty and dirty, the musk of exertion wafting through the air as they jockeyed over rock fields and raced across an unending stretch of white sand.

Waking up next to a sleep-tousled Bram was a fantasy Oliver wanted to live every day of his life, even if their first night had been a companionable sleepover. The sight of Bram's perfect vintage formal wear becoming rumpled and undone during their evening was a delicious memory he would relive over and over.

They'd settled into the sumptuous cotton, the mattress comfortable enough to make Bram groan at the luxury of it all and yet firm enough to make Oliver think about how much the bed could take when put to the test.

Those thoughts did not soothe Oliver. He listened for Bram's breath to fall into the deep cadence of sleep, but it hadn't come for almost an hour.

He was grateful now for Bram's athleticism. Especially his calves, splattered with sand and mud from their hike. They were sweat-streaked and messy against a naturally pristine backdrop, but Oliver craved more. He wanted Bram in all the filthy ways he could imagine in the sparse days on the island.

When they collapsed on the deck of their bungalow, the shockingly invisible staff had their lunch set out in a bright display of fresh fruits, veggies, and fish.

"Yes," Bram said, moaning. "I'm claiming the mango. All of it"—he pointed a finger at Oliver—"is mine."

A surge of pride flowed through him. He had added Bram's favorite fruit to their meals when they arrived.

"Can I have one slice?"

"Well," Bram said, making a show of considering his options, "you brought me to a luxurious private island, so I suppose."

Oliver nodded and grabbed a spear of the peppery fruit. "Do you want to eat here or inside?"

"Here is great. Plus, I need to look at the pictures I took this morning."

"After we eat?" At Bram's questioning look, Oliver clarified. "Can you look at the pictures after we eat?" Oliver had mentally cataloged every nibble of Bram's lip and tug of his hair as he worked through the minefield of comments about their new fake-lationship. He had also struggled with Isley's constant focus on her phone. She was an influencer by trade, but he enjoyed communal meals. Attempting to engage her while she giggled at a screen and commented on posts was exhausting.

Bram blinked, seeming to connect why he'd made the request. "Of course." He set his phone at the far end of the buffet. "Let's eat."

The spread was enormous, as was the depth of their conversation, and Oliver enjoyed the lively twists and turns. The latest football stats. The tech used to craft hybrid charter jets. How the chef had created the spice palette, and if they had a garden or relied on local farms.

"I need more of that hummus." Bram took one final swipe through the dip with a carrot then settled back with a satisfied groan. "I need to stop or my stuffed body, anchored to the ocean floor, will ruin our scuba excursion."

"The ocean is forgiving and offers buoyancy."

"So kind," Bram said before taking a long drink of water.

Oliver had to peel his gaze away from Bram. Watching Bram's throat work fed the need to feel those muscles under his tongue.

"Oliver?"

"Hmm?"

Bram's fingers were loosely tangled against his belly, his head back, his lickable neck on full display. "Do you think she would have appreciated what you've done here?"

Oliver's mouth fell open, but nothing emerged.

"It's just that this is beautiful. I'm grateful for this experience, but all of this is extravagantly planned. I'm not sure why you would agree to this so quickly when you clearly care about her happiness."

"This, as in agreeing to the lie that we are open?" At Bram's nod, Oliver couldn't dismiss the earnest observation with another lie. "We haven't been good for a while. The gala was the first time we were going to see each other in about a month."

"A month?" Bram's eyes went wide. "She's present on socials."

"But never at the office." The laugh that pushed from his chest wasn't happy. "Maggie was always tense when she came to the office. Her feelings about Izzy were clear. When I asked Maggie to give her a chance, she reluctantly agreed."

"Is that Margaret's place? To give relationship advice."

"Maggie has been with me since Kent Technologies was a scratched-out plan on notebook paper. She's a force, but she always has my best interest in mind. Besides, are you going to tell Maggie to mind her own business?"

Bram chuckled. "She resurrected me from the bowels of my couch to wear a seventy-year-old man's suit while she battled the plague. I'm not the best example of standing one's ground against Margaret."

"She likes you. That's why she called."

"She likes my skills." Bram waggled his brows. "My aptitudes."

"She appreciated your work. I enjoy your aptitudes."

Bram's gaze flitted to Oliver before he shifted in his seat. "Speaking of which," he said with a jaunty lilt, "I got some great photos during our hike. The island is gorgeous, and you are looking rugged and well-worn, which everyone will love." Bram retrieved his phone from the buffet and set it next to Oliver. With a flick of his finger, he gestured for him to swipe the screen. "Pick your favorite and I'll post it for your adoring fans."

Oliver didn't need to swipe, he knew they wouldn't cut it. "*We need to be shared.*" He enjoyed the slightest flinch from Bram. "Why are you hesitating?"

Bram shifted again in his seat, turning his profile to Oliver. He fought the urge to press his mouth to the tender skin under the sharp line of Bram's jaw.

"Bram?" Even with Oliver's coaxing, Bram still wouldn't look at him. "I see your interest in me." The cool admission caused Bram's eyes to flare wide. "I hope you can see mine, too."

"I didn't know," Bram said, hedging, "that you knew … or that you reciprocated."

"I know this has been crafted to hide Isley's infidelity, but I've wanted to know how soft your lips are for longer than I care to admit."

"You never seemed interested … like that." Bram's voice held the airy wisp of disbelief.

"I was your boss. In some circles, lusting after your intern is a no-no."

"But fake dating is okay?"

"I'm not your boss anymore. And this is real. I want us to be real." Oliver parsed Bram's silence. "Do you want that with me?"

Bram's nod was tight. "Yes."

In all the games that Oliver designed, satisfaction always came when the task was complete. Otter cleaned the beach. The lawn was mowed, trimmed, or cut into beautiful patterns. The bookshelves, designed however the player desired, were organized by size, color, or genre.

Bram's nod was all of those things.

He was the satisfied feeling when the hard work was over.

Oliver wanted that good feeling everywhere.

"Can I kiss you?"

Bram's visible shudder triggered silver-tipped bolts of desire through Oliver, and he nodded as his pink tongue skated along his lower lip. Bram's teeth then pinned his lip as his gaze settled on Oliver's mouth.

"Keep that up," Oliver warned as he stood from his chair and leaned over Bram, "and we'll never get to scuba dive."

Bram allowed space for Oliver to move closer. It was too much, and yet, not enough. Oliver carded his fingers through Bram's hair before gently cupping his face.

Another tremor shivered through Bram as Oliver skimmed his thumb along the curve of his lip.

"Just a kiss for now." Bram's breathless words fanned Oliver's lust. "Okay?"

Oliver cleared his throat, swallowing down the need to cancel every plan he'd made and explore Bram instead.

"For now, this is enough." His lips hovered just over Bram's. "More later?"

Bram nodded. His breathy "yes" was all Oliver needed before capturing the mouth he'd fantasized about for months.

CHAPTER
ELEVEN

BRAM

Even after several hours in the water exploring the beautiful reefs along the shore, Bram was eager to slip into their bungalow's private pool.

The infinity edge provided a seamless view of the clear blue-green water. He felt limitless. Bram was enjoying a private vacation with Oliver, who had kissed him with a hunger that matched his own.

They'd been late for scuba diving. Despite Bram's focus on punctuality and respect for other people's schedules, when Oliver's tongue swept across his own, and he *groaned* into Bram's mouth, he'd no longer cared.

They were on a private island, and the heat in Oliver's eyes left nothing to question.

Oliver seemed open to exploring. The alarm bells Bram heard at the start of this mess had been soothed by the sound of crystal waves lapping at the white sand.

"Sir." A staff member nodded in greeting before setting down a large tray on the surface of the water.

"Oh, uh, I can get out," he started to say, but the man set down two more and walked away.

Bram stood, shocked, as the trays, loaded with fruit, meat, and vegetables, floated on the water.

"Cool, right?" Bram didn't have to look up to know Oliver was smiling.

When he did, he was gifted the sight of Oliver in loose swim trunks that hung low on his hips, his body lean and muscled from years of yoga.

Bram traced the line of Oliver's abdomen with his eyes, soaking in the smattering of hair that disappeared below the waist of his trunks before remembering himself.

"Definitely." He gestured to the trays. "I've never had a floating meal before."

"Same," Oliver agreed as he slipped into the pool. He popped a cucumber slice into his mouth, humming in satisfaction. "Could you imagine this setup while watching the playoffs?"

"Which playoffs?"

"It doesn't matter." Oliver gestured for Bram to eat. "Regardless of the game, you're chilled out because you're in the water. Get pissed at a missed play and thrash around in here, nothing gets inadvertently broken. The team wins, you have a splash fest. All of it works."

"That is why you are a successful entrepreneur."

Oliver seemed to absorb the compliment as they both ate, sharing their favorite moments from scuba diving and talking about the next day's excursions.

When they had polished off the trays, a final one with juicy strawberries and bubbly champagne flutes, complete with tiny, twinkling tea lights, floated toward them.

"Darling," Bram cooed, "you shouldn't have."

"I do aim to please." Oliver had the audacity to look sheepish. "I didn't have time to ask them for whiskey and blondies."

Bram swallowed his shock. Whiskey was always his spirit of choice. Blondies were his favorite indulgence. "How did you know that?"

Oliver chuckled. "You mentioned something about Rosa making them for you once. You suggested them on the survey for staff meeting lunch options. I figured you liked them."

"Very much." Bram's chest felt warm. "I didn't realize you paid such close attention."

Oliver shrugged. "I always thought you were handsome. Isley is right. I totally have a thing for blonds." His sly wink made Bram laugh. "The more time we spent together, and the better I got to know you, the more I realized you checked all my boxes."

"We get along well," Bram said, conceding. "Margaret could never discuss playoff baseball like I do."

"Maggie hates sports, and despite my annual notation of such incompetence on her employee review, she continues to not improve."

"Steadfast in her ignorance," Bram said in confirmation. "Never tell her I said that."

Oliver laughed. "She'd never believe me if I did. She can be terrifying, but she likes you."

"As much as you like me?" It was a cheap ploy, but Bram was still thrumming from their kiss. He'd shared kisses before, but Oliver's felt different.

"I like you in a very different way, Bram." He lifted a brow. "You know what did it for me?" At his coaxing hum, Oliver continued. "The *Otter's River Cleanup* launch." Oliver lounged against the side of the pool, his arms resting wide along the invisible edge. "You were so proud. So excited. I knew you understood what I was trying to do. You worked to make that vision happen."

Bram shrugged. "It's my job to make sure you shine. That's my purpose."

"Right, but it's how you did it. You knew what I wanted. Do you remember when you came to me and asked to bring in the zoologist from the otter rehab center to provide an educational session for the launch? It was like we were sharing a brain. Izzy never understood that part of me." Oliver's expression shuttered as he looked out over the ocean. "When I think about it, she didn't understand a lot."

Bram's irritation with Isley ratcheted up. "I'm sorry, Oliver. I thought you two were happy."

He sighed. "We were at one point. She's great, but she's not my person. We have similar desires, but different comfort levels with achieving those desires."

Bram felt his own body tighten at Oliver's disclosure. "She couldn't give you what you needed?"

"She was open to try, but she told me it wasn't for her." Oliver took a sip of champagne. "She wasn't into it. I could feel her distance the moment we started." Oliver was quiet for a moment. "Things unraveled after that."

The knowledge that Oliver had been in a vulnerable moment with Isley and felt disconnected from his partner made Bram want to rage. "I'm sorry that happened to you. No one should feel like that in an intimate moment. She should have stopped if she didn't want to engage anymore."

"I told her the same thing." Oliver looked upset all over again. "In all fairness, I didn't stop it either. It's one thing to not like what you're doing and stopping. It's another thing to not like what you're doing but still feel compelled to keep going for the other person. I felt like shit for weeks after. She bounced back in a day."

For Bram, Isley would always be single-service: she was for herself. "I take it she didn't want to explore after that."

"She's not very flexible with the desires of her bisexual boyfriend." Oliver huffed. "I think that was her issue. If I was with her, I shouldn't crave the feelings I could have with a male partner. She didn't understand me in that way."

"She should have respected your needs, Oliver."

Oliver looked at him over the thin rim of the champagne flute as he took another sip. "Are you flexible, Bram?"

"Not like you … I can touch my toes, but that yoga pretzel move you had me post to social media a month ago would have me limping for days."

Oliver looked as serious as a man in a pool, with a champagne flute dangling from his fingers, could. "That's not what I mean, and you know it."

Bram felt his cheeks flush. Oliver wanted this conversation. They both needed it. "I usually bottom, but I'm open to whatever brings you pleasure."

"Would topping me, when I crave that?"

Bram couldn't hide anymore. Here it was, the truth of his desires laid bare. "Anything you need, regardless of who is giving and who is receiving, would bring me pleasure."

Oliver pushed off the side of the pool, a look of bold determination on his face. "You just keep getting better and better."

CHAPTER
TWELVE

OLIVER

In the waist-high water of the infinity pool, Oliver marveled at the droplets that clung to Bram's shoulders. He hovered, with mere inches between them. "Can we explore?"

At Bram's shaky inhale, Oliver's confidence waffled. He wanted Bram, but he would not live through the shame and embarrassment he slogged through after asking Isley to peg him. Her initial enthusiasm was breathtaking but, in the moment, he'd felt incredibly alone.

"Do you want to kiss me again?" Bram asked between heavy breaths, his chest lifting and falling.

"I never wanted to stop the first time." He enjoyed the catch of Bram's breath too much. "Yes, I want to kiss you. I want to touch you."

"Where?" The word gusted over Oliver's shoulder. Bram's fingers threaded through the water.

"Where do you like to be touched, Bram?" Oliver tangled their fingers together, lifting their joined hands, marveling at the ribbon of water that ran down Bram's muscular forearm and cascaded back into the pool. It was a delight Oliver committed to memory. "Show me."

Oliver shifted their grip to allow Bram to extend his pointer finger, dragging the tip of Bram's finger along his own collarbone. "Do you like to be touched here?"

Bram's gaze was fixated on the place where his finger touched Oliver's skin, his tongue licking, and teeth nibbling, at his own lips. "Yes."

"You are going to kill me." Oliver chuckled as he lifted his other hand and trailed a touch along Bram's collarbone. "Where to next?"

Bram swallowed and drifted their joined hands up the column of Oliver's neck and along the underside of his jaw. "I like attention here." Oliver felt the gravel in Bram's voice abrade every inch of his body.

"Attention here?" Oliver confirmed by tracing the path Bram set on his skin. When Bram shivered, Oliver untangled their fingers but laid his hand to Bram's shoulder. Oliver stepped closer pressing a chase kiss to his collarbone, then drifting to the tender place below Bram's jaw.

The strained hum, the sharp buck of Bram's hips, nearly triggered a feral response in Oliver. He pulled back. "I need us to take our time." He cleared his throat, his own arousal fogging his brain. "Show me where else."

Bram shook his head, then closed his eyes, pushing a breath through his nose before focusing on Oliver again. His fingers drifted down Oliver's chest, tracing the line of his pecs before brushing a light touch over Oliver's nipples. "You are so hot."

Bram's touch had Oliver bucking against the shapeless water.

At Oliver's growl, Bram chuckled. "How about this?" Under the water, Bram pulled at Oliver's hip, nestling their bodies close.

"Am I really going to dry hump you right now?"

"Well"—Bram shrugged—"technically, it's a wet hump because we're in a pool."

Oliver reveled in Bram's gasp as he pushed their bodies together, their hard arousal rubbing slick against each other in the cool water. He was moments from losing his mind over this man.

"I want you in my mouth." Oliver punched every word with a thrust of his hips. "I want you begging for everything I'm going to give you."

At Oliver's heady demand, Bram carded his fingers through his hair and devoured his mouth, their kisses rough as they ground against each other. When Bram's hand snaked under the waistband of his swim trunks, fingers skimming his sensitive skin, Oliver gasped.

"Is this okay?" Bram's voice held a bold edge. "We're not doing anything that doesn't feel good for you. For us."

"Yes." Oliver pushed a breath through his nose in a futile attempt to calm his body. Of course, he didn't do himself any favors when he covered Bram's hand with his own to grip his cock. "Let me watch you."

Oliver was pinned to the sight of Bram stroking his body. The deep rumble that flowed from Bram's chest had Oliver jerking and shuttling into Bram's touch. "Fuck. So good."

The heavy pressure of Bram's attention triggered Oliver's body to coil and burn with need.

"Yes, that," Oliver choked out. "Harder." His body moved of its own volition, chasing Bram's touch, rutting into his hand. A single swipe of Bram's thumb over the head of his cock had him spiraling out of control.

Bram bracketed his body the moment he careened over the edge, continuing to pump him, kisses absorbing the rough groans of heady pleasure. Gentle presses of his mouth against his chest and neck immediately soothed Bram's rough treatment, his hands caressing his shoulders and arms.

"Good?" Oliver could hear the smile Bram pressed into his neck.

"We're never leaving this pool." Oliver enjoyed Bram's laugh, but delighted in his quiet gasp when he said, "I need a few minutes, then I'm going to make you scream my name."

CHAPTER
THIRTEEN

BRAM

Bram uploaded a new reel from the previous day's shipwreck snorkeling tour to Oliver's account, mindful not to share how he'd had a slight freak-out about the possibility that shipwrecks were haunted, and that they would violate some ghost code by gawking at the wreckage of a very sad turn of events.

Once their guide patiently talked him down, they enjoyed their swim, even if Bram didn't venture near the sunken boats.

What he did was post a selfie of himself and Oliver enjoying an afternoon on the beach. Both of them sun-kissed, their hair fluffy from the sea breeze. He loved the picture. They looked happy and relaxed. They looked like a couple on vacation.

Sexy boys on a sexy beach
    How is the water? It looks beautiful!
    You two are walking f**k me signs I hate you both for being so damn hot

Bram skated through the comments, basking in the compliments and deleting the trolls. When Isley's comment floated to the top, he paused. *Romance wins! Can't wait to see you!*

Romance *wins*? As in, she can have a romance without telling Oliver? Or she can tell Oliver his needs will be respected and met while she's getting off with another man?

"Are you almost ready?" Oliver called from the suite, dragging Bram out of his thoughts. "The boat is about ten minutes out."

"Yeah." Bram couldn't parse Isley's post. "Hey, do you have plans to see Isley?"

"No. I thought once I got back from Singapore there'd be an official announcement that Isley and I are no longer." He walked to Bram and leaned close, landing a kiss on his cheek before looking at the screen.

"That's what I thought." Bram pointed to the comment. "This seems weird."

"Who knows. I'm sure she's just trying to smooth over the situation." Oliver smacked the marble countertop. "You know, now that I think about it, you could come to Singapore with me." He added a jaunty wink, as if to seal the deal.

"I would love to, but I'm graduating. After years of funneling every dollar into that institution, I'm snatching my diploma out of the dean's hand and marching across that stage. For all the time and money I spent on my degree, especially when they promised job placement and I am still unemployed, they owe me a catwalk experience."

"Ugh." Oliver wrinkled his nose. "If you need the spotlight so badly." His attempt to chastise dissolved into laughter. "I agree you should take part in graduation. You know Kent Technologies could always use a social media manager." Oliver's gaze was hopeful.

"You were worried about the boss sleeping with the intern, but it's okay to get the job because I'm sleeping with the boss?"

"When you put it like that ...." Oliver grimaced. "Maybe you could clean up Wombat's socials."

"Not for all the money in the world."

"I would have to protest that application. Loudly." Oliver toyed with the cuff of Bram's T-shirt. "Something will come along."

"Agreed." Bram closed his computer and peered out at the water. "There's our boat. Ready to fish?"

. . .

The brisk boat ride over the rich blue water was enchanting. Once they settled on a spot and the crew handed over their fishing lines, Bram and Oliver raced to hook the biggest catch. Working in tandem, sharing creative ideas and plans, was always fun. The challenge of a competitive outing, where the only real prize was bragging rights and a fresh fish dinner, settled Bram. For years, he was always focused, determined to meet his goal. With Oliver sharing trash talk and vibrant celebrations when a fat fish was pulled in, Bram felt light and happy. Like a new level had been unlocked.

He'd overcome his worries and now he reaped the rewards. Bram glanced across the bow of the boat, grateful for the cover of his sunglasses and hat as he soaked in the sight of Oliver reeling in a powerful catch. The rod bowed under the pressure of Oliver's grip and the fish's fight. Hollering that he would not be bested, his smile was bright and bold. A faint shimmer of exertion from the hot sun and the challenge of the catch reflected on his skin.

Bram exhaled a shaky breath, not realizing he'd been holding himself still.

Oliver—the man he'd lusted after from afar, and then had the joy of working next to—only to be tangled in a drama-filled fake-dating ruse that had morphed into actual feelings so real they pressed on his chest with a painfully exhilarating crush.

Bram joined in with the excited cheers of the mates as Oliver held up his catch. "Our dinner." His triumphant grin sparked a wobble in Bram's stomach.

Moving around Oliver to get the best shot for socials, Bram smothered the feelings that pulsed down his arms and legs.

He loved Oliver. Every part of him. And their time together was ebbing away.

Oliver settled under the canopy of the fishing boat and cracked open a bottle of water. His knees falling wide, one arm slung over the back of the bench. "I won," he called, before tipping his head toward the space next to him. "Come here and tell me how great I am."

Oliver's cheesy bravado, on full display since arriving on the island, was Bram's kryptonite. Oliver had never been arrogant or egotistical. But he could be demanding, and that suited Bram.

"How do you want to celebrate our last night?" Oliver shifted closer as Bram settled next to him.

"I have a few ideas for posts." Bram hesitated, looking around to make sure the mates weren't within earshot. Even with the rush of the wind and water, he wanted to keep some things private. "Then I want to spend the night with you."

Oliver's jaw rolled, his lips pursing and plumping, his gaze firmly rooted on Bram. "We've been spending the nights together." Oliver's voice was playfully ground down.

Bram leaned forward, knowing what Oliver wanted. "I want you. Not just hands. Not just your mouth. All of you."

Oliver's tongue played along the line of his teeth, like a wolf prepared to devour its prey. The shift in Oliver's hips offered a glimpse of his growing arousal beneath his airy shorts. "Well, then"—he cleared his throat—"I'm yours."

CHAPTER
FOURTEEN

OLIVER

"What am I supposed to do again?" Oliver stood on the edge of the platform that extended from the bungalow's deck and hovered over the water. It was a king-sized net that offered one the illusion they were laying atop the water. He had viewed images of influencers laying fluffy white comforters over the mesh to create a bed. Oliver had planned to set the scene of an outdoor sleepover for Isley, then take photos of them.

"Look like you, but hotter," Bram directed from the opposite side of the net. "Like you're thinking some deep thoughts."

"I'm thinking," Oliver said as he balanced on the edge, "that if I fall into the ocean after I've already showered, I'm pulling you in."

"C'mon, think sexy thoughts." Bram watched him through his phone. "You're a sexy man. On a sexy beach. The sunset is gorgeous. Make people want you."

Oliver didn't need pictures for anyone else. He wanted them to be for Bram.

When they'd docked, the resort staff were ever-present, finishing the day's housekeeping, making their meal, and cleaning the boat.

It wasn't until halfway through dinner that Oliver told them they had the night off. As soon as he had, Bram shoved him out on the deck for a sunset photoshoot. Despite tempting him with one last night, Bram was drawing out the evening to-do list like one giant tease. Oliver wanted him so badly it hurt.

"Take your shirt off."

The timber of Bram's husky command flowed through Oliver. "Is that what you want?"

"Yes, and you know it."

Oliver enjoyed Bram's low grunt as he pulled his shirt wide, flexing the muscles in his forearms and back as he guided the thin fabric over his head. He let the cotton dangle from his fingertips. Months in a relationship with an influencer had taught Oliver how to pose his body at the right angle for the best image. "Good?"

"Now the shorts."

His voice, breathy and sensual, made Oliver shiver. He looked over his shoulder to see Bram lobbing his phone onto a deck lounger.

"Get your shot?"

"I'm taking it right now. Shorts."

Oliver's chest pounded with anticipation of nothing separating them. No technology. No clothing. No space. "I thought you wanted me to take charge tonight."

"Oh, I do," Bram said with a sigh. "I need to see you in your naked glory against this beautiful backdrop before you touch me and I melt into a gelatinous, sex-addled man."

"I enjoy making you sex-addled." To punctuate his point, Oliver tugged at the button of his shorts and shimmied them over his hips. "And I don't think any part of you is gelatinous." Oliver paused. "Are we staying out here?"

Bram considered the netting, then the deck and its wide sofa. "I would like that."

A wild pulse consumed Oliver. He was nearly naked, in his boxers at Bram's request, in the middle of an island paradise, and he was about to enjoy this man on a bed of ropes above crystal-blue water. "Get over here. Now."

Bram crossed the firm netting and fell into Oliver's embrace. A heady groan rolled from his chest at the press of Bram's stiff arousal against his own, the delicious ache blooming as Bram tipped his face to receive Oliver's hungry kiss. "This," he said against Bram's mouth as he tugged at his shirt, "off."

Bram groaned as Oliver nibbled and sucked his neck. "I brought what we need."

"Of course you did." Oliver swooned, because that was Bram. Prepared, attentive, and—based on the tight peak of his nipples—Bram was eager for more.

Oliver turned Bram, settling them back to chest. With one arm barred across Bram's front, Oliver slipped his fingers below Bram's waistband. He reveled in the gasp that flowed from Bram when his hand closed around his length. "Tell me what you found for us."

Bram rocked against Oliver's painful erection in time with his methodical strokes.

"Tell me," Oliver mumbled into Bram's shoulder. "Condoms?"

"Yes." Bram's hips pushed against every stroke.

"Lube?" Oliver's teeth grazed Bram's earlobe, triggering a full-body vibration.

"Oliver." Bram's voice was a plea.

"Can I get you off like this, or when we're together?" Oliver asked, lightening his touch.

"Together. You and me."

The words sparked a primal need in Oliver as he tumbled them onto the netting. They rolled, growling into each other's kiss as they stripped away their clothes. Nestled between Bram's legs, the sensation of their cocks rubbing against each other stole the breath from Oliver's lungs.

Bram skated his fingers along Oliver's back and hips, dragging ribbons of sensation across his skin. The dizzying headiness of Bram canting his hips to grind their bodies closer was too much.

"I'm dying for this to last," he panted, "but I can't wait."

"Yes, now." Bram reached to grab the small container of lube from the side of the net. During the nights they'd spent on their island getaway, Oliver had marveled at Bram's openness, his willingness to engage in their intimacy. Now, he watched Bram shift his knees wide, a heel anchored against the tight webbing as he tilted his hips and dipped his lubed fingers into his own body.

The scene—Bram splayed wide and preparing himself for Oliver—cracked him in half.

A feral throb triggered low in his abdomen. Oliver swiped the lube from Bram. "Both hands on the net."

"Let me touch you," he whined as he snaked his hands through the ropes, his abs flexing as he moved.

"You will." Oliver pressed a digit into his sensitive skin, relishing the sight of Bram's arousal glistening on his belly. "You are so fucking hot."

"Please." Bram bucked against Oliver's methodical touch.

"Hmm." Oliver added a second finger, nearly ruining their whole escapade when Bram writhed beneath him. Bram's biceps rippled with exertion as he gripped the ropes, his hips lifting in a silent plea. "How about this?" Oliver lowered his mouth, his tongue teasing the head of Bram's cock.

"I'm going to ... Fuck!" His broken groan melted as Oliver sucked him into his mouth. Oliver fought to maintain control as Bram's body pulsed around his fingers, his hips bucking between Oliver's lips.

"I'm close." Bram's voice turned desperate. "Please, Oliver."

He levied a bruising suck before releasing Bram. "When we do this again"—he ran his nose along the juncture of Bram's thigh, inhaling his musky scent—"I'm making you beg for everything. My mouth. My hands. My cock. Everything." He sat back to rest on his knees, Bram's thighs draped over his. "Touch me," he commanded, reaching for the condoms.

Bram obliged, sitting up to stroke Oliver. He sagged, a groan caught in his throat, at the perfect pressure of Bram's grip. "Too good." He pushed Bram's hand away and tried to settle his breath as he sheathed himself.

Oliver pushed Bram's knees up and back, the head of his cock tapping against Bram's ass. "This is going to go fast, but we have all night."

"All night." Bram's voice broke as Oliver pressed into him.

Their shouts of ecstasy collided as Oliver settled against Bram, giving them time to adjust.

The heat of Bram's body was consuming. Greedy nips and kisses were something he could no longer live without. He needed to calm down and focus, or their time together would be over. "You feel so good," Oliver mumbled. "You're perfect." He lingered, slowing their pace to enjoy the sensation of Bram taking all of him, but Bram had other plans. "You need to stop trying to fuck yourself on my cock. You're going to make me come."

Bram's laugh was heady. "Keep talking to me like that, and I'm going to make a mess of both of us."

"I will *never* stop saying things like that." Oliver shifted back and drank in the sight of their intimate connection as he sank into Bram. "You look so good on my cock. I think we should make a mess of each other." Oliver felt Bram's body tighten and throb. "Are you ready?"

"So close." Bram moaned. "Harder. More." He scrabbled to grip the netting, absorbing Oliver's thrusts.

"You are everything," Oliver said, rocking his hips with every word.

"Yes. I'm there," Bram keened.

Oliver drove into Bram, nearing the moment he'd break with pleasure. Bram crying his name and bucking against his body tested Oliver's thready control. Bram was thoroughly fucked, lips swollen from their kisses, belly slick with the evidence of their play, and still looked breathtaking.

Before Oliver could form words, Bram gripped Oliver's ass, urging him into motion. "Give me everything you've got. I want to hear my name on your tongue when you come."

Oliver's body jerked against the molten stab of desire. He felt Bram everywhere. The warmth of his body, the pressure of his hands, and teasing kisses followed by sharp, playful nibbles.

Bram's name spilled into an incoherent mash of sounds as relentless pressure triggered an avalanche of pleasure, Oliver's hips rutting, seeking release. He tumbled, chasing the heavy pulse of each blistering wave. Oliver's world narrowed into a comfortable rightness when Bram pulled him close for a soothing, centering kiss.

In the waning daylight, Oliver felt weightless and grounded in Bram's embrace as their breath slowed, hovering over the gentle lapping of the Indian Ocean.

Oliver gingerly pulled from Bram and removed the condom. They used a towel to wipe themselves clean before collapsing against each other.

"That was ..."

"Yeah," Bram agreed with a sleepy yawn. "Let's rest and do it again."

Oliver felt a keen satisfaction at being the one responsible for Bram's sated tone. "Good. Because we're going to wreck that bed before we leave."

As Bram snoozed in the gentle comfort of the canopy, Oliver watched the sky shift from a bright pink-orange to inky night. Their days had been blissfully long and heart-wrenchingly quick. His time with Bram felt like he'd awoken from a dream. He'd been in a place where he questioned himself, who he was, and what he needed in a relationship, not realizing that the person he'd thought would never be for him shared his passions openly.

Oliver's feelings were big and bold and too quick. His planned trip to Singapore would give both of them time to think and reflect on their time together.

Would this side quest—a few days of enjoying Bram in the privacy of a secluded island—end as soon as it started? Could he really love Bram after only a few days together?

Bram shifted in his sleep, his body relaxed and hair messy from Oliver's greedy touch. If it wasn't love he felt, Oliver didn't know how else to label the ache in his chest. Their adventure was over.

CHAPTER
FIFTEEN

BRAM

Oliver reviewed the text message Bram had sent as they traveled to the airport. "Is it strange that you know my itinerary for Singapore?"

"Not really." Bram watched the landscape blur from private oasis to inhabited town as they neared the tarmac. He was relieved when Oliver shared their departure plan included a boat ride and a scenic drive instead of another tuna-can flight. "I helped plan the trip and made a list of places for you to take pictures for your socials. If you don't want to post them, just send them to me and I'll do it."

"Or you could come with me."

It was tempting to ghost an entire institution of higher education, but those hallowed halls owed him something more than debt and an ulcer. "Are we really going to talk about how depriving me of my moment in the spotlight will ruin my life?"

Oliver's charismatic smile was a drug. "I'll give you a spotlight to shine under."

"Let's hope it's still burning bright when you're home." Ten days felt like an eternity.

Oliver shrugged. "It's an LED. It'll last forever."

"Good to know." Bram shifted in his seat, the delicious soreness from last night a constant reminder of Oliver. "I'm going to miss you."

"Same." Oliver tangled their fingers. "If they cancel graduation, I have a ticket with your name on it."

Bram's face warmed. "You'll be the first one I call."

"Sirs," the driver announced, "we've arrived."

Their car pulled onto a private part of the airfield, where the hybrid charter plane that had whisked them to their private island waited to take Oliver to Singapore. The driver exited, leaving them alone.

"Bram?" Oliver's tone pulled his gaze away from the plane. "When I get back, can we talk about this?" He gestured between their bodies. "Us. I want to talk about us."

All the liquid in the world couldn't soothe Bram's desperately dry mouth. "Yeah." The words were gritty. "I think we have to, don't we?"

"We should. I know this whole arrangement was a messy start, but I really enjoyed these past few days." Oliver looked stressed. More stressed than he'd been the entire time. "I always knew we got along well, but this trip was powerful."

"I agree." Bram felt a wave of relief. "We deserve the opportunity to talk and figure out what our next steps could be."

Oliver nodded. "I want those next steps to be together. There's no question about that for me." He took a breath, seeming to bolster himself. "Bram, I think I lo—"

"Hey, guys!" A chipper female voice called out from the tarmac. "I know it's been a few days, but we're here and ready for the next leg of our trip!"

Oliver's eyes flared wide at the sight of Isley Berns prancing alongside the body of the plane as she chatted at her screen.

"She's live." Bram's observation felt flat.

"What the hell?" Oliver growled as he undid his seatbelt and reached for the door.

"Wait." He had no clue what was going on, but this was strange. "If she doesn't get off that stream, her viewers will see everything. You need to keep your game face on. I'm sure her audience is enormous right now."

"Why is she here?" Oliver asked, then he shrieked as a furious knock pounded against the window.

"Open this door right now!" a voice hissed through the glass.

"Maggie?" Oliver's shock reflected Bram's as the crisply dressed assistant tumbled into the car.

"Don't you check your email?" she snapped in their general direction.

"Uh, no." Bram snorted.

"Maggie," Oliver said, attempting to soothe, "I'm so glad you're feeling better. We were on vacation, therefore no email."

"No, you two were on a sex fest and couldn't think about damage control."

"I think *sex fest* is a bit much," Bram said, hedging the issue.

"I think that's about right," Oliver countered, showing zero care. "Why is she here? And before you complain about email, you had both our phone numbers and there was not a single call or text."

Margaret's face soured at Oliver's observation. "She's here because she's going to Singapore with you."

The words landed on Bram like a punch. "What?"

"No."

"Oliver, from what her team is telling me, she's upset about the way things fell apart. Isley wants the opportunity to talk about what happened."

"She let another man put his face in her crotch while at an award ceremony honoring me. There is nothing to discuss. She's not going to Singapore. We're done."

"You'll have to work that out on the flight." She canted her gaze toward Bram. "The university has been up my ass about the validity of your internship placement given this"—she cleared her throat— "public presentation."

Bram felt his world screech to a halt. "Come again?"

"They have called an academic review meeting."

"For when?" Oliver huffed. "Bram's graduating on Saturday. It's a moot point."

"Thursday. The meeting determines if the course is valid. They can revoke his ability to walk in the ceremony or confer his diploma."

His entire body crumpled forward. Time, money, and years of tap-dancing around antiquated policies that had limited relevance in a modern world were theirs for the taking. "Fuck me."

"Oh, I think they want to." Margaret's sharp gaze flicked to Oliver. "You need to get on that plane with Isley and figure this out."

Oliver sat back in his seat, arms crossed. "I'm not doing this."

Bram despised the thought, but he knew what had to happen. "She has to go."

"The hell she does," Oliver yelled. "You're the only one I need on that trip."

Margaret's face crumpled, mirroring Bram's understanding. "Isley has woven the story that you're in an open relationship. If word gets out that you're cutting her off after a vacation with one of your partners, it'll look like you've left her hanging."

At Oliver's blistering protest, Bram held up his hand. "I don't like it either, but this is an image war now. She knows that Oliver Kent's brand floats on openness and honesty. If you don't give her the chance, she can pull your company's mission and values into question."

"I told you," Margaret bit out as she reached across Bram to pinch Oliver's leg. Despite his yelp, she continued, "She's trouble. You wouldn't hear it."

"Not now, Maggie," Oliver groused. "Can you get her off that live so I can talk to her?"

Margaret tapped out a text message. A group of people huddled in the shade of the nearby plane focused on their phones, like meerkats scanning the horizon, when the message landed.

"You can text them, but we get an email?" Bram knew it wasn't his place, but he didn't care. Oliver was again in a terrible position and the entire situation had robbed them of time to say goodbye.

"No dice," Margaret replied, ignoring Bram's comment. "They want you on the feed. For continuity."

Oliver rolled his eyes and slumped against the door. "Continuity."

Bram's irritation flared. "This is bullshit." When Margaret and Oliver's gaze settled on him, he nearly screamed. "You don't have to step into that stream, Oliver."

"But she has to go to Singapore?" he barked. He leaned forward, cradling his head. "Damn it. I'm sorry. That was not ... I shouldn't have said it like that." Oliver slumped back, his beautiful blue eyes shimmering. "This is not how I wanted this to end."

The scene was twisted. Oliver had done nothing but be recognized for his hard work and then planned a beautiful vacation to celebrate. He'd been cheated on, asked to lie, and then made to perpetuate that lie for one person's curated image.

"Would she have appreciated it?" At Oliver's questioning look, Bram pushed. "The adventures. The meals. The beauty of the reef. The haunted shipwrecks—"

"They were not haunted—"

"The gorgeous sand. The stunning sunsets. Would she have appreciated any of it? Or would it have all been for her followers?"

"Bram." Oliver hesitated. "This is a smear on my brand. Your entire academic career is on the line. I need to get us out of this. All of us."

"You're letting her get away with disrespecting who you are for her own gain." The air in the car turned stuffy. "You're more than the image she curates. You always have been."

Margaret's phone vibrated with a message. "She's prepping her people. It's time."

Oliver swiped a watery streak from his face before hardening his features. "We'll talk when I get back," he said in a rush before opening the door and stepping into the bright morning light.

Bram followed Oliver's path, only to be held back by Margaret. "Wait here."

Isley squealed and jumped with delight at the sight of Oliver walking toward her. He turned his face away just as she tried to kiss him on the mouth, her lips smearing pink across his cheek.

Bram's stomach twisted as Oliver allowed Isley to ring her arms around his waist. They chatted for what felt like an eternity before they waved at the screen and signed off.

"Now go," Margaret said, releasing Bram like a hound unleashed to chase a fox.

"Oh," Isley cooed when Bram approached, "I didn't realize you'd be here."

"Of course he's here. We just came from the island," Oliver replied coolly. "You're not coming with me, Isley."

Her blond hair rippled as she absorbed the shock. "I've spent days prepping my followers for this trip. My luggage is on board. I'm going."

Oliver glared at her team. "She's not staying with me. Find her alternative sleeping arrangements."

Isley huffed, turning her attention to Bram. "You could help me here, you know."

Bram itched to confront her spoiled entitlement. "No, I really can't."

"We've arranged for her to be in the same hotel but on a different floor," one of her team chimed in.

"We're not talking on this flight," Oliver bit out. "Later, maybe, but not now. I'm not ready to talk to you and this stunt is just that. A way for you to parade yourself in front of anyone who will watch."

"What the hell, Oliver?" Isley demanded. "You fuck Bram and you're ready to throw everything we have away."

Bram's rancid "We're *not* going there" collided with Oliver's jolly "I did and it was *so* good!"

"That's enough." Margaret stepped in with the authority of a schoolmarm who still believed in the value of corporal punishment. "Oliver, go to Singapore. Isley, you'll respect the boundaries that Oliver puts in place or we'll expose this farce faster than you can change your lipstick. I don't care what you do while you're there, but Oliver has planned this trip as a research expedition. You will not interfere with that for your own benefit."

"What about him?" Isley gestured loosely in Bram's direction.

"He's graduating this weekend," Oliver offered with none of the celebration the event deserved.

Isley's mouth pursed with a sinister smile. "Congratulations."

"Thanks." Bram felt hollow because his reason for not going had the possibility of being yet another lie. He had to defend years of hard work to a panel that didn't have an inkling about what he'd done.

Under the blazing sun of the Maldives, he felt cold and alone.

They stood in pained silence until the pilot confirmed the flight was still on, encouraging them to board to keep on their scheduled flight plan.

Their bags were pulled from the cars and tossed into cargo holds.

A rushed, back-slapping half hug was all they got before the flight crew guided Oliver and Isley toward the stairs. Bram watched Oliver thread his fingers through his hair as he ducked into the cabin.

Isley lingered at the bottom, then pulled Bram into a tight hug. When he attempted to put space between them, she held tight with the strength of a woman who kicked ass at Pilates.

"He needed to get you out of his system." She pulled back, a sweet, grateful smile curving her mouth. "Thanks for helping us get through this, Bram."

Before he could respond, Isley scampered up the steps, waggling her fingers in a jaunty goodbye as the cabin door closed.

CHAPTER
SIXTEEN

BRAM

"You're home!" Rosa's proclamation could have been heard from space. "Con, our Bram is home!" She ushered him into their immaculate apartment, looking out into the hall. "Where is our Oliver?"

"Our boys are home?" Con cheered, straightening his hair with the small black comb he kept in his back pocket as he shuffled down the hallway.

Bram's heart crumbled a little more. "Just me." He held up the dry cleaning bag. "I had your suit cleaned and your shoes buffed."

"You didn't need to do that," Con said as he marveled at the bags.

"I did. Between the gala and the flights, they were more creases than clothing." Bram shrugged. "It's the least I could do for how perfectly you saved my red-carpet debut."

"You did look handsome." Rosa nodded and gave a small clap of her hands. "How was the trip? We saw the pictures on the 'gram. That's what they say, right?" She kept her voice low, as if it wasn't just the three of them. "Anyway," she said, waving away the question, "it looked very nice."

It was half a question, half a request for juicy details, and all the loving prying of a sweet grandmother who Bram suspected read historical romance novels to keep her young.

"It was"—Bram inhaled a shaky breath—"the best trip I have ever been on."

"Great!" Con patted him on the back. "Will Oliver be coming to graduation?"

The wobbly feeling Bram had been navigating since he and Margaret returned home made his knees weak. He hadn't heard from Oliver since the airport.

No texts. No calls. No messages.

Not that he'd sent any either.

Isley's parting words lingered in his mind, settling into a fear that now seemed true. He'd had a fling with a man he cared for deeply. If he was honest with himself, he shouldn't have agreed in the first place. He'd felt too much going into their side quest to pretend he couldn't fall in love with Oliver Kent.

"He's on a work trip to Singapore." Bram needed to state the facts, get back to his apartment, and order a King Ramen, Special #2 because drinking himself into an oblivion wouldn't cure his aching heart. Calcify it in delicious sodium? Possibly. He was willing to take the risk.

Rosa clucked in irritation as she tapped the screen of her phone. "Why is that girl with him?"

The images Rosa was scrolling through were burned in Bram's mind: Isley artfully posed in a wide window overlooking a bustling metropolitan street, her beautiful face turned toward the camera, smiling as she soaked up the sun. And—of course—a post featuring one of her meals. The food image wouldn't have bothered him if Oliver hadn't been featured.

It was at a meeting with fellow gamers, people Bram recognized from social media, in a large open market. Plates of food clogged the tabletop, the bodies seated around the edge crammed together as they reached for their helpings.

It was enough to crack the veneer Bram had settled into on the flight home.

He was going to wait for Oliver to return. He was going to be calm about the whole thing. He was an adult, with a master's degree, and was in control of his life.

Then he'd seen Oliver and Isley tucked into the bustling scene, bodies smashed next to each other. Their faces tanned, smiling, laughing, enjoying the moment, and looking happy.

For the first time in years, Bram cried over a man. He had felt heartbreak and longing before, but this? Oliver had dealt a heavy blow to his heart and Bram worried he might never recover.

"I'm not sure why she's there." He inhaled a deep breath for the millionth time since returning home. He needed to proceed as if success was inevitable or he was going to fall apart.

"Con, can you help me with an outfit for Saturday?"

Con's salt-and-pepper brows arched in joyful delight. "The design team of Con & Rosa would be delighted to style you for graduation."

Bram took three deep breaths as he paced an awkward path outside the conference room door. The panel of faculty ranged from his advisor, to the dean, to the head of student conduct. It was a sea of people and he was drowning.

Sharp clicks echoed down the cavernous hall. Bram stepped aside for the woman making fastidious strides in his general direction. He already felt trampled. He didn't need heel marks pocking his face.

"Stop fidgeting." Margaret pulled to an abrupt halt next to him. She looked fierce in a sleek pantsuit, her shirt speckled with tiny otters, recycling symbols, and plastic bottles.

"Are you wearing an *Otter's River Cleanup* blouse?" Bram could barely rationalize Margaret's presence, but seeing her speckled with adorable otters was a sight to behold.

"I am. My boss might be an idiot, but he gives thoughtful gifts." She shifted in place. "It's my favorite game."

"It is good." Bram's chest ached at her presence. "Why are you here?"

Margaret gave him a withering look. "I'm the Kent Technologies representative at this meeting. You were our intern. I'm here to represent the company."

"Oh." The realization that Kent Technologies would be present never crossed his mind. Oliver sent Margaret because he was in Singapore. With Isley. The weight on his chest gained another pound just as the heavy wooden door creaked open and a man Bram barely recognized as his advisor appeared.

"We're ready for you," he said without really looking at Bram.

Introductions were made around the table, leaving Bram and Margaret for last. The titles and departments blurred as Bram tried to capture some semblance of what was about to occur. The whole time, Margaret tapped on her phone.

"Bram Ridley. Graduate student in the Master of Social Media Marketing program."

Margaret set her phone on the table. "Margaret Stratton, administrator for Kent Technologies, Incorporated."

From Margaret's phone, a tinny voice pushed into the room. "Oliver Kent. Founder and CEO of Kent Technologies, Incorporated, and Bram's internship supervisor."

The room buzzed with hushed murmurs, which didn't soothe the sucker punch that landed in Bram's gut. He looked at Margaret, who stared placidly across the table.

"Mr. Kent," Bram's advisor said, speaking into the room, "we didn't expect you to join us today."

"You've called my company's business practices into question. It would be inappropriate for me not to be on this call." Bram shivered at the overt irritation in Oliver's voice. He was upset. "I am on a work trip currently, so if we could begin, and cease wasting everyone's time, that would be nice."

Oliver had never engaged in any form of higher education, so the unspoken rule about kissing faculty's ass no matter how much bullshit they shoveled was lost on him. Bram savored every scandalized look the faculty members drilled at Margaret's phone.

"Of course, Mr. Kent." Bram's advisor cleared his throat. "Mr. Ridley, we are here today to understand the roles and responsibilities of your internship placement as it relates to the nature of your relationship with Mr. Kent."

"My role at Kent Technologies was to design and execute a social media marketing plan for an upcoming game launch in addition to marketing both existing and developing products. By implementing my strategy, *Otter's River Cleanup* became one of the highest-grossing cozy video games on its release day—worldwide, and across all demographic targets."

"And your relationship with Mr. Kent?"

Bram knew when bait was dangled. "He provided the intended outcomes of all projects, which were reviewed at weekly team meetings. Every session comprised of myself, Oliver, and other team members. Minutes for every meeting are documented and on record."

"Were you paid for this work?" asked a white-haired man in a suit that looked like he wore it every day.

"Yes." Bram could feel his irritation ratchet up. "Tuition is expensive. It's nice to eat more than pasta and beans when you're responsible for creative work."

"To clarify, you were being paid to do this job while you and Mr. Kent were engaged in a romantic relationship?"

"I can speak to my income in relation to the work produced for Kent Technologies. I would need further clarification how any other inquiry beyond that would be relevant in this discussion."

"Mr. Ridley." In chastising Bram's rebuttal, his advisor seemed to find two additional syllables in his name. "If you and Mr. Kent were engaged in a romantic relationship when you were paid for your services, the ethical foundation of your academic experience is in question."

"Can I clarify something?" Oliver's sharp tone pushed through the phone. "Are you asking if Bram was working for me and I was paying him to keep our relationship quiet?"

"We need to ensure that any relationship you had did not impact Mr. Ridley's academic experience." The dean of the college looked deadly serious. "And that the relationship was consensual."

Bram looked at Margaret, whose eyes had grown wide, her cheeks puffed out with a heavy breath.

"Consensual!" Bram winced at Oliver's tone. The volume alone nearly cracked the plaster on the walls. "Are you seriously asking Bram if I paid him for sex?"

"Mr. Kent, you will have your oppour—"

"No. I'm not waiting. This is the type of farce that gives higher education a bad name. Bram is brilliant. You are *lucky* to have his name on your roster of graduates. His undergraduate and graduate records reflect not only his commitment to your institution, but he's paid through the nose for his education. The issue here is that you witnessed—through some online filter—what you think is a relationship. At no point in time did you attempt to clarify what was happening before calling this meeting and threatening his livelihood."

Bram's advisor began to hedge the accusation. "Mr. Kent, that's not what this—"

"The fuck it's not. His work is impeccable. Bram's project management skills are exemplary. He got the job done, and then some. He asked to leave Kent Technologies early to start job hunting, a task that your esteemed institution has done nothing to help him with. If his degree is denied because of your issue with two adults taking part in a consensual relationship, maybe we should question if your issue is with two men being in that relationship."

Even if Oliver heard the shocked bluster that flowed through the room, he pushed on.

"Please know that I have a legal team ready to rip you apart if these allegations go any further. A defamation suit with a hefty dose of human rights violations won't look good for incoming students." Oliver paused, his voice dipping to a chill Bram had never heard before. "And if that prospect isn't terrifying enough, I have close to ten million followers. A fan base cultivated by your own industrious graduate student. I have close partners with an equally staggering number of followers. They're aware of the position you've put Bram in and they're itching to make this biased hearing go viral."

The king of cool. The master of mellow moods.

The creator of calming outlets was pissed.

It was the first time Bram had witnessed Oliver tip into anger. He was sharp and terrifying, and Bram wasn't going to feel too guilty about the fact that he found it pretty hot.

The dean cleared her throat. "I think we have met the goals of this meeting. Mr. Kent, thank you for your insight and clarification of the facts. Mr. Ridley, we look forward to seeing you on Saturday."

CHAPTER
SEVENTEEN

OLIVER

"How did he look?"

"Like hell." Maggie paused. "Handsome, of course, but like someone had roughed up his tender heart and left him in a smelly alley." At Oliver's groan, she twisted the knife. "You did that. You roughed him up. You left him in a smelly alley."

"Don't you think I know that!"

"Do you know there are rats in that alley? Hmm? Fat ones."

Oliver sucked in a breath. "Is this how you parent your children?"

"I employ Lucy for a reason."

The sun was setting, but the Singapore streets were alive with pedestrians and motorbikes. "You need to pay her more."

"You need to pay *me* more. I'm lucky they didn't kick me out of that meeting."

"Like you'd let them. I'm sure you took them by surprise, too. The good news is, it's done. He's graduating."

Maggie hummed in agreement, the sound of shuffling papers filtering over the line. "I sent him some leads for potential jobs this morning." Oliver wanted to question for who and what the job was, but he didn't. "How's Singapore?"

"Beautiful. Fun." He didn't dare say he was lonely in a country of millions, despite how he felt.

"Isley?"

His breath stuttered. "She's Isley."

"Are you two …?"

"Never. It took longer than I expected, but she understands where I'm at. We're trying to figure out the best way to share that we're done. You know, conscious uncoupling or mindful separation."

"How about you say, 'This was great but now it's not. Buh-bye!'"

Maggie was a viper and Oliver loved it. "That might be my next post."

"You know what else wasn't great? How you disconnected before talking to him. He grabbed my phone as soon as that meeting broke. Then he told me with a *wobbly voice* that there has been nothing from you. He sees you tucked into a street vendor smorgasbord with her and you say nothing. Bram nearly cried, you jerk! I almost had to deal with tears!"

"That meetup was set before I knew she was tagging along. I had no clue she was going to show up." When he'd felt a body slide next to his on the crowded bench, he never imagined it would be her. He'd swallowed down his irritation then spent most of the meal envisioning a pane of glass between them.

"That wonderful man loves your dumb ass, Oliver."

It would have hurt less if she told him that his games were stupid, or that he was a joke, or if she threw searingly hot coffee in his face.

"I think I love him, too." Oliver swallowed past the lump in his throat. "I was so angry during that call, Maggie. They suggested he did something dirty and unethical and I wanted to destroy everything in that room."

"Yep, that sounds like love to me."

"Right." Oliver worried his bottom lip between his teeth. "Can I tell you something?"

"Of course."

"I'm worried that I manipulated him." The pain of the admission knocked the wind from his chest. Of all the things he'd thought about since he and Bram left each other, he kept coming back to the same conclusion. "What if I'm no better than Isley?"

"Huh." Maggie was quiet for a moment. "I don't see it that way, Oliver. She cheated on you, then put both of you in a bad situation. Bram agreed to walk into that arrangement. You asked, he answered."

It was rational and not untrue, but Oliver still worried over all the ways he could have hurt such a wonderful person. "I still can't believe they tried to revoke his credits."

Maggie snorted. "I can. You should have seen Professor Dewson when you went off. He was a grouchy jerk when I had him, too. I thought he was going to pinch his face so tightly he'd become his own black hole."

Oliver blinked. "Wait, you knew those people?"

"Of course. I'm alumna of Berkstone University. I handpicked Bram because I know what that program is. No one would have had the educational background to support what you needed. He was good on good; an excellent program, stellar recommendations, dean's list."

"If you knew those people, why didn't you smooth this over for him?"

"I have some pull but this was your fight, not mine." Oliver could hear her smile over the phone. "It was inspiring to watch you rise to the challenge."

Oliver glanced around his hotel room. It was opulent, draped in luxury linens and studded with high-end fixtures. The view was breathtaking. There were endless edible delights. But for all the swank and swag, something was missing.

"Maggie, I need you to do me a favor."

CHAPTER
EIGHTEEN

BRAM

Bram—

Con and I are getting a car now to beat the traffic.

Do you need anything before we leave?

Love, Rosa

Bram's heart pinched every time Rosa, or Con, sent a text. He didn't have the heart to correct their letter-writing hardwiring.

Hi Rosa! I'm good. Tell Con the cufflinks look great.

I'll grab a ride home with you after the ceremony if that's okay.

See you there!

A quick rap at the door forced Bram to laugh. Of course Con was coming to check on him one last time. After returning from the feat-of-strengths academic meeting, Rosa and Con welcomed him home, where he'd promptly dissolved into tears of frustration, heartbreak, and sweet relief.

Even if his heart was broken, even if he had submitted his resume to what felt like every company on the planet with no callbacks, he would have his degree. One out of three would have to be good enough for now.

Rosa had also made him a massive pan of blondies, which he'd consumed in less than a day.

Heartbreak needs healing, she told him, and sometimes that remedy is only found in baked goods.

"Coming," he called at a second impatient knock. Bram tugged at his cuffs, smoothing the line of his shirt under his jacket. Con had dressed him in the university's colors: a warm maroon jacket, white shirt, and sleek black pants accented with touches of gold.

Bram was annoyed that he had to wear a graduation gown and cover up Con's masterpiece during his catwalk.

"How do I look?" Bram asked as he pulled the door wide.

The amused huff took a moment to settle. "Perfect."

Oliver, in dress pants, a tie in the same *Otter's River Cleanup* pattern as Margaret's blouse, and a button-down shirt rolled up to expose his tanned forearms, rocked on his heels in the hallway.

Bram felt his legs wobble, then braced himself in the doorway. "What are you doing here?"

Oliver nodded, his mouth pressed to a thin line as if contemplating his words. "I never should have gotten on that plane without you." Bram could hear the crack in his voice. "I should have come home and faced those people with you. I should have shoved every disgusting question they asked you back down their throats." He breathed in a stuttering breath. "I severed things with Isley. It should have been done the night of the gala." Oliver took a tentative step closer, rubbing his hands together before shoving them into his pockets. "I need to be here to watch you graduate and tell you how breathtaking you are in vintage."

Bram swallowed down the rocky wobble of excitement and lifted his hand to touch Oliver's tie. "Margaret has a shirt with this pattern. You have a tie. I have nothing."

Oliver's brows brushed his hairline. "I leave Singapore to surprise you, pour my heart out in this very institutional hallway, and you complain you don't have video game swag?"

Bram couldn't help but laugh. "I'm so happy you're here." Tugging Oliver into his apartment by his tie eliminated the space between them. "You realize," Bram said through a kiss, "that graduation is a ticketed event. It's sold out."

Oliver pulled back, a devilish twinkle in his eye. "It's a good thing

I've got this." He extracted a very official and rather fancy ticket to the December commencement.

Bram's mouth fell open. "There are people fighting to get extra tickets. Where did you find one?"

"Magg— Uh, *Margaret* got it for me. She pulled some strings."

"You're calling Margaret by her name?"

"It was part of the deal. She terrifies her alma mater and gets me a ticket to commencement, I call her Margaret for the rest of our lives. Pretty even deal if you ask me."

"I guess," Bram said as he played with the edge of Oliver's hair. "I can't believe you're here."

"Me too." Oliver roped his arms around Bram's waist, pulling him close. "Can I tell you something?"

"Anything."

"I think I love you."

Bram felt warmth flow across his cheeks. "I think I love you, too."

Oliver muscled back a satisfied smile. "Good. Now, let's get you graduated. Then"—he paused for dramatic effect—"King Ramen, Special #2."

"Of course." Bram leaned in to kiss Oliver soundly. "There is no other."

ABOUT PIPER MALONE

Piper Malone's award-winning novels enchant readers with heartfelt, authentic romances. Her stories include a cast of unforgettable characters in a variety of romantic pairings. With snappy one-liners and witty banter, Piper wants her readers to laugh, swoon, and enjoy a well-deserved vacation.

Connect with Piper at www.pipermalone.net

ALSO BY PIPER MALONE

If you enjoyed Milo and Jackson's savory second chance in The Fry Guy from Beachside, you'll love their holiday happily ever after in Hawaii.

North Shore Nuptials: Holidays in Hawaii

When Jackson proposed a Hawaiian destination wedding on New Year's Day, he knew the end of the year would be festive. What he didn't realize was his laid-back, merry-and-bright style would be dwarfed by the dazzling spectacle of the Cusano family's plentiful traditions. Between exuberant celebrations, wedding planning, and reuniting with his former team for a charity surf tournament, Jackson feels the pressures of the season.

After Milo fries a massive Thanksgiving turkey, finds the perfect evergreen tree, lights up an ugly sweater competition, and plans a ceremony to marry his sexy surfer boyfriend, he's ready for a tropical getaway. In Hawaii, the sparkling sun can't outshine the rollicking adventures that started in Beachside. What's a more magical way to close the year than hula lessons, hiking excursions, and a Secret Santa gift exchange on the beach?

But as Jackson prepares to ride the North Shore waves, Milo struggles to embrace the joyful celebrations surrounding his fiancé's return to the same waters where a shark attack brought his surfing legacy to a violent halt. Even worse, the reunion with his team sparks rumors about Jackson rejoining the professional circuit—the career he left for a life in Beachside with Milo.

As the days tick down to their New Year's Day nuptials, and relationship-shattering secrets are revealed, Milo and Jackson must decide: Will they begin the New Year as newlyweds, or newly single?

North Shore Nuptials *is the fifth installment in The Beachside Boys series, featuring Milo and Jackson's path to happily ever after. This merry romp invites you to celebrate Thanksgiving, Christmas, and that weird week between exchanging gifts and ringing in the New Year with all your favorites—Zeke and Heidi, Leo and Arie, the parents, and (of course!) Nana—on the gorgeous Hawaiian island of Oahu.*

(And Nana would like to reassure you there are hot surfing Santa dudes, as well . . . Happy Holidays indeed!)

Get your copy of North Shore Nuptials: Holidays in Hawaii at https://books2read.com/NorthShoreNuptials

.

HOLD ON FOREVER

SUSAN SCOTT SHELLEY

ABOUT HOLD ON FOREVER

London Best has spent the last ten years pouring everything he has into the rock band he formed with his best friends. Signing with a new label has brought them newfound success and their star is rising. Fresh off recording their latest album, he's excited to return to performing. Reuniting with musician in crisis Maddox Muldoon throws him off balance, and London rides to the rescue of his friend's brother, issuing an invitation that will affect his upcoming festival shows, and keep him in close proximity with Maddox, who has captivated London for years.

Maddox Muldoon has spent the last twelve years as a member of a wildly popular boy band, with his life revolving around other people calling all the shots and the public watching his every move. Deciding to switch genres from pop to rock costs him his band, record label, and friendships he'd depended on. Alone and disheartened, he jumps at London's offer to join him for a weekend away at a music festival, and for the first time in years, has uninterrupted hours with his longtime crush, and a chance to spread his creative wings into the genre of his heart.

As London and Maddox's relationship grows into more, they learn how well they complement each other, onstage and off. But with the spotlight growing uncomfortably brighter, these friends to lovers will need to decide if they can stay in tune, or they'll risk becoming a one-hit wonder.

CHAPTER
ONE

LONDON

"London, over here!"

The flashes of dozens of cameras accompany the calls from photographers. I hand my autograph to a beaming fan and take my place on the red carpet, waiting for my bandmates to join me. Excitement vibrates in the warm summer evening.

Pan, Andrew, and Garrett group around me and I grin when I realize we're in the same order as our latest album cover. The crush of fans screaming our names both energizes and gratifies me. Since signing our deal with Furious Records last year, we've hit another level of success. Feels like we've finally made it, ten years after we first formed.

Sunlight teases out the red highlights in Pan's long brown hair and in his beard. He casts a glance at the crowd and shakes his head with a laugh. "I still can't believe we're actually here."

This is the first time we've walked the carpet of the music industry's biggest awards show. It's crowded and *loud*, and I love it. "Right? Or that we're presenting an award."

I'm starstruck at the music legends strolling past, nodding at us like they think we belong here. I wave to a few, glad I listened to Pan and changed into the dark purple suit he threw at me after seeing the jeans and tee I'd originally intended to wear.

A reporter from one of the networks live-streaming the red carpet event thrusts a microphone in my face. "London, let's hear an update. What's been going on with Satyr's Kiss?"

I love being around the fans and other artists, but reporters, not so much. In an aim to look casual, I slap on a smile and tuck my hands into the front pockets of my pants. Interviews are my least favorite thing. Reporters have burned us before, cherry picking sound bites to cause drama and drive clicks. "We've been working hard on the new album and can't wait for our fans to hear it."

"We spoke to Luke Thompson and Zander Rostov from The Fury earlier. They told us you're playing at their festival next weekend. Can you tell us about that?" Her smile is encouraging as she looks from me to Pan, then to Garrett and Andrew.

I lean into Pan, our signal that I'm ready for our frontman to take over. "Yeah, we're excited to play there. The festival is all bands signed under Furious Records. It's always fun sharing the stage with them."

Pan puts his hand on my shoulder, keeping me by his side, and motions for Andrew and Garrett to move in closer so they stay in the shot and receive as much attention as the two of us. "Every song on our new record was a chance to stretch our creative wings and push the boundaries of our songwriting, while still having that Satyr's Kiss edge. We're really proud of it. We'll be playing the new songs at the festival and we'll have a full tour announcement coming soon."

"Thanks for the time, guys. Enjoy your evening."

Ever the drummer, Garrett's fingers tap a repetitive beat along his thigh as we move down the carpet. "Even though we've been rehearsing for the last two weeks, I already have pre-show butterflies."

Andrew, our bassist, raises a brow as he pushes his glasses into place. The green frames coordinate with his forest-shaded suit, appropriate for our nature lover. "You kidding me? I can't wait to get on stage again. I'm so ready to go."

Garrett playfully shoves Andrew forward a step. "I bet you're already packed too."

"I am. It's been a minute since the last time we shared a tour bus." His smile turns sly. "I hope you're over the phase of talking in your sleep, Gar."

"I hope you're not." I nudge my shoulder into Garrett's and he laughs. "It's entertaining."

With all the time spent recording the album, we haven't played on stage together in a while, so I understand his worry. I'm a little nervous too, but we have four days until we leave, so that's more time to rehearse.

To my right, the flurry of flashes start again for whoever is walking the carpet behind us, followed by cheers from the crowd. I glance over and see Maddox Muldoon, former lead singer for the wildly popular boy band MTKC, posing and smiling for the cameras.

In place of his habitual bright colors, black leather pants encase his long legs, a black tee shows off a tattoo sleeve he did *not* have the last time I saw him, he's grown out his close-cropped haircut to past his shoulders, and dyed a strip of his dark brown hair platinum blond.

"Whoa…"

The sexy, edgy look is catching the attention of every photographer, reporter, and attendee.

Maddox turns his head and meets my gaze. His brows lift and his smile grows softer. Awareness sparks through me, a tingling rush over my skin.

Something about him has always pulled at something deep inside me, but with his band's commitments and mine, we haven't had the opportunity to spend a lot of time together over the last few years. Plus, his older brother is one of my oldest friends, and I don't know what Randy would think of me having feelings for Maddox.

"Dude." Garrett elbows me in the side. "We need to keep moving."

"Sorry. I just saw Maddox. I almost didn't recognize him with his new look." I give Mads a quick wave, Garrett and Pan do too, then follow my bandmates toward the venue's doors. But my attention keeps going to Maddox.

The trio of artists in line several feet behind Maddox make up the rest of his former band. His smile is strained as he gives in to several fans' shouted requests that he pose with the guys. He stands slightly apart, while the other three have their arms around each other. The studs adorning Mads's ear and wrist cuff glitter in the lights flashing around the space, but the hunch of his shoulders and the downturn of his mouth don't match the evening's festive mood. The smile he had for me is gone.

I stop walking. Stepping aside to avoid Andrew banging into me, I catch the dagger gaze of Trevor Berry slicing into Maddox's back and Mads shrinking away from whatever Trevor just said to him. "I'm guessing his former bandmates aren't taking his exit well. I'm gonna see how he's doing."

"Hold up." With a wince of sympathy, Pan claps me on the shoulder. Behind him, a member of the event staff waits, glancing at her watch. "Presenting the first award, remember? They need us backstage now. We'll find him after the show, yeah?"

I'm not comfortable with that at all. "Give me one minute?"

I turn around, but Maddox is gone. Maybe he ducked inside another door? He could've gotten lost in the sea of people streaming around us.

"We'll find him after the show," Pan says again.

Nodding, I force myself to walk into the building. The excitement over presenting the award dims under my concern for Mads and the desire to find him as soon as I can.

CHAPTER
TWO

MADDOX

The music industry's biggest names and brightest stars crowd the after party. The room vibrates with the energy of people high off of a win and excited to be in a room filled with their peers. There are too many conversations, questions, and way too much staring. If I don't get some air soon, I'm going to choke. I should just go home, but that would be letting my old bandmates win. And that can't happen.

Dodging glances, I cut a path through the ornate decorations, hundreds of flowers, and twinkling lights and duck through an open door leading onto the balcony. Warm air rushes over my skin. It's quiet out here and I'm alone.

The tension that's snaked around my body all night eases. I suck in a long, greedy breath, gazing at Los Angeles glittering around me. Damn, I need to get away.

Caleb, Trevor, and Kell don't understand my decision to leave the band. We met when I was twelve, in a national singing competition that changed our lives. The judges put us together as a foursome, and we won the whole thing, including a recording contract. As MTKC, we were touring by the time I turned thirteen. We grew up together. I thought we were friends in addition to being bandmates, but they aren't acting friendly now. Icy fury describes them perfectly. And it sucks.

I've felt more alone tonight, and in the two months since the official announcement of my decision, than I have in years.

Sighing, I lean on the railing and stare at the sky. I feel lost, and I hate that.

Soft footsteps and a hint of leather and spice drifts from my right. My heart thrills at the sight of London Best walking toward me.

His short blond hair is tousled, and he's opened the first two buttons of his black shirt, giving an enticing glimpse of skin. The dark purple suit with its subtle shine looks amazing on his muscular body. Light emanating from the wall sconces washes over him, lighting up his sea green eyes. "Hey, Mads."

"Hi." My voice rasps the word. He's gorgeous. I've always thought so, but we haven't been in the same room together in a few years and I'd forgotten how powerful a punch the guitarist packs with his presence.

He stops beside me, resting one hand on the railing. Lines of concern crease his forehead. "Are you all right? You don't look very happy."

"I'm fine." I find a smile for him, but don't think he's buying it. "What are you doing out here? I thought you and your bandmates would be hanging out with The Fury."

"We are. Or I was, until I saw you heading out here. I've been looking for you the whole time we've been at this party. You looked upset earlier, on the red carpet. I was worried."

I'm surprised he noticed, and stunned he'd care enough to come find me. "Oh."

He bends his head so we're eye to eye, and lays a warm hand on my shoulder. "What's going on?"

His concern has me shifting between shades of vulnerability and giving away far more than I normally would. "Did you ever feel like what you wanted doesn't matter?"

"What do you mean?" A shadowed line forms between his brows.

"Does this have anything to do with you and your band, and that stuff on the carpet?"

"Yeah. I left the band."

His lips quirk in a half-smile. "I know. You dominated headlines for days. The statement said something about it being time for you to embark on new adventures?"

"When we first formed, I thought MTKC would only last a few years, but we blew up, became this massive thing. Touring the world, playing to sold out stadiums, and having amazing fans is awesome, but bubble gum pop never fit me." I catch myself playing with the spikes on my wrist cuff and drop my hand. "It's been twelve years. For most of that time, I've felt trapped, creatively, legally, and emotionally. Leaving was the only option."

London rubs my shoulder in a soothing gesture. "What do you want to do instead?"

My gaze travels over his face and I bite my lip, bracing for his dismissal. "I want to change my music and my brand from pop to rock. Rock fits me. It's who I am."

His gaze turns thoughtful. "That's a radical switch from the vibe you've had going on for over the last decade. But I like it for you. You look the part already."

Relief at his easy acceptance washes over me like a warm wave. I gesture at my clothes, tats, and hair. "The label wouldn't allow any of this, or to let me make the switch with music. I'll be twenty-five next month, London. It's time to start being true to myself."

Twenty-five, though at times, I feel far more ancient than my years. London is six years older than me. Thirty-one, the same age as my older brother. I feel like I've known him forever, and opening up to him is easier than I imagined.

The tip of his thumb brushes my neck, and I suck in a breath at the contact of skin on skin. He pauses, his focus dropping to that small connection, before he drags his gaze back to mine. "Let me guess, from what I saw earlier, your former bandmates aren't on board with your leaving?"

The horrible things Trevor said flit through my mind. I cast a dark look over my shoulder at the glittery room and find the trio laughing together with an A-list actress near the bar. My anger crumbles into a despair threatening to swallow me whole. "They knew I hadn't been happy for the last several years, so I'd hoped they'd understand or maybe even saw it coming. But no. It's been two months, and they're still treating me like I sliced out their hearts with my guitar pick. I thought we could stay friends, but I guess I thought wrong."

London's hand tightens and flexes on my shoulder as he glares at my former friends. Shaking his head, he turns to me, and, with a smooth step, adjusts his stance so he's blocking my view of them. "I'm sorry."

Shrugging, I try for a smile. I've unloaded on him enough for tonight. Though I want to stay here with him, I should make an excuse so he can get back to his friends. "It's not your fault. Thanks for checking on me. I should—"

"Come with us to the festival next weekend." His words hang in the air, dangling like a lifeline. Grinning, he rubs his hand over the back of his neck. "Good music, great people, food, drinking. Fun. You need to get away from this toxicity."

That sounds like a phenomenally good idea. Plus, being in such close proximity to London for an extended period of time is tempting. "Come with you? Really?"

"Sure. We're driving up on Thursday, the festival is Friday, Saturday, and Sunday, and we drive home on Monday. We can hang out. You can relax." He shoves his hand in his pocket and rocks back on his heels. "I'd really like you to come."

"I want to, but what about your bandmates? I can't just insert myself into your lives without their okay."

The balcony doors open wider and Pan Macleod steps out, followed by Garrett White and Andrew Perfetti. Tall and lanky, Pan tugs his hair into a ponytail as he crosses to us. "Good, you found him. Are you okay, Mads? We were concerned."

Being surrounded by familiar, friendly faces is so soothing. I hug him, then Andrew and Garrett. They were my brother's friends first, but I consider them mine too. "I'm okay."

London drapes his arm around my shoulders. "He's not okay.

Caleb, Trevor, and Kell are being major dicks. So I invited Mads to come with us to the festival. He needs a break."

Pan holds London's gaze for a beat and something passes between them. When he focuses on me, his hazel eyes warm and he reminds me of my brother. "Do you want to come, Mads?"

"Yeah." Leaning against London's side, I soak up surety from his solid frame. "Is that okay?"

"Fine with me." Pan swings his head towards Garrett and Andrew. "Guys?"

The lights strung around the balcony reflect in Andrew's glasses as he raises his champagne flute to his lips. "Good with me."

"Me too." Garrett steals Andrew's drink, earning a glare for his efforts. Beneath his shaggy brown hair, his gray eyes light with mischief. "It's been too long since we spent time with you."

"Then it's settled. We're leaving at eleven o'clock on Thursday morning, Mads. There's room for you on the tour bus." Pan pulls out his phone. "We need to give Luke and Zander a head's up about this, since it's their festival."

London tightens his arm around me. "I already thought about that. I was going to contact the tour manager tomorrow. I know Mads will need the same passes we have."

With one raised brow, Pan continues typing the text. "I'm thinking more along the lines of the guys might want to add more security, for one thing. Maddox's fans are... let's go with extremely motivated."

I feel safe and happy with these guys, and don't want anything to prevent me from tagging along. "I can pay for additional security."

"Luke and Zander should be here in a second." Pan pockets his phone.

Nerves shoot through me. Meeting the music titans on their own is one thing. But in this situation, the stakes are higher. "I don't want to be a problem."

The feel of London's fingers squeezing my shoulder in support is nothing compared to the gentle comfort in his eyes. "You're not. Don't worry, I'm right here. Whatever happens, we'll figure something out."

The door opens and Zander Rostov strides outside with Luke Thompson beside him. The pair have trusted people in place to run

Furious Records, but the talent they sign is up to Luke, Zander, and their bandmates Landry and Brendan.

"Maddox, I'm Zander Rostov. Good to meet you." With a warm smile, Zander shakes my hand. "This is Luke Thompson."

Luke shakes my hand too. "So, you'll be joining us for the festival?"

"London invited me. I hope that's okay." I square my shoulders against the urge to shrink back and hide in London's protection.

"We're happy to have you there, but don't want any problems with Excite Records thinking we're trying to poach their talent." Luke glances from me to London. "So, how are we explaining your presence at a Furious Records festival? Friends? Boyfriends?"

Boyfriends with London? I wish. "I'm not with Excite anymore. We had creative differences. With my band's last two records, I tried venturing into a harder and heavier sound, but the label pushed back. My bandmates did too. I've fulfilled my contract. Excite only wants me in a boy band role. I want to make the type of music you do."

Luke's eyes fill with glee. He crosses his arms over his chest and nudges his elbow into Zander's side. "This has taken an interesting turn. We had our problems with Excite before venturing out to create our own label. No love lost there. Maddox, at Furious Records, a harder and heavier sound is music to our ears. If you're interested."

My heartbeat ticks faster and thuds harder. "I don't have a demo yet. That's why I haven't reached out to you. But I have a video of me jamming with my brother's band before they left for their tour. I can show you what I'd like to do." I dig my phone out of my pants pocket. If I can just show them…

"I want to see this." Zander gestures for me to go ahead.

I hit play as the guys crowd around me and focus on the screen. Randy on drums, his buddy on bass, with me on guitar and taking the lead on vocals. How happy I look singing and playing the hard rock anthem slams into me.

Nerves clawing at my stomach, I worry the video is too raw and unpolished. Nothing like what I'd present were I fully prepared.

London's hand touches the center of my back and fans out, like he knows I need comfort. Grateful, I lean into him and dare a peek at his bandmates to gauge their reactions to the song. Andrew nodding his head to the beat, Garrett drumming his fingers in time with Randy, and Pan smiling at the screen reassures me.

The song ends. My pulse racing and breath caught in my chest, I tuck my phone away, waiting for their feedback.

Zander beams at me. "Soulful voice, backed by sick guitar riffs and rapid-fire drums. It's sexy, powerful, and draws me in immediately."

"Me too. Damn, you can sing." Luke claps me on the shoulder.

Admiration fills London's eyes. "I didn't know you could shred like that." His hand slides up my back, raising nerve endings, and I shiver.

The weight of his palm and fingers on my shoulder and his forearm resting on my back, the fact that his arm is around me once more, is as good as the praise. Pleasure lighting through me, I settle against his side. "Randy taught me to play."

Luke and Zander share a look and both grin before turning to me. Then Zander says, "We'd love to talk more with you about the music you want to create and how Furious Records can help make that happen. Are you free to meet this week?"

Gaping at him, I'm unable to speak for a moment. I can't believe my luck and the timing of this, after everything that's happened. My limbs feeling like liquid, I lean harder on London. "You're serious?"

"Very." Luke gives me a sharp nod. "You're talented as hell and I can't believe Excite let you walk away. Not signing you would be incredibly stupid. And we're not stupid."

Zander slips his buzzing phone from his pocket and swipes away a notification. "Since you're coming to the festival, do you want to join our band on stage for a song during one of our sets? We'll put you on the billing as a special guest."

"That's... wow. Yes, please."

London playfully locks his other arm around my waist, pulling me into a loose embrace. "Hold on. He's *our* friend. You don't have a monopoly on Mads. We want him to play with us too."

"Great idea." Pan rubs his hands together, his eyes sparking as if plans are already spinning around in his head. "We'll do the same thing. Maddox, we can toss around ideas for songs during the drive."

Hugging London's arm against me, elation has me feeling as high as a satellite. To be sharing the stage with The Fury *and* my friends in Satyr's Kiss? Wow. "Two hours ago, I was alone and kind of hopeless, and now I'm getting the chance to be on stage with people I really admire, and the opportunity to create something I've wanted for a long time. You don't know how much I appreciate it."

Zander hands me his phone. "Enter your contact details. We'll be in touch tomorrow morning."

London releases me so I can do as Zander asks. After I pass the phone back, Zander texts me so I have his info too. I'm excited to talk more with them, and having lawyers I trust to hammer out contract details is one less worry.

More people spill out onto the balcony, filling it with laughter and conversation. Luke and Zander bid us goodnight, and the rest of London's band follows them into the ballroom, with plans for us to get a drink together.

I grab London's hand to hold him back. He's standing so close our chests brush in the crowded space, and that blue green intensity in his gaze sends a thrill through my blood. There's something special about him, something that draws me in and makes me want to stay. Though I want to keep holding his hand, I release it. "Thank you for finding me and for listening to me earlier."

"Anytime."

We smile at each other under the twinkling lights. London's gaze darts to my lips and lingers there. I wonder how his would taste, pressed against mine.

He tucks my hair behind my ear. "It sounds like good things will happen with Furious Records."

"Thank you for that too."

He shakes his head, his gaze fond and roaming over my face. "My invite may have gotten them out here to talk, but the rest was all you."

It's been an emotional night. I'm exhausted now, and can't get the idea of kissing him out of my mind. "I'm looking forward to this weekend. Maybe the two of us can—"

"Hey, London. Mads." Garrett's voice barrels in, crashing the moment like offbeat cymbals. "Are you coming?"

London jerks back a step, as though he was as lost in our moment as me and forgot the rest of the world existed. "Right behind you, Gar."

He gestures for me to go ahead of him. I enter the ballroom, grateful for the weight of his presence sticking close. I appreciate his protective vibes, and am relieved I don't see my former friends anywhere.

Maybe us being interrupted tonight is for the best, but I'm looking forward to this weekend with him. The chance to make music, sing with special people, and hopefully, have the chance to kiss London before it's over.

CHAPTER
THREE

LONDON

The tour bus bumps along the road, but the ride is smooth enough not to spill my coffee. Stretched out on the small sofa, I take a sip. Sunlight streams in through the windows as the California landscape rolls by. Coffee may not have been the wisest choice. I'm already bursting with energy, eager to get where we're going, and thrilled Maddox is here with us.

I glance at him, sitting cross-legged at the L-shaped bench across the aisle where he's playing a strategy card game with Andrew and Garrett, and catch him looking at me. Those chocolate brown eyes widen slightly before he gives me the same soft smile I remember from the red carpet, and my heart skips a beat.

His blue hoodie is at least two sizes too big and his gray sweats look so soft and comfortable, I can't stop picturing cuddling with him. Though the hoodie's purpose, covering him from the prying eyes of the photographers staking out his house when I picked him up this morning, bugs me. He shouldn't have to live like that. No one should.

"Kicking everyone's ass at this game is thirsty work." Andrew sets his cards facedown on the table. Keeping a watchful gaze on Garrett, he walks to the refrigerator and helps himself to one of the beers Pan brought. "Want one, Mads?"

Maddox fumbles his cards as he swings his focus to Andrew. "Sure. Thanks."

Garrett throws a card on one of the neat piles lined at the table's center. "On your way back, you can draw two more cards. I just played the one that reverses your last action."

Pan comes down the short aisle between the beds and heads for the electric kettle. He's exchanged his jeans for sweats. His shirt sports the logo of his brother Poe's football team, and the logo of his brother Puck's baseball team decorates the left thigh of his pants. We're Team Philly always, but even more so with his brothers playing for our hometown teams. "How do you end up with that card every time we play?"

"Luck?" Garrett asks.

"Cheating." Andrew coughs the word.

Pan drops a tea bag into a mug then hits the button for the water to boil. "Who's left in the game?"

"I've been out since the last round." I salute him with my coffee. "Andrew, Garrett, and Mads are still in."

When Andrew sits and picks up his cards again, Garrett leans over and takes Andrew's beer. He downs a mouthful, grimaces, and yanks the bottle away from his face to glare at the label. "Ugh. That's not so good."

Andrew's lips twitch. Behind his glasses, lines fan at the corners of his eyes with his smile. "It would probably taste better if you weren't also drinking coffee. And, you can stop stealing my drinks anytime now."

Garrett tips his head to the side in consideration, the fingers of his left hand drumming along the table's edge. "Nah. We both like it when I do that."

"Do we?" Andrew raises a brow. And they grin at each other.

It's only a matter of time before they start hooking up. Maybe they already are.

Garrett passes the beer to Andrew. He lifts his coffee mug, drinks deep, then sits back with a grateful sigh. "London, thanks for bringing the good coffee."

There are faint shadows under Maddox's eyes, but the gleam in them is bright. He takes a pull from his bottle. "What's the good coffee?"

"Any kind Garrett doesn't have to brew himself." I roll off the sofa and join him at the table, sliding into the space he makes for me. "You look tired."

"I didn't sleep much last night. I was too excited about today." He shifts his leg and his knee comes into contact with my thigh, resting there.

We're separated by a layer of cotton and another of denim, so that tiny touch shouldn't affect me as much as it does. Laying my hand on his knee feels like such a natural response. As soon as my fingers touch the soft heather gray, something in me settles. Though, I still want more. If he were mine, I'd cup my hand around his knee and shift him so his thigh lay atop mine. "Same here."

Holding the beer, he relaxes into the cushion at his back, glances at my fingers touching his knee, and turns the full power of his smile on me. "Want to jump into the game again? We can team up."

"That's not in the rules." Garrett tosses down a card forcing Andrew to forfeit his turn.

With a growl, Andrew smacks him in the shoulder. "Neither is you hiding cards in your pockets so you can use them against me."

"You saw that?" Garrett's gray eyes grow comically wide.

Chuckling, Pan turns off the kettle, then pours the steaming water into his mug. "Welcome to travels with Satyr's Kiss, Mads. Card games —*any* card games—are always this way."

"I'm having fun." Leaning against my side, Maddox shows me the cards fanned out in his hand. "Which one do you think?"

His scent surrounds me and my dick is half hard from his nearness. I pluck out a card to play against Garrett that will set our cheating drummer behind everyone in points.

Nodding at my choice, Maddox takes it, then reaches over me, balancing a hand on my thigh, to set the card on the farthest pile. "How'd you come up with the band name?"

"Well, Pan being Pan, he leaned heavily into his namesake. And me being me, I went along with him because he's my best friend." I draw in a breath and will my body to calm down and stop reacting so strongly to his touch. "Forming the band was his idea, and the best name I could come up with as a sleep-deprived college senior during finals was Pan's Band. Satyr's Kiss is much better. Andrew and Garrett agreed."

Pan's lips stretch into a smile. "I like the way you tell that story. The real answer is my brother Puck came up with it."

His green eyes locked on Garrett making the next card selection, Andrew sips his beer. "Mads, the song you and Pan are doing on Saturday is the one Puck's using this season for his walkup song when he goes up to bat."

"Then I'm even happier we're doing that one. I can't wait to sing with you." Maddox grins at Pan, then turns to me. "Either of you."

Our discussion during the early part of the ride about which songs would work best for Maddox to join us on stage ended with the decision that Pan and Mads will sing together on Saturday night and Mads will sing with me on Sunday. He's singing a song with The Fury during their set on Friday night.

"It'll be epic." I tip my mug to his beer bottle with a *clink*. Half of my attention is focused on his hand on my thigh and how much my cock likes it.

Maddox's phone, tucked into his hoodie's pocket, rings and vibrates against my side. He glances at the screen, smiles, and shoves the cards into my hands. "My brother. I'm gonna take it."

I stand so I'm not blocking him from sliding off the bench. He gives my arm a pat as he passes me, and I swear he holds on a few seconds longer than necessary.

"Tell him we said hi," Pan calls as Maddox heads for the privacy of the bus's back room.

Captivated, I watch him go. My system is a whirlwind of sensations, all thanks to Mads.

Once the door closes, Pan slides into Maddox's vacated seat. "How long have you had feelings for him, London?"

My heart jolts and my hand crumples the cards in my fist. Three flutter out, falling to the table and floor. Trying to keep my features neutral, I pick them up. "What are you talking about?"

He eyes me over his mug. "Are you really going to pretend you don't?"

We've been friends since we were five years old. I can't hide anything from him. And his knowing look says I'd be stupid to try. "Okay, fine. A while."

Pan acknowledges that with a nod.

I reclaim my seat, shuffling the cards in my hands over and over, but I can't concentrate on any game strategy. "I didn't invite him here expecting anything to happen. You saw how upset he was the other night. I wanted to help him. Randy would expect us to. And okay, I admit, I wanted to spend time with him. But I'd never try to take advantage."

"He watches you too. The same way you watch him." Pan takes the cards from me. He selects one and lays it on top of the center pile.

My breath gets caught in my lungs. Hands flat on the table, I soak up the coolness of the surface. "He does?"

Garrett splits the discard pile in two, preparing to shuffle them. "Big time."

"I've noticed that for years now," Andrew adds, smiling at me.

The revelations stun me silent. I think about several of our latest encounters. My focus goes to the closed door at the back of the bus. "I thought we had a few moments that could've been something, especially at the after party and today, but worried I was reading too much into things."

Pausing in the middle of taking one of Andrew's cards, Garrett says, "There were totally vibes when I doubled back to get you two for drinks, and with you sitting together right here."

I study my hands, the calluses on my fingers from years of playing guitar, the broken knuckle earned in a fight years ago defending Pan, and wonder if I have enough softness for Maddox. As tough as an exterior as he wants to project, I see the vulnerability and want to protect him. "If it stays with Mads and me only being friends, fine. But if there's a chance for more, I want to take it."

———

The setting sun turns the sky shades of pink and orange. Our tour bus is parked beside the one for Failing Midnight, and Pan, Garrett, and Andrew are outside, chatting with its members. Sprawled on the recliner, I scroll through social media feeds, liking the comments our fans have posted about the festival.

Most of the bands have arrived, their buses scattered across the large parking lot. We've been here for half an hour, and though I want to head out, catch up with friends, and meet new ones, I don't want Maddox, sleeping in the bed below mine, to wake up to an empty bus, wondering where we are.

His bed's closed curtains rustle, then draw open. Maddox swings his legs to the floor, combing his hand through his hair. His gaze finds mine. "We're not moving anymore."

"Nope. We're here." I thumb over my shoulder at the door behind me. "The guys are outside. Most of the other bands are here too."

He stands, tugging at his rumpled tee. The red color echoes the flush in his cheeks. "How long was I asleep?"

I glance at the ridiculous amp clock with the guitar pendulum Pan insisted on buying when we were in New Orleans last year. "About an hour and a half."

"I looked at my phone when I woke up." He pads toward the kitchenette, picking up cups and decks of cards from various games then placing them down. "There are photos of you and me leaving my house this morning, and an article speculating about what we are to each other."

"Oh." I don't know what to think about that, but the warmth in my stomach and twitch of my cock tells me what my body thinks. None of those photos crossed my feed. Nervous energy radiates from Mads as he moves from window to window, straightening things that don't need straightening. Concern wriggles through me. "Does that article upset you?"

He sucks in a breath then lets it out slowly, brushing his fingers over his hoodie hanging on the hook by the window, next to my leather jacket. "I wasn't thinking. I shouldn't have let you pick me up."

I stand, aching to pull him close and soothe his worries. "I wanted to."

"But now, they might start showing up and following you around too. They can be really intrusive." Pacing the small space, he drags his hands through his hair. "I don't want you to have to deal with them."

That his discomfort is because he's worried about my possible future discomfort endears him to me even more. "They'll get bored with me. And I'm not as photogenic as you are."

"You're gorgeous." He stops moving, his expression an interesting mix of confident and shy. Then he shrugs and gestures at me. "Well, you are."

My heart pounds like Garrett's bass drum with the thrill of his words. "Thanks. Don't worry about the article. Everything will be okay. This weekend is for relaxing, remember? Playing music, making friends, taking a break from everyday life. Just focus on those things. I want you to have a good time, Mads."

The slow bloom of his smile accompanies the softening of the tension in his shoulders. He rests his hip against the counter and his fingers pluck the hem of his shirt. "I'll try. I know we should go meet everyone...."

I cross the space and lean on the counter beside him. "It's okay if you're not ready yet."

"I'm excited about being here. Thrilled I'm being given a chance. But I'm nervous too."

"I think most of us feel that way. I love live performances but always get anxious before shows."

He shakes his head. "It's more than that. Yeah, I want to do well performing, but I also want to show the fans, Furious Records, the people who believe in me, and the people who doubted me that I can pull this off."

I gently bump my shoulder into his. "That's understandable."

"And I want to impress you." The soft words curl between us.

He's worried about impressing me? Staggered, I grip the counter to steady myself. "You dazzle me."

Brown eyes rounding, he blinks at me, his mouth opening and

closing a few times, like I've stunned him speechless. A small smile tugs at his lips. "I do? How? I'm just... me."

"You're talented, yet you still work hard and don't try to coast on anything. You're a star but don't have the arrogant attitude that usually comes along with being one . You're still kind to everyone. You don't use people. You're genuine."

His gaze drops to his socks and his foot absently traces the lines on the soft rug. "I don't know what to say to that. You make me sound good." Cheeks rosy, he looks at me again. "I'm kind of needy, and it's hard for me to trust people. I never know whether they like me for myself or for what they think I can do for them."

"I get that. I've been burned before too. This business makes having a relationship tough. It's difficult opening up to someone when you're unsure if you can trust them." I swallow, my throat dry, my tone holding a weariness I don't often notice.

We look at each other as the light of the setting sun shifts and evening shadows take on different shapes. Our vulnerability is on display. Opening up to him is easy and feels natural. I haven't had that feeling for anyone outside of my bandmates and a few other friends in years.

Maddox's gaze is eloquent, searching mine. He rests his hand on the counter and slides forward until our fingers touch. "I trust you. Just thought I should put that out there."

Tension I didn't realize I was holding drains from my limbs and shoulders, squeezed out by the revitalizing warmth of his declaration. I lay my hand over his, my thumb caressing the soft skin of his inner wrist. "I trust you too."

"Good." His voice is soft, his Adam's apple bobbing when he swallows. He inches closer to me, gaze shifting from my eyes to my lips, back and forth again.

Everything in me throbs with the desire to kiss him.

Maddox's eyes close for a moment and his body sways toward me. When his eyes open, desire and need shimmer in the brown depths. "You're going to kiss me, right? Please say you're going to kiss me. I've been thinking about it for years."

I move until there is only a sliver of space between us. "Years?"

"Yeah. Is that okay?"

"More than okay." I cup his face, brushing my thumb over his lower lip. "I've been thinking about you for years too."

His slow, sexy smile blooms like the opening notes of a love ballad. Being at the center of his attention is a heady rush.

My heartbeat thudding as energy races through me, I lean down. Maddox's hand curls into my shirt as I cup his shoulder. The warmth of his skin seeping through the thin cotton and fresh scent of his body wash combined with the leather of my jacket beside us reminds me of warm spring days riding my motorcycle in the sunshine. I can picture him holding on tight, arms wrapped around me, the wind in our faces, as I take us to my favorite places.

His lips part and I pause, drinking in the perfection standing in front of me.

He's gorgeous, and looking at me like I'm the only person in the world who matters. I've never had that before.

The slight tug on my shirt pulls me forward. I touch my lips to his. He tastes like citrus and softness and my world tilts beneath me.

Slanting my mouth for a deeper taste, a more intimate touch, I stroke across his lips until they part again and let me inside. The feel of his tongue teasing mine, the sound of his sigh and the way he shifts closer, spikes my need further. I slide my free hand to his back, and bury the other in his hair. His arms band around me like they have no intention of letting go, like they could hold me forever.

Kissing Maddox is freeing. Amazing. I could compose songs about it for eternity and never run out of things to say.

When breathing becomes necessary, I raise my head, drawing in more of his scent.

Maddox smiles at me, tracing his fingertips over my jaw. "That was worth waiting for."

My heart melting, I cuddle him closer. "Definitely worth waiting for. And better than I imagined."

His hold on me tightens. So much emotion swirls in his eyes. "I hoped I'd get the chance to kiss you this weekend. I didn't think it would happen on our first night here."

"Neither did I."

"We can do it again, right?"

Leaning into his touch, I press my lips to the soft skin on the inside of his wrist. "As much as you want."

CHAPTER
FOUR

MADDOX

The roar of the crowd and the blare of music coming from the stage paint the night air with a verve pulsing like lightning in every heart-beat. The festival's venue space is an open roof sports stadium my former band and I played on our last tour. Back then, I took the stage without any qualms.

But tonight, waiting in the wings to step on stage, nerves needle me, tiny pinpricks of anxiety mixing with adrenaline. It's almost dizzying.

The Fury are on stage, giving an electric performance. The song I'm singing with them is up next. My nails biting my palms, I draw in a deep breath. Then another.

What if they announce me and the audience responds with boos? The comments on social media this week, following the announce-ments of my signing with Furious Records and that I was joining this festival, were mixed. Hard rock fans wondering if I'm serious about this change or just playing at it because I'm bored. Other people suggesting I should stay in my lane and not try to branch out. And still others, wanting to see me fail.

Some MTKC fans are here, wearing our t-shirts and holding signs bearing my name. Thanks to them, the festival is sold out. They crashed the ticket site, and the demand for more tickets was so high, the venue opened up another parking lot, selling it out as lawn seating.

These fans seem like they're sticking with me, and I don't want to let them down. But how will they react to this different style of music?

London emerges from one of the dressing rooms with Craig and Cody from Failing Midnight. I met them last night over burgers and beers and we clicked right away. The trio make their way toward me.

Craig claps me on the shoulder. "Break a leg, man."

Cody barrels right in and hugs me. "You'll be awesome."

"Thanks guys." My nerves recede a bit, like a wave ebbing into the ocean. I've been thinking of the sea a lot lately, thanks to London's eyes. "I'll see you after."

They nod and continue toward the corridor leading to our parking lot.

London's hand cups the back of my neck and lightly squeezes. "Are you ready?"

I lean into his touch. "Excited and nervous as hell."

"You've got this." His gaze falls to the space between us. I follow it to find my fingers playing with his bracelet.

Heat flaming into my cheeks, I disentangle myself from the leather strap woven through thick silver links. I don't have my wrist cuff to play with. It might have fallen out of my bag at home because I couldn't find it on the bus. "Sorry."

He works the clasp open and then takes my hand and fastens the bracelet around my wrist. "In case you need it out there."

The gesture swamps me with sweetness. Pressing his hand to my chest, holding it against my heart, I trail the fingertips of my other hand along the prickling stubble on his cheek. "Thank you. Will you stay?"

His fingers hooking my collar, he draws me forward. "I'll wait right here."

He keeps our gazes connected as he brings his lips to mine. The touch is electric, shooting through me with the immediacy of touching a live wire.

No matter what happens on stage, London is here.

That settles me.

He pulls back and grins. "Now go be a rockstar."

On stage, Luke is chatting with the audience. He meets my gaze and gives me a nod.

I nod back. Ready or not, we're doing this.

Zander rips into the frenetic pace of the next song, then Brendan joins on drums, followed by Landry on bass to complete the controlled chaos. Luke belts out the first line and the fans cheer. He gestures for me to come on stage. One of the techs hands me a mic. Sucking in a breath, I step into the spotlight.

The cheers grow louder. I see metalheads in the pit at the front of the stage, eyeing me skeptically beside MTKC fans screaming my name, and worry neither group will like what I'm trying to do. Luke holds out his arm for me to join him. He gives me a half-hug as fierce as the man himself, before releasing me so I can sing the next verse.

I pour everything I have into the words. We rehearsed this song a lot on Wednesday, and I'm comfortable with it. The music spirals and swirls, moving around and through me, and I'm hit with how right being out here feels. The warm circle of London's bracelet sliding down my forearm is a reminder he believes in me, too.

Luke saunters away from rocking out next to Zander and meets me at center stage. The five of us sing the chorus together. Singing with this famous foursome is surreal. I never could've imagined experiencing something like this with my old band. The adrenaline rush is different, now that it's music I love.

Zander waves me over to his side of the stage. His guitar tech hands me one of Zander's backup guitars and I slip the strap over my shoulder. Zander had suggested we add in a small solo to show the fans what I can do, an incredibly generous offer and I need to make the most of it.

I launch into a sonic guitar-shredding solo that would make any metal head proud. Heart pumping wildly, I focus on the notes, fueled by determination, adrenaline, and nerves. I have something to prove tonight. I *do* belong here.

Breathless, I conclude the solo then return to the final chorus of the song.

The crowd's cheers grow louder and louder. Some of the people who'd looked at me skeptically when I stepped on stage are now flashing me the horns.

Zander thumps my back in hearty praise as the song ends. Luke gestures to me and says into his mic, "We're proud to welcome Maddox Muldoon to Furious Records. What do you guys think about that?"

More cheers ring out.

Elation and relief bolstering me like I'm crowd surfing, I wave to the fans. Waiting in the wings, London grins, with Pan, Garrett, and Andrew beside him.

Luke hugs me, and after I hand off the guitar to Zander's tech, I hurry off stage with one last wave.

London is still beaming. He opens his arms, his glittering gaze roaming my body as potent as an actual touch. "You were amazing."

I launch myself into his welcoming hold, wrapping my arms around his shoulders, and bury my face in the crook of his neck, inhaling the leather from his jacket and the spicy wildness of his body wash. "Thanks for earlier. The bracelet was good luck."

His hands are hot on my back, pressing me into him. "You didn't need luck. But you can keep the bracelet."

Flying high from the performance, I nose along his cheek until my lips land on his. Kissing him sends me higher. Licking into my mouth, he takes the kiss deeper, and his hands lower to cup my ass, nudging me closer so the bulge in his jeans presses against mine. My pulse is throbbing, I'm fully hard and aching for more.

Behind us, someone clears their throat. I lift my mouth from London's. He slides his hands to my waist and we both twist toward the sound.

Arms crossed over his chest, Pan angles his head in the direction of the event staff bustling around. "You never know who might be taking pics or videos. I wasn't sure if you were keeping this," he gestures at us, "private or not."

It's only been two days, and a few amazing kisses. Too soon to

222 SUSAN SCOTT SHELLEY

discuss anything yet. But I don't want to stop touching London, and since he's still holding onto me, I doubt he wants to stop either. Even so, we should be a bit careful.

London smooths his palms up and down my back, leaving a trail of heat. "We should get out of everyone's way here, regardless."

He's right. The Fury are the last to perform tonight and they only have a couple more songs to go. The crew won't want us in their way.

Garrett slings his arm around Andrew's shoulders, pulling him out of the tour manager's path. "Let's get down to the buses. A lot of the other bands are already there hanging out."

"Good idea." Andrew grins at me. "Come on, Mads, let's get a drink to celebrate your performance."

I slide out of London's hold. As much as I want uninterrupted time with him, it's important to make connections with the other bands, and to spend time with the friends standing around us. "Sure, I could use a drink. Maybe some food."

We follow the long corridors and exit the stadium, bidding good-night to the security guard stationed at the door. Beyond the fence on one side, a few photographers linger. They've been there all day, and I'm afraid they'll be around all weekend. I'm glad our tour bus is at the opposite end of our parking lot, hidden by the other buses, and out of their view. They've seen so much of my life, private moments and mundane ones. I hold up my hand to block my face from them.

London hands me his jacket. "Here. For cover, if you want it."

"Thanks." The gesture means a lot to me. I use the soft leather as a shield, breathing in his scent, feeling safer with it wrapped around me. Nighttime makes hiding easier too. Once we get to the maze of buses, I slip the jacket off then pass it back to him.

Hooking his jacket over his shoulder, he wraps his arm around me. "Anytime you want it, it's yours."

We find Craig, Cody, and their bandmates Devon and Patrick sprawling in camp chairs in the space between our bus and theirs. They've set out five additional chairs for us, like they did last night.

Cody spots us first. "Hey! Pull up a chair. We have beer and quesadillas. Great job on the song, Mads."

"Thanks." I claim the empty chair beside the short, dark-haired singer. After he passes me a beer, I drag my chair over a few inches so London can fit his chair between mine and Pan's. He stretches out with a beer in one hand and a quesadilla in the other and offers me a bite.

Thanks to Devon, I end up with my own plate of food and Devon, Cody, and I talk with Craig about the songs he's written for other artists. All around me, people are chatting and mingling. More bands wander by and I meet so many people, their names and faces blur.

A pang of loneliness hits me like an arrow to the chest, seeing the obvious friendships Craig, Cody, Devon, and Patrick share, and Pan, London, Andrew, and Garrett too. I can't help thinking about my former band. It's been a hard few months, a hard few years if I'm honest, and I miss that things aren't the same anymore.

But things are getting better. A lot better. The guys keep including me in conversations, and I can see myself forming new friendships here. I genuinely like these people and I'm getting good vibes.

Leaning forward, I catch Craig's attention. "If you have some time, I'd like to talk with you about collaborating on a song or two. I know you're busy with your band, but—"

He holds up his hand, grinning. "Working together would be awesome. When you're back in LA, hit me up. I might be less available to meet in person, but we can do a call. The guy I'm seeing lives in Buffalo, so I'm planning on spending a lot of time there and being bi-coastal."

"Long distance can be tough."

"I don't like having three thousand miles between us." He raises his gaze to the sky, but I catch his yearning expression before the shadows hide it away. "He'll be here tomorrow. I can't wait."

"I hope I get the chance to meet him."

Cody leans into me and whispers, "Craig and Ty only have eyes for each other. It's really sweet. Kind of like you and London."

My swallow of beer gets stuck in my throat, and I sputter and cough as I gape at him. "What…"

He pats me on the back, his eyes narrowing with worry. "Did you think no one else would notice or are you surprised because you didn't realize you look at each other that way?"

"Um…" I suck in a breath, then cough again. "Both, I guess. I know what I feel when I see him, but it's so new, I'm not sure what he feels. I'm trying not to get my hopes up."

Head tilted to the side, he studies me, his dark eyes reflecting my own image at me. "But your hopes *are* up."

"Yeah. They are." I run my finger over the bracelet. On my other side, London has moved his chair closer to Pan's, and bits of their discussion with Patrick drift over.

The scrape of Craig's chair on the concrete drags my attention to him. He tosses his empty plate into the trash, then glances at the stadium. "This weekend will be the largest crowd we've ever played. Mads, I know you're used to playing bigger ones. Any advice?"

"I tell myself it's no different than playing in a small club, that large crowds are just a lot of small ones put together."

He tips his beer back. "That's a good way of looking at it."

After setting the remains of my quesadillas aside, I lean back in my chair. "It wasn't always that easy though. I was pretty young when I started touring with my old band, and the sold out stadiums and arenas overwhelmed me, freezing me to the spot backstage. From doing community theater with my parents back in Philly, I was used to performing in front of an audience, but not on that level."

London sets his chair beside mine again, lining them up without any space between us, then slides his arm around me. Resting my head on his shoulder, I like the way I fit here.

His fingers play with my hair. "How'd they get you to overcome the stage fright?"

"My brother taught me breathing exercises. I still do them. And my parents told me to find one person in the crowd to focus on, and let the others melt into the background. That helped." The touch is so relaxing, my eyes flutter closed. "What about you? You come from a line of performers too. Did your parents give you any advice?"

He shrugs. "Regardless of crowd size, I'm nervous before every show, wanting everything to go well so the fans feel like their time was well spent. My parents never gave any specific advice, but I saw how hard they worked preparing for performances. That rubbed off on me."

I wonder if he ever feels like the odd one out in his family, with his opera singer parents and grandmother, and concert pianist sister. "Did they ever pressure you to do something other than what you wanted?"

"No. Music was always a huge thing in our house. They're happy my sister and I are able to pursue it professionally. Rock's always been my genre, but I can appreciate opera and classical music. When I was really little, I apparently would run around the house wearing bits from different Halloween costumes and imitating whatever operas my parents were doing."

"I bet you were really cute."

Chuckling, he shakes his head. "I probably drove them crazy."

The others are talking among themselves, so I roll toward London and lay my hand on his chest. The warmth of his skin under his tee soaks into my palm. Talking with him like this, in the dim, shadowed light, is cozy. "Randy is really why I got into rock. I followed him around, wanting to do everything he did, listening to everything he listened to, and probably drove him crazy too. Even so, he gave me guitar lessons for years."

His touch gentle, he combs his hand through my hair. "He liked teaching you. He talks about it sometimes. I don't think you realize how touched he was that you wanted to be like him."

I'm glad Randy didn't see me as an annoying pain in ass. We've become good friends now that we're adults. I wish he were here too. With him on tour in Australia for the past month, connecting for phone calls and texts has been tough with the time difference. "He's a good brother. And he has great taste in friends."

A smile curls the edges of his lips. The desire and intimacy flickering in his eyes brings me right back to being on the balcony with him. The way he took care of me and the way he looked at me like I was someone who mattered to him. "I like being with you out here like this."

"I do too." Kissing him again consumes me. And though we're only two days into our time together, I already know I want more with him than this single weekend.

CHAPTER
FIVE

LONDON

The crowd is lively and our energy is fierce. From my place on the left side of the stage, I tear into the next song, a live wire of adrenaline running through me as the crowd gets louder, recognizing what's coming next. My friends are on fire tonight, our set has been amazing, and thousands of people are singing along to our songs. I never get tired of this feeling.

Music flows as I coax notes out of the guitar. To my left, Garrett lays down a beat. The drum beat starts slow, and progressively gets more intense. I increase my pace too. He grins, his gray eyes lighting with happiness. My lips stretch into a smile. Every worry, about the performance, about how I need to talk to Randy about my feelings for his brother, about how much I want to keep seeing Maddox after this weekend is over, fades.

Across the stage, Pan launches into the lyrics. He has something special, both in himself and in his voice, that captures people's attention. Working the crowd, he encourages them to sing along, making them feel like a part of the show.

Maddox watches me from the wings, dark eyes tracking my every movement, his fingers tracing over the links of the bracelet I gave him. Awareness prickles along my skin, deepening into arousal that runs my blood hot. I meet his gaze. Hold it. And see an echo of what I'm feeling in his expression.

Over the last few days, I've watched Maddox playing and laughing with Pan, Garrett, Andrew, and myself, and how he's opening up more to Cody and Craig. Far less alone than when I found him on the balcony last weekend. I'm thrilled to see it. I need him to be happy in the same way I need music.

We hit the midpoint of the song, and the drum breakdown turns into a full out drum solo. I love how Garrett puts his whole body into his performance. Andrew saunters closer to the drum kit. Their gazes meet and hold, and they both smile. The solo ends, and silence reigns for a few seconds, drowned out by the crowd's roar. Pan and I grin at each other.

Garrett lays down the beat, resuming the song. Andrew joins in, and I follow. Pan is last, grabbing the mic. "How about Garrett back there?"

Cheers roll over us like a tidal wave. We keep playing and Pan sings the last verse. For the final chorus, he holds his mic out to the crowd, letting them finish it off.

When the cheers die down, Pan leans into his mic. "This next song is from our new album. It's called "Seeking Strangers" and we have our friend, Maddox Muldoon, to help us out with it."

Maddox steps onto the stage, brushing his hand across my back as he passes me. The crowd goes wild. I spy signs with his name and teens wearing shirts with his former band's logo, and wonder what they'll think of this new sound, if they'll like it as much as the fans from last night.

I play the opening riff, moving around my side of the stage, interacting with the fans as Pan bursts into the first verse. The audience jams along with us, people dancing in the throng. The atmosphere is so electric and alive.

Maddox's voice takes over. Dressed in black jeans, boots, and a black tee showing off his tattoo sleeve, his hair flowing and wild, he looks like a dark angel. I ache with wanting him.

I'm used to Pan's voice singing this song. Maddox caresses the notes and lyrics in a different way. He looks at home and happier than any performance he's done with MTKC in the last several years.

He's awesome and amazing. From the cheers and screams, the fans are into it. And when he and Pan sing together for the third verse, the way their voices blend is so freaking good.

Garrett meets my gaze. He grins, not missing a beat, sweat trickling down his face.

Andrew leaves his side of the stage, meeting Pan, going back to back as he joins the chorus. I add my voice to the mix. There is absolutely nothing else I'd rather do with my life than create music with my friends. And now with Maddox too.

At the song's end, Maddox hugs Pan, nods at Andrew and Garrett, waves to the crowd, and then crosses to me. His smile is huge, he brushes his fingers along my arm as he passes by.

We have one more song to go. I play, but my attention is split, half on the music and half on Maddox waiting for me at the side of the stage.

Finally, the song reaches its end and Pan thanks the audience for being a great crowd. Amid the cheers, I hand my guitar off to the tech then walk to the front of the stage. Garrett, Andrew, and Pan join me. We link hands and take a bow.

Sweating from the stage lights and riding the wave of adrenaline, I follow the others offstage. We high-five the tour manager and a few members of the crew. Once we're out of their way, we gather into a group hug. We've been through a lot together, ups and downs over the last ten years, but every show begins and ends the same way. The four of us huddled together.

I love them like they're my brothers and wouldn't want anyone else by my side. "I'm so proud of us. Great set, guys."

Pan squeezes me tighter. "We're doing it, brother. Let's celebrate."

Luke and Zander are hosting a get together outside their tour bus tonight for the bands. I've been looking forward to drinking, relaxing, and maybe dancing with Mads. Maybe more.

We separate from our huddle. I turn in a circle, scanning the flurry of people for Maddox.

"There he is." Garrett points to Mads talking with one of the staff near the dressing rooms.

We head toward him, and my friends crowd around Mads, wrapping him in hugs and congratulations on his performance. He lights up with each one. I wish he'll always remember how happy and supported he feels in this moment. Maybe it'll help make up for the dark and lonely months he felt so isolated from his former band.

The others step back and Maddox turns to me. His eyes are shining, happiness radiating from him like sunbeams. "That was an amazing set, London."

"You weren't too bad on the mic either, Mads." I open my arms and he throws himself into my embrace.

His lips land on mine. The kiss is hard, desperate, and laced with need. High on the excitement and energy of performance, and high on Maddox himself, I clutch him against me.

All day long, I've ached for time alone with him. Listening to him sleep in the bed below mine, drinking coffee with him this morning while we shed the cobwebs of sleep, seeing him smile at me from across a room, watching him sing as he joined Cody for an impromptu rendition of songs by 90's grunge bands in the parking lot this afternoon, knowing how he feels in my arms and the taste of his kisses. And now, I get to have it.

Maddox lightens the kiss and leans back, his gaze so hot I wouldn't be surprised if I ignited. His fingers slide out of my hair and onto my neck, stroking a patch of skin above my collar.

Kissing him here, backstage like this, is like a repeat or continuation of what happened yesterday after his song with The Fury. I'd love it if every time he or I exited a stage, we'd have the other person waiting for us. The rush of feelings is unreal. Just like last night, I want to grab him and hide away from everyone else.

A tangle of voices spill out of the dressing room as the four members of The Fury head into the hallway. They're the final act tonight. They wave as they walk toward the stage, and Zander calls out, "We'll see you at the party."

Pan clasps my shoulder. "We should head out."

"Yeah." Shifting our embrace, I snake my arm around Maddox's waist, loving the way he snuggles into me. Holding him is always amazing, but since I don't have my jacket with me tonight, I want to be there if he needs cover from the photographers hanging around outside.

We make our way to the exit, passing by the security guard stationed at the door. A warm breeze dances over our skin and the driving beat of The Fury on stage echoes from the stadium. I don't see the photographers in their usual place tonight. Both Mads and I relax.

Near The Fury's tour bus, several grills are set up along with colorful coolers filled with drinks. There are food trucks too, different ones from the previous two nights. The scents of beer, fries, and barbecued food waft in the air.

Cody, Patrick, and Devon stand near one of the coolers, beers in hand.

With my finger hooked through a loop on Maddox's jeans, I lead us in that direction, greeting people we've met over the past two days on the way. There have been comments from some fans on social media questioning Maddox's transition into the realm of rock, but everyone here acts like he belongs.

Devon sees us before his bandmates do and shifts closer to Cody and Patrick so there's room for us. "Hey, guys. Grab a drink."

Andrew hands out beers before grabbing one for himself. "Where's Craig?"

"Spending the night with Ty." Cody jerks his thumb in the direction of their tour bus, though he could also mean the hotel two blocks away.

They have the right idea. I should sneak away with Mads.

Leaning into me, Maddox looks toward our bus and raises a brow in question. My hand on his hip, I skate a thumb along the edge of his waistband, brushing warm, soft skin in invitation.

He gives me a nod, presses closer to kiss me, then surprises me by turning to Patrick and asking him about one of the songs Failing Midnight played during their set today. Maybe he thinks it's too early for us to slip away.

"Here." Pan thrusts a plate loaded with chicken and fries into my hand. He sits on top of an empty cooler, balancing his plate on his lap. "Eat."

"Thanks." I set my beer on a ledge and dig in, grateful he always looks out for us.

Garrett returns with a ton of food, yet steals a fry from Andrew's plate. I laugh, almost choking on my mouthful of beer at his obvious, not at all cloak and dagger move. Andrew's amused smile is fond. The two bicker about stolen beers and fries, laughing and sampling foods off each other's plates.

The fries are crisp and hot and the chicken is seasoned with a spicy rub. I share bites with Maddox. Though he keeps in conversation with various people who happen by, he also keeps contact with me, leaning against my side and resting his hand on my shoulder. I soak up every little touch, each moment of connection.

The Fury's last song fades into silence and the fans' cheering is so loud it sounds like thunder emanating from the stadium.

After that dies down, the din of fans leaving the stadium and cars driving by, horns honking, becomes the backbeat to our conversations.

Music pours out of speakers set up near the bus. The atmosphere is happy with people dancing and singing along. Maddox rocks out beside me, bumping his hip against mine in time with the beat.

Cheers erupt from the people closest to the stadium's door when Luke, Zander, Landry, and Brendan emerge. The guys make their way across the lot, taking the time to chat with each band. They treat everyone equally, and while I appreciate their consideration, tonight my impatience burns bright.

Maddox continues dancing, sending me teasing glances laced with heat. Our hands keep wandering, discrete touches turning daring, driving us higher.

Once the guys in The Fury have greeted us and moved on, Maddox angles his head to the side, his attention on my face, and draws me in closer. "Want to get out of here?"

"I do. Are you sure you're ready? I don't want to drag you away if you want to meet more people."

His hands slide up my chest, slow and steady, before descending to rake over my stomach, sensations spiraling in his wake and turning my cock to granite. "The two of us spending time together is important too. I want you to myself, London."

With a groan, I capture his lips in a heated kiss. They taste of spice and beer and the promise of more. "I want that too. Let's go."

My arm locks around his waist as we hustle from the crowd. The music and din of conversations grow softer, and the night seems almost too quiet.

Maddox slides his hand into my back pocket. The heat in his gaze pushes me to walk faster.

A few of the tour buses have lights on. We reach ours and I manage to get the door unlocked without letting go of Mads.

We stumble inside. I turn to lock the door, my hand fumbling as Maddox kisses the back of my neck.

His eyes shining in the dim light, he pulls me toward the room at the back of the bus. "More space here."

I kick the door closed behind us. Two couches run the length of the small room. Maddox switches on a light, dimming it to a soft golden glow.

He's gorgeous in any light. But standing before me here, on the precipice of taking our relationship to the next level, he's breathtaking.

We fall into each other's arms. Our mouths meet and I groan at how he opens for me. His hair is loose, tangling in my fingers. Angling my head, I take the kisses deeper.

My shirt pulls as Maddox tightens his grip, fisting the material. His sigh is needy and heavy as his tongue laps at mine. My body reacts, hardening and warming. I move my lips along his jawline, trailing soft kisses over clean-shaven skin.

He tugs my shirt up my torso. "Need this off. Want to see you."

I yank the tee off and toss it onto the couch. Maddox gets rid of his too. He has a wiry build, thin and strong. More tattoos spill across the side of his stomach, a mix of music notes and Celtic knot work I long to trace with my fingers.

His gaze roams over my chest. "I knew you'd look good like this."

"Half dressed?" I smirk, pulling him against me.

"Halfway undressed. For me." The hungry look in his eyes and the way his hands drag across my skin, like I belong to him, makes me wish for it. More than I've wished for anything in a long time.

My fingers trailing along those tattoos, I ghost more kisses over his lips. "I'd do anything for you, Mads."

Surprise coats the desire darkening his features. He makes a soft sound in his throat and bands his arms around me. There's fierceness and almost a desperation in how tight he hugs me. Stroking my hands up and down his back, I'm overwhelmed by how much I want to give him everything, to be there for him for as long as he'll have me.

His sigh breezes over my shoulder as he pulls back. Vulnerability shimmers in that chocolate gaze. His fingers tremble as they trace the edge of my lower lip. "No one's ever said that to me before."

I swallow against the thickness in my throat. "I've never said it to anyone."

He nips my lip, drawing my bottom lip between his teeth. His focus drops to my stomach, and lingers on the two-inch scar decorating my skin. "What happened here?"

"I took a stick blade to the stomach playing hockey with Pan and his brothers a few years ago."

The tip of his index finger follows the path of the silvery line with tender care. Then he stoops and touches his lips to the spot. My heart aches with the sweetness of the gesture, even as the image of him almost on his knees before me is a fantasy come to life.

His hair curtains his face. I sift my fingers through the silky strands, pushing them behind his ears. He peeks at me, biting his lip. "I'd do anything for you, too."

"No one's ever said that to me before either." That ache in my chest blooms again. This man... Sweet and generous and kind. My hands tightening around his shoulders, I pull him upright. With lips, teeth, and tongue, I try to show him how much his words mean to me. He could hold my heart in his hand, and I trust him with it.

As we kiss, the sweetness of the moment sinks low as sultry desire surges high. Maddox works his fingers between us and pops open the buttons on our jeans. His knuckles drag over my covered cock as he lowers his zipper, then with a twist of his wrist, he lowers mine.

"Pants off. Boxers too." He pants the order between kisses along my jaw.

Rock hard, I rush to do as he asks. We separate, working the denim and cotton down our thighs, freeing ourselves of boots and socks too. I steal glances as I kick free of my clothes. He's gorgeous, long lean lines, and dark hair spilling over his shoulders.

Banked fire flares in his eyes as he stalks toward me. "Look at you. Even better than the half-undressed version."

I stand taller under his appreciative gaze. "If I look to you even half as good as you look to me, I'll consider myself lucky."

"I have something for us." He holds up a packet of lube.

My cock throbs at the sight of it. "I love people who come prepared."

A smile flashes across his face lightning fast. "We'll both be coming."

"Yes, we will." Gripping his hand, I tug him forward. He tumbles into my chest and our cocks rub together. We both groan. The feel of being skin to skin with him is unbelievable.

Having Maddox in my arms like this… I need the closeness and I want to make him soar.

His scent, his heat, his breaths and gasps and whispers, I crave them all. I clamp my hands on his hips, rocking us against each other. My pulse races with the thrill.

I want to touch him everywhere, roam and explore, learning every secret and sigh and what makes his body sing. We don't have time tonight for everything I want to try with him. Hopefully, there'll be a lot more times together.

He's warm and throbbing against me. I'm hard as a rock, leaking for him. Desire pulses through me in time with every heartbeat.

Maddox tears the lube open. He drizzles the clear fluid over our cocks then takes hold of my hand and pours more into my palm. The rest ends up on his fingers before he tosses the empty packet aside.

I wrap my hand around us, working our shafts, groaning at the friction and the reality that Maddox Muldoon, the object of my fantasies for years, is here with me now, helping to edge us closer to shared orgasms.

His hand covers mine, pumping up and down, while he chases my kisses and drives me wild playing with my balls. "I want to make you feel good."

"You are." Each new area he explores pushes me closer to the edge. My other hand bites into his hip, tightening as he teases his fingers farther back. "So good. I want to do that for you, too."

"You always make me feel good." His gaze is eloquent and his words wrap around my heart.

I skate my hand from his hip to his ass, kneading the firm globe, teasing my fingers closer to his hole. Trailing kisses over his neck, I land on a spot that makes him shiver. And *suck*.

Maddox throws his head back, gasping then moaning, thrusting into our hold. His fingers tighten over mine. "I'm close."

Pumping our cocks faster and harder, I circle my finger over his rim then edge the tip of it inside him. "You're gorgeous like this."

"London." My name is a plea. His other hand grips my shoulder like I'm the only thing holding him together.

"That's it, Mads. Come for me."

He stiffens, mouth open, then his release erupts over our stomachs. I work him through it, giving him as much pleasure as possible until he sags against me.

The heat and smell of his release, the fact that it's Mads, is too much. I'm losing control. My fist is a blur, flying over my cock.

Eyes heavy lidded, he pushes my hand away. "I want to do it."

Completely on board with that, I clutch his hip and shoulder, leaking for him, thrusting into his grasp.

He works his thumb over my cock head and his other hand jacks my shaft, tight as a vise. "You feel so good. I love touching you like this. Love the way you made me feel."

"Mads." Gasping his name, I ride the spine-shattering sensations shooting through me like a starburst. In seconds, I'm falling over the edge, soaring on pleasure, coating our cocks and his hands with my release.

Maddox continues stroking me, pressing kisses to my jaw. "Very sexy, London. Very, very sexy, watching that. Feeling that."

"Yeah?" Boneless and floaty, I pull back, catch his sated smile, then kiss him again. I love how he opens for me, kissing like he savors it as much as I do.

The stickiness on my hands and stomach is a reminder we need to clean up. My shirt is the closest thing to grab. I rub it over myself, then hand it to Mads. The bus is still quiet. No one else is back yet.

Mads finishes using the tee, then sets it on the floor. He glances at me, smiling. Though he's only a few feet away, that's too far. I need to hold him.

"Come here." Gripping his hips, I haul him with me onto the couch, settling him on my lap. His thighs straddle mine and his cock rests against my stomach.

My body is still humming from my release. I could sit like this, our arms around each other, forever.

His hands roam my chest in lazy exploration. I sigh at how good it feels, slide my fingers to the back of his neck, and pull him until his lips meet mine. Kissing him is both comforting and exhilarating.

Leaning back so we can see each other, I draw my own patterns on his skin. "I've wanted you for a long time. Before this weekend, I never imagined we'd end up here. But I'm happy we did."

Maddox's eyes, so dark, so serious, so earnest, hold me enraptured. "I had the biggest crush on you for the longest time. Whenever I had the chance to talk to you, I got butterflies. You're strong, talented, smart, and supportive. And being with you now... It's everything. I'm so lucky."

"You..." I shake my head and my throat works as I swallow hard. "You're amazing. I'm the lucky one."

He leans into me. Our lips meet and the depth of emotion welling in my chest overflows. He's a far more gentle soul than I'd known. And his words, sputtered honesty, raw and real, humble me.

I *am* the lucky one, if someone as special as him feels this way about someone like me. I don't ever want to lose this. Or him.

CHAPTER
SIX

MADDOX

Waiting in the wings is no easier now than it was on Friday night. Holding my water bottle, I tap my foot in time with the beat and concentrate on my breathing. I'll be singing with London tonight.

The pressure is on.

At center stage, Pan sings, his body swaying from the power he's pouring into the performance. My gaze keeps skipping to London, his muscles flexing as he plays, only a few feet away from me.

With London, it feels like a light has been turned on in my life. Tonight's the last night of the festival and I'm not ready for our time together to end. I slept in his arms last night, and maybe it's too soon, but I want that every night.

Luke joins me and watches Satyr's Kiss with the satisfied smugness of someone who knows he made a good choice in signing them. "You ready?"

"I can't wait to get out there."

"Zander said he caught some of your rehearsal this morning. He likes the way you and London sound together. We want to talk to you and these guys," he gestures to London and crew, "about recording the song together."

I gape at him until the sensation of my water bottle slipping through my fingers jars me into putting my surprised thoughts into words. "I'd love to get into the studio with them."

"Good." He glances behind me as someone in the sea of people backstage catches his attention. "Zander and I had a good feeling when we met you. And we were right. You fit in well with us. We're happy you're part of the Furious Records family."

Family.

I already feel at home.

My throat thickens. I swallow, searching for words to express my appreciation. But I fall short and the best I can do is, "Thank you for giving me the opportunity."

He claps me on the back. "Everyone deserves a chance to do what they want. And everyone deserves to have someone who believes in them."

The backs of my eyes sting. I'm damn lucky I found people who do. Luke and Zander. London. His band. And the new friends I've made this weekend. I manage a nod. "I feel like I'm a part of something special here, with all of you."

He pats me on the back again. "I'll get out of your way. My wife's waiting for me. See you tonight?"

"I'll be there." The get together at the bar inside the stadium will be our last chance to see everyone before we head home tomorrow.

The blaring music on stage comes to a stop and cheers ring out. Pan sets the mic on the stand then steals a sip of water from the bottle set near one of the amps.

London hands his guitar off to a tech, struts to center stage, and winks at me. He leans into the mic and beams a smile at the crowd. "How're you all doing tonight?"

The audience cheers.

"We're bringing out a special guest to sing a song with me. So please put your hands together for our friend, Maddox Muldoon."

My heart pounding, I step onto the stage. An avalanche of screams pours over me. Like yesterday and Friday, there are MTKC shirts and teens holding signs with my name. I want to keep these fans. Waving and smiling, I cross to London and pick up the mic set out for me.

His mic in one hand, London runs his other hand down my back. "Ready?"

I nod. And the music begins. Pan is in London's usual place, a yellow guitar strapped to his chest. Garrett beams at me from behind the drum kit, and with a jerk of his head, Andrew welcomes me to his side of the stage.

London takes the first verse. Tight jeans, black tee, and dark boots, he looks every inch the rock star he is. Lights play over his muscles, his angular face, and his golden hair. He's seriously sexy. And his voice… he doesn't sing lead often, but damn, he totally could if he wanted to. There's a huskiness to it, a roughness that sends tingles over my skin.

Rooted to the spot, I watch him. Enthralled by the way he moves his body to the music, and captivated by his voice, drenched in longing and need. The words skate along my spine, pulling at something deep within that calls me closer to him. I cross the stage, drawn to the man who takes up so many of my thoughts.

He holds out his hand. My heartbeat thundering, I grasp hold, linking our fingers together. The music swells around us. For a moment, the crowd melts away, and he's all I see. Gorgeous, generous, talented, caring, and protective, and I want him to be mine.

I raise the mic. Singing of desire and love and holding onto each other, I could be making these promises to him. It feels like I am.

He joins me for the chorus. I love the way our voices blend together. He's smiling and my lips curve too. I want so many more moments with him like this. Sharing a song and the stage, and the intimacy lacing around us despite an audience of thousands.

His seascape eyes glitter with desire and something warmer that's been present since the night on the balcony. Maybe it's too soon to be love, but it could be love on some level. Like our hearts waking up to feelings that have been growing for years.

Playing the type of music I feel I should've been playing from the beginning, and sharing this passion with someone I feel I should be with going forward, makes this moment completely euphoric.

We hold the last note, standing so close together, if I drew a deeper breath our chests would touch. I lower my mic and he follows, placing his on the stand. The cheers from the crowd are an ocean of sound, waves lapping over each other.

Still keeping hold of my hand, he draws me against him. I raise my face, my pulse pounding, and meet his waiting lips.

The noise level triples.

His heart beats against mine, his breath ghosts over my lips, and I taste salt from his sweat and mint from the tea he had before the band's set. His hold on me is light, but tethers me to him as I fly high on adrenaline.

I laugh against his lips. "They liked it."

"Great job, boys." Clapping me on the shoulder, Pan slips the mic from my hand. He shifts a few feet away and addresses the crowd. "Give it up for London and Maddox!"

More cheers wash over us. Holding London's hand, I take a bow, then wave. The band has two more songs, and I don't want to linger and possibly be a distraction.

London releases my hand. "Wait for me?"

I nod, then stride offstage.

Cody, Craig, Patrick, and Devon are huddled together, their arms around each other, heads in close, prepping to take the stage next. I silently wish them a great set. Craig's boyfriend, Ty, is somewhere in the crowd. I met him this afternoon and Cody was right. The pair only have eyes for each other.

I continue down the corridor. The dressing room smells of lemon and mint from the teas Pan and London had pre-performance. Andrew's water bottle and Garrett's iced coffee sit on a table. I settle onto a comfortable couch, and sipping the rest of London's tea, scroll through social media. There are comments about me on the festival's page from people who loved the music and people who want me to get back together with my former band.

The feed refreshes and a new photo, uploaded seconds ago by an audience member, appears. London and me, kissing.

Happiness and trepidation fill me. I haven't spoken to Randy yet about my feelings for London, and I don't know how he'll react. And I need to talk to London. I don't want to hide our relationship, but once we tell the world we're involved, there's no going back. Though with this photo released, and probably video of it coming soon too, the protected bubble we've been living in this weekend is already shattered.

I frown at the tea, needing something stronger.

The door opens and London strides in. "Hey. Zander said there's a new food truck in our lot today that has wood-fired pizzas. Want to get some?"

"Yeah, definitely." Standing, I set the empty bottle in the recycle bin. "I need to talk to you."

His brows draw together. "Anything wrong?"

"Not wrong. Just…" Nervous energy coiling tighter and tighter around me, I drag my hands through my hair. "The picture of us kissing is making the rounds. We need to figure out a game plan."

He nods, and tentatively reaches out his hand. "Okay, let's talk. Away from here. The guys'll be in any second."

His hand holding mine always settles something in me. I link our hands together and we walk into the corridor.

The bustle of backstage diminishes the farther we trek along the winding hallways. Less people cross our path and more piles of road equipment line the way. Soon, the echo of our footsteps is our only soundtrack. It's just London and me.

We turn the final corner leading to the exit.

Three men spring into our path, blocking us from passing. They don't have passes around their necks, and they aren't dressed like any of the event staff or the employees we've seen.

With a tug on my hand, London pulls me behind him, angling himself to face off with the biggest of the three. "Move."

The guy thrusts his phone in front of London's face, and the two beside him have cameras. "We just want a word, London. Are you two officially a couple? You were spotted leaving together from Maddox's home on Thursday, walking together this weekend, and kissing onstage tonight."

Oh shit. Reporters of the worst kind. Tabloids.

How did these guys get in? I can see the exit door. The security guard who's been stationed there all weekend is gone. I slide my phone from my pocket and text the number Luke gave us to use if we felt unsafe this weekend. Hopefully, security will be here soon.

London pulls me along with him as we try to sidestep the men, but they move with us, a human barricade.

The one with the phone is toe to toe with London. "Are you the real reason Maddox left MTKC? Did you drive a wedge between him and the rest of the band? Are you using Maddox as a publicity stunt to raise your band's profile?"

"Are you kidding?" London's muscles are tense and his hand goes slack in mine. "How'd you concoct those outrageous theories?"

Rage rushes through me. I push forward, standing side by side with London. My free hand forms a fist, but I can't throw a punch, not while the cameras are recording. I wish I could break both of them too. Glaring at the guys falls far short of what I want to do. "Come on, really?"

London's grip turns firm once again. "Mads…"

His low plea tears through me. I think he wants me to run, but I won't abandon him, not to deal with these guys alone. He'd never leave me either.

Squeezing reassurance into his hand, I stare the guy down. I'm mad as hell anyone would falsely paint London, *my* London, in a bad light for clickbait. "London using me is laughable. He's my friend. A real one. Someone I can actually count on to have my back. He has nothing to do with why I left my old band. So leave my friend alone, man. You have me here. Ask *me* your questions."

The smarmy so-called reporter lights up. "Are you saying Trevor Berry doesn't have your back?"

I snort a laugh. "Do you see Trevor wishing me well anywhere? He hasn't done that publicly or privately."

"What about Caleb and Kell?"

"What about them? If they have my back, it's news to me. And before you ask, I wish them *all* well, whether they continue on as TKC minus my M, replace me, or if they venture out on their own." These comments will cause drama with my old bandmates, but I don't care. I'm feeling salty. And strategically, this may take the gossip away from London and me.

The reporter's gaze flicks to our joined hands. "Are you two dating?"

I heave a sigh. Guess my plan didn't work. "Next question."

"What about that kiss?"

"Nope." My phone keeps buzzing in my pocket. I hope it's security responding they're on the way. "Ask me something not having to do with my personal life."

"How do you feel about the fans who aren't taking your leap into the rock genre seriously, or worse, are mocking you for it?"

My smile is as fake as this guy's journalistic integrity. "I'm completely serious about it, and hope they'll give me a chance. I'm a metalhead at heart and I've wanted to do this for a long time. If it turns out I'm not as successful, so what? Should I be too afraid to try? What type of message does that send?"

"What about the fans who feel abandoned and heartbroken by your decision to leave MTKC? Don't you care about them?"

Anger and frustration burn through my veins as I glare at the dude. The solid weight of London's torso pressing into my side gives me strength and reminds me to hold myself in check. "I love those fans. I'm showing them that going after your dreams is a good thing to do."

The exit door wrenches open and a security guard sprints toward us. Rushing footfalls thundering behind us bring two more guards. The largest one grabs hold of the reporter's elbow and the others lock on his partners. "All right, man. Let's get you out of here."

"But I paid for my ticket." He sputters, fighting the hold.

The guard jerks him away from us. "A ticket doesn't get you in here. Having one of your associates distract our staff so you could sneak by is reason enough to toss you. But harassing our artists? Yeah man, you're out."

They frogmarch the men toward the exit.

"Thank you," I call after them. My heart's still pounding and adrenaline thrums through my system. Taking a breath, I turn to London, determined to shake off the skin-crawling sensation of dealing with that reporter. "Are you okay?"

He nods, but his lips pinch and his shoulders hunch in a tight ball.

"I don't like that they were here. Or getting ambushed. I hate being caught off guard. Are you okay? I know you hate it too."

"I usually don't engage with them. I know better. They'll say anything, trying to get a soundbite or have you make an expression that'll get them clicks. My responses might come back to bite me, but when he said those things to you, I couldn't let it go."

"No matter what we say, there's nothing stopping them from writing whatever they want." Lines of strain fan around his eyes.

I trace my fingertips over them to soothe him. "I know. But what kind of guy would I be if I didn't stand up for you? After all, you've been taking care of me since the awards show."

Calloused fingers graze my palm before his hand engulfs mine in hard heat, keeping me trapped against him, right where I want to be. "Thanks for defending me."

"Anytime. You defended me too, putting your body between me and them."

"I like taking care of you." London brushes his nose against mine, so sweet, it weakens me. "This thing between us, it's different from anything I've had before."

"Same here." Holding his hands, I lean into him, chest to chest, heart to heart. "So what do we do?"

His smile deepens, revealing a dimple in one cheek. "I want to tell people we're seeing each other."

"Me too." Nervous and excited, I suck in a breath. "We'll need to talk about handling, um, the more difficult aspects."

I don't want to mention reporters and photographers by name, it could ruin the moment.

"I know." Understanding lighting his gaze, he brushes his lips over mine. "We will. Let's enjoy the rest of today, okay? I want to bask in just being with you."

The temptation to take the kiss deeper thrums through me. "I do too. Instead of pizza, let's go back to the tour bus. Get to basking. In your bed."

"Good idea." London wraps his arm around my waist, and I tuck myself into the shelter of his side as we walk.

The security guard for the exit door has resumed their post. In seconds, we're outside in the private lot. The heat is worse today compared to yesterday. Not many people are milling around. I refuse to look at the fence line to see if any photographers remain. With each step that sends us deeper into the maze of tour buses, I relax a degree. Finally, we reach the back of the lot.

Our tour bus door flies open. Pan slams it closed then hurries down the steps. He sees us and his long legs speedily swallow the distance. His hands raised in a stop gesture, his expression is caught between surprise and laughter. "You can't go in there."

We slow to a stop. London's hold on me tightens. "What's going on?"

"Garrett said he was beat after the set and coming here to crash. As I went in, I heard him talking and thought he was doing it in his sleep again. But he was talking to Andrew. They're hooking up in there. The curtains for his bed aren't closed. I got an eyeful."

I stifle my laugh into London's shoulder. "Whoa. I didn't know they did that."

"Me either. Today could've been the first time or the fiftieth."

A smile pulls at London's lips as he casts a knowing look at the bus. "The way they've been acting, I'm not shocked. Did they see you?"

"Yeah. I don't know which of the three of us was more surprised. I apologized and got the hell out of there." Pan presses the heels of his palms to his eyes like he's trying to blot out the image. "Though, thinking about it now, I'm pretty sure I told them to have fun as I backed out. Not that they needed my direction."

The three of us start laughing.

"Let's get pizza." I point to the food trucks and we head toward them. "Are you worried about how it'll affect the band?"

Shaking his head like it's no big deal, Pan tucks his hands into his front pockets. "Whatever happens, we'll deal with it together. Those two have been into each other for a while. Hopefully, it works out."

I can't help looking at London and thinking about the earlier interview and his reaction to the cameras and questions.

Hopefully, it works out for us too. Though I'm afraid I'll lose him if he decides he can't cope with the constant attention that follows me everywhere. I don't know if he'll think I'm worth putting up with all the bad that comes with the good.

CHAPTER
SEVEN

LONDON

Sunlight streams through puffy clouds and palm trees, spilling sunbeams over the road, lighting the way home. Palming the steering wheel, I make a left turn. Maddox is beside me. The weekend is over, the festival is done, and we have an entire week of downtime. And plans to spend most, if not all, of it together.

Just looking at him makes me smile. He catches me looking and smiles too. Though his is a few shades dimmer than usual, and has been since that jerk reporter's article came out a few hours ago, while we were heading down the highway in the tour bus, celebrating the festival, Mads and me getting together, and Garrett and Andrew being all cute and cuddly now that their secret is out. Totally killed the vibe.

Opening with the "exclusive scoop" that I'm Maddox's boyfriend, it went on to list all the things Mads had said about his former band-mates, then ended with an accusation that we had the dude unfairly ejected from the festival. Luke texted us both, promising someone from the label's PR department would handle setting the record straight.

A hollowness carved into my gut when Mads pulled on his hoodie after reading the article. He's still wearing it. I can't wait to get him home and relaxed. We'll need to talk more about what Mads calls the more difficult aspects, but I'm hoping we can have a chill night first.

I lay my hand on his thigh, thrilled he covers it with his own. "What do you feel like doing for dinner?"

"Trying out your pizza oven." He takes a sip of water from the bottle nestled in the console between us. "I know we just had pizza yesterday, but it was so good. And since you have that oven..."

I'm happy to recreate the wood-fired experience for Mads. "Not using it would be a shame. I really like the pizzas it makes."

His phone chimes with a text notification. Tucking his hair behind his ear, he opens it and laughs. "Randy. He sent it to you, too."

My phone is in the pocket of my duffel bag, which is in the backseat. "What's up?"

"He says he saw the clip of us kissing on stage yesterday, and though we don't need his seal of approval if we're dating or whatever, he's giving it to us anyway."

That lightens one of my worries. I focus on getting around a minivan going much slower than the speed limit. "Things happened so fast. I wanted to talk to him about it. I'm happy he's okay with us. We should call him later."

"Yeah, I think so too." His thumbs fly over the keypad. "I'm telling him we'll try calling him tomorrow. It'll be so much easier when we're back in the same time zone."

"Only a few weeks to go until then. We can all go to dinner." I turn onto my street. There's a crowd of people gathered in the middle of the block. Outside of *my* house. I slow down. "What the hell."

Not regular people. Tabloid photographers.

"Why are they... Never mind." I can answer my own question. They're here for Maddox. And maybe me too, given the photo and video of our kiss on stage yesterday. And that article.

They spot us and are clicking away.

His features etched with dread, Maddox slinks in his seat with a groan. He slips his sunglasses on and pulls his hood up, concealing his hair and the sides of his face. "London, there's no barrier between us and them if we get out of the car. They're too close to the house. I don't want to get out. I don't like this."

"Neither do I."

There isn't a gate around my house. It's separated from the road by only a narrow cement sidewalk. The photographers are essentially right against the house. There's no way to get in without them accosting us. I don't feel safe bringing Maddox here now.

Annoyance heating my blood, I drive past the house and speed up. Some of the photographers chase after us, blocking cars coming down the street.

His fingers plucking at the sleeve of his hoodie, Maddox twists toward me. "I'm sorry. I'd hoped they wouldn't find out where you live. At least not this soon. I hate being unprepared. I should've had security with us."

I lay my hand over his. "This isn't your fault. I didn't think they'd be here. I expected them to stake out your house, not mine. That article's only been out a few hours. They work fast."

I've never had anything like this happen before. I'm not yet at the same level of fame as Maddox or Zander and Luke. Needing security guards or anything more complicated than an alarm system isn't something I've had to worry about, but I'll have to now. Because Maddox should never feel unsafe.

"I don't always have security with me. I do things like going for drives and to the farmers market alone. Other stuff too." Maddox shoves his sunglasses into his hair. Lines of worry crease his face. "I really didn't think coming home would be a problem. But after what happened yesterday, I should've been prepared. I've had enough experience with tabloids over the years."

Squeezing his hand, I bring it to my lips and brush a kiss over his knuckles. "Let's make a deal, you stop kicking yourself over it, and I'll stop kicking myself over it. Okay?"

He nods, but the tightness in his shoulders doesn't ease. "Okay."

"Since they were at my place, I'm sure they're at yours too. Do you want to go there or do you want to go to a hotel instead?"

His hand is cold under mine. Biting his lip, he pierces me with brown eyes edged with unease. "My place. I want you there. Will you stay for a few days?"

"I'll stay." For as long as he wants me.

He's too quiet, so I turn on the radio, hoping it will relax us both. My thoughts jump from going through the clothes I have in my bags, to what else I might need during my stay, and what I can do to alleviate the stress of encountering that unwelcome crowd.

My trepidation rises as I turn onto his street. Here, the houses are large and most have a gate or wall surrounding the property. Maddox's is the same. White walls, taller than me, are topped with decorative spikes that would hurt like hell if they scraped skin. Beyond the wall, trees tower skyward. Another layer of privacy.

The number of photographers camped outside his place is absurd. I glance at Mads slinking in his seat. "You ready? I can keep driving if you want. Maybe they'll get bored and leave."

His stare is too weary. "They won't leave. Let's go in."

The photographers fan out as we arrive at the gate, their cameras raised. Maddox pulls the collar of his hoodie higher, covering half his face. He opens the app on his phone that controls the gate.

Bodies crowd close to the car.

"Are you two dating?" The person near my window shouts.

There are other questions, called out on top of each other, but they're too tangled together to hear clearly.

The gate opens and I drive onto the winding driveway, glancing in the rearview mirror. My muscles are tight. I worry about someone attempting to slip inside. The gate closes behind us, the lock engages, the photographers stay out, and the clenched feeling in my stomach and chest eases.

The house is set farther back, with more trees and plants ringing it. Maddox has created as much privacy as possible. I hate that he needs the level he does, but I'm happy he has it.

He hits another icon in the app, and the garage door opens. I pull in next to his SUV and turn off the ignition. "Coming here was the better idea. They're like vultures, aren't they?"

Huffing a long sigh, he shoves his hood off of his head. "Yeah. Or sharks at a feeding frenzy. I'm sorry."

"You don't have to be sorry. It's not your fault." I climb out of the car and grab our bags from the backseat. Maddox claims the remaining bag then hits another icon to turn off the house alarm.

He opens the door, leading the way into a mudroom. "We can leave our shoes here."

The air inside the house is cool and everything is quiet. I follow him into the kitchen. It's decorated in tones of black, gray, and white. Once the luggage is set down, he tugs off his hoodie.

Needing to hold him, I pull him into my arms and press a kiss to his temple. The shape of him soaks into me, nurturing my ravaged and unsteady parts. "We made it."

His arms fold around me, but his body stays rigid instead of relaxing into mine. "Yeah. For now."

"For now? What do you mean? Are you worried about whenever we next leave the house?" I draw back so I can see his face, and shift my hands to his shoulders, massaging muscles as hard as granite. "I don't like that they're out there or knowing they might follow us or show up places we aren't expecting them. We'll just have to make the best of it. I'll hire security like you do. Hell, I'll move to a different house if I have to."

"I'm worried about all those things. And more."

I did a lot of thinking last night while he slept in my arms, and again today on the bus. "Whatever it takes for us to be safe and happy, I'll make it happen."

Lines form on his forehead and between his brows. He slides his hands to my chest, resting them over my pecs. "So much scrutiny can be overwhelming and exhausting."

Wishing I could take away the misery coloring his features, I keep rubbing his shoulders. "I've seen what you, Zander, and Luke go through. Getting a taste of it for myself yesterday and today wasn't fun. And I know it was only a taste, nothing compared to the scale of what you guys deal with."

A whimper sounds in his throat and he lowers his focus to where his hands are splayed on my chest. "I'm sorry they're bothering you too."

Regret that I opened my big, stupid mouth clobbers me. Gently touching my fingers to his chin, I raise it until his eyes meet mine. "It's okay. I only meant that I can relate better now. I'm sorry you have to deal with it on the level you do."

With a gentle clink, the bracelet I gave him slips up his arm. He runs a fingertip over the links, his breaths coming faster and shorter. "I'm… used to it. I don't like it, but I'm used to it. But now that we're involved, you'll be forced to deal with the same level as me. You hated what happened yesterday. The photographs and questions happen all the time. I'm scared this—us—could go away, because of people watching and clamoring for more."

"That's not going to happen." My words are as fierce and firm as I can make them. They bite into the air, strong and sure. I need him to believe me. "I can deal with photographers and questions. They might be frustrating and annoying, but they won't chase me away."

"I'm scared you'll eventually get tired of having to deal with them and leave." His tone broken, he drops his head to rest against my chest and curls his fingers into my shirt. "I don't want you to leave."

The earnest words claw at my heart. Cradling him tighter against me, I stroke his hair. "I'm not going anywhere. No matter the amount of paparazzi causing chaos. No matter what. I finally have you, Mads. There's no way I'm letting go."

He raises his head. A light of hope shines in his dark eyes. "Do you promise?"

"I promise. You make me happy." My heart cracking wide open, I frame his face with my hands. "I want to be by your side. On stage. Off. However you'll have me."

All of the tension releases from his muscles as he melts into me. His smile trembles as it grows. "I want all of that. Want you, London, more than I've wanted anything or anyone. You make me happy too."

I bend my neck, slowly closing the space between us, loving how he strains toward me. My hands slide into his hair and I comb one hand through the soft strands before gliding down his chest and coming to a rest over his heart. "I'm staying. I'll prove it to you, whatever it takes."

"Whatever it takes," he echoes. He presses his lips to mine, eager and needy, then sensual, then sweet.

Here, in my arms, is everything I need.

Maddox raises his head. His fingers brush along my cheek. "When we're holding onto each other, I believe we can do this. Have it all."

"I *know* we can." Gazing at the man I'm falling in love with, I'm ready to give him everything I have and all that I am. "It's probably too soon to say this, but I'll say it anyway. I'm ready to hold on forever."

"Me too." Beaming brighter than the brightest spotlight, he flings his arms around me and jumps up, wrapping his legs around my waist. Laughing, I catch him, securing him in my arms. We sink into a kiss, his heart beating in time with mine.

CHAPTER
EIGHT

LONDON

"London, over here!"

The flashes of dozens of cameras accompany the calls from reporters. I hand my autograph to a beaming fan and take my place on the red carpet, waiting for my bandmates to join me.

Pan, Andrew, and Garrett group around me and we smile for the cameras. Today is my first time back in a suit since we walked this carpet at last year's awards show. I traded purple for black this time, so I'll better match Maddox.

I'm still starstruck by the music legends strolling past us, but now, newer acts are looking at *us* in that way too. Such a surreal moment.

A reporter from one of the networks live-streaming the red carpet event thrusts a microphone in my face. "London, tell us what's been going on with Satyr's Kiss."

Interviews, especially impromptu ones, are still my least favorite thing. After a year of dating Maddox, I'm better about not tensing up as much, but it still happens."We just finished our US tour. Next month, we're kicking off our shows in Europe. We can't wait to meet our fans there."

"We spoke to the members of Failing Midnight earlier this evening. They told us they'll be joining you for the European tour. Are you excited to have them along?"

"Definitely. We love those guys. Touring with them is like traveling with family." We've gotten together with Cody, Craig, Devon, and Patrick several times over the last year. Wondering if now is an okay time to make the announcement, I glance at Pan and receive the go ahead nod. "Maddox Muldoon will be a special guest on the tour too. We haven't announced that anywhere yet."

"You heard it here first, folks." Her smile is encouraging as she points to the platinum band on my ring finger. "And wedding bells are coming your way soon, right?"

Every time I see the shine of my ring and feel its weight, I'm reminded of my man, and I love it. "We're getting married next weekend."

To my right, the flurry of flashes start again, followed by cheers from the crowd. I know who was in line, ready to walk the carpet behind us. I glance over. Maddox poses and smiles for the cameras beside his brother.

I lean into Pan, signaling that I'm ready for him to take over talking. He gently nudges me aside so he can continue chatting with the reporter. Free from answering more questions, my heart beating faster, I glance at my fiancé.

Black leather pants encase his long legs, the sleeves of his black button-down are rolled to the elbows, showing off the tattoo sleeve he's been adding to over the past year. He still wears the bracelet I gave him, and his engagement band shines in the flashing lights.

His sexy, edgy look is every inch the rock star he's become, catching the attention of every photographer, reporter, and attendee.

Maddox turns his head and meets my gaze. His brows lift and his smile grows softer. As always, awareness sparks through me, and I'm hit with a rush of love for this man.

"Dude." Garrett nudges my shoulder. "The interview's over."

"Awesome." I make a beeline for Maddox. I haven't seen him since this morning, and though we hadn't been apart for that long, I missed him.

He twists toward me, beams, and rushes to close the distance between us. Flashes from cameras and calls from reporters fade into the background as our arms come around each other and our lips meet. Kissing him is fire and air and water and earth, consuming and soaring and soothing and grounding. It's everything.

I draw in his scent, reveling in the feel of his arms around me and the satisfying whisper of my name upon his lips. Loosening my embrace, I lean back so I can see his face. "Did you have a good day in the studio?"

His fingers tease into my hair. "Yeah, we recorded both songs. Then Randy came over for dinner. He helped clear a spot on the patio for the pizza oven."

I turn to pull my soon to be brother-in-law into a hug. The pizza oven is his wedding gift to us. "Thanks bud, I would've done that."

"Eh, it was the least I could do." Randy claps me on the back. "Since I expect to be eating several pizzas."

"Anytime you want. You're always welcome."

"London, Maddox!" One of the photographers calls. "Can we get a photo of you together?"

"Have fun, love birds." Randy leaves us with a grin, meeting up with Pan and the guys. I spot Craig, Cody, Patrick, and Devon milling around behind them. I know Luke and Zander are somewhere here too. All of our friends are together. I can't wait for the afterparty.

I slide my arm around Maddox's shoulders and he snakes his arm around my waist. We're locked together, our torsos touching, heads tilted close, smiling for cameras, and I think about how things were a year ago, with me watching Mads on this very carpet and worrying about him, unable to get to him and see if he was okay.

He rests his left hand on my chest, his ring winking in the lights. Now, we share a home and a label, friends who have become our family, and even a love song. One we wrote and recorded together. "Hold on Forever" is nominated for Song of the Year.

Whatever happens when they open the envelope to read who's taking home the trophy, I feel like I've already won. I have Maddox and nothing else compares to that.

Maddox tilts his head up and presses a kiss to my jaw. "Love you."

"I love you too." My heart wells with how much I do. Overflowing always for the man who's made my life so much richer.

"And I can't wait to marry you." His eyes shine, competing for brightness with his smile. "This time last year, I was a miserable mess, then you found me and everything turned around. Everything's better with you, London. My life, my career, me."

For a moment, I can't speak. Too many emotions clog my throat, and sting the backs of my eyes, and riot into a storm swirling inside my chest. "Everything's better with you too. Amazing. Incredible. I feel lucky every single day. And I can't wait to experience even more. You own my heart, Mads."

"You own mine too." He slides his hand into my hair then guides me down to meet his waiting lips.

I link hands with Maddox and we walk toward the venue. Our friends crowd around us, enveloping us in hugs and so much love. I can't wait for the awards, and the wedding, and the tour, and spending the rest of our lives together.

ABOUT SUSAN SCOTT SHELLEY

Susan Scott Shelley

USA TODAY Bestselling Author Susan Scott Shelley writes romance with heat and heart that celebrates love without limits. She enjoys watching hockey, training for her next run, reading romance novels, and binging episodes of her favorite British TV shows. Susan lives in Philadelphia with her husband and also works as a professional voice over artist. A city girl who likes being out in nature as often as possible, she has yet to meet a plant she hasn't wanted to take home and she really wants a pet crow.

Visit Susan's website, where you can sign up for her reader newsletter, check out all of her books, see the places and ways to follow her, and more: https://susanscottshelley.com

OUR FIRST LOVE

CHANTAL MER

ABOUT OUR FIRST LOVE

Sunnie St. James has spent years focusing on school and building a therapeutic practice, just like she planned. Sure, she thought her college roommate and friend, Annalise, would be with her, but sometimes life doesn't care about your plans. When she meets Jo, Sunnie welcomes their instant attraction, and their whirlwind romance changes Sunnie's life in ways she never imagined.

With a career as a food critic for the top travel publication in the country, Annalise Hart has more than she ever expected. Except someone to share it with. When Jo contacts Annalise years after their first meeting at a concert with her onetime friend, Sunnie, Annalise gets caught up with promises of love and connection.

Discovering they are married to the same woman upends Annalise and Sunnie's worlds. As the women navigate deception and heartbreak, they mend their broken friendship. But can they learn to open their guarded hearts to trust each other and love again?

PROLOGUE

SUNNIE

I bounce and jump in my spot with the rest of the crowd as we belt out the last line of the chorus. Perspiration dots my forehead, and my vocal cords scratch from shouting out lyrics and talking over the crowd. Arms in the air and singing as loud as the rest of us, Jo bumps my shoulder, her grin the same brilliance as the first time she smiled at me over a crowded coffee shop four weeks ago.

It had been raining, and my umbrella, sacrificed to the winds, left my hair drooping in my face, my blouse plastered to my chest, and my shoes so filled with water they squelched with each step. All I'd wanted was to sit down, but there wasn't a free table anywhere. As I scanned the small shop, anticipating who might leave soon, Jo's gaze hit me. It was like being warmed from the inside out. Even in pink scrubs, she was sleek and sophisticated. With her peaches and cream cheeks and perfect blond ringlets, she looked fresh and approachable. So, when she pushed out the empty chair at her table with raised brows, asking if I wanted to join her, the only answer was yes. That, and every yes after, has been bliss.

The final chord from the guitar reverberates over the crowd and the lights go dark.

"Wooooo!" I clap and whistle. My heart pounds and my breaths come fast. It's like being in college again, where my biggest worry was passing mid-terms. Not in my mid-thirties with a car payment, house payment, payroll for a growing therapy practice, and making sure I have enough billable hours to cover everything.

The lights flash back on and Rain, the lead singer, says, "We're taking a break. Get some drinks and don't go anywhere because we'll be back."

"Want another?" Jo's breath hits my skin and I stretch my neck, offering it up. She presses closer, takes my empty beer bottle from my hand, and brushes her lips to my hammering pulse, trailing her tongue along my over-sensitive skin. "Or we can go home."

My body is all for the idea. With those topaz eyes transfixed on me and her pale pink lips glistening from the beer, I'm *thiiis* close to saying, yes. But... "I promised Rain we'd stay for both sets."

"Another beer it is." She plants a quick kiss on my lips, before making her way to the bar, squeezing her way through bodies. I watch, unable to tear my gaze from the white tank that hugs her curves and shows off defined arms.

"She's not your typical type." From behind me, Rain's baritone voice has me spinning and throwing my arms around his neck.

"You sounded great. Thanks for inviting us." I drop my arms and push my curls off my forehead.

He presses a kiss to my cheek. "I invite you to all my gigs."

"I know." A part of me feels bad for finally making time only after hearing Annalise was in town and coming.

He rests his hand on his hip and, with the same exaggeration as the teens I work with, says, "I suppose I can forgive you. But really, *Dr.* St. James, how much longer can you use the excuse of helping people and doing good in the world? It's getting tiresome."

I snort and smack his chest. "Har, har."

"I'm glad you're here." He slings his arm over my shoulders like he's done since freshmen orientation in college. "Now tell me about this new woman of yours."

I search the crowd for Jo's blond head and sigh a happy sigh. "She's amazing."

"How long have you known her?" His gaze stays pinned to her, scrutinizing with the same intensity I've seen when he's in songwriting mode.

"A month."

His attention darts back to me. "And she's living with you already?"

"She's not *living* with me. They found black mold in the apartment she was renting, so I offered to let her crash at my place until she finds something." She's totally living with me, but it's been so nice to have someone as attentive and unafraid to express her feelings around. Someone to come home to. Someone to share my space with. Someone to ask how my day was and listen when I tell her.

"Still... It seems a little fast for you." A fine line forms between his brows, and his lips purse as he crosses his arms over his chest, his tee stretching with the movement.

I shrug. "Sometimes you just know. Ya know?"

"Nope." He jostles when a tall guy with chestnut hair and a close-cropped beard that makes him look like he just rolled out of bed and couldn't bother with shaving bumps his elbow and holds up a beer. Rain takes it, reads the label, then smiles. "My favorite. Thanks, Dacker."

"No problem." The guy plows his way through the crowd, a gaggle of women and a few men following him like he's a hot pied piper.

Rain takes a pull from his beer, his eyes glued to the guy's denim-clad ass until he's swallowed up by the crowd. "And her new place is ready when?"

My stomach fluttering, I concentrate on picking non-existent lint off the hem of my shirt. "She's only in town for another month. It's hard to find something for a short lease like that."

"Hmm..." Instead of continuing, he spots someone in the crowd and his face lights up. Raising his arm, he waves. "Lise. Over here."

"Lise?" My heart skips, and I stand on my tiptoes, straining to see the woman with whom I once shared all my fears and dreams.

As she gets closer, I spot the same dark hair pulled into the same low bun. The dim light of the bar highlights her shiny hair the color of the richest cup of coffee, and my skipping heart trips over itself. Looking as gorgeous as she did when we were in college, Annalise Hart's beaming face appears.

"Rain!" She throws herself at our friend, and he deftly catches her, while keeping hold of his beer. "God, it's good to see you."

"You too." He kisses the top of her head. "Glad you could make it." He sets her down and spins her to face me. "Look who else's here."

Eyes the same color of the sky before a summer storm but far more welcoming, widen and ruby lips spread, exposing teeth that glow in the light. "You came."

"Lise." Her name rasps from my throat. "I told you I would." There was no way I could miss seeing her.

She pulls me into a hug as years of memories flood my brain. Promises to stay in touch when she moved to Los Angels and visits that never happened as our busy lives drifted further and further apart. The hole in my chest after she left grew with every day, week, month, year she was gone until there was a canyon so vast my chest threatened to cave in on itself.

"I can't believe it." She gives me a tight squeeze before releasing me. The scent of vanilla ensconces me, conjuring more memories of late nights studying in our apartment. And nights falling asleep watching television together, snuggled on the couch we salvaged from the curb.

Tons of questions race through my brain, but there are so many, pinning more than one down is impossible. The brief text she'd be in town and coming to Rain's show was as much as I got from her. "How long are you here?"

She blows a stray strand of hair out of her face, and I watch it flutter, digging my nails into my palms, not wanting to embarrass myself by reaching over and tucking it behind her ear. "I leave tomorrow. But when I found out this one," she tucks her arm through Rain's, "was playing, I had to see him."

"It beats going back to your lonely hotel room and writing up whatever article you're working on." Rain tips his beer toward her, then brings it to his lips.

"Hey." Beers in hand, Jo squeezes next to me. "Sorry it took so long. It's a madhouse." She hands me a bottle, then hands one to Annalise.

Dark sculpted brows raised, Annalise takes the offered bottle. "Thanks?"

"I noticed you'd joined the group and didn't have a drink." Jo wraps her arm around my waist, resting her palm on my hip.

Guiltily, my gaze zips to Annalise, but I reprimand myself. There is no reason for her to care who I'm seeing. No reason for regret. And this is why Jo is so freaking amazing. She's observant and takes care of not only me, but my friends. I press into Jo, loving the feel of her soft curves, and introduce her. "Rain, Lise, this is my..." We haven't defined what we are, so I say, "My Jo. Jo, these two made my four years of college the best years of my life."

"Until now." Jo's smile is as soft as barbed wire and she presses her arm down, pinning me to her.

I wiggle my arm and she loosens her hold. She gazes at me with a stoniness I haven't seen in the month we've been together. Meeting people I have a history with may be hard for someone with Jo's traumatic past. I palm her cheek, recalling the night she opened up to me about losing her parents in a house fire, then being shuffled from one foster home to another. She never had a chance to develop close relationships, so seeing her insecurities surface now isn't unusual for someone with her experiences.

"How long have you been together?" Annalise's expression and tone are overly bright, like she's trying to sound cheerful when really she's battered. Just like every conversation she had with her shitty family when we were in college.

I want to reach out and comfort her, but that's not who we are anymore. Not who we've been in over a decade. "We're—"

"Very serious." Jo's gaze is so intense it lassos me, catching and tugging me closer and closer until I only see her. She nuzzles my ear, her nose breathing me in, then her lips press to it. "I love you."

Those three words slam into my chest, stunning me silent while also invoking a thrill to be claimed. To be the one who evokes the kind of passion that makes someone as gorgeous and accomplished as this woman emboldened to express such feelings.

"That's…" Annalise's gaze darts between Jo and me, and for a moment, I think she heard what Jo whispered into my ear.

"Unexpected." Rain guzzles his beer, then tips his bottle toward Jo. "Sunnie isn't known for throwing caution to the wind. So hearing you two are living together after a month is a surprise." He turns his attention to me. His demeanor is seemingly carefree, but I know him better than that and see the concern behind it.

I love him for caring, but I want to reassure him there's no need to worry. Jo and I connected instantly. I wasn't joking when I told him sometimes, you just know. And with Jo, I know.

"Do you still have your life plan?" Rain points his beer at me.

"Oh my god. I remember that." Annalise covers her laughter with her hand, and I notice her red nail polish perfectly matches her lipstick. "It was in a teal binder."

"And all the pages were laminated," Rain adds.

Jo raises her brow. "I need to see this."

"You all are the worst." I bite my lip to keep from laughing and pin my so-called friends with a look. "I was planning on waiting until at least our one-year anniversary before I shared *all* my idiosyncrasies."

Tugging me to her, Jo kisses me, her lips grinning and cold from the beer. My body relaxes into her softness as I open to her. The taste of hops and peppermint fill my senses.

"As lovely as it is to watch you two make out, I've got to head back." Rain's dry tone straddles the line between amused and sarcastic.

I slow the kiss and pull away, my cheeks warm. From the kiss or embarrassment for the level of PDA, I don't know. Annalise hugs him, and I follow. Tugging me back into the warmth of her embrace, Jo lifts her chin, and we wish him a good set. When he disappears to the front, where the makeshift stage is, Annalise turns her attention to me, her expression as open and friendly as the day I walked into our dorm room, and she offered to share her Chinese takeout.

"So, tell me how you met," she says in a sing-song tone, swaying her hips.

Jo tucks her hair behind her ear, her pouty lips shaping into a smile. "I had only been in town for a couple of weeks when I was getting coffee and saw her." She looks down at me and entire galaxies shimmer in her eyes. "Letting her leave without swinging my shot was impossible."

I rest my palm on the spot between her bellybutton and the waist of her low-slung jeans, hoping it will ground me after her bombshell admission that she loves me. "Jo's a traveling nurse, and she'd just started working at Roxborough Memorial Hospital."

"Wow. How does that work?" Always curious, Annalise's eyes light with interest so familiar a pang hits my chest. She shifts closer, tilting her head to better hear Jo over the conversations taking place around us.

Jo tightens her hold around my shoulders as if she knows how hard saying goodbye will be. "My contracts are usually thirteen weeks. Sometimes twenty-six. I've always loved being in a different location and getting to know the area and people. But now…"

"We're figuring it out." I pat Jo's stomach to let her know I'm all in.

Am I all in?

I study the woman who has been through so much, yet still has the capacity to be open and to love. She could have anyone and she's choosing me.

"Well, if you ever find yourself in LA, message me and I'll show you around." Annalise pulls out her phone and opens Facebook. "I'll friend you now."

Jo stiffens. Her distaste for social media coming out in a physical response. "I'm not on social media."

"No worries." Annalise fishes in the black wristlet hanging from her wrist, then holds out a business card. "Here's my card. I may not be in town because I travel a lot too, but if you're there for three months, I'm sure we can find a time to get dinner at least."

I give Jo's hip a gentle squeeze. Thanks to Lise, my palate expanded as we tasted our way through Philadelphia. "You'll definitely get a good meal. Annalise is a food critic for *Eat, Sleep, Go*."

"I dragged this one all over the city whenever I got a lead on a good restaurant. Mind you, we were in college and had no money, so they were mostly hole-in-the-wall places—"

"Remember that Puerto Rican place in North Philly?" My mouth waters at the memory of fried plantains topped with nothing more than garlic, and I lick my lips.

Annalise's silky smooth chuckle is a spark of nostalgia that wraps around me, warm and familiar. "I felt so bad for the owner's son." Keeping Jo involved in the conversation, Annalise directs her next comments to her. "The woman kept trying to marry your girlfriend off to her son. The poor guy was mortified."

"And more interested in Rain than either of us." My cheeks heat at how much I've missed laughing with Annalise.

"But those tostones were amazing." She licks her lips like she can taste the crispy golden plantains and warmth suffuses my neck.

As if Jo can somehow sense my reaction, she lifts her hand to the nape of my neck and the necklace she gave me tightens as she plays with the delicate chain. "How long are you in town?"

"My flight leaves tomorrow morning." Annalise brings the beer bottle to her lips and closes her eyes like she always did whenever she tried any food or beverage. "I'm going to be dead on my feet, but I couldn't resist seeing Rain. And seeing Sunnie is the icing on the cake."

The lights dim and conversations taper off at Rain's voice, thanking us for sticking around, and I don't have time to wonder why for the millionth time how Lise and I grew so far apart.

The music starts and Jo squeezes me to her front, wrapping her arm around my middle, and whispers into my ear. "Did you have a thing for her?"

How to answer that?

Did we date?

No.

Did we fool around?

Once.

Did it break my heart when my best friend moved across the country and our friendship was never the same?

It took me years to admit, but yes. I always thought we'd end up together, only to realize my feelings both romantically and regarding our friendship were far more intense than Lise's. I glance at her out of the side of my eye. Her wide, toothy grin and the same comfort in her own skin she had in college still shines like a beacon in a stormy night.

"A little." I hold Jo's hand, anchoring her to me. I tip my head back and she gives a playful peck to the tip of my nose. "Then this gorgeous woman asked me if I wanted to share a table with her, and I fell head over ass in love."

"Hmmm... so you're saying I have competition?" While it sounds like she's joking, the pinch of her lips implies otherwise.

Turning until the plush of her breasts brush against mine, I want to smooth away her insecurities. "The only competition you have is with yourself." I press my mouth to hers and everyone around us disappears. "I love you, too."

"We should do something about that."

I sway with her to the music. Exhaustion from years of focusing on only work and school recedes with the unexpected turn my life has taken. "Like what?"

"Marry me?" Another whispered ambush that abducts my breath.

I gaze into her eyes, sure and steady as they look on eagerly. "You're serious?"

"I've never been more serious in my life." She frames my face with her hands. "I was going to woo you with a romantic proposal. But you overwhelm me and I couldn't wait. We'll pick out the biggest, most beautiful diamond—"

I press my lips to hers, stopping her. She moans into my mouth and tugs me closer, our bodies moving to music only we can hear. "Yes."

"Yeah?" Her smile sends me toppling and no flapping of my arms will slow me from careening to earth.

"Let's do it." I just hope the fall doesn't break me.

CHAPTER
ONE

SUNNIE

Three years later.

Muted sun strains to shine, but the clouds have other plans. The overcast day fits my mood as I read Jo's text.

Jo: *Can you cancel your flight?*

Jo: *Just found out I'm working a double this weekend.*

Instead of writing case notes from my last session with a teen and her mother, I'm at my desk pondering how, yet again, my wife has changed plans for us to see each other. When we got married, she talked of weekend visits, then settling in Philadelphia, so we wouldn't be apart. Wrapped in each other, we made plans. So many plans. And I believed every sugar coated word she fed me.

I sigh and type.

Me: *No problem.*

Her response is immediate.

Jo: *You're the best.*

Jo: *Love you.* <3

I'm too pissed to respond. But I have a three o'clock that's due to show up any minute and addressing my personal issues will have to wait. Instead, I scroll through social media.

Because that's healthy.

Things with Jo have been off for months. Who am I kidding? Things have been off since month three of our marriage.

I heart a video Rain posted of his band opening for Outrage during the North American stint of Outrage's world tour. Seeing his dream come to fruition, I can't help but smile.

It's nice. The lightness that fills me at my friend's success radiates to the long neglected parts of my psyche. It feels like a lifetime since anything other than stress and second-guessing were at the forefront. And this little piece of joy is a welcomed respite from what has been a tension-filled few of years.

My sigh hits the most cavernous depths of my soul. I'm so damn tired. I close my eyes, grateful that at least I can watch what I want, and order takeout from my favorite Indian place without worrying that my wife is going to have a tantrum or give me the silent treatment.

Thinking about a weekend without walking on eggshells, my muscles relax and I unclench my jaw. I exhale. At least I won't have to deal with airports or insecurities. Silver lining and all that.

What does it say about me and about my marriage to be relieved Jo canceled our plans again? More so, what does it say that I'm relieved when she leaves for another job? Or worse, when she goes straight from one job to the next without coming home first?

"Hey." Angela, the receptionist of the therapeutic practice I started with two other therapists four years ago, sticks her head around the open door. "Your three o'clock just called and canceled. Apparently, pissed off geese took over MLK Boulevard, and they've been staring down cars in both directions. Traffic's been at a standstill for the last twenty minutes."

I huff a chuckle. "Only Philly geese."

"Check out Channel 6. They have footage of the geese surrounding one car, pecking at it." She turns to leave but stops and pins me with one of her I-know-something's-wrong looks she's known for. "You okay?"

I examine the ceiling, noting a lone cobweb swinging from the ceiling fan like a spinning trapeze artist. I've been too embarrassed to express my concerns to anyone, for fear I'll get the *I told you so* I know all my family and friends have been dying to say since the day I moved Jo into my place. But the longer I hold it in, the more it festers, eating away at me. Angela is as good as anyone. Close enough to know about my whirlwind romance and marriage, but professional enough to keep her opinion about my rash decision to herself.

At least I hope so.

"It's Jo," I hedge. When Angela slips into my office and quietly closes the door, her expression curious but lacking any judgment, I continue, "I think I made a mistake." Air whooshes from my lungs. The relief of finally saying the words I've been thinking out loud pours over me like a cool waterfall after a day sweating in the sun.

"How so?" Her cocked head is one of interest.

I straighten the picture of Jo tipping me back in a movie type kiss in front of City Hall. A white pantsuit wasn't what I'd envisioned wearing on my wedding day, but with only seventy-two hours to find something, that's what I came up with. "Moved too fast. Didn't really know her. Believed everything she said. Should have asked myself why I was so eager... You name it."

Angela nods, but uses silence like a seasoned therapist, and I'm a little jealous of how good she is at it. Finally, she speaks. "Seems like you have a couple of choices." She holds up a finger. "Stay in the marriage." A second finger joins the first. "Or leave."

"It's not that simple." I groan and flop my head back, tracking the stupid cobweb doing its twirling performance.

"Actually, it is." She pats her middle. "Listen to your gut. It knows."

I tap my stomach. My brain has been rationalizing for so long, I'm not sure my gut and I speak the same language anymore.

"I'll leave you to it." She slips out the door, but before closing it, she sticks her head in again. "If you need to talk, I'm always here." She gives me a wink and the door *snicks* closed behind her.

The hum of the white noise machine does nothing to drown out racing thoughts. Divorce would mean I failed. We haven't physically lived together for more than a couple of weeks at a time, and some of those weeks were vacations. Maybe if I approach Jo about finding a position in the area, again… It's been months since we've had that argument, we're due for another one. But the thought of her being in my home, my space permanently sends my stomach into a rolling mess.

Apparently, my gut is not a fan of the idea.

I pick up my phone and scroll, getting lost in the mindlessness of GIFs, rants, and photos before clicking on the public profile I follow, even though I know it's unhealthy. Telling myself it's to catch up on the latest restaurant review or recipe is a lie, but when I feel shitty, I cling to the delusion.

And then, my breath ceases.

I click on the picture, enlarging it, and the rolling in my stomach swirls to full-on sea-sickness. My hand shoots to my mouth as the muscles in my stomach spasm. I drop the phone, yank the trash bin from under the desk, and shove my head in it. Contractions consume me and I heave, once, twice, three times, but all I get for the effort is bile. Head in the can, I breathe in the scent of orange peels from my lunch lying on the bottom, and ignore the white spots behind my eyelids and the vice squeezing my heart.

Focus on breathing. That's all I have to do right now.

Just breathe.

In and out.

In… and out…

In… and… out…

I can do this. How many times have I walked clients having a panic attack through breathing techniques?

Focused on only the breaths filling and leaving my lungs, the nausea abates. When I feel confident enough not to spew the contents of my stomach all over my desk, I slowly lift my head out of the trashcan and sit back. With trembling hands, I pick up my phone and stare at the picture of *my wife* with her arms wrapped around the middle of another woman from behind and, what looks like, whispering into her ear. Eyes closed, full lips painted ruby turned up in a way that screams bliss, the other woman's expression is one I recognize from years of memorizing every nuance of her face. They look like an island of utopia in the middle of sweaty dancing bodies.

The caption under the picture reads: *Annalise Hart and wife enjoying our great local band.#ClassOf2010Reunion*

"What the fuck?" My whispered question crashes down like a lead weight, crushing my chest. I rip the necklace from my neck and dump it in the trashcan as my breaths come short and fast, not enough for me to gather the oxygen needed to fill my lungs. A sharp pain launches from my chest to my throat, and my hand shoots to the base of my neck but does nothing to ease the agony.

How could she?

After years of sharing triumphs and failures, dreams and fears, how could she do this to me? The picture blurs and I swipe the wetness from my cheeks with trembling fingers. But I can't tear my gaze from the betrayal.

What the hell do I do now?

CHAPTER
TWO

ANNALISE

"Finished." I tap the period key, then sit back and crack my neck. Friday afternoon, my last article completed, no upcoming deadlines, and I have the weekend ahead of me. I kick my feet up and relish the feel of a having weekend without a deadline looming over my head. The only thing that would make this better would be having Jo here. Unfortunately, she was called to work a double.

This isn't the first time she's been scheduled for a last-minute shift, and I've talked to her about how they're taking advantage of her, but she has such a giving heart. She says the patients would suffer and she wouldn't be able to live with herself if something happened because she didn't help when she could.

How can I possibly argue with that?

But after only four months of marriage, I'm already over the long separations. She said she'll start looking for a permanent position here in California once this contract is up.

I can't wait.

My co-worker, Whitley, skirts into my office and closes the door, peering through the sliver she's left open. Keeping her eye glued to the hallway, she whispers, "Elora's on a rampage. Janice broke her leg skiing and is too hopped up on pain medication to finish her story on that new resort in Vermont. Elora's looking for someone to fill the spot."

"Shit." I drop my feet and crawl under my desk.

Whitley glances over her shoulder. "Are you hiding?"

"Yes."

"Brilliant." She scurries behind my desk and squeezes under, bumping my shoulder and jabbing her bony knee into my toes.

"Ouch." I push her. "Find your own spot."

She presses her finger to her lips. "Shhh."

Arms wrapped around my bent knees, squished under a desk that's barely big enough to hide one person, let alone two, I sigh. Whitley shoots me a side-eye and I return her glare. "I've got to rethink my life."

"Shhh." Her shushing is louder than my words, and I stick my tongue out at her. She covers her mouth, her shoulders shaking, and I bump her foot with the toe of my sandal.

The knock on my door silences both of us, and I slow my breathing and contemplate which exit will prevent me from running into Elora when I leave.

"You know I can see you." The pointy tips of leopard print pumps appear at the front of my desk.

"Shit," Whitley mouths, her eyebrows high on her head, looking at me like we were just caught by our mom throwing an underage kegger.

I roll my eyes and edge myself out, brushing the front of my linen pants as I stand and paint on a smile. "Hi Elora. What brings you here?"

She points at the front of my desk. "There's a six-inch gap. Did you not think I'd see you?"

"We were meeting?" Whitley pops up next to me.

"Really?" Elora crosses her arms, her coral lips pinched. "About what?"

Panic grabs Whitley's face, and her mouth hangs open. After

several beats, she nudges me, like I can save us from this ridiculous situation.

"U-um…" I tap the tablet Whitley's holding to her chest like it's a shield that will ward off Elora's demands for a replacement article. "Whitley's investigating the new trend of napping under your desk."

Lips still drawn together, Elora looks the part of the demanding boss, but I spot the flash of amusement in her eyes. She actually has a good sense of humor. Not that she lets many see it. "How interesting…"

"It's nothing. Just a fad. Won't go anywhere." Whitley pinches my side and I fight my laughter. "Okay. Well. Yep." She claps her hands together once and scurries around my desk and our boss. "This was fun. Thanks for your help, Annalise." The last is called from halfway down the hall.

Elora's expression is inscrutable, which is probably one of the many reasons she's the longest standing editor in *Eat, Sleep, Go*'s history. I don't move. Being in her cross hairs is a lot like a rabbit being hunted. Seconds tick by and her mask fractures with a quirk at the corner of her mouth. "Napping under desks?"

I lift a shoulder. "There was a *Seinfeld* rerun on last night."

A cross between a snort and a gasp wrenches from her throat. It's only because I've worked with Elora for so many years that I know the sound is her actual laugh. The first time I heard it, I thought she was choking and tried to do the Heimlich on her. It also happened to be my interview. She lived—though she was less than impressed that I wrinkled her perfectly pressed Michael Kors suit—and I was hired, so everything worked out.

She sits in the low-slung swivel chair in front of my desk, crossing her long legs at the ankle and looking elegant enough to have tea with a queen. "I'm sure you heard about Janice."

"Whitley mentioned something." I plop into my desk chair, internally mourning my weekend with a silent sigh. *Goodbye lazy weekend, it was nice while it lasted.*

Another quirk of her mouth. "I'm sure she did."

She wakes her tablet. It's like watching armed pirates storm a yacht from the shore with your binoculars. You know they're hijacking the vessel, but the only thing you can do is scream for help. In this case, yelling for help would be less beneficial. Heck, it would probably piss off the Prada-wearing pirate currently tapping away at her screen. "That leaves me with a gap in the—"

"How could you?" The softly spoken words interrupting Elora may as well have been screamed from the wrath that's behind them.

Elora whips her head around and my gaze shoots from my boss to the woman standing in the doorway. Curls of dark hair fallen loose from the puff atop her head flutter around a face lined with a cornucopia of emotions, but there's no doubt fury is one of them.

"Sunnie?" My chest clenches. I haven't seen or spoken to her in three years. The same night I first met Jo. We'd promised to stay in touch, but just like after college, she tossed the promise aside. Only this time, it was radio silence. Not a response after my Happy Birthday text. No Merry Christmas or Happy New Year texts.

Nothing.

"How could you?" She moves farther into my office, wheeling a small suitcase behind her. Her black sweatshirt and leggings are the opposite of the bright colors she wore in college, but they fit the grim mood now blanketing the room. "Did you think I wouldn't find out?"

I stand, as much to brace myself for whatever she throws my way as to give me some much needed confidence. Seeing Sunnie upset was always staggering, and my wobbly knees are proof it still holds true.

Elora folds her arms over her silk blouse and leans back like she's as interested to see what happens next as I am.

The edge of the desk presses into my palms. A piece of MDF from when I dropped a metal tumbler of water and chipped it, digs in to my skin.

Jo should be here. I shouldn't be doing this by myself.

As if I can summon courage from mere air, I inhale a lungful and lift my chin. The MDF jabs deeper into my palm. "I'm sorry things between you and Jo didn't work out."

"Didn't work out?" The disgust in her tone matches her scrunched-up face.

My skin heats with her attitude. They dated three years ago. I don't owe Sunnie St. James a damn thing. "Look, it's not like we planned this. Jo still had my card and contacted me when she was here for a job." I glance at Elora, wanting her to leave so I don't have to do this in front of an audience—especially my boss—but praying she stays because being alone with Sunnie is something I'd rather not experience right now. She looks... broken. Nothing like the workaholic who cared more about her patients than her girlfriend and ignored said girlfriend's pleas for attention. "Besides, it had been, what? Two-and-a-half, three years since you two dated?"

Sunnie's eyes flutter so fast, I think she's having a seizure or heart attack.

Do I remember how to use the defib machine from last year's company wide First Aid and CPR training?

"Dated?" The word sounds like it's being scraped from her throat, snagging on barbed wire on the way out.

So, no need for CPR, yet. That's good. I take another breath, but my lungs won't expand fully. "Yes." I press my palm to my sternum. "Jo was devastated when you broke up with her. It took her years to date again."

Holding Jo as she sobbed over Sunnie's callus disregard of her—which I could relate to—and the sincerity of Jo's heartbreak jump-started our relationship. Unable to bear her tears, I kissed them away, reminding my now wife of all her wonderful qualities.

Ready for this reunion to end, I keep that to myself.

Stone-still, but for the rapid blinking again, Sunnie stares at me. Then, without warning, a squeal of laughter bursts from her. Elora flinches and I jump.

Head thrown back, Sunnie says to the ceiling, "Dated." Another peel of laughter. "So it's true. You married her."

"Yes." I soften my voice in hopes it cushions the blow. No matter how her relationship with Jo ended, Sunnie and I were once close. Without her to ground me, remind me that there was a time to study in addition to having fun, I would have failed out of school. And it was Sunnie who suggested I take my love of food and journalism degree and combine them. For that, I will always be grateful.

She grabs her middle and bends over. Cackling; she sounds this side of hysterical. I try not to remember nights falling asleep with my head in her lap to her lyrical laugh as we watched '90s sitcom reruns on the lumpy-ass sofa we roped Rain into helping us carry to our apartment at three in the morning.

My gaze meets Elora, who raises one penciled-on blond brow. I shake my head, then point my attention back to my onetime friend. Rising from her hunched over position, her eyes tearing, she asks, "Do you have a marriage license?"

I blink. "Of course."

"And a lawyer?" She wipes her face with the sleeve of her sweatshirt as a mixture of laughter and crying sounds pop the quiet office.

Every muscle in my body restricts.

What is she after? Revenge?

No, that isn't Sunnie. Is it?

Keeping my tone conversational takes a level of restraint I didn't know I had. If she's having a breakdown of some sort, I don't want to rile her up anymore than she already is. "Why would I need an attorney?"

"Because, my friend, it looks like we're married to the same woman." She pulls out a piece of paper from the bag slung over her shoulder and slaps it down on the desk.

"What..." I draw out the word, not sure where she's going with this, but I can't bring myself to look at the paper on my desk.

Her gaze bores into me. It's the same look she gave me when she told me our freshman year how worried she was that I was drinking and partying too much. The same look when she told me her mom had cancer. The same look before commencement when she told me our friendship was the most important part of her college experience. Anytime she had something important to impart, she gave me that look. And for a second, I consider throwing my hands over my ears, not wanting to hear whatever it is she has to say, but I wait her out.

"Married..." The exaggerated way she mimics me zaps my patience, but before I can insist she leave or I'll call security to escort her out, she says, "Jo asked me to marry her at Rain's show. We got married four days later. We are *still* married. Ergo, you and I are both currently married to the same woman." Her finger stabs at the paper.

There's a sharp inhale of breath and my gaze darts to Elora, who rises with hurried elegance from the chair. "I'll leave you two." She nods at Sunnie as she strides past her.

I look down at the paper and see, *Certificate of Marriage*. Jo's name. Sunnie's name. The license number… I run my fingertips over the raised seal. "This is… I-I can't…"

Questions swirl in my head, making the room spin. I slam my eyes shut, but still the questions bump into my skull like the worst kind of bumper car ride.

"Perhaps it would be best if you take this discussion somewhere more private." I force open my eyes to find Elora with her hand on the doorknob. She peers at me and lowers her chin to her chest. "Call me day or night if you need anything."

"Thank you." Frozen in place, I watch her leave and close the door. On the other side, life continues. Chattering voices and laughter, a phone ringing, sounds of the street, while inside this room Sunnie detonated a bomb, and I'm standing in the middle of the destruction that was once my life.

"I'm sorry." The soft words pierce my spinning brain. "It's a lot, I know." She flops into the chair Elora abandoned and the same anger, bafflement, and grief that is swirling through me fills her sigh. "I just found out two days ago."

"How?" I collapse into my chair, rubbing the small hole in my palm.

Sunnie flicks the edge of the marriage license as if it's an unwanted bug. "I saw a picture of you at your high school reunion on Facebook."

I nod. "Guess that explains why she's so adamant about not being on social media."

"Yeah." Sunnie snorts, then tips her head to the side, examining me. "I thought I'd have to do more to convince you."

"You'd think, wouldn't you?" I stare at the marriage certificate. Even after completely dropping out of my life without explanation and all the shit Jo talked about Sunnie, I believe her over my so-called wife. Suddenly, the air's too thin, my clothes too tight, and the walls feel like they're closing in. I jump up and grab my purse. "Let's get out of here, and you can explain this nightmare we're living."

Wheeling her suitcase, Sunnie follows me. Shoulders hunched, movements slow and deliberate, everything about her reeks of exhaustion. "Somewhere with vast amounts of alcohol."

"Good idea."

Two hours, four shots, and a pitcher of beer later, Sunnie and I tuck into a corner booth at the bar where I first kissed Jo. Sunnie props her head on her arm as she stacks one shot glass on top of another. "I should have known better."

"Nah." I pat her arm with a hand that weighs at least two hundred pounds, but it's no heavier than the rest of my limbs. "How could anyone know? This is made-for-television level shit."

She looks up from the glass pyramid she's building, cheeks flush from the alcohol we've consumed, and puff askew. "But I'm a therapist." She smacks her chest. "I'm supposed to be able to decipher when people are bullshitting me."

She drops her forehead onto the table and bangs it once, twice, three times. I rub my heavy hand up and down her arm, trying to provide some kind of comfort. But how do you comfort your wife's wife, when you've just found out you're both married to a bigamist at best and a con-artist at worst? "I can't believe she told both of us she had to work a double this weekend."

"Makes me wonder who else she's married to." Forehead pressed to the table, Sunnie's slurred words cuff me from behind.

My head falls to the sticky table with a *thunk*. Shit. "Do you really think there could be more?"

"Why wouldn't there be?" She turns her head, looking at me like somehow I can make it better. For a beat, we're twenty again and she just received the call from her dad about her mom's ovarian cancer diagnosis. She pushes herself up, exhaustion apparent in her every move. "Do you know how many arguments we had about her settling in Philadelphia?" She blows at the stray hairs surrounding her beautiful face, sending them fluttering. "In the beginning, she promised she didn't want to travel anymore. That she wanted to come home every night. Start a family."

I recoil from her words, but they hit like a punch in the gut. Hearing Jo's promises from Sunnie's lips almost verbatim is as disappointing as going to a Michelin star restaurant and having a shitty meal. I sit up too fast and drop my spinning head onto Sunnie's shoulder, her clean, crisp scent like a homecoming. "She made me the same promises."

"I knew it was too good to be true. I should have listened to my gut." She rests her cheek on the top of my head, sitting like we did so many times after a bad date, bombing a test, or when one of us had a crap day. "But she was so good at being there for me. And I was lonely. I thought I'd found my soulmate."

A rainbow glistens over the shot glass pyramid from the overhead lights. I down the last of my beer, then raise my hand to our server, indicating another pitcher. "I should have known the stories she told were bullshit. And questioned why she pushed to move so fast."

"It's the love bombing the keeps you off-kilter." Sunnie points to the empty shot glasses and holds up two fingers. Our server takes a long look at the two of us, then nods.

"I should have contacted you, no matter how hurt I was that you ghosted me."

She bolts up, her back ramrod straight, and her eyes narrowed and assessing. "I didn't ghost you. *You* ghosted *me*."

Head too fuzzy with drink to deal with more than one lie at a time, I ignore her remark. "What I can't figure out is how we got a marriage license."

She doesn't push the ghosting issue. Instead, she nudges my shoulder and I sit up. Reaching across the booth to where she parked her suitcase, she unzips the front pocket of her shoulder bag attached and pulls out a file folder the color of sunshine and covered in pictures of orange slices. She flips through some papers, then plucks out the marriage certificate she tossed onto my desk earlier.

Sunnie taps her pale pink polished fingertip at a name: *Josephine Joanna Smith*. "Is this the name she used?"

My vision blurs as hot tears threaten to drown me. My stomach churns and an overwhelming urge to run home, cocoon under my comforter, and order takeout from my favorite Vietnamese restaurant devours me as I absorb what I'm seeing. "She used Joanna Josephine Smith on our license."

"Jo Smith," Sunnie spits our wife's name like it's a curse.

Our server returns with two frosted mugs, a new pitcher, and two more shots. We nod our thanks as she fills the mugs and takes our old ones, and Sunnie continues. "She couldn't even be honest about her fucking name."

"I wonder what her real name is." Jaw clamped so tight I'll need to schedule an appointment with the dentist to fix my molars from the grinding, anger blazes through my veins. "How dare she use us. How dare she take advantage of you."

"And you." Sunnie raises her shot glass. Her nostrils flare, and her indignation on my behalf smooths some of the sting of the betrayal.

I clink my glass to hers, and we both chug. The potent liquid burns my throat and soothes my ragged nerves, but all I taste is bitterness, anger, and the need for revenge. I slam the glass down onto the scarred tabletop with a loud thud. "She's not getting away with this."

"Absolutely s-not." Sunnie's words wobble and slur, but the vehemence behind them is strong and steady.

"We'll confront her." I hold my hand out, palm up.

Sunnie clasps it with a loud clap and squeezes. "Together."

"Together," I repeat. "We just need a plan."

CHAPTER
THREE

SUNNIE

I slide the charcuterie board to the left corner of the coffee table, then step back and inspect the scene.

"No," I say, more to myself than the woman sitting across from me, then move it to the center again. I fan out the napkins, step back to give it another once over and wipe my damp palms on my pants.

"Sit." Annalise pats the cushion next to her and hands me the martini she made, insisting we needed something strong to cut through the crap we were about to deal with. "You're making me more nervous than I already am."

I take the glass and sit down, appreciating the burn of the vodka. For a second, I forget the cacophony of emotions skewering my insides for what has felt like an eternity. "Same."

In the two weeks since I first confronted Annalise at her office, we've been in constant contact. Once we realized our wife used software to intercept texts, which explained why we both thought the other had stopped reaching out, communicating without raising suspicion has been remarkably easy. Joe's supposedly completing a contract in Michigan. At least that's what she's told both of us. We've texted and video-conferenced most days, planning when and where to confront Jo.

And it's been… nice. Like the years apart never happened.

I take Lise's hand and squeeze. "I missed you."

"Me too." She squeezes back. "If nothing else, I'm glad our lives are imploding together."

I huff a humorless laugh. "Yeah." I close my eyes and pinch the bridge of my nose in an effort to ward off the headache that's been a constant since first seeing the picture that started the avalanche careening down on us. "At least we have each other."

"I'm sorry." The whispered words are so quiet, were I not sitting next to her, I wouldn't have heard them.

Needing to read her expressions, I shift so I'm facing Annalise. "For what?"

She smooths her hands over perfectly smooth hair secured in a perfect low bun, and I don't miss the slight tremble of them. "For not contacting you. For believing everything she said, even when it didn't match up with the person I knew."

"Lise…" I open my arms and she folds herself into me. The scent of vanilla and berries stirs up memories of how close we were. "She looked for our vulnerabilities and played into them. When we saw you at Stealthy Spirits, she knew how happy I was to see you. But I see now how she manipulated me into believing she was all I needed. I let her drive a wedge between Rain and me, too."

Warm breath strokes my neck, then she drops her forehead to my shoulder. "I never showed you the texts I sent you after that night."

She pulls out her phone and opens the message app, holding it up so I can see the text.

Annalise: Great seeing you yesterday. Let's do better about staying in touch. I miss you!

Two days later, there's another text.

Annalise: Hope you're doing well. I'm going to be in New York next month. Maybe we can meet up?

I scan the feed. Message after message from Annalise to me until they finally end. The last one from over a year ago, wishing me a happy birthday. The vodka sours in my stomach and I press my palm to it, then hand her my phone. "What an insecure bitch."

She crosses her arms, absently rubbing them as she skims the messages I sent her. Brows scrunched, mouth down-turned, she shakes her head faster and faster, until red blotches work their way up the porcelain skin of her neck. "I can't bel—"

At the sound of a key fumbling in the lock, I pocket my phone and inhale a shaky breath. Annalise straightens and guzzles her drink. Her face is taut, but she gives me a nod just as the doorbell rings.

"Sunnie?" There's a knock. "Babe, something's wrong with my key."

Another breath and I stand and walk to the door. This is it. Hand on the knob, I suck in one final gulp of air like it's my last and open the door.

"Hey. Have you been having problems with the lock? We should call a locksmith." She kisses my cheek as she comes in. "Missed you."

Even knowing what I know, I have a hard time deciphering anything other than genuineness in her features and movements.

And it pisses me off.

A storm of emotions swirls and twirls, picking up speed until a tornado of anger, betrayal, disgust, regret, shame, grief, and every other emotion imaginable rotate so violently they threaten to demolish anyone in my way, and possibly destroy me in the process. But I put a cap on them and through sheer force of will, I smile at my lying, cheating, manipulative, asshole of a wife. "Missed you too."

Her duffel bag drops to the floor, and she snakes her arm around my waist. She grazes her mouth along my neck and my blood freezes in my veins. There was a time I would have stripped her as soon as she walked in, eager to reconnect. Now, I want to cover her with honey and dump her in a field of hornets. Preferably of the murdering kind.

"We've got the weekend to make up for lost time." Her hand slides up my side and she palms my boob.

I push her away, and from her expression, I may have used a bit more force than necessary. "We have company."

"You invited people over when you knew I was coming home?"

The irritation in her tone—like I'm the one who's in the wrong—grates on my every last nerve.

"I think you'll enjoy seeing this person." I slip around her and stroll into the living area.

Legs tucked under her and martini glass in hand, Annalise looks relaxed and at home on the plush couch. Jo rounds the corner and freezes. Lise wiggles her fingers in a wave, and I gesture at her with open arms. "Surprise."

Silence.

Behind her rounded eyes, I can see the gears moving faster and faster as our wife tries to twist the situation.

With purpose, Annalise stands and walks toward Jo. Her grin is sugar sweet and syrupy. And fake as the last three years of my life. She tips onto her toes and kisses Jo on the cheek. "Hi, *babe*. I figured since you couldn't make it home for a visit this weekend, I'd come and see you."

Scarlet mars the peaches and cream cheeks I once found so appealing. The scarlet travels up and up and up until Jo's entire face and ears are the same shade as the red bikini she bought me on our trip to Turks and Caicos. Eyes narrow and her jaw ticks. "I can't believe you two would do this."

"Do what exactly?" Annalise crosses her arms over her chest, her voice low, daring. I scoot closer to her, providing a visual of our united front.

"This." With exasperation, Jo jerks her hands in our direction. "You're ganging up on me."

My laughter is high and loud as I throw my head back. The nerve of this chick. Finally free, I let loose and step closer. The gentle touch of Lise's hand on my forearm keeps me from getting totally up in Jo's face.

"Don't. Say. Another. Word," I grit out.

With way more calm and control than I can muster, Lise says, "We've notified the authorities, and you'll be hearing from our attorneys."

Jo snorts. "For what? Because I fell in love with two amazing women?"

"Oh my god." My eyes roll so far back in my head, I feel the strain. "Are you fucking kidding me? It's called bigamy."

Jo holds her hands up in surrender. "Maybe I got carried away. But who can blame me?" She tips her head, and like that, the caring, loving woman I married appears. "Sunheart."

A clog the size of a monolith turned sideways invades my throat at the use of the pet name she would whisper in my ear when we snuggled together. When I believed the bullshit she spewed. My hand shoots up. "Don't. You're caught. And you can't sweet talk your way out of this."

The mask falls as fast as she erected it, and Jo scowls at Lise and me, like this is our fault. "I'll just get my things."

"I took the liberty of collecting them for you," I say, then wait a beat just for the drama of it. "And donated everything to a charity that works with women experiencing homelessness."

Annalise shifts so our shoulders touch. "I did the same thing. I also had the locks changed and notified the neighbors to call the police if they see you anywhere near the house."

"Fuck you both." Jo spins on her heel and storms out. The door slams, causing the pictures on the walls to shake.

Annalise and I stare at the empty space where moments before our wife stood.

"That was…" She turns her gaze to me as if I'll have the words.

I don't.

I collapse into her arms, all the emotions of the last two weeks spilling out in a pulverizing rush of quaking limbs and quivering voice. "Now what?"

———

My eyes flutter open but I slam them closed, shutting out the sliver of light shining through a slit between the blackout shades and window's edge. Inside my skull, a hammering pounds my brain, and my heart feels… Not as shattered as I thought it would.

Behind me, a low moan rumbles. Soft warmth wraps around my

back and an arm slings over my side, palming my middle. "Can you do something about the spinning room?"

"Think it's too late for that." I rest my hand over Annalise's, grateful not to be waking up alone.

Apparently, *now what?* was Lise making more martinis, ordering enough shawarma, butter chicken, vegetable pakoda, dosa, and garlic naan to feed a rugby team, and commiserating until we stumbled to my room, passing out. Neither of us wanted to sleep alone, and having spent four years falling asleep together in college, sharing a bed was as natural as communicating with Annalise every day for the last two weeks has been.

I snuggle closer. "Coffee?"

"Can't move." Her curves are softer than when we were in our early twenties, but she fits perfectly.

I yawn, comfortable in our cozy cocoon. "We have all day."

"Yeah." The word puffs over the back of my neck and before long, her breathing slows and her limbs relax.

I trail the pad of my thumb over her smooth knuckles, back and forth, until my eyes grow heavy.

When I wake again, my mouth still tastes like a garbage truck dumped its contents in it, but the warm body I'm wrapped in eases the dull thudding in my head. I stretch out my legs, but keep my arms around Lise.

"Should we try coffee now?" Her voice is gritty from sleep and a night of drinking, but it's still better than hearing my favorite song.

I open one eye, then the other. No spear piercing my brain. So, that's a plus. "I think I can manage. You?"

"Have to get up at some point," she says, but doesn't sound like she believes it.

After brushing my teeth and splashing water on my face, I feel like I can at least make it down the stairs to the kitchen. While the coffee brews, I fill two large glasses with water and hand Annalise two aspirin.

"Thanks," she says, then pops the pills and guzzles the water. I follow suit, refilling our glasses as the coffee maker gurgles, and a rich nutty aroma fills the room.

"I'm glad I had the foresight to make these." I remove a pan of cinnamon rolls from the fridge and preheat the oven.

With the last sputtering sigh of the coffee pot, Lise finds the mugs and fills them. Pulling the half-and-half from the refrigerator, she says, "You still take cream and sugar?"

"Yep. Thanks." I take the mug she passes me, holding it in both palms and soaking in the warmth. Closing my eyes, I inhale the robust scent before bringing the cup to my lips. The bold flavor warms my throat, and the punch of caffeine calms the marching band tramping through my head. "Mmmm. God, that's good."

The oven beeps, and I pop the rolls in. Lise makes herself at home at the round table for two that sits next to a small window. A cardinal swoops in and lands on the bird feeder. It's all so *normal* and I wonder how our friendship went from telling each other everything to nothing more than a quick text each year on our birthdays, to letting a con-artist infiltrate and nearly destroy it.

As if she can read my mind, Annalise says, "Leaving you was the hardest thing I've ever done."

"Including finding out your wife is married to someone else?" I joke.

She lifts a brow.

"Too soon?"

She tucks her knees under her oversized sleep shirt and rests her chin on them as she gazes at the birds quarreling at the feeder. As wild as Annalise was, she was always good at giving careful consideration and thought when necessary. "You'd think it would be too soon, but all I feel is… relief. I'm glad we were only married a few months." She reaches across the table and clasps my hand. "What about you?"

"That I felt more betrayed by you than Jo, speaks volumes. I wasn't happy and hadn't been since almost the beginning. But leaving was scary and I think I was too proud to do it." I give her hand a squeeze, then bring my mug to my lips.

She hugs her legs and nods. "All my years in LA and I've never had a friendship like I had with you."

I ask that question that's bothered me for years. "What happened? How did we end up little more than strangers?"

"When I first moved, I'd walk around wishing you were with me to share all the new experiences." She drops her legs, sitting cross-legged and picks up her coffee. "The more I talked to you, the more I missed you."

"And even though I was happy for you and the opportunity you had, there was a part of me that was crushed you didn't stay." She opens her mouth to say something and I hold up a hand. "I know I encouraged you. I'm not saying it was rational, but I get it."

"We can't let distance interfere with us this time." She sets down her mug and grabs my hand, squeezing hard to emphasize her point.

I squeeze back just as hard. "Agreed."

Because moving forward without Annalise feels like an impossibility.

CHAPTER
FOUR

ANNALISE

With a thud, the wheels of the plane hit the runway, and my head jerks forward with the force. I glance at the woman next to me and she grimaces, then says, "A crap landing for a crap flight. How appropriate."

"Worst flight I've been on in ages." I should have known it was going to suck when there was a three-hour delay because they couldn't locate the pilot. And it only got worse when the attendants announced there was no coffee because it was missing—probably the same place as the pilot—but there was plenty of alcohol. Then the guy in 10B shared his vocal talents with the plane as he sang the score to *Annie*. Unfortunately, there was no amount of requesting, threatening, or cajoling that could make him stop until he finished the complete score. "At least 10B's performance put the crying baby to sleep."

My seatmate chuckles. "That poor mom."

"Yeah." I tuck my tablet into my bag and turn my phone off airplane mode. Within seconds, a rapid succession of pings sound. I ignore the messages from the office. Elora can wait. The entire trip to Chicago was a shit show, but for Long Change, the Tex-Mex restaurant owned by retired hockey player Ash Ariti, my restaurant experiences were less than stellar. Not to mention, reviewing six places in three days is a lot. Since it was Elora's grand idea to feature a city in each issue along with an assortment of restaurant reviews to "capture the feel of the city", I'm in no hurry to hear what other "inspired" ideas she has.

I tap on the messages from Sunnie while we wait for security to escort 10B off the plane. My legs are crampy and my head aches, but I appreciate 10B's rendition of *So Long, Farewell* from The Sound of Music. He's really not half bad.

Sunnie: *I know you're flying, but I'm having a shitty day.*
Sunnie: *Had to hospitalize a suicidal teen.*
Sunnie: *His parents were less than supportive.*
Sunnie: *What the hell? Your kid's basically screaming for help and you think "it's a phase"?*

As we shuffle off the plane, I text her. Since she showed up in my office three months ago, looking beaten and dispirited, we've texted and video chatted every day. Usually multiple times a day. Remarkably, we've restored our friendship, as if the ten years between was an aberration.

Me: *Just landed.*
Me: *That sucks. How are you?*
Me: *How's the kid?*

Thankful I don't have a checked bag, I make my way to the exit. All I want is a shower, my bed, a pint of double dark chocolate ice cream… And Sunnie.

My phone pings.

Sunnie: *Stabilized. How was the flight?*
Me: *No better than the rest of the trip.*

My phone rings, and inside my chest the same tiny flutter that first occurred when she walked into our first shared meal of Chinese food, sitting on my bed in the dorms, materializes. And like every other time, I'm caught off guard for a fraction of a second.

"Hey," I say as I get in the cab line. "How are you?"

I hear the deep sigh and I can picture her gathering her hair off her neck and holding it at the top of her head before letting it all drop. "Fine. It's never easy seeing a kid in so much pain. And it's worse when their parents are too scared or ignorant to support them the way they need."

"It's good they have you." The couple in front of me hop into a cab, and I step forward as the next one pulls up. "Hold on," I say to Sunnie as I slide in, then give the driver my address. "Okay, I'm back."

"I should have waited until you got home." Guilt weighs heavily in Sunnie's voice.

I lean my head back on the cracked leather and settle in for a long ride. It doesn't matter the time of day, it's always rush hour in LA. "By the time I get home, you'd be sound asleep."

"Don't think I'll be doing much sleeping tonight. I'm too wired." What sounds like her comforter being pulled up, rolls over the line, and I wish I was there with her. "On top of everything, my dad called. He wants me to go there for the holidays."

From what I remember, Sunnie's parents were supportive, but after her mom died right before our junior year, Sunnie put a lot of pressure on herself to succeed. It was like she didn't want to be a burden on her dad while he was grieving. "And you don't want to?"

"It's just that…" A deep sigh. "I don't know if I can face them yet."

I understand completely. Tension-free holidays are just one benefit of not being in contact with my family anymore. The relief and peace I felt when I removed myself from them is another. "Because of Jo?"

"I found another credit card opened in my name." Jo did the same thing to me, opening credit cards in both of our names. Fortunately for me, there was only one, and she hadn't had time to run the balance up too much. Sunnie hasn't been as lucky.

"I'm just so… embarrassed," she continues. "How can I face my family and tell them, not only did I fall for a woman who lied to me, but she's also ruined my credit and put me further into debt? That I was so needy I fell for someone who told me everything I wanted to hear?" Without seeing her, I know Sunnie's worrying her bottom lip with her teeth.

"You're human. Perfection is impossible to achieve." We pass yet another billboard advertising a plastic surgeon's services, which illustrates my point. "Your family loves you."

Another sigh. "I know. But my dad's new fiancée will be there. Don't get me wrong, she's lovely, but I don't think I can handle their lovey-dovey stuff. Plus, my sister will be there with her perfect husband and their perfect children. And then there are all my aunties, uncles, and cousins... I'd rather soak in the sun, sipping fruity drinks on the beach than answer their questions. Or worse, listen to their unsolicited advice."

"Then, let's do it," I say.

There's a pause. "Do what?"

"Let's go on vacation the week of Christmas." The idea takes hold, jolting me to sitting. Spending a week alone with my gorgeous friend feels necessary.

"You're serious?"

My fingertips rap my knee in a nervous beat. Sunnie agreeing seems more essential than my career, the tiny condo I scraped and saved for, even my next breath. "Yeah."

"Can we do that?" Her voice is unsure, but underneath the hesitation I hear banked excitement.

"Of course we can. We can do an all-inclusive, so we won't have to leave the resort." The foot of my crossed leg bobs faster than my rapping fingers. "I think we deserve to treat ourselves."

The patter of footsteps sounds like she's wandering her bedroom, pacing, just like she used to do in college when mulling over a decision. "That's tempting. But can we get something on such short notice? Christmas is only two weeks away."

"You know who you're talking to, right? I have connections. Not to mention, the week of Christmas isn't typically busy for resort towns." The more I think about it, the more I want it. Going away with Sunnie and forgetting about the complications of life for seven days sounds glorious. "What do you say, Sun?"

There's a long pause and just when I think she's going to tell me how busy she is or there's no way she can leave her patients on such short notice, she blows out a breath and says, "Let's do it."

"You're serious?" I screech and bounce in my seat. The driver frowns and glares at me in the review mirror, and I wave an apology.

"Yes!" I can practically feel her exuberance vibrating through the phone and it only enhances my own excitement. "But nothing too expensive."

I snub out the boiling desire to track Jo down and strangle her for the unease I hear in Sunnie's voice. Even if it's in passing, it shouldn't be there. "Not to worry. Once I get home and settled, I'll start researching and send you options."

She giggles, and for the first time in three months, she sounds unburdened. "I'm excited."

"Me too." And I plan to do everything in my power to keep her laughing because there's no better sound in the world.

CHAPTER
FIVE

SUNNIE

"Wow. This is gorgeous." I gape at the enormous palm fronds fanning over a soothing aqua water flowing over rugged boulders of earth, making it seem like the lobby was created around an oasis.

The bellhop stands straighter as if the rainbow of tropical plants and flowers growing from the rocks and around the pool of water are his children, and he's proud of each one of them. "There is no other resort as beautiful as ours."

"I believe it." The photos Annalise sent me from the resort's website did not do justice to its beauty. The indoor and outdoor spaces merge until there's no distinction. Sunbeams glimmer through the ceiling of windows onto polished marble floors, glistening like the shimmering water it surrounds. Plush loveseats paired with rattan chairs with overstuffed cushions create intimate seating areas where couples relax with tropical drinks. Spray painted branches made into the shapes of Christmas trees, snowmen, and animals, along with what must be hundreds of poinsettias, decorate the lobby, giving it a Christmas feel. I breathe in the sweet scent of flowers and sea, and the last three years melt away.

Before we reach the check-in desk, a woman in a pale gray pencil skirt and teal resort issued blouse with the Harmonious Sea Resort Concierge embroidered on the left pocket approaches us with a glass of champagne. "Dr. St. James?"

"Yes."

She extends the champagne and gladly I take it. "Ms. Hart asked that you join her by the pool."

I look down at my black leggings and boots, then at the bellhop with my suitcase. It was a damp thirty-eight degrees when I left Philadelphia. My attire doesn't fit eighty-five and sunny.

"Not to worry," the concierge continues with a welcoming smile. "Ernesto will bring your luggage to the suite, and there is a change of clothes in your private cabana."

"I can take those if you'd like." Ernesto tips his head at my down jacket and the cardigan I removed in the shuttle.

"Thank you." I hand him my coat and sweater but keep my tote bag and follow Danita through the expansive lobby. The air perfumed with citrus and honeyed scented blossoms seeps deep into my soul, and already I feel its healing effects.

She leads me along the winding pool. "The pool runs through the entire property. There are two swim-up bars." She points to one as we pass it. "But there are many quiet nooks where you can enjoy privacy."

Loungers dot the parameter of the turquoise water, and covered cabanas tucked beneath one-hundred-foot-tall palm trees sprinkle the area. Each white tent is an oasis within an oasis. "When I left Philadelphia, they were calling for one to three inches of snow tomorrow."

"Let's hope it is melted by the time you return." Danita halts in front of a secluded cabana. "Here we are."

In white bikini bottoms and a red tank top that hugs her slender frame, Annalise hops up from the lounger and throws her arms around my neck. "You made it."

I fold myself into her, tightening my hold and capturing a lungful of coconut and sunshine. "We're here."

"Enjoy your stay at Harmonious Sea. Should you need anything, our staff is happy to assist you." Danita spins on her wedged espadrilles, leaving us to ourselves with nothing but a lovely breeze and a view of the ocean.

Careful not to spill champagne, I unwrap myself from my friend, then drop my bag next to the lounger. Gazing at the horizon, infinite shades of blue unfold before us. "This is amazing."

"Wait 'til you see our room. I was able to get an upgrade to a suite." My eyes widen, but Lise lifts her hand, halting my protest before it forms. "It doesn't cost us a thing. I told you, these resorts are dead the week of Christmas. They're happy to have guests." She points to the back of the cabana where a flat screen television hangs across from a small sofa and another charamico, this one a white Christmas tree. "There's a suit for you behind the screen."

"I brought a suit." I set my glass on the square table between the lounges.

She swats my shoulder with the back of her hand, then gives me a little push toward the screen in the back. "Knowing you, you only brought one. We're here for a week, and I don't plan on moving too far from this spot."

"I hate it when you're right," I say over my shoulder. Any attempt to fight her melted away the minute I laid eyes on her in that bikini bottom. Wanting to untie the strings at her hips with my teeth has me clamping them closed.

Minutes later, I'm on the double lounge sipping a pina colada while Annalise smooths sunscreen over my shoulders and back. The sweet tartness of pineapple tickles my tongue, but the caramelized flavor of the rum softens the taste. I take a bigger sip, hoping the rum will calm the dolphins frolicking in my stomach and knocking at my chest with every touch of Annalise's fingers.

Ignoring the fact that legally ending my marriage to Jo and sorting out my finances has proved to be more challenging than one would imagine, the last three months have been some of the best in way too long. And it's because of the woman with the magic fingers.

"Done." She scoots over, stretches her long legs out, and picks up her drink, plucking the pineapple garnish from the rim of the glass and taking a bite. Her eyes flutter closed and a droplet of pineapple juice dribbles down her chin. "God that's good."

"You've got..." I catch the bead of juice from dripping down her neck, swiping it from her chin with my thumb, then sucking it off. Lise's eyes darken and my gaze glues to the pink tip of her tongue as she sweeps it over her plump lips. The dolphins in my stomach morph into a school of humpback whales breeching the surface, their enormous bodies flying into the air before crashing back into the depths of the ocean.

The corner of her luscious mouth quirks. She wiggles her bottom, settling into the plush cushion. "Thanks."

"Sure." I bite on the straw, then suck. The icy drink is a bullet train to my brain. "Shit." My eyes slam shut and I pinch the bridge of my nose. "Brain freeze."

Sweet laughter rises with the waves and, not for the first time, I realize how much I've missed my friend. "So, what should we do this week?"

I let my head fall back, resting it on the pillow headrest. "Whatever you want. I'm just glad to be here."

"Me too." She bumps her shoulder into mine and the warmth singes me. "My annulment went through."

"Lucky." I sigh because until I find out if my wife has any other wives, and if she was married to them before me, I don't know if I need to get an annulment or a divorce. "I'm still waiting to see if the PI uncovers any other spouses."

She laces her fingers through mine. "I'm sorry."

"I just want it over. You know?" I tighten my grip. Lise's hold is my anchor and I fear if I let go, I'll float away and eventually drown.

"Yeah." We sit in silence, soaking in the tropical beauty before us. Annalise's eyes droop close and when I think she's asleep, she says, "No more talk of Jo. This week is about you and me. We're going to eat too much, drink too much, and get too much sun. And when we return to reality, we'll be ready to deal with whatever shit she's left us." She opens her eyes and her head lulls to the side so she's looking at me. "Deal?"

I bump her foot with mine and squeeze her hand. "Deal."

"Then let's get a start on eating too much." She sits up and scans the QR code for the resort's bar menu.

Whatever awaits us after this trip, I know I won't have to handle it alone.

CHAPTER
SIX

ANNALISE

"You didn't tell me there was only one bed." Sunnie stands in front of the king size bed, with her hands on her hips and chewing her bottom lip. The white gauze curtains draped on the four posters flutter in the warm sea breeze coming in through the slatted doors.

A curl dislodged from her hair tie waves with the curtains, and my fingers tingle with need to tuck it behind her ear. "If it bothers you, I can sleep on the couch in the sitting room."

"Why would it bother me?" Keeping her gaze on the bed, she absently pats her center.

"Our other room was a garden view and this…" I throw open the French doors and fling my arms wide at the view. "We get to wake up to this every day."

She spins and takes in the pristine white sand beach and water that seamlessly unfolds into a sky so blue it looks more like an artist's rendering than real. "Yeah. I can get used to this."

"I don't want to sleep by myself." My admission is barely audible over the crash of waves and chatter of wildlife, but the truth rushes out in a way that only happens with Sunnie. I move closer, pressing my shoulder to hers. The heat from hours by the pool seeps from her skin to mine.

She wraps her hand around my waist, her fingertips playing with the edge of my tank. "Why is it so hard? It's not like she was around."

"Knowing we're alone when we thought we had a partner makes a difference, I think. Now, we're just alone." I clasp the hand at my waist, anchoring her to me. Or me to her. I'm not sure which, but it doesn't matter. Having someone, especially this woman, understand the roller coaster of emotions that have railed me since Jo's lies surfaced is a relief.

She flips her hand and laces our fingers together. "This week we have each other."

Lips with a hint of shine from lip balm she applied in the elevator, turn up. They're full and look soft enough to sleep on. Her curl teases, fluttering again with another rush of warm air, and I can no longer keep my hands to myself. I tuck the rogue curl behind her ear and trail a finger along the column of her neck. The stutter of her expelled breath brushes my cheek, and I watch in fascination as goose bumps erupt along the silky smooth skin. She erases the space between us, the soft cushion of her chest pushing against my smaller, nearly non-existent breasts. In an instant, my nipples harden, poking against the thin fabric of my bathing suit, begging for attention.

"What are we doing?" The question is a whisper, but I hear the yearning in the tremble of her voice. At least to my hopeful ears, that's what it sounds like.

"Whatever you want." I press my lips to the corner of her mouth and it's like sticking my finger in an electrical socket. The chaste, barely there kiss jolts volts of electricity through my system, causing every nerve ending to light up and my breath to catch.

She plants a quick, smacking kiss on my mouth and disengages from my hold. The abrupt change leaves me spinning.

"Let's eat." She strides across the room and opens her suitcase, pulling out clothes, hanging them, and stuffing them into drawers as she speaks. "We can check out the restaurant near the club. And after, we can go dancing."

I nudge her shoulder with mine as I pull undergarments from the drawer I snagged earlier. "You think you can keep up with me?"

Sunnie always loved to dance. Whenever we went out with friends, one by one they'd drop, exhausted, until she was the only one of us left on the dance floor. Her skin glistening and face beaming brighter than her name, and her sweet voice begging me to stay with her, no matter how badly my feet hurt in the heels I inevitably dreaded wearing the minute I walked more than a block, I could never disappoint her.

"We'll find out soon enough." Her chuckle follows me as I slip into the bathroom, and I can't help but grin like a besotted fool.

———

Lights flash in beat to the bass vibrating with *Girls Just Want to Have Fun*, illuminating Sunnie's hair, making it look like black silk. Arms waving over her head and her hips swaying as she belts out the words, the grin she blasts in my directions stuns me. I trip over my feet, but she catches me and pulls me close to her. The tawny skin of her shoulders shimmers with the light film of dampness from two hours of dancing.

"Easy," she says as she slides her hand until it rests just above the low waist of the skirt that's hung in the back of my closet for two years. I bought it on a whim, because I couldn't resist the red silk that ended at mid thigh and showed off the best parts of my legs. It never occurred to me to wear it for Jo, but was the first thing I thought about packing for this trip.

I'm plucked from the bleak thoughts by the sway of Sunnie's body, the feel of her hand, and the ringing of her laughter. A thrill drills deep, fueling a long shuttered need within, tickling my core and infusing an excitement that dampens my panties. There are a million reasons why I should curb the attraction that's always flitted at the edges of our friendship. The biggest being I was an idiot and bought every lie Jo sold me about Sunnie. But I push those thoughts aside and enjoy the moment.

Resting my arms on her shoulders, I let my fingertips skim the back of her neck and relish her slight tremble.

Slender fingers skim the sensitive skin exposed by my crop top. Gold flecks spark in honey-colored eyes as familiar and welcoming as the first time I met her at eighteen. Those eyes stare into mine, and my heart vaults to my throat.

What does she see?

Who does she see?

The woman who wanted to spend every waking moment with her? The woman who moved across the country taking a chance on a career instead of taking a chance on a relationship? The woman who pushed friendship aside because it was easier than confronting the possibility I'd made a mistake? Or the woman who had such little regard for our onetime friendship and the person I knew she was that the lies Jo spewed blinded me?

"I'm sorry." Emotion thickens my words. Shame that's nestled into my chest, taunting and jeering me for months—no, years—scales the walls I've methodically built, crumbling them with its weight. My eyes sting, pricking with every flutter of my eyelids.

The pad of her thumb swipes under my eye at a stray tear. Her lips follow as she places a soft kiss on the same spot. "I'm not."

My head jolts back, and my gaze volleys back and forth between eyes that were once the only ones I sought in a crowd. The lights fade with the slowing beat as the opening notes of *Crazy for You* play. "How?"

"If it weren't for Jo, we wouldn't be here." Her palms skim my waist, then rest on my hips. She presses her cheek to mine and I breathe in the sweet citrus that is Sunnie. "We may not have any luck with our wife, but I can't help being grateful to have you back in my life."

Unable to voice the myriad of emotions twirling through me—hell, I can't even identify them all—I nod and let her lead me around the dance floor. When *Nothing Can Come Between Us* comes on, I swear the universe is speaking to me through eighties night at the hotel dance club in the Dominican Republic. Every step, every rock side-to-side, every skim of Sunnie's fingertips is a pardon, a reconciliation, a rekindling of the relationship we've been cultivating and renewing since the mutual annihilation of our marriages.

"I missed you." Still cheek-to-cheek, her words tickle my ear and arouse feelings that were long dormant, but always ever close to the surface.

I shift my head until my gaze meets hers. The need to have her *feel* my words as much as hear them is more important than when I first signed with *Eat, Sleep, Go*. "Missed you so much."

Her smile is the sunrise and sunset, white sand beaches and crystal blue seas all in one. Only better. Sade's velvety voice croons, declaring nothing can come between us, and the words embed themselves deep in my being.

When the peppy beat of *It's Raining Men* overtakes the last notes of Sade, Sunnie takes my hand and tugs. "That's our cue to skedaddle."

"Skedaddle? Who are you? My grandmother."

She scrunches her nose and sticks out her tongue, and she's so damn cute, I can't help but pull her to me. She comes willingly, and her sweet laughter and sweeter scent engulf me like the coziest blanket. Then, I do what I've wanted to do for forever.

Our mouths meet, and it's like catching lightning in a bottle. White sparks flash behind my eyelids. Her sweet tongue traces the seam of my lips and an electrical current strong enough to knock me off my feet sizzles my skin. I let her in, and our tongues tangle, dancing to a song of their own. My breath hitches and a keening moan escapes my throat. Time ceases and the earth stills its rotation. If I did nothing more than kiss her for the remainder of my days, I'd be happier than I've ever been.

Sunnie grunts and shuffles into me, breaking our kiss. I catch her in time to see two men, arms around each other, weaving, and I'm not sure who's holding up who.

"Sorry," one of them slurs.

I nod as they stagger around us, then grab Sunnie's hand. "C'mon."

We speed walk to the elevators, which thankfully are empty. The doors slide closed, I crowd Sunnie to the back wall and nibble the skin behind her left ear where a mini constellation of freckles lives. Salty sweetness seduces my taste buds. Her hands trail up the outside of my thighs, working their way under my skirt, and her pert nipples poke through the thin fabric of her halter top, rubbing against me and making my own nipples harder.

The elevator lurches, there's a ping, and the doors open. Sunnie pushes off the wall, catches my hand, and pulls me behind her as she runs down the hall. Our giggles echo through the quiet hallway, intertwining much like our lives. Panting, I pull the keycard from the back pocket of her white jeans, and within seconds we're inside the suite, lips and hands—mine, hers—everywhere. The door shuts with a slam, and Sunnie pushes me against it.

"Want you," she says against my mouth.

"Yes." My head is nodding like a bobble head, and my hands are frantic in their mission to feel every centimeter of her golden skin. "Yes."

She hikes my skirt until it's bunched at my waist. Her hands palm my ass and one slender finger trails the thong between my cheeks. Her groan sounds as desperate as I feel. "I dream of this ass."

Kissing my way along her collarbone, I hum and untie her halter, lifting my head only to watch the fabric fall, exposing the gorgeous mounds beneath. Brown nipples stand at attention against skin slightly lighter than the rest of her after an afternoon soaking in the sun. I tear my gaze from her chest and I'm struck by the heat in eyes that were once as familiar to me as my own.

"Beautiful," I say, before sucking one nipple into my mouth.

Her breath shudders, and her fingers dig into my backside. "More." Her head falls back, exposing the delicate skin of her neck. "More."

Swirling my tongue around the hardened peak, I increase the suction. Her low keening is a torpedo to my center. If I thought my panties were wet before, I was sorely mistaken. Her hands roam my back, setting mini fires where her palms touch my bare skin, reducing my self-control to nothing more than a droplet of water.

I rip my mouth from her, pushing her onto the loveseat in the living room of our suite. Before her bottom hits the cushions, I unbutton her jeans and wrench them down and off her legs. I groan at the sight of the tiny lace bikinis covering her waxed pussy. I drop to my knees, and she spreads her legs in invitation. Her fingertips trail through my hair, grasping tightly when I run my nose along her inner thigh, inhaling the fragrant musk that I will forever associate with Sunnie. When I reach the apex of her thigh, I flick my tongue at the seam of her underwear and slide it along the smooth skin. Pushing the fabric aside, I swipe her center, lapping up the luscious confection.

"Hurry." Her voice, breathy and needy, has an edge to it. One hand leaves my head and I glance up to see her palming her breast and tweaking her nipple. "I need more."

Same. I need more of her. I've always needed more of Sunnie St. James, but I never believed I was enough for her. And those insecurities led me to the other side of the country to make something of myself.

"What do you want, baby?" My tongue circles her clit and her hips jut up, seeking more.

"That. More of that."

Another circle while I reach up and massage her neglected breast. I pick up the pace, putting more pressure on her sensitive nub before licking her down the center. Her taste, more decadent that the richest chocolate, the smoothest cheesecake, or the finest wine. She shoves my face into her mound, and I'm nearly suffocated, but I keep lapping up her juices and playing with her swollen bud. Every moan, every touch, every taste heats me hotter and hotter until I'm an inferno on the brink of incinerating.

My hand drops, and I slide my thong to the side, fingering myself.

"Want. To. Do. That." Each word is a huff of breath. "Feel. You."

Her hips buck, and I know she's close. The only thing I want right now is to make Sunnie lose control. So, I don't say a word, instead picking up the pace and pressure of my tongue and my hand. We have an entire week ahead of us, and I plan on finding all the ways to make both of us scream. Her thighs close around my head, snaring me in her warmth and scent, and annihilating life before this moment.

"Yes. Yes. There. Yes." Eyes wild, her head shakes from side to side. "Fuuuck." Chest heaving, she pushes her breasts together and bites down on her bottom lip before grabbing my head and holding it in place while she grinds into me, my name a howl from her gorgeous mouth.

The violence of her climax ravages her body with jolts and quakes.

All of it taunts my orgasm to the surface and I insert a finger into my hot, wet channel, grinding down on my clit while juices from Sunnie's sweet pussy drip down my chin. Within seconds, I'm toppling over the edge, and it's Sunnie's name that cascades from my lips.

I collapse forward. The heat of Sunnie's thigh burns my boiling cheek, but moving from her would be more devastating than anything Jo has done or could do. So, I stay there, catching my breath. Never wanting to leave.

CHAPTER
SEVEN

SUNNIE

"This. Is. Awesome," Lise calls over the wind. Her smile wide even as she white-knuckles the harness.

Four hundred feet below us, the boat is a dot speeding along the shoreline. After a week relaxing which included sharing a Christmas Eve buffet filled with traditional holiday food of roast pork, banana leaves stuffed with meat, turrón pudding, rice, bread, and more with the other guests, then spending Christmas day lounging in bed and on our balcony, making love, and ordering room service, one would think I'd be used to the beauty. But from up here, the beach looks like sugar and the ocean like glass. The enormous palm trees could be children playing, their fronds of hair blowing in the breeze.

"I knew you'd like it." I stretch my legs out and tip back slightly, enjoying the sun on my face. My loose curls tickle my cheeks, and I know my hair will be a hot mess when our ride ends, but I don't care. This is our last full day in paradise.

The last day that I'll spend with Annalise until… I don't know when.

The last night to sleep in the same bed, waking to her arm slipped through mine and her leg pinning me down as if in sleep she's afraid I'll leave her. But that's just it... I don't want to leave her. I didn't want to part from her when we were in our twenties, and I don't want to now.

I shake the thoughts away until they're flitting along the current with the seagulls and take in the view. "It's so peaceful up here."

"I wouldn't want to share this with anyone else." Lise pries her fingers from the harness and holds her hand out to me.

I grasp it, and we stay that way, sailing side-by-side until we start our descent. Choking back the churning in my stomach, I fortify myself for when we say goodbye tomorrow.

After returning to the resort and thanking the crew for a wonderful ride, Lise threads her fingers through mine and leads me to the cabana that has been our home base this week. When we arrive, two daiquiris and water wait for us.

"Danita is good." Annalise removes her coverup and slides her feet from her hot pink flip-flops.

I grab the tube of sunscreen and toss it to her. "I suppose since she was the one who arranged the para sailing, she knew when we'd return."

"Yep." She catches the tube, but with our feet back on the ground, the wonder of flying dissipates. Lise's effervescence seems muted, like champagne that sat uncorked over night.

I fold my coverup and set it on the love seat, then sink onto the chaise and look out at the translucent water. "You okay?"

A sigh gusts from her lips, heavy enough to make my chest feel like a whale is lying on it. "I don't want to leave."

"I don't either." I pick up a drink and swirl the straw in the frozen ruby slush. "Being here... Being with you... has been a haven from reality. Going back to deal with..." I wave my hand in the air. "Every-thing... Isn't something I'm looking forward to."

"Have you heard anything more from your attorney?"

My phone pings, and I glance at it. A notification for an email from Demarco Baker, my attorney. I hold up my phone. "It's like he heard you."

"Have you received that ten million dollars yet?"

I tilt my head. "What are you talking about?"

"Nothing?" She shrugs her shoulders. "Figured it was worth a shot. An email about some long-lost relative leaving you money has to be better than hearing from Demarco."

I chuckle. "You're not wrong." I don't want to talk about Jo. I don't want to think about Jo. I'm sick of her. She's taken up too much space in my head and too many years of my life already. But I'm not the only one whose life the con-artist has hijacked. So, I open the email and read. "Shit."

"What is it?" Eyes wide with concern, Lise scoots to the edge of her lounge.

I blink and the words on the screen stop swirling. "Looks like we're not the only ones. He said he's found another woman."

"Wife?" She pokes my leg and I scoot over as she climbs onto my chaise.

"Wife." My head spins and I rub my temples. I'm so damned tired. "Married approximately a year after Jo and I got married."

Annalise takes my phone and reads the email, cursing under her breath. "That bitch."

"I don't want to talk about her." I pluck the phone from her fingers and toss it under my chair. "She will not ruin our last day in paradise."

Lise passes me the lotion, then turns her back to me. I sit up, giving her more room. "Not like it's not already ruined," she mumbles, talking more to herself than to me. She straightens as if she's gathering her courage. "It's…"

I squirt lotion into my palm, waiting for her to continue. Birds chatter, waves kiss the shore, and steel drums play in the distance, but silence hangs in between each of the sounds. As a therapist, I'm comfortable with silences. Know how to use them, how to sit with them. But the longer Annalise remains quiet, allowing the hush to roost between us, the more it feels like an invisible gag. I wiggle in my seat and try to focus on spreading the lotion evenly over her fair shoulders until the fear of being extinguished by the muzzle pummels my gut with such force I rip it off, blurting, "What? It's, *what?*"

"I don't want to leave you." Back still to me, her admission is barely audible, but the slight hunch in her shoulders, like she's waiting for a blow, is noticeable.

I move until I'm sitting next to her and twist until I catch her downward gaze. Everything Annalise has, everything she is, she's done on her own and despite her family. For the entirety of her childhood, she was told she was nothing and would amount to even less. And from the bits she shared, the better she did, the more she succeeded, the harder they hammered her with negativity. That was a big part of why I encouraged her to take the opportunity with *Eat, Sleep, Go* when it arose. She deserved to be acknowledged for what she'd created.

With my finger, I tip her chin until she's looking at me. "This week has been the best I've had in..." I shake my head. "College? I can't remember. I want to continue this. Us. But—"

"We live on opposite sides of the country. But you can't uproot and leave Philadelphia when you've worked so hard to build the practice you have. But I have a career most in my position would kill for. But..." Her chin wobbles and for the first time since the clusterfuck with Jo, the enormity of it seems to hit her.

I pull her into an awkward hug. "We'll keep in touch like we have. Texts, video calls, vacations. You're the only other person who *really* understands what I'm going through." I lean back until she looks at me. "Well, you and wife number three."

The corner of her mouth tips up, but it's as wobbly as a newborn deer. "Technically, I'm number three. She's number two."

"For now. Who knows how many more there are?" I tug her back into a hug. "There's no way I'm losing you again."

"I hate my job." She sniffles into my neck.

I pull away so I can see her again and gape. "But I thought it was your dream job."

"It *was*." Blinking away the glistening tears, she fans her face with her hand. "But lately... I hate LA. I miss knowing a city and finding all the gems tucked away where you'd least expect to find them. The mom-and-pop and the hole-in-the-wall places that don't get credit because they're just doing their thing, not worrying about making connections."

I slow blink, trying to process her words. My brain feels like it's trudging through the thick jungle carrying a butter knife instead of a machete. "What are you saying?"

"I don't know. But I don't want things to go back the way they were." She smooths her thumb across my cheek. "Philadelphia always felt like home. Maybe because it's where you are. Maybe it's something about the city. I don't know... But I'm tired of feeling out of place. And I'm tired of working my ass off for someone else. I miss my blog. Writing about what I want to write about."

"What about your Facebook page?"

"It's not the same."

The pounding in my chest makes it difficult to catch my breath. "You're considering moving back?"

"I've played with the idea for years. Now," she twists one of my wayward curls around her finger, "I have more incentive."

I hold my hands up like I'm talking down a criminal with their gun pointed at me. As much as I would love to have Annalise closer, the last thing I want is for her to drop her life, only to regret it in the future. Or worse, resent me. "Let's talk about this."

She clasps one hand and brings it to her lips, placing delicate kisses on each knuckle. "Don't freak out."

"I'm not freaking out." *I'm totally freaking out.*

"Yes, you are."

My shoulders slump and I nod as the pressure in my chest loosens. "I know."

"*If* I move back to Philadelphia, it won't be because of you." She quirks a grin and shoots me a look from the corner of her eye. "Though knowing you're there helps."

She twists around so she's reclining on the lounger, leaving enough room for me, and pats the empty space. "When I first moved to LA, I thought once I got to know the area and was established, I'd make friends and I'd feel... like I belonged." Her gaze stays focused on the water and she crosses her ankles. "But when I came back to Philly—"

"When I introduced you to Jo?" I slip onto the cushions and stretch out beside her. My thoughts cast to the moment they met in the bar. I know I couldn't have foreseen any of the bullshit Jo put us through, but guilt and regret pin me to the chair, so heavy I can't even lift my gaze to meet hers.

She nods and clasps my hand to her chest. "That's when I realized how much I was missing."

"Why didn't you move back then?" Our intertwined hands pressed so close to her heart is both casual and intimate and when she presses a kiss to my palm, I feel it all the way to my toes.

After a week of sunbathing, dots of brown decorate her creamy skin, and I want to kiss every freckle on the shoulder she raises to her ear. "Fear?" She rolls her head until her gaze penetrates me. "But with you..." She blows out a breath. "With you, I've always felt fearless. Which is why I'm going to fight for us this time."

"This time?" I try to swallow, but swallowing cut glass would be easier.

"I was too young and too scared to understand what was important in life. You were still reeling after your mom died, and I didn't know what to do, which is hard as hell to admit, because it shows what a coward I was. But now... after everything... I know..." She leans in, her lips brushing my ear. "Friendship, doing what you love, and trust are the important things."

My nails dig into my palms and I lick my suddenly dry lips. "If you move back, would you..."

How do I express I don't want her to move in with me without sounding like I don't want her? Because I *do* want her. I've always wanted Annalise.

"Don't worry." She presses her lips to my temple. "I'll get my own place. Not making that mistake again."

I huff a relieved breath and sink into her. "Thank god."

Our arms, hips, and thighs press together, and she rests her head on my shoulder. "We'll take things slow."

"So we're what? Dating? Girlfriends?" I kiss the top of her head.

"We're Sunnie and Lise. Like we used to be."

Her hair is warm on my cheek as I gaze at the line where the ocean meets the sky. "Only better."

"Sunnie and Lise 2.0." She tilts her head up and pops a kiss on my jaw.

I snort a laugh, though the thought of Annalise and me together sparkles through me, twinkling brighter than the Christmas lights decorating the resort. I playfully tip her sunhat over her face. "Dork."

"You love it." Smiling, she hangs the hat on the back of the lounger, then settles against me once more.

I do.

And I love her.

Always have.

Later that night, when Annalise takes me, it's not with the frantic hunger like when we thought a week was all we had. Every kiss is a promise, enshrining what we were, what we are, what we will become. Her lips worship my body, coaxing whimpers and moans, tingles and shivers, heart pounding sighs and stomach somersaulting flutters.

Scented with the ocean, the sheer panels hanging from the bed flap in the warm evening air. Stradling her, my hands roam supple skin, every curve and dip a treasure trove of bliss. Her protruding nipples brush against my sensitive breast and we both groan. The heat of her wet core as I grind against her is heaven and hell. But it's her unwavering steel gaze that invades and conquers. The intensity is so great, it almost hurts, and I want to look away.

But I don't.

I can't. Everything I want to say is reflected back to me in her gaze. Every fear, every hope, every promise, she cradles in her stormy blue-gray eyes.

I cup her face, brushing her cheek with the pad of my thumb, then press my mouth to hers. Our tongues and bodies move in rhythm. Her fingers glide over my hip to my stomach, triggering a quiver. With a groan, her mouth slips from the kiss, and she pushes my boobs together, sucking between one nipple and the other. With every nip, I'm annihilated, only to be revived with each suck.

I push up on my knees, the hot air feeling cool against my blazing pussy, and trail my first and second fingers along her swollen lips and around her clit.

"You're so wet." I reverse the motion, sliding my fingers through the wiry trimmed hair, damp with her arousal, and over her vulva, slow and steady.

Seeking more pressure, she grinds into my fingers. "More."

Fingers soaked with her juices, I insert one, then two.

"Fuck, yes." Her hips buck, and she bites down on my breast. The pain licks the surface before transforming into all that is sublime.

My pussy aches for more, but with every plea, every tug of Lise's teeth on my nipple, and the grip of her fingers on my hips, I know she's close. And she's fucking beautiful. Long, dark hair mussed from my fingers, chest red from my mouth, lips glistening from my kisses.

"That's right, baby," I croon, then pull away so I can devour her mouth. I work my fingers in and out of her. "So beautiful." She grabs my ass cheeks, massaging them as her hips gyrate and mash my hand, pulling my fingers deeper and deeper into her heat. "Like that. Let me see you."

Words fall from my mouth, and I'm not sure what I'm saying. Not that it seems to matter because as soon as I tap her clit with my thumb and say, "Come for me," she explodes, coating my fingers in her warm fluids. A flush blooms along her skin and her head falls back as she shouts my name. She shudders and shudders again. Her hot breaths come in a rush against my neck, spawning a string of goosebumps behind them.

Before I can appreciate her post-orgasm glow, Lise falls back, tugging me with her. Her mouth devours me with a greediness that has me crying out within seconds as my orgasm blasts through my body, exterminating everything before.

And I wouldn't have it any other way.

EPILOGUE

ANNALISE

Nine months later…

I stand in the well-appointed kitchen. Looking out the window onto the cute garden in the postage-stamp sized backyard. "This'll work."

"Really?" Sunnie bounces on her toes, her grin beaming.

Rain's grandfather smacks his hands together with one thunderous clap. "Excellent. I'll feel better knowing my home will be well taken care of."

"And you're sure you don't want more for rent?" I can totally see myself living here, but I worry Pop's generosity and huge heart carried a lot of weight when arriving at the amount of money I'll be paying him each month.

"Lise," Rain pipes up before his grandfather can say anything. "You're doing both of us a favor."

Wringing my hands, I shuffle across the tiled floor, breathing in the scents of mint and rosemary from the pots on the windowsill. "It just seems like I'm taking advantage of you."

Pop takes my hand and squeezes, his hazel eyes bright and shining with more mischief than a man half his age has. "Rain is correct. Without you, I'd have to enlist the services of a management company and would spend the tour worrying rather than enjoying this time I have with my grandson."

When Rain found out I was planning on moving back to Philly, he called to see if I wanted to rent his grandfather's house in Manayunk while they were touring. A renowned jazz musician, Pop convinced Rain and his punk band to accompany him on a year-long world tour. Knowing Rain, he would have gone with or without his band because he'd do anything for his pop.

"It's perfect." Sunnie wraps her arm around my waist, and Pop drops my hands. "You'll have your own place, but you're close."

"Now we just need to find me somewhere to live." Iggy, the wife Sunnie and I found out about while we were on vacation, wraps her arms around her center. She contacted Sunnie shortly after Demarco told her about us. Though the three of us lived in different cities, it didn't take long to create a sort-of-support group. Or, as Iggy likes to call us, the No Jo Luck Club.

Sunnie holds out her arm, and Iggy falls into her. I wrap my arm around Iggy, the three of us forming a huddle of sorts. Iggy rests her head on Sunnie's shoulder and tightens her hold on me. Younger than the two of us, Iggy's had a harder time coming to terms with Jo's betrayal. I imagine had I not had Sunnie, I would have been the same. Fortunately, Iggy lives in New York City, so she and Sunnie have been able to meet up in person more frequently than I have. I think her decision to move to Philadelphia after I announced my plans was to start anew and be closer to Sunnie and me.

Over Iggy's head, I meet Sunnie's gaze and she nods. We've discussed the possibility of Iggy rooming with me. It would help with expenses while I'm building my brand, and would give Iggy stability.

I take a breath. "I could use a roommate." My gaze darts to Pop and Rain. Shit, I never discussed it with them. "If that's okay with you?"

Understanding how difficult it's been for Iggy, Rain—our sweet, supportive friend—smiles and booms in his baritone voice. "The more the merrier."

"You'll probably take better care of the place than this one when he and his buddies crashed here for a summer." Pop jerks his thumb toward Rain.

Rain holds up his hands. "We were twenty-three and thought we were the shit because we landed a consistent weekend gig at the Rusty Rudder in Dewey Beach."

Sniffling, Iggy releases her hold, but her eyes are clear and her smile steady when she looks at us. "Are you serious?"

"Absolutely," Sunnie and I say in unison, causing all of us to chuckle.

"Yes!" Iggy jumps up and down, hugging Sunnie, me, Rain, then Pop. "I can't believe it."

I pat Sunnie's hand on my waist. "Only three more months."

As terrified as I was to tell Elora that I didn't plan on renewing my contract with *Eat, Sleep, Go*, she was supportive. And never one to miss an opportunity, she worked with me to develop a new bi-monthly column called *Philly Eats*. Apparently, after the Chicago spread did so well, and the response we got from readers wanting more places to eat, she was looking at tweaking the direction of the magazine. Wanting to cater to locals and travelers, she's starting with *LA Eats* and *Philly Eats*. Whitley was thrilled to be tapped to write the Los Angeles version. And I get to move and have at least some consistent income while I build my blog back up and do more freelance work.

Working in television, Iggy encouraged me to start posting videos of me cooking. An extension of the shorter videos I was posting on Facebook. Thus, *The Food Critic Cooks?* was born and is turning out to be far more popular than I imagined. The videos I posted with Sunnie when she came out to visit and when I came here were my highest viewed posts to date. The audience loves our chemistry. Although they also enjoy when Iggy joins us and apparently find it hilarious when the two of them critique my masterpieces with less than glowing terms.

"I can't wait." Sunnie pecks a smiling kiss on my lips, her eyes reflecting the happiness in mine.

"Me either." Our future is bright and exciting and I'm looking forward to sharing a life with her here.

The sound of Sunnie's phone vibrating and ringing has us all turning our heads. Sunnie releases me, and I miss her closeness, as I have since we parted at the airport in the Dominican Republic. We've done the long-distance thing, which was scary as hell since we'd both done that with Jo, but it turns out when your partner respects you, she actually wants to talk to you, see you, and spend time with you.

As Pop, Rain, Iggy, and I discuss the logistics of my move and their tour, I hear Sunnie in the background. "Are you serious?"

I turn to find her shaking her head, her eyes closed. It's the look she gets when she's processing information that is hard for her to believe. Without thinking, I cross the kitchen and rest a hand on her lower back.

Eyes still closed, she leans into me. "Yeah. Okay. Give her my number if she wants to talk. Thanks, Demarco."

She ends the call and opens her eyes to look at me. "Demarco found another one."

"Wife?" Iggy's tone is indignant.

"Are you fucking kidding me?" This from Rain.

Anger ties with pity whenever I think of Jo, and a part of me is still stunned that she can go around blatantly lying about who she is, racking up marriages like balls on a pool table, and leaving broken hearts in her wake. I trace my fingers up and down Sunnie's back, soothing her as much as myself. "Where does she find the time?"

"Who knows?" Sunnie turns and tucks her face into the crook of my neck, her arms holding as tightly to me as I do to her. No matter how wonderful my life is now, it's like getting my guts yanked out every time another wife appears.

Pop opens the wine fridge and pulls out a bottle of white. He holds it up. "I don't have anything stronger. Will this due?"

Sunnie kisses my neck, extraditing herself from the hug, but inter-twining our fingers together. The connection, the love I feel for this woman, washes over me, a balm healing the scars of the past. Keeping my feelings to myself suddenly seizes and shackles me. And I want to break free.

Free from my insecurities.

Free from fear.

Free from not trusting my instincts.

"Will you excuse us for a minute?" I tug Sunnie to the back door the leads to the garden. "I want to show Sunnie something."

"Take your time." Pop waves us away, pulling out stemless wine glasses and handing them to Rain and Iggy, who looks shell-shocked, but when Rain drapes his arm over her shoulder and gives me a nod, I know she's in good hands.

Once outside, Sunnie pulls me into another hug, and I'm wrapped in her citrus scent. "It will be okay. One more to add to our club."

I chuckle and pull away. "At this point, we should start charging dues."

"And rent out a proper meeting space. Do you think the Convention Center is available?" Sunnie teases.

The sun's rays bring out auburn highlights in her hair, and the blush in the apples of her cheeks. The scent of roses and cut grass mingle with her perfume and in her, I see my future standing before me. "I know we said we wouldn't jump into anything quickly. But it's been too many years of me being a fool. Of me loving you and being too scared to admit it to myself, let alone tell you. And I'm done being afraid because of some manipulative con-artist. It's okay if you don't have the same feelings. It's okay if you're not ready. I'm here for the long haul and I'll wait until you are. Hell, I'll wait even if you're never ready. But I need you to know that I love you. I'm *in* love with you. I thought Philadelphia was my home, but I realized it's you. Sunnie, you are my home."

"Thank god." She collapses into me. "I've wanted to tell you how freaking much I'm in love with you for forever. But I didn't want to freak you out."

Her words resuscitate me after years of suffocation. "Are you kidding? Nothing you do could freak me out." I tip her chin until our mouths meet, and I'm suffused with a love I thought was only in fairy-tales. But this is real.

No matter the time apart, the number of states separating us, or the woman we married, we're still Sunnie and Lise.

Nothing and no one can change that.

The End

ABOUT CHANTAL MER

Chantal Mer never set out to write books. Yet here she is, and she's having a blast. Happily ever afters for everyone makes her heart sing.

When she's not writing, Chantal can be found walking her adorable dog, going to musical theater with her daughter, observing the night sky with her husband and his telescope, and learning about the latest advances in video games with her son. Give her a book and a glass of wine and she's in her happy place. Chantal lives outside of Philadelphia with her husband, two teens, her sweet pup, Miss Toffee and her big orange tabby, Simba.

Chantal's website: https://www.chantalmer.com/
    Facebook: https://www.facebook.com/chantalmerauthor
    Instagram: https://www.instagram.com/chantalmer/
    BookBub: https://www.bookbub.com/profile/chantal-mer

FALLEN

XIO AXELROD

ABOUT FALLEN

Some stars fall with purpose. Many forget they ever fell at all.

Fallen is a short story about a world that lies just alongside our own.

CHAPTER
ONE

DEATH HAD COME *to take the soul, to flee the body and leave it cold.*

———

Adea became aware.

The colors hit first, swaths of dark, vibrant brights and everything in between. Colors they had no name for on the celestial plane. Adea knew the names of the things, but not the colors themselves.

There were trees, and the color of trees.

There was grass, and the color of grass. Similar to the trees but more luminous.

There was the sky above and the sea below, which were also similar but not the same.

Then there were the sounds. The wind was wind, but softer somehow. The very sounds of life overwhelmed Adea. So many hearts beating. So many voices.

Landing atop the listing waves of an ocean, Adea looked down at the corporeal form that contained them. Long appendages stretched toward the water, dark and smooth as a starless night. Adea willed them to move, and they did, like ribbons of space undulating in the open air. There were more on the sides, and Adea moved those, too. A curious sensation, Adea could feel the wind brush against these extremities. How odd, to feel that all the time as humans must. How distracting it must have been.

But it was pleasurable, like being caressed by the breath of the Origin.

The rest of the form baffled Adea. Soft curves and even more dark, smooth flesh.

Names, words, definitions. Adea lacked them all. This was unacceptable. It had been millennia since they had inhabited the earthly realm, had come into contact with the life there. Adea had forgotten all that they had ever known about the place. Unacceptable.

Humanity was clever, though, and had cast its existence into the universe like a net. Ready to trap anyone who ventured close.

Adea allowed the net to settle over this body, letting the information seep into its cells.

Languages. *Verden er ikke perfekt.* So many. *The only thing to fear is fear itself.* How could these beings communicate? *Je t'adore.*

The knowledge of things came quickly now.

Apples.

Cars.

Phones.

Clothing.

Adea learned of men and women, and those who were both or neither. Of children. Of parents and forbears.

Generals.

Doctors.

Actors.

Learned of Race and identity. Action and inaction.

Emotions. Desire. Love. Hate.

Hate.

A lot of that one.

But also love, joy, pleasure...so much pleasure.

Adea looked down at this body and realized it was likely to be perceived as female. A she.

She, her, he, him.

Very confining, these binary genders.

Adea moved her limbs again and brought the things called hands to the thing called her face. Moved them down this body, over the things called tits. Breasts. Boobs. So many words for them, but soft was Adea's word. This body was soft and pleasing to the touch. Stroking certain areas sent ripples of sensation across a thousand nerve endings. Maybe it wouldn't be so horrible to stay in this form while on earth, she thought.

Willing herself to move, Adea floated down closer to the water. It lapped at the ends of her legs. Feet. Toes, they were toes. Adea touched the toes to the surface and registered the cold, the energy traveling through her like an electrical current. Gathering that energy, pulling it toward her, Adea fed and felt her mind clear.

She knew where she was and when, and she knew the one she had come to claim was close. Adea gathered nature's will around her and went off in search of her target.

It didn't take long to find him.

Stars were beautiful, dotting the velvet curtain of the universe like musical notes. They were, after all, the jewels of the universe. Chalices of light. Adea might not admit it on the celestial plane, but fallen stars burned brighter. And fallen stars would attract the hedonists. The sybarites. The lonely. The lost. The lustful.

This body's lust led her right to him. An aching between her thighs pulsed, driving her along the river to where he sat. Waiting, whether he knew it or not.

***

Between the music in his ears, the alcohol on his lips, and the E in his veins, Loris Stern felt far better than he should. Definitely better than he deserved.

The wind whipped his hair around and threatened to topple him off his precarious perch on the corner of the roof. His view of the Savannah River was unobstructed, save for the spots dancing at the corners of his vision.

On the outdoor deck, one story below, the party raged on.

Matt looked down upon his acolytes, all there to suckle at the teet of fame and fortune. His fame and fortune.

His money had rented out the upper two floors of the Rosa Hotel and Resort. His money had paid for the booze and the drugs, both of which flowed freely throughout the crowd. His money had lured a top DJ to sleepy Savannah, and his money afforded the best food for his guests, ninety-nine percent of which he didn't even know.

All to celebrate the wunderkind that was Loris Stern, though Edden wasn't a kid anymore. He was thirty-three now.

Thirty-fucking-three.

Below his feet, the crowd cheered and chanted his name. *Loris, Loris.*

"Happy Birthday to me."

He spoke only to the wind. He hadn't expected it to answer.

"Birthdays are curious things."

Loris lurched away from the voice, too close to his ear to make sense. He lost his balance and would have fallen off the edge were it not for a band of pressure around his chest that seemed to pull him back to safety.

"Great," he groaned, his voice shaking with the rest of him. "Now I'm hearing things." Loris raked a hand over his face.

"Only me, my lovely one."

He froze, the warm Georgia air doing nothing to stave off the chill that ran down his spine.

"*Hva faen?*"

"Hmm, Swedish? No, Norwegian." The voice cooed. "You are a northern star."

Soft laughter filled the air, sending goosebumps racing along his arms.

Loris held his next breath. If this were some sort of hallucination, it was a damn strong one, though it really shouldn't have been. He'd only popped a couple of E, and he was only on his first bottle of vodka. Other than hitting a few joints, he'd been a good boy. No coke. No smack.

Maybe someone was playing a prank. He swept his gaze along the length of the roof before turning to see who might be behind him. No one. He got up, careful not to take a header over the edge. The pool was below, but he wasn't sure it was deep enough to absorb the impact of a six-foot-four-inch cannonball.

Loose gravel crunched under his feet as he got to them and looked around again to confirm that he was indeed alone.

He groaned, raking a hand through his hair. "Fuck, I'm losing it."

"Losing what?"

This time, Loris got a good sense of where the voice was coming from, but it just didn't compute. He looked out across the winding, black river. Scanned the countryside again. The lights from various boats and small craft bobbed along its surface like drunken stars.

"Hello?" Loris cupped his ears, waiting for the wind to answer.

"Hello, Loris Stern." The voice was warm honey, whiskey, and smoke, and the sound of it went straight to his groin.

Jesus Christ. I'm horny for a voice in my head.

"Not in your head. I am Adea," it whispered, and Loris heard laughter in the words.

"Adea." The word rolled off his tongue with a familiarity he didn't understand.

Loris walked toward the edge and peered over. Down below, the party churned on. The dance floor was practically one giant orgy. Bodies writhed to the thumping bass-and-drum track blaring from the speakers. The sound was muted, though. One story up, he was in a bubble.

Though not alone.

"Where are you?"

"I am across from you, but at a distance."

He squinted into the darkness. "How?"

"You will not trust my explanation."

"Try me."

"We...I am suspended in your air, above your waters."

"*My* waters?"

"This planet's."

Okay, this was now well into what-the-actual-fuck territory. Anger flared at the center of his chest. "Are you trying to screw with my head? I don't need help in that department."

"I did not know it could be done that way. Curious."

"What?" Loris stepped as close to the edge as he dared and shielded his eyes from the light pollution coming from the pool party. "Why don't you come closer if you're really out there?"

"I am really out here."

"Well, then?" He challenged. "Come here."

"I will, but I am waiting for you to adjust."

"To what?"

"To the idea of us. Of me."

Loris closed his eyes and took a deep breath. If he was hallucinating, it meant he was having a conversation with himself on the roof of a hotel where hundreds of partygoers could witness his imminent breakdown.

"You are not hallucinating, Loris Stern."

He opened his eyes and glared in the direction of the voice. "Why do you keep using my full name? And who the fuck are you? Why are you here..there?"

"I am upsetting you."

"You think?"

He thought he heard a sigh, or maybe it was just the breeze that lifted the fine, blond hair from his forehead and curled around the side of his face. If he didn't know better, he would have thought someone had touched him. Caressed him.

A spike of desire knocked the breath out of his lungs.

"What the...?"

"Look out over the horizon," Adea said. "Look straight ahead at the darkened sky."

Unsure why he was playing along, Loris obeyed. He concentrated on the vast, black expanse of the heavens. And then he saw it.

Or rather, her.

The silhouette of a woman drifted toward him, her skin as dark as the sky above and the river below. She was nude, her breasts round and high and her hips full. Ribbons of white swirled across her skin, along her jawline, over her eyebrows, around her ears, and down her neck. They outlined her collarbone and skimmed along her waist. The contrast was striking.

She was probably the most beautiful thing he'd ever seen, and then she opened her eyes.

He gasped and stumbled back a few steps.

Adea's gaze burned into him, twin violet flames whose heat he felt over every inch of his skin. She smiled, another perfect white crescent curving into the velvet black.

"Jesus."

"No, Adea." Honey-infused whiskey, that was her voice, and Loris felt like he'd just taken a shot. "That's better."

"Wh-what is?" His head swam, but he continued to move back as she floated toward him. "Who are you? *What* are you?"

Delicate feet touched down on the roof without a sound. Loris watched, mute, as Adea glided toward him. She moved slowly, carefully, as if she were approaching a feral cat.

"Are you all right?"

He barked a bitter laugh. "I think not."

She frowned. "Is there something I can do?"

He straightened as best he could. Meeting her gaze was difficult, nearly impossible, but it was better than taking in all of her glorious curves. The desire to reach out and touch her, take her, was nearly crippling.

"Who the fuck are you?" He pronounced each word with great care and with more than a little difficulty.

Adea's smile faded, and he felt a pang of guilt. It was a lovely smile. A thicket of black curls sprang from her head and framed her heart-shaped face. There was absolutely no shame in her expression despite being as naked as the day she was born.

All of his annoyance and disorientation aside, Loris couldn't stop staring at her. He got lost for long moments in the curve of her waist, the hollow at her throat, or the tip of one onyx nipple. Adea was… beautiful wasn't a strong enough word. *Consumable* was more accurate. He wanted to devour her.

He was harder than he'd ever been in his life, and his cock throbbed insistently between his legs. God, he wanted her.

"Thank you," she whispered, smiling.

"I-I didn't..".

"Sorry, I can hear your thoughts." There was almost a blush in her apology. "But, I should not listen when you do not speak. I am sorry."

"Please. I-I-I don't understand what's happening."

"Of course," she smiled again. "I am here for you."

"For me?"

"You're a star."

This statement snapped Loris out of whatever trance she'd put him under. He rolled his eyes. "Yeah, and are you my number one fan? Is this some sort of elaborate stalking technique?"

He glanced up, looking for wires, a harness, something. Anything to make this make sense. Anything to strip his gaze from the enticing sight between her legs.

"If so, I have to say, you're the best I've ever encountered."

Adea frowned. "I do not understand what you are saying."

Weary of the game, Loris ran two hands through his unruly hair. "Look, Adea, it's been a long day. Hell, a long month. I'm at the end of my tour, and my band is downstairs with a few hundred of my closest friends."

"You do not know those people."

He narrowed his eyes at her. "Well, I know them a hell of a lot better than I know you. Where did you come from?"

Adea smiled again. "If I told you, you would not accept the truth."

"Lie."

She seemed to think about that. "I have been watching you for a very long time."

"A fan, then?"

Adea nodded. "I suppose you could say that."

She moved closer, and he was once again assaulted by her physical beauty. His cock thickened to the point of pain, and he tore his gaze away from her all-too-enticing form.

"Let me get you a t-shirt or a-a-a robe or something."

"My appearance displeases you?"

"No, fuck. It pleases me. It pleases me too goddamn much." He turned away before it got truly embarrassing. "*Faen*, didn't you bring a swimsuit?"

"Should I cover myself?"

"Please." Loris started to remove his hoodie. He was too warm with it anyway. Before he could lift it over his head, her voice interrupted him.

"There."

It wasn't much of an improvement. Adea had somehow manifested a gauzy chemise that did nothing more than accentuate all of her considerable assets. Her nipples poked at the fabric, and it took all of his willpower not to reach out for her. He closed his eyes.

"I know you have no preference for your sexual partners."

She didn't sound judgmental, only pragmatic, which eased some of the tension in his shoulders.

"I can change into the form of the man you lay with this morning if need be."

Loris opened his eyes and found Adea standing in front of him. She was tall, nearly as tall as him. "Wait, how did--"

"You want *this* body."

Maybe the hard-on knocking at the zipper of his jeans had given it away, Loris thought wryly.

"It's good," she said, sounding almost relieved. "It will make this easier."

"Make what easier?"

"You're sad here, Loris Stern. You have given to this world, and this world has only taken from you."

She reached out, and he instinctively moved back.

Adea's hand hung in the air between them. "Please. I won't hurt you. It won't hurt."

Violet eyes locked onto him, and he fought the urge to run as she drew closer. Every fiber of his being screamed for him to get away. Well, not *every* fiber. His dick was more than happy to have her closer.

The first touch was a shock to his system. A wave of desire so strong that his knees nearly gave out.

"Fuck."

Adea cupped his face between her palms, and Loris wanted to weep. He could feel her in every cell, hear her in every thought. But it was more than her. It was… It was too much.

"I-I don't... I can't... What...?"

"You are a star," she said as if that were news to him. "You are a billion, billion years of light poured into an envelope of flesh."

"I've certainly never heard it put that way before." Loris was surprised his voice worked at all.

She frowned. "You've drawn so many to you, and yet you are so alone. It's because these people, these beings, they cannot know you. This place cannot fulfill you. But you can go home. I can set you free."

Loris wanted to ask her what the holy hell she was talking about, but he knew. As she curled long fingers into his hair, her blunt nails raking over his scalp, he felt the universe move through him. He saw it all. Creation, destruction, birth, and death. None of it in the sense of humanity. All of it in the sense of infinity.

She grabbed the hem of his hoodie and gently pulled.

Loris lifted his arms and let her remove it, and his t-shirt soon followed. Her hands on his skin had him reeling. She unbuckled his belt, slid his zipper down, and cupped his length. It was bliss.

He blinked at her. There was light all around them, and he was shocked to find it was emanating from him, a faint glow. "What... What is happening to me?"

Adea smiled. "I told you, you are a star."

She curled her fingers around his rigid cock, and he lurched forward, steadying himself with a hand on her shoulder. The pleasure was so intense that he thought he might lose consciousness. Adea knew how to touch him, somehow. Knew what he liked, and how he liked it. She brought her lips to his ear and spoke. It was like drinking vodka straight from the bottle.

"I was there when you burst into life." She tugged at his flesh with one hand and tugged at his jeans with the other. They pooled at his feet. "I was there when your light first reached the earth, and you peered down in wonder at the emergence of these creatures."

Loris found himself on his back. He clothing provided a scant cushion between his skin and the gravel-covered roof, but the discomfort was distant. Like the buzz of a mosquito in the breeze.

Adea straddled him. Without preamble, she positioned him between her legs and sank down over him, impaling herself. He roared.

Her flesh was hot. Hot like fire, but he welcomed the burn.

"I was there when you fell, and now I understand why you remained," she said, arching her back as she rode him. "This carnal pleasure is enough to make me consider it."

He had no idea what she meant. Loris only knew that he needed more of her, this woman, or whatever she was.

As if she could hear his thoughts, which, he supposed, she could, she reached behind, and he felt slim fingers cup his balls. Loris only had a moment to wonder what was happening before she grazed his hole.

He gasped as she penetrated him, her fingers thickening into something else. Something long, hot, slick, and pulsing.

"Oh, fuck."

It was so thick and filled him up so well.

Loris skimmed his hands up her thighs, over her stomach, and cupped her breasts. Her nipples beckoned like ripe blackberries, and he leaned up, taking one into his mouth as he fucked her, as she fucked him right back.

Music filled his ears, all of it from her. She sang for him as he took control, rolling them until Adea was on her back. He thrust into her, and she thrust back, seizing him from every angle. Every stab sent him soaring. It had never been like this. Had never, ever been like this.

Adea laughed. "Oh, my star. Yes!"

Loris slammed back onto her fingers, cock, whatever the hell it was. He slammed forward into her, letting go of any control he may have ever had. It was incredible. Unearthly. His release hit him hard and fast. Started at the base of his spine and traveled with lightning speed to his balls, drawing them up tight against his body until he spilled over into her and felt her spilling into him. A ribbon of starlight filled him up.

She laughed and laughed and laughed as he collapsed over her, dragging air into his lungs as he tried to process everything that had just happened. Everything that she'd said, that he now remembered.

Felt in his bones.

"I thought I'd imagined it, the feeling of not belonging here." He spoke against her shoulder, damp with sweat and cool from the night air.

Adea brought her arms around him and stroked his skin. "You did not."

"I'm not supposed to be here."

"You are not."

Loris lifted his head to meet her eyes, more lilac now than amethyst, the color subdued.

"There are things I love here, things I want to do."

"But you would be so much happier if you let me take you."

"Take me where exactly? Would I be fixed in the sky again?"

Adea smiled, and it was sad. "No. As far as you might understand it, you would cease."

Loris reared back.

"Cease? You mean I'd die?"

"No." After contemplating that a moment, Adea nodded. "Yes."

He pushed up, moving away from her, as cold dread stole over him. "You're here to-to kill me?"

"I am here to return your essence to the place from whence it came. You, as you know you, would cease. So, yes. I suppose you're right." She smiled again as if she hadn't just pronounced a death sentence. As if they had been discussing the weather.

"You're... What are you in all of this?"

"I am...an angel, in the vernacular."

Loris cocked his head, studying her. "You're an angel. Of death? You're the fucking Reaper!"

Adea's laughter did not warm him this time. "Oh yes, that is a good word. Reaper. I reap so that others may sow."

"I don't give a shit what you call it, or me for that matter. I don't want to die. This life may not be perfect, but it's the only one I have now."

"But..." She frowned, confused. "You could be reborn. You could shine again as you were meant to."

"*Could?* Meaning there's no guarantee?"

Peering down over the edge to the party below, she offered another sad smile. "You sound like one of them."

"Because I *am* one of them."

Her smile was sad this time. "You should never have stayed here this long. It has dimmed your light."

"I disagree," Loris looked down at the party. "I may not be all celestial and pure, but I still shine. I create art here, sort of. Music that people like. I bring joy to their lives. And if you know anything about this world, it's that they need art and music and joy. Now, more than ever."

Adea shook her head and sighed. "It doesn't matter, I have a mission. I have to take you."

"Or," Loris countered, grasping for the only logic he thought might get through to a being like her. "You could stay here. With me."

Adea turned to look at him, her surprise evident. "What?"

The more he thought about it, the more the idea appealed to him.

"Stay. Like you said, there's no one here for me. I can never be fulfilled with a human companion, but you… You are not human."

She shook her head. "I am not."

"Is there a time limit on this reaping? Like, did they tell you to be back by midnight or something?"

"No." She drew the word out. "Time works differently here."

"So, technically, we could stay as long as we want, and you could take me later. Say, in eighty years."

Her smile was luminous. "You have learned to be as wily as they are."

"They have taught me a lot." Loris cupped her cheek, and Adea leaned into the touch. The heat returned, warming his palm where they connected. Would it always be like that?

"Yes," she answered his thought. "Between us, it would always be this way. We are made of the same light."

He leaned in and brushed his lips over hers. Adea startled, but allowed him to kiss her. It started sweetly, softly, before deepening into something all-consuming.

Loris swept his tongue into her mouth and swallowed her moans and musical sighs.

By the time they broke apart, Adea was glowing. "I think I like that almost as much as the sexing."

He grinned. "Sex. It's just sex. Or fucking."

"Fucking." She nodded. "I like the way that word feels with this mouth."

Loris kissed her because he liked that mouth, too. "Let's stay. For a little while."

She eyed him warily. "A little while?"

"A decade or ten."

"Fine. But I want to sing," she declared, surprising him.

He shrugged. "You can. We will, together."

"And I want to fuck you again."

Loris laughed, pulling her closer. "We will definitely do a lot of that. In, uh, any form you want to take."

"Right now?" Leaning back, Adea turned a fiery gaze on him, her eyes luminescing as her body transformed. Delicate limbs gave way to powerful arms and legs. The soft mound between her thighs elongated into a gloriously thick cock.

Stifling a moan, Loris flopped down onto their makeshift pallet and turned over onto his stomach, staring at Adea over his shoulder. "Oh, yeah. Right the fuck now."

THANK YOU FOR READING FALLEN

I had so much fun revisiting this short story from several years ago.

Who knows, I may expand it into something more someday. What do you think?

Xio

ABOUT XIO AXELROD

Xio Axelrod is a *USA TODAY* Bestselling author of love stories, contemporary romance and (what she likes to call) strange, twisted tales.

Xio grew up in the music industry and began recording at a young age. When she isn't writing stories, she can be found in the studio, writing songs, or performing as her fictional band, The Lillys.

She lives in Philadelphia with one full-time husband and twopart-time cats.

Find all things Xio at www.linktr.ee/xioaxelrod

THE MAIDEN AND THE CRONE

R.L. MERRILL

ABOUT THE MAIDEN AND THE CRONE

Grad student Elia has one last project to complete before earning her degree—a paper deconstructing the feminine archetypes. The perfect opportunity for an interview presents itself during a trip home for spring break. Rosalind Ford is new in town and "a woman of a certain age." She's purchased the outrageous mansion built by a country music superstar in Elia's small hometown, making her a mystery Elia can't wait to solve. She's nothing like Elia expected, and their conversations throw Elia's plans for her future into the air. Roz offers Elia an enticing opportunity, one that will give her a shot gaining valuable experience while working closely with the attractive older woman, or it could draw her into Roz's personal tragedy. What's the right move for a maiden who is smitten with a crone?

To all of the female-identifying folks who fight for those who cannot fight for themselves.

CHAPTER
ONE

PROCRASTINATION WILL PROBABLY BE LISTED as my top skill on my curriculum vitae...that is, if I ever complete my graduate degree in Women's Studies. Procrastination made it necessary to extend my degree an extra semester, and then an extra year. Procrastination had me sitting in front of my advisor's office the Thursday before spring break, pleading for help with a final project. I should be finishing grad school in June and entering the world of academia in the fall, but my faculty position would soon be gone if I didn't finish this one last paper to complete my master's degree.

"You've really backed yourself into a corner. Even considering you have a break coming up, you need to have this practicum finished in the next six weeks, or you're looking at summer, or fall—"

"I'm literally out of money. If I don't finish my degree, there goes my position in the fall, which is the only way I'll be able to dig myself out of this hole of debt..."

"Have you thought about why you're so resistant to moving forward with your study of the archetypes?"

I liked Kimbra Moriguchi a lot. She'd held my hand through all of life's ups and downs over the past three years. But she never let me skate past accountability.

"Yeah, I've thought about it. I can't *stop* thinking about it, and now

I'm stuck. Frozen. As a woman in the tail end of her maiden phase, according to the literature anyway, I'm supposed to be excited about creating and preparing myself to move into the mother phase. I can't get past my own bullshit to create, much less consider nurturing anyone else. I'm a lesbian who doesn't want children of my own, so what does that say about the next stage of my life? I think I'm having an existential crisis way before my time."

Kimbra gave me a sad smile. "I know it's overwhelming. You're about the fifth student I've had in this semester who's going through the same stuff. How about this? You're going home for break, aren't you?"

"Yeah. My aunt and uncles are expecting me." And expecting answers to the "what the hell are you doing with your life" question.

"Your aunt is still raising children, correct? So she could be your interview about the mother phase of the feminine archetypes. Are there any women in your hometown you'd consider part of the crone archetype?"

And then, inspiration hit. *Finally.*

"You know what? We had the strangest thing happen last summer, right before I came back to school." Kimbra had always loved to hear my tales of small-town America. To her, a born-and-bred city girl from San Francisco, my life experience was almost mythical in its cliched existence.

I'd had to vigorously defend my first grad-level paper on the survival of the small-town lifestyle because I'd argued that there were still places in America where you could find the farmers chatting on a bench in front of the drug store, no traffic lights, barn-raising parties, churches full on Sundays, and homes where folks never locked their doors.

I went so far as to create a whole multimedia presentation of life back in Calaveras, and my class had gotten a kick out of it. It also cemented me a place in Kimbra's good graces.

"Do tell," she said, sipping her herbal tea. She loved to share her latest concoctions with me. Her office smelled like brown sugar and lemon, and knowing she'd have a warm drink for me and a place to talk made this harrowing phase of my life a little easier.

"So you've seen those Rowdy Real Estate posts, right? The ones where they show these homes that are outrageous? Well, Calaveras happens to have one of those. You ever heard of country singer Owen Buckley? Well, after he made gazillions of dollars off that one song, 'Boots and Booties'—"

"Which seems to have finally died a death of obscurity. That song was the most painful earworm."

"It was, but it made him stupid rich and he built a massive compound in Calaveras. A huge house on seven acres. It did a lot for our little town. Tourism picked up, and Buckley donated money to build a youth community center and then a skate park. Can't say I was mad about it. But anyway, he built this big ole funky house, filled it with all kinds of bizarre things supposedly, although I've never been inside. He ended up moving to Nashville, though, after only living there two years. Commuting was too much of a pain because he had to drive two hours to the nearest airport.

"Anyway, the house has been empty for about six years and someone bought it over the summer! An older woman, single. No one knows much about her. She moved in and barely anyone has seen or talked to her. She gets all of her food and supplies delivered, and what she can't, she buys at the local drug store, but she goes in right before closing or when the store opens to avoid running into people."

"If that's the case, how do you know if she's a crone?"

My cheeks flushed. "She's got silver hair? Like, wild silver hair. That's practically all I know about her. Well, that and she's armed. Mr. Tompkins, whose property is adjacent to hers, kept complaining to my uncle—he's one of five police officers in town—that he hears gunfire from her property, but my uncle Ernie said she's within her rights to have a gun range on her property. Anyway, the whole town's been titillated about her since she arrived, making up stories. There's even an Instagram account that posts sightings of her."

"Sounds like a nightmare for her," Kimbra said, and that made sense, but Kimbra had repeatedly explained that she lived in a place where new people came and went and most people didn't know their neighbors.

"All part of small-town living, even if one buys a wacky mansion and wants to be a recluse."

"If you're going to make your deadline—and you know I believe you can do it—you need to get her to talk to you. You have a way of disarming people with that folksy charm you can put on like a uniform for a tour guide at a national park." She snickered as I sputtered in protest.

"Folksy charm? I'll have you know that the panel for my thesis presentation on the role of true crime aficionados in female-presenting empowerment would disagree with me being charming at all."

Kimber laughed heartily. "Because you invited a panel of old white men in law enforcement and then belittled their attempts at justifying their lack of meaningful action regarding victim advocacy. *I* was cheering you on, but I think the balls of every man in that packed hall shriveled a little."

"I was pretty damned proud of that presentation. Too bad I haven't found any police departments willing to take a look at my ideas."

"Patience, grasshopper," she said. "Don't give up just yet. I think you should take your presentation on the road. Speak at law enforcement conferences and public health forums. Someone is bound to see your proposal as viable."

My thesis project, which focused on the need for more entry points for victim advocacy in crimes against female-presenting persons, was the culmination of my grief after losing my mother. I could talk about the Violence Against Women Act all day long, but it was still incredibly painful to discuss how it felt to hold my mother's hand as she bled out on the floor of her living room after an ex-boyfriend got out of prison, returned to Calaveras, and showed up at our house.

"Go home and use that fire to ignite your passion for deconstructing the feminine archetypes." She snorted at my expression. "Don't let a little old lady keep you from your degree, huh?"

CHAPTER
TWO

TURNED OUT, Rosalind Ford was no little old lady.

As I stalked her through the aisles of the local CVS just before closing, I couldn't help but notice several pertinent details:

She was not old, despite her wild mane of long, curly, silver hair.

She was ripped, her arms and shoulder muscles perfectly toned beneath her tank top and the stretched-out and frayed, knitted sweater that hung off her shoulders. She wore cut-off jeans that hit her mid-calf and were more a tangle of loose threads than actual denim. Her outfit was finished off by a pair of ratty black work boots that were unlaced at the tops and looked too big for her.

In my hurry to make the four-hour drive home in time for my aunt's Saturday night dinner, I'd forgotten my facewash and moisturizer for my eczema, which was threatening to take over due to my current stress level. Instead of rushing, I took my time watching Rosalind cursing to herself in the stationary aisle. She wore dark glasses despite it being 8:47 p.m.

"Brandon, I thought you ordered more Post-its for me," she hollered to the assistant manager. I used to babysit Brandon, and I was trying really hard to avoid him seeing me.

Her voice was Angie-Harmon-deep and husky. It curled my damn toes. Her olive complexion was darkened by the sun and smooth. She had faint tan lines on her shoulders, a few lines on her face, and thin lips…but man. She was gorgeous.

"I did, Ms. Ford. They're in back. Hold on, I'll grab them for you."

I was so busy watching her, I didn't move in time, and when Brandon barreled around the corner in a hurry to fetch the mysterious woman's supplies, he ran right into me.

"Aurelia Muse! Boy, it's been a while. How are you?"

The gangly teenager pulled me in for a hug, and I stumbled forward into him.

"Brandon. Hi." I patted his back clumsily.

He pulled back with a smile. "I didn't know you were in town! Let me grab Ms. Ford's items and we can catch up."

"That's all right, I—"

But he'd already trotted through the doors to the store room.

"Muse? As in Deputy Sheriff Muse?"

"My uncle," I said, turning to face her. My…*crone*? She was a little taller than me, slender but strong, as opposed to my soft, academic body. Drop-dead stunning. "I'm Elia."

I held out my right hand, all polite like the small-town girl I'd been. In the before-times.

She looked down at my hand, then at the load of notebooks, Post-its, Sharpies and tape she had clutched to her chest.

"Tell Ernie I said to come by tomorrow."

I started to ask her a question…but what would I say to her? "Hey, you're a woman of a certain age, can I interview you about being a crone?" I hadn't mapped out how I could get her talking, but that sounded hella rude. Should I tell her what I was doing, or maybe just try a normal conversation? Should I ask on a curious getting-to-know-you premise? You know, two single women becoming acquainted over coffee? Or drinks? God, that would sound like I was hitting on her. Was she even gay? Sometimes I was a disaster at peopling.

And what did she want with my uncle? My mother's youngest brother, Ernesto Muse was one of the last innocent good ole boys left in this world. One of the last optimistic and generally positive cops left in this world. He'd spent four years working for the Stockton Police

Department before coming back to Calaveras to take up the small-town cop life.

"Here you are, Ms. Ford. A case of rainbow Post-its. That's a lot of—"

"Thanks." She cut him off and frowned at me before she carried her load over to the check stand by the front door.

"Just let me know if you need more. I can put in orders at any time. We usually get the stuff in within a couple of days—"

"Thanks. I'm all set."

Brandon continued to attempt conversation with her but she was on her way out before he could even thank her for shopping at CVS.

"Man, she's a tough nut to crack," he said to me as he reached for my items. "She comes in at least once a week and cleans out the stationary aisle. What could she possibly need to do with all that stuff?"

"Some people prefer that analog life, what can I say?"

He grinned at me. "You look great. How's the big city treating you?"

I laughed. "If by big city you mean graduate school, it's kicking my ass. I'm almost done though."

"Oh yeah? Then what?"

I blew out a breath and went to slide my debit card into the kiosk... where I found hers.

"Oh no," I said, pulling hers out. "Let me see if she's still here." I left my things with Brandon and ran out to the parking lot, but there were no cars there besides mine. I walked back in.

"I can take this to my uncle," I said, suddenly realizing I'd found my way into a conversation with her. "Since apparently he's going to see her tomorrow?"

Brandon was just at that young enough age that he didn't question me, the deputy's niece. It was a good thing for Ms. Ford that I was only a nosy, desperate grad student and not a dangerous person.

I finished purchasing my things, promised Brandon I'd say goodbye before I left town, and pointed my old Ranger pickup to Uncle Ernie's house. I arrived in the middle of poker night with his buddies.

"You bring beer, kid?" He pulled me in for a hug and kissed my hair.

"Of course. I grabbed some of that hard cider from Fieldwork that you liked last time you came to visit me." I'd packed up a case in a cooler before leaving my San Leandro apartment that morning for the drive up to Calaveras. It was my ticket to the guys' card game, and I didn't want to miss out on all the gossip, especially now.

"Good girl," Uncle Ernie said, tugging on my longish dark brown hair. Ernie was more like a big brother than an uncle. He was only eight years older than me. He'd lived with Mom and me when he was a teenager. Their parents thought he should be helping his sister and his niece. He didn't mind one bit. Despite being a teen single mom, Cristina Muse had things under control, so while he did watch me occasionally, he ended up with more freedom than he would have had with his Mexican mother—my abuela Bonita—watching his every move.

Papa Herman was a white man, a retired career Marine, so that meant their house was full of rules growing up and both kids had been ready for freedom by the time they hit their teens.

Mom may not have planned on having a baby at sixteen, but she graduated early, got a good job working for the County of Calaveras, and Abuela watched me during the day. As much as Papa was frustrated with his children's choices, he loved me. I could do no wrong in his eyes, unlike Mom, Uncle Ernie, and Uncle Teddy.

"Girl, where's that beer?" Uncle Teddy called out from the poker table, where he was shuffling the cards. "You know your Auntie Rachel won't let me have it at the house."

Auntie Rachel ran her teetotaler home with the efficiency of a practiced stay-at-home mother of four. Teddy followed Papa into the Marines, but an injury in the line of duty sidelined his military career. Now he spent his days giving tattoos and selling his art in his busy shop downtown, sneaking beer wherever he could get it.

"I know. I gotchoo." I'd moved in with Teddy and Rachel after Mom died because they had the space—a converted attic in their turn-of-the-century home—and they wanted me to have a home base in

Calaveras. You know, in hopes I would return after I finished school. That wasn't likely to happen, but I appreciated the effort.

I wheeled the cooler into the kitchen, pulled out four of Fieldworks' best brews, and brought them in for Ernie, Teddy, and their two buddies, Tony and Angel.

"Órale, Elia, ven aquí con las cervezas!"

"Yeah, yeah." I was used to the razzing I got from these guys.

"Looking good," Angel said as he stood to hug me and accept a hard cider. "Still gay?"

"Lo siento, Angel. Sí. I still love women."

He made a ridiculous show of being disappointed as I hugged Tony and handed him his cider. "Rainbow shit? Do they only have gay beer down there in the Bay? Maybe if you drank some tequila it would straighten you out."

I groaned as he winked at me. "Thanks, but can you blame me for only liking women? If I were into guys, I'd be sitting home alone on Saturday nights while you fools play cards."

Their razzing was the only negativity I'd experienced coming out, and it never felt negative. During my college visits—especially after losing my mom—they'd all stepped up and made me feel like one of the guys.

They all laughed as I perched on the arm of the couch, the movement reminding me of my stolen property. I reached into my hip pocket and held the card out.

"Ernie, I'm supposed to tell you that Ms. Ford would like you to come see her tomorrow."

"So she gave you her credit card?"

"No, she told me to tell you, then she left the card in the slot at the store. I told Brandon I'd give it to you."

Ernie frowned. "He should have kept it, locked it in the store safe, rather than trust some random chick—ouch!"

I didn't care if he was a deputy or the damn king of Spain, I smacked him upside the head. "I'll have you know I used to babysit Brandon and his little sisters. I'm trustworthy."

"Man, that vieja loves you, Ernesto," Tony said. He made kissing sounds at Ernie, who flicked a cashew at him.

"She's a lesbian, dumbass." Ernie ran his thumb over the credit card numbers and frowned. "She's a former cop, you know that?"

The guys got quiet around the table.

"No shit," Teddy said. "I knew you'd been up there a couple times talking to her. Is she loca like they say?"

"Nah," Ernie said, taking a drink of the cider and giving a groan of approval. "I won't say a whole lot, cause it's her business, but let's just say she's been through it. Sucks that people here are treating her like a freak show rather than a neighbor, you know?"

"She's always cool when I see her, like she says 'thank you' when I drop off her mail and shit," Tony said with a shrug. "Saw her out there cleaning spray paint off her wall the other day."

Ernie swore under his breath. "Some asshole kids tagged her place, calling her a bruja."

"A witch?" I felt for the woman. There were a lot of kids around Calaveras with nothing better to do, but that slur hit close to home. In my studies, I'd done a lot of research on how that particular label was used to control women, take power from them, and how many women had started to reclaim it, practicing various forms of witchcraft as an act of defiance. A way to take their power back. I was all for that type of empowerment. Fuck the patriarchy.

Well, my brothers and these two weirdos were okay, but the rest could kiss my ass.

"It's bullshit," Teddy said, dealing the cards. "You want in, Elia?"

I held up a hand. "I promised Natalia and Miguelito I'd tuck them in tonight." The eldest two of Rachel and Teddy's kids knew me the best, as I'd been around when they were little. Lealie and Oscar were born after I left for college. I hated missing out on the early times with them. I loved the littles so much, which was another reason I was torn about finishing my degree program and taking a faculty position. I'd only see them over breaks. I'd miss out on so much.

"They love it when you're home," Teddy said with a warm smile. "We all do. Especially when you bring the good brew. If you'd just come home, we could make it ourselves."

"You know it." *And I would love to spend time with you.*

We toasted each other, and I watched as they all played shitty hands. In all these years, they were still the worst poker players I'd ever seen. "Maybe y'all should go out to the casino and take some lessons," I finally said after five hands of trash.

"What, you can play better? Bring it," Angel said, but I took one last swig of my cider and stood from the couch.

"Not tonight. The kids are waiting on me. You guys still play Wednesdays too?"

They grumbled that yes, they did, and then got back to shit-talking each other. I said my goodbyes a few minutes later and Ernie followed me out.

"I don't suppose you'd take me with you when you go out to her place tomorrow, would you?"

Ernie raised an eyebrow. "She's a little old for you, don't you think?"

I socked him in the gut, and he laughed. "I'll tell you why, and then you tell me if I should go or not."

He crossed his arms over his chest in his cop stance.

"I need to interview a woman of a certain age for my very last practicum. I have to do this for my degree."

"Why her? Aren't there other old women in town?"

"I don't want it to be tainted by my history with them. I'm already talking to Auntie Rachel, but I need someone…beyond childbearing years. That doesn't mean old. I don't know if she'll even talk to me, but—"

"She might. She's really cool. Been through hell, though. Her fiancé disappeared while she was in the middle of a wrongful termination lawsuit, I can tell you that much, as it's public record. But Elia, I'm the only person in town she talks to, so I don't want to upset her. She's had enough people be assholes to her since she came to town."

"I swear, I just want to meet her. Make the introduction and then if she wants me gone, I'll leave her alone and go talk to one of the old women at Casa De Oro. Auntie Rachel volunteers over there, she'll know someone." But I didn't want to talk to some random old woman.

I wanted to talk to *her*. Rosalind Ford.

"All right. I'll pick you up at ten. She doesn't get up early. She's kind of a night owl."

"Great. Should I bake for her? Take her some of abuelita's mole sauce?"

"Nah, then she'll be suspicious. I'll tell her the truth, that you're doing a ride-along with me, you know, what you need to be doing for your *other* project." He raised an eyebrow. "You're still working on your proposal, aren't you? It's such a good idea."

"I am, I swear. After I graduate, I'll have more time."

"All right. I'll pick you up in the morning."

"Thank you. Want me to make you breakfast?"

He gave a sheepish grin. "Please?"

I shook my head. "Someday you need to find someone to cook for you."

He shrugged. "But you're so good at it."

"Wow, what, are we going to be the old spinsters together?"

His eyes widened a little too excitedly. "We *could*…if you came home. Man, I miss you. It's not the same without you here."

I sighed and hugged him tight again. I did miss my family, but I'd worked so hard for a career in academia. *Shouldn't I see it through?*

"I don't know what I'm doing. I'll be screwed if I don't finish this practicum though, so please, help me talk to her?"

"All right, but watch your step. She'll freeze up quick if she thinks you're like everyone else."

"Like *what* like everyone else?"

"Nosy."

CHAPTER
THREE

I GOT UP EARLY, made chocolate chip pancakes and bacon for the littles, and then made a big batch of breakfast burritos for Ernie, as well as some to take to Rosalind. Food helped people open up, no matter what Ernie said. At least that had always been my experience, and I was a damn good cook. I learned from my abuelita.

I showered, straightened my naturally wavy hair—which brought out the auburn highlights, thanks to my mixed heritage—and dressed in tan leggings, a long, white, sleeveless shirt, and Chucks. My skin was so pale, though. I needed some sun this week, that was for damned sure.

"Auntie Rachel? I'm headed out with Ernie for a bit, but I'll be back later in case you and Teddy want to go out for a bit? Catch a movie?"

Rachel sat on the couch with her Kindle and a cup of coffee. "Maybe. But the thought of getting dressed today seems like too much work. I kinda want to read all day."

I laughed. "Then you should do that. Teddy will keep the kids busy and I'll cook dinner."

She smiled up at me. "I'm so glad you're here. We all miss you."

I squeezed her shoulder. "I've missed you too. And the kids. Man, they change so much when I'm gone."

She raised an eyebrow at me but sipped her coffee.

"I know, I know. I'll be back later."

I grabbed the bag with the burritos and mole sauce and met Ernie on the street in front of the house. Rachel and Teddy's place was two blocks off the main street of the town, which had been around since the gold rush. Many of the houses and buildings downtown had survived, but the population had only made a comeback in the past twenty years from its heyday. It was less touristy than neighboring towns, like Murphys or Angels Camp, which had become popular for their wine-tasting offerings from local vineyards, but it had an equally rustic charm.

I did miss that charm when I was in the Bay Area. I loved knowing that everyone here knew me, even if that meant they knew the worst of my life. I sometimes wondered why I'd been in such a rush to leave.

"Oh, man, that smells so good," Ernie said as I climbed into his cruiser.

"You want yours now or are you going to sit someplace and eat this like a civilized person? I made the mole sauce, so—"

"I got this."

He drove us across town to Mark Twain Park, where our little community gathered for all kinds of festivals that we've been cele-brating for at least a century. Snail races, homely dog pageants, and Halloween parades, along with Octoberfest, Fourth of July, Frog Jumping and on and on. The picnic area was well-maintained and fairly empty, since the various church congregations in town were still in session. Ernie carried his burrito over to a table in the sunshine, and I sat across from him.

"So how is it that you've struck up a friendship—"

"An acquaintance. I told you that Mr. Tompkins kept complaining about her shooting, right? Seriously, she's using the area farthest back on her property and well away from him. She's within her rights, and it's not like she's doing it every day or anything. When I went over to talk to her the first time…" he began with a smile. He took a bite of the burrito and his eyes rolled back in his head. The sounds coming from him were ridiculous. "She was real short with me at first, but then she was like, 'I've been where you've been. I'm sorry this is creating more work for you.' I reassured her that Tompkins complained about Buckley's noise way more often, which led to her asking about Owen Buckley, and letting me know about some of the more bizarre things she'd found in the house."

"Oh my God, did she give you a tour? I've always wondered about the bits of the house that weren't shown in the magazine spreads."

He laughed and finished chewing. "Yeah, she showed me around. Not all of the place. She said there were still rooms she hadn't spent any time in. She signed an agreement with Buckley's manager that if she came across any intellectual property, she'd pass it along. She also said that if there was anything they wanted, they had six months to claim it or she was going to auction it off for charity."

"That's so wild! I can't imagine living someplace where you don't know every last thing you have in your house. Mom...well, she kept our place sparse, never liked clutter, and Auntie Rachel is like that. My place is miniscule. There aren't any hiding places."

Ernie took a sip of water. "Think you're going to stay there?"

I slumped in my seat. "I don't know. I thought I would. I was offered a faculty position in the fall, that is if I finish my damned degree on time."

"That's great, mija. But?"

"But...I don't know! I feel like I'm still learning, you know? Growing. I don't know that I'm ready. I'll be like all the profs in undergrad that I couldn't stand because they'd been in their positions for decades and hadn't had actual contact with the subjects they were teaching. And like, what does a twenty-five-year-old have to offer to people who've been out there living their lives?"

"Not to push either way, but you *have* been through more than the majority of students you'll be teaching."

Had I, though? Sure, I'd been a victim of trauma on more than one occasion, but so had millions of other people, especially those who identify as female, trans, or non-binary. I was no one special. Perhaps I'd thought that by allowing my trauma to fuel my fire in academic pursuits, I was using my pain to bring about good, but was that true? Or was it a way to hide?

"Maybe my experience and skills could be put to use in a better capacity. Maybe I should wait until *I'm* a woman of a certain age and have a bit more life experience under my belt. Then I'd be a better candidate."

He shrugged and finished the last of his burrito. "Sounds like the school thinks you're a good candidate now if they offered you the position."

"Maybe."

"And maybe you're having a bit of imposter syndrome."

"Maybe."

He laughed. "And maybe I still want you to come work with me."

"Ahhhhh, the truth finally!"

He threw his wadded-up burrito wrapper at me. "Come on, you know you'd be a great cop, and we could use a female-identifying officer. And I could use someone I trust at my back." He gave a small shrug. "I want you to do whatever is going to make you happy, El, you know that. No harm in keeping your options open."

"I know. You know Abuelita would have had a cow."

His smile turned sad. "Your papa too. But they'd be proud of you no matter what you do. We're all proud of you. You're a survivor, El."

I rolled my eyes at that. "Enough, already. Now, how should I play this visit? Should I come right out and ask if I can interview her?"

Ernie polished off his can of water and his brows met in the middle. "Let's see what mood she's in today."

And with that, he cleaned up his mess and radioed that he was code 10-62—meeting a citizen—at the Ford place.

At which point the dispatcher asked, "Which place?"

Ernie heaved an exaggerated sigh, gave the proper address, and the dispatcher answered "10-4."

"They'd prefer to still call it Buckley's house, but he's long gone. Roz deserves better than the town treating her like some freaky shut-in or a witch."

"I'm sure you're right," I said. I couldn't wait to meet her for real, on her own somewhat-legendary turf.

CHAPTER
FOUR

LIKE EVERYONE ELSE IN CALAVERAS, I'd ridden my bike by the Buckley house during construction and after Owen Buckley moved in. We'd been told by our parents to stay away, to give the man his peace, but we were nosy. We wanted to know if it was true there was a waterslide that went from the top floor all the way down to the pool.

Sadly, we couldn't see that from the road. I knew better than to hop the fence and sneak around. Papa had warned me not to, and Mom threatened me with perpetual punishment if I put one toe over that property line, and that was enough to keep me away.

Eventually, Buckley opened the grounds to the public for a few special occasions, and we were disappointed to see that the pool was actually indoors and couldn't be seen from the outside at all. I'd fallen in love with the gardens, however, and the roses had been some of the best-smelling flowers I'd ever encountered.

Pre-teen Aurelia was internally squealing with delight that I might finally catch a glimpse inside the place.

When we pulled up to the gate, Ernie entered a code and the gates opened.

I was saddened to see that the gorgeous landscaping Buckley had kept up, even after he'd left for Nashville, was overgrown. The flowers needed deadheading, the roses were nearly overrun with passion-flower vines, and the lawns were overgrown. Poppies sprouted from every corner of the yard, brightening the space with pops of orange that gave me hope the gardens could still be saved. Angel's brother ran a gardening service. Maybe Ernie could convince her to get them out here.

Ernie parked the cruiser to the right of the house in the circular driveway, in front of the tennis courts. I could see around to the back of the house from this angle. Rosalind was sitting on a lounge chair on the back patio, which I remembered had been done in large mosaic panels. She wore a huge floppy hat like the kind you might see in a European travel brochure. When I opened the cruiser door, I could hear music pouring out of the house. I recognized The Ramones. So she liked punk. *All right.*

"Think Mr. Tompkins can hear the music at his place?" I asked as I walked beside Ernie.

He snorted. "I'm tempted to tamper with his hearing aids so he'll leave the poor woman alone."

I raised my eyebrows. "You wouldn't."

He shrugged. "She's got good taste in music at least. Hey, Roz," he called out, in case she hadn't heard us pull in.

She turned in her chair and waved to him.

"Hold on, let me turn it down." She pointed a remote at the window and the music faded to a low roar. "I've still got to figure out how to hook my phone up to the Bluetooth speakers that are sprinkled around the garden. The tech that country bumpkin left was just advanced enough at the time he installed it to now be barely work-able." She stood from her chair and dusted peanut shells off her knit overalls.

Then she noticed me.

"Didn't know you had a deputy, Deputy."

Ernie smiled at her and shook her hand. "Roz, this is my niece—"

"Elia. We've met." She had a blank look on her face, but something in her eyes twinkled when she said my name. I swear I wasn't imag-ining it. But it seemed like the kind of twinkle that came before mischief. The good kind of twinkle. *Hmm.*

"You left your credit card at the store last night," I blurted out. "I tried to catch you, but you were already gone."

Ernie pulled the card out of his shirt pocket and handed it to her.

"Thanks," she said, frowning at the card. "Guess I was distracted." She glanced at me and then she looked square at Ernie. "You hear anything?"

He shook his head slowly. "'Fraid not. I'll keep trying."

A crease appeared between her brows, but then it disappeared. "I need help with that other thing," she said, her eyes darting to me.

Ernie stood straighter. "Oh, well, you're in luck. I brought Elia along. She's way better than me at computer stuff."

She crossed her arms over her chest. I was momentarily mesmerized by her long fingers grasping her bronzed biceps. Her skin was so, so lovely, and her hands were—

"What makes you qualified?"

"For?" I obviously missed something.

She dropped her arms and turned for the house. "Might as well come in. I'm dead in the water unless I get this damn thing to work."

I looked to Ernie, and he simply gestured for me to follow her in.

Her bare feet slapped on the patio and then on the wood floors in the room we entered, which could, I suppose, be called a great room, only it was mostly empty. The cavernous wooden space resembled a saloon from the Old West, complete with loads of antlers mounted everywhere. I could see a modern stainless-steel kitchen through a set of saloon-type doors, but the large space was only occupied by a long solid-wood bar with about twenty stools tucked underneath.

"I know there's a lot more I can accomplish if I can just figure out how to get these extra monitors set up."

We came to a doorway with more double doors and she pushed through. The room on the other side was a fairly normal living room, except there was deep green shag carpet all around and big, bulky leather furniture that obviously a country dude would pick out, and the wallpaper had...cowboy hats and tumbleweeds on it? Did he actually pay someone to decorate this place?

"I'm telling you, Roz, I can have the consignment shop come and pick up any of this...furniture." Ernie curled his lip. I was grateful he'd said something. If he would have complimented the room, I would have barfed all over the green shag.

She waved a hand and kept walking. "Eventually. His six months are nearly up and then I'll do something. I'd like to have an auction, but that's work I don't have time for. The carpet's gotta go, though. I bought one of those vacuum robot things and it got tangled, this shit's so tall."

"I mean, they weren't made to tackle the grasslands." *Fuck*, I didn't mean to say that out loud.

Ernie snickered. Rosalind stopped in front of a section of mirrored wall. I couldn't tell if I'd offended her by her expression.

"*You* buy a house this size and then let's see how quickly *you* address its less-than-appealing elements." She smirked and then waved her hand in front of the mirror. "Shit." She stepped two steps to the left and tried again. "Dammit." Four steps to the right, she waved her hand, and a keypad appeared to light up behind the glass.

"*Say whaaat?*" I muttered, stunned. She punched in a code, messed it up twice, and then finally got it on the last try. A seam appeared in the glass, and the wall moved back about a foot, opening up a dark hallway.

"Pretty neat, huh?" Rosalind said. "Only problem is, for a safe room, it's not practical. If you mark the spot where the keypad is, you've given away its existence. And if you have to hunt for it in an emergency, that's precious seconds lost. Eventually I'll switch out the dumb keypad. It doesn't pick up touch very well anymore. I'll get a thumbprint scanner or something. Anyway, I'm set up in here for now, but I'm gonna need more space soon."

She led us down a short, dark hallway, and I was just about to whip out my phone for a light source when she flipped a switch.

There we were, in a narrow Cape Canaveral-style computer control room. There were about twenty screens on one wall, showing views of the whole property. On the opposite wall, there was a table with three large computer monitors still in their boxes, two keyboards, three mice, and a boatload of notebooks, folders, and Post-its strewn all over the surface.

There was also a fridge stashed in here, a cot, and a wardrobe. The room, while small, was still bigger than my apartment in San Leandro.

"The operation is growing, huh?" Ernie asked her.

"Word got out. I've got a lot of former contacts who are taking advantage of my free time. The problem is that everything is much more sophisticated now, and I'm used to a more tactile approach."

"How many cold cases are you working on?"

My ears perked up.

She sighed. "I've lost count. I've got two more rooms full of file boxes and crime scene recreations, boards, you name it. I've got the space, but it's getting too big for just me. I thought putting it on the computer might help, but it's not organic for me to work that way. Plus, the fastest wi-fi is in here, but I can't stand being cooped up in here with no windows." She threw her hands up. "I can't even hook up these monitors, let alone get them all working the way I want."

"El and I can take a look," Ernie said, raising his eyebrows at me.

"Sure," I said. "I run a research program in the Women's Studies department at East Bay University. I've had to become my own IT person."

She looked between us and raised her eyebrows. "Have at it."

It took less than an hour for Ernie and me to get everything hooked up properly and for him to show Roz how she could use each monitor to run certain programs and be able to look between them easily. As we were getting things set up, my curiosity grew. She was working on cold cases? Like for actual police departments or on her own, I wondered? Ernie asked her a lot of questions, and I tried to pay attention without seeming like I was too involved.

"I've checked, there was nothing after she left. I've talked to every family member and co-worker I can come across, but no one has heard from her. It's been two years and nothing."

"Have you tried Websleuths or Reddit Bureau of Investigation? A social media scrub?"

I'd been using some zip-ties I found in a box on the floor to clean up her cords and spoke without thinking whether or not my contribution would be welcome. I crawled out from under the table to find her staring at me. I'd expected snark, but her face was soft, and she'd removed her dark glasses to reveal the most incredible blue-green eyes I'd ever seen.

"I've looked at Websleuths a time or two, but it's so complicated. And Reddit? Isn't that just for conspiracy theorists?"

"It's a mixed bag of folks. Sometimes you can find good info there."

Roz looked at Ernie and then back at me. "How do you know all this stuff?"

Ernie spoke before I could string words together.

"El did her master's thesis on resources and programs to help empower female-identifying victims of crime and their families. She's got a lot of great ideas—"

"That I'm sure were really popular with law enforcement?" Roz chuckled and set down a stack of folders she was moving. "That's the kind of shit that got me in hot water in my department."

I shrugged. "It was a strong thesis but I could see their arguments. I'm still working out the kinks."

Roz nodded at me for several beats. "Right. Well, thanks for helping me get this set up. Maybe I'll actually make some headway. Thank you for coming out."

Ernie tipped his head to his shoulder and listened to his radio for a moment, then stepped out of the room to talk to dispatch.

I was running out of time to ask her if I could interview her for my project. I was just about to say something when Ernie poked his head back in.

"I gotta head into town," he said. "El, I can drop you back at home."

"Actually," Roz said. "Elia, would you mind sticking around for a bit? I can run you home later?"

I looked at my watch. I'd planned on helping out Rachel with the kids, but she'd made it clear she didn't want to go out. Maybe I *could* stick around. "If it's no trouble."

She rolled her eyes. "Thanks, Ernie. I'll bring her home."

He raised his eyebrows, tapped his fingers on the doorway twice. "You sure?"

It seemed like that was more for me than for Roz.

I nodded. "It's no problem. I'll text Rachel."

"All right then." He waved and turned to leave as his radio squawked loudly.

"Your uncle is the most overworked and underappreciated cop I've ever known, and that's saying something." Roz turned her intense gaze on me, and my chest fluttered. "I don't know what you know about me."

I was startled. "Uh, you were a cop? You bought this house? That's about all."

She nodded and crossed her arms over her chest again. Her hands distracted me for a moment once more, but I tried to keep my eyes on hers.

"Nothing about the money, huh?"

I shrugged. "Inheritance? Win the lotto?"

"Wrongful termination and defamation lawsuit."

"Oh. Wow. Okay."

"Yeah," Roz said. "Right. Well, here's the deal. I had a really fucked-up situation at my previous job. I was the lead detective on the case of a trans kid who was assaulted. A series of odd turns happened, and they took the case away from me. I had a little pull with command, so I kept it, but when they found out my suspects were a couple of off-duty cops and I refused to let it slide, they fired me."

"That's awful," I said, my stomach clenching. "That must have been horrible for you."

She turned to look at the computer screens showing footage from cameras set up around the property. "Horrible for a lot of people."

"I'm glad that you were compensated at least. Although, no offense, you could have gone anywhere. Why Calaveras?"

"Why Women's Studies?" She'd turned to face me, and we were standing so close, the movement stirred the air next to my bare shoulder and I broke out in goose bumps.

"Why?"

She nodded.

I stood a little taller. "Did Ernie tell you about my mom?"

She nodded again.

"Then you know."

"Maybe. Depends on what you do with it. Freaking poetry? Art? Something like that?"

I laughed at her disdain. "What would be wrong with that?"

"Nothing," she said with her own laugh. "Other than it's boring as shit."

"I'm not a huge fan of poetry, so no. My work has been geared toward helping female-identifying people overcome trauma. Resiliency, advocacy, and empowerment have been my focus."

"Interesting. I'm a fan of all three. And that's kind of the answer to your question."

"Why here?"

"I guess I, too, went through a traumatic experience after years of helping other people deal with trauma, and while I needed some time to be angry and selfish, I'm ready to get back to work."

"Yeah? As a police officer?"

She wrinkled her nose. "I think I can be of more use helping departments as a consultant. I'm good at what I do. I had one of the best closure rates of any detective in my precinct in Denver, but I decided that I'd rather do what I'm good at without giving up too much of myself."

"That's very resilient of you," I said with a grin.

"Touché," she said. "But I'm realizing I'm in over my head."

"How do you mean?"

"Exhibit A," she says, gesturing to the room around her. "I have nearly unlimited resources at my disposal, but I'm not the most organized person. I was fortunate to always have partners who were very organized, but now it's just me and…yeah. I know there are programs out there—"

Something caught her eye on the camera feed, and she walked closer to one of the monitors.

"Those little shits," she said, and she darted out of the room.

"Roz?" I called out to her. I looked up at the screen, and in the bright midday sun, there were two pre-teen boys I didn't recognize. They had ridden up to the front gates on their bikes and were pulling spray cans out of backpacks. There was no sound to the feed but I could tell they were laughing.

"Those little shits!" I echoed.

They were just about to start tagging the stone wall when suddenly they looked up, soundlessly screamed, and then went running toward their bikes. They pedaled away as if the Hounds of Hell were chasing them.

Roz returned a few moments later, cackling.

"What happened?" I asked, as she seemed quite pleased with herself.

"I may be lousy with computers, but I did pick up a few skills in the department before being fired—including piloting drones." She pulled out her phone, tapped it a few times, and then stood next to me, holding it out. "Exhibit B."

The drone she'd used had a camera feed that she could view on her phone.

"I used a voice modifier to give them a little scare, and I attached a laser pointer to the drone...and pointed it right at their scrawny little chests."

I covered my mouth. "Oh my God." I couldn't help laughing. Served them right.

"I kinda don't blame the kids for starting rumors about me. After the first time I caught them on camera trying to climb over the gate, I started hiding out in the bushes in a skeleton mask and jumping out at them. One of the kids' parents called Ernie to complain about me. First Tompkins, then the kids. He didn't know what to do with me. He came out here all frowny, you know how he is."

"I do," I said. My uncle was a damn good cop, but if you didn't know him, you'd take his serious expression as evidence of him being an insufferable prick. He wasn't, thank God. I couldn't handle having a huge dick in the family.

"Once I showed him the footage, he just gave that resigned exhale he does. He asked me for a copy, I sent it to him, and he told me he'd take care of it. He started coming out about once a week after that, checking to make sure everyone was leaving me alone. Then he asked me for help on one of his cases, I asked him for help on another matter... He's the closest thing I have to a friend here."

I smiled. "He's pretty great."

She got that twinkle again. "He told me all about you, by the way. I told him to bring you up here sometime."

"Me? Why?"

She shrugged. "Curiosity. Guess I wanted to meet the Muse who got away from Calaveras."

I snorted. "I guess? I miss it, though."

"Your family misses you, too. At least your uncle. I haven't met the rest of them yet, although apparently I have an open invitation to poker night?"

I laughed. "That's awesome. Just so you know, your money is probably pretty safe because they all suck at cards."

"All right then. Perhaps I'll check it out."

We stood there for a beat longer before she backed away. "Right—"

"So—"

"The thing is—"

"How can I—?"

And we both laughed.

"How can I be of assistance?" I asked, trying to enunciate slowly so I wouldn't trip over my words. We'd definitely had a moment there, but I had no idea how to interpret it.

"Sorry. I've been spending too much time on my own, I think I've forgotten how to converse. I thought I'd be living the dream, you know? By myself, no one to hassle me, well, except for the neighbor. What's the deal with that Tompkins guy anyway?"

"Mr. Tompkins has been a hundred years old my whole life, it seems. The Tompkins family has been in the area probably since the late eighteen hundreds. They used to own the whole area. The state got them to cough up the land for the town so it could be the county seat for Calaveras County. They weren't happy the town wasn't named after them, but at least they got to name a street."

"They did? Where?"

I snorted. "It leads out to the dump from the other side of their property."

Roz threw her head back and laughed. "Serves him right," she said. "I'm sorry, I don't know if you're friends—"

"No, don't worry about it. I don't think there has ever been much love between the Muses and the Tompkins clan."

"Okay. Well, I thought I'd pick your brain about some of the tools you mentioned."

"Oh. Sure. Okay."

She frowned and flicked her hand at me. "I'm not a hundred percent ready to give up my Post-its and bulletin boards, but I need… something. I feel like if I could look at these cases holistically…I don't know. I need a system, and I don't have one and it's driving me nuts. "

"I think I get it. I do. Let's sit and you can walk me through some of your needs. Maybe we can come up with something together."

CHAPTER
FIVE

THREE HOURS LATER, I was on my second Diet Coke and I was surrounded by candy wrappers.

"This way you've got all the things in one place and you can branch off from there."

We'd used a program called Notion to create a workspace for every case she was working on, and I was showing her how to access everything from a single data point.

"You can have a task list, contacts list, a calendar for each case that also links to your main calendar here," I said, clicking over to the master calendar. "You can set reminders here that will connect with the calendar on your phone, so you always have access."

"This is really cool," she said, leaning over my shoulder. "Now, how do I see the whole list of them?"

She automatically reached for the mouse and my hand was still on it.

"Oh, sorry." I pulled my hand back when her skin brushed mine. She smiled down at me. I was close enough to catch the scent on her skin. She smelled like strawberries and cream...and I needed space before I did something stupid.

"Hey, how about we take a break? Can I feed you?"

I turned to look at her and was at eye level with her rosy lips.

"My burritos! *Dammit.*" I turned the chair around, and she stood in front of me with her hands on her hips.

"Excuse me?"

"Oh, I just realized, I left the batch of breakfast burritos I made in Ernie's car. I hope he refrigerated them."

She laughed. "You better text him. It would be criminal to waste a batch of burritos." She grinned and stepped back from my chair.

"Is there…can I use your restroom?"

"Oh, yeah. Sorry. Uh…do you want to use the plain boring one in here or one of the fun bathrooms?"

I laughed. "Fun. Definitely."

She rolled her eyes. "I'm not sure what's more ridiculous, that he built this place or that I bought it. Step right this way."

She led me back through the funky cowboy living room to the saloon and pointed to the right corner.

"Some of the bathrooms in this place…you're taking your life into your hands, but the ones in here are pretty safe."

"How many bathrooms are there?" I asked as I walked toward the side-by-side doors.

"I think ten, not counting these two, but I swear there's one I found once and haven't found again."

"How is that possible?" I muttered to myself as I made it past the bar to a short hallway. There were two doors, each with stick figures of the traditional male and female variety but wearing cowboy hats. But there were also pictures taped to the bathroom doors of what I'd describe as non-binary and/or trans folks. From David Bowie, to Kristen Stewart as Joan Jett, to Harry Styles in a dress. It was the best thing I'd seen about the place so far.

Inside the bathroom was a single stall with a half door made out of wood. When I opened it, I found myself looking at an outhouse-type setup like something you'd see in a horror movie, complete with plastic snakes and scorpions on the bench, on the floor, and even hanging from the ceiling. There was an animal skull hanging over the brass toilet seat in the middle of the bench. I wondered how much of the decor came with the house and what, if any, had been added by the current owner.

Roz was such a paradox. As we worked, she was tough as nails, on task, and completely businesslike in her approach to the cases she was working on. She was mostly focused on missing persons involving women, children, queer and trans folks. We hadn't talked a whole lot about what she was going to be doing, exactly, but I got the sense she was trying to establish her own ways of examining the cases because she didn't trust the systems in place for law enforcement.

But then I recalled the stories she told about messing with the nosy kids, and she seemed like she had a mischievous streak, like she knew how to have a good time. I knew from Ernie that cops tended to goof off when they were between calls, and I'd seen some of their hijinks for myself when I'd visited the station. Roz did not seem like the kind of person who didn't like people and wanted to be isolated.

So why move into this giant house by herself? What happened to her must have been so awful to make her want to literally leave everything behind.

My project loomed, so sure, my internal interrogation had to do with that, but I also wondered on a human level...what was driving her? Helping her just little bit had me wondering, what would it be like to know your purpose and be so good at it, embrace it, and run with it? Maybe that was the major difference between the maiden archetype and that of the mother and the crone.

I washed my hands in the trough sink and looked around. There was a stack of cloth hand towels, and nearby, a small card that said "Use Me," written in Sharpie. After use, I spotted a hole in the wall with a similar sign that said "Abuse Me." I reached out to put the towel into the hole and it was sucked right out of my hands, causing me to shout in surprise.

When I came out of the bathroom, a little shaken, Roz was standing at the end of the hallway laughing.

"Gotcha! I swear, I thought that whole laundry-sucking thing was bullshit when I saw the ads on social media, but it works! I had a system installed when I moved in. You'd think I'd have bigger priorities, I know, but laundry is my least favorite thing ever."

"The reptiles and arthropods were a nice touch." I rubbed my hands on my leggings as I approached her.

"How could I not? If this place is supposed to be an authentic saloon, I thought I'd add some realism."

"Right? I mean, why wouldn't you?" I laughed.

"Right. Well. Hungry?"

"Sure. I don't want to put you out though."

She gave me an incredulous look. "After the work you did? You've saved me countless hours of pouring over papers and slicing up my hands with papercuts. The least I can do is feed you."

She led me around the bar and into the industrial-sized kitchen.

"Wow, this place looks like it could feed an army."

"Probably it could. There's a smaller kitchen on the far side of the house, which is kind of set up like a little mansionette? Like maybe Buckley planned on moving someone in over there at some point, or maybe he just didn't want to walk the half mile over to the saloon. I swear. I have no idea what he was thinking with this place. Which is to say, I often wonder what the hell I was thinking *buying* this place."

"Have to admit I was wondering the same."

She nodded as she opened the fridge. The door was lined with green tea drinks, sparkling water, and canned wine.

"Hmm. Right. Pasta okay? I get meal deliveries. I'm not a huge fan of cooking."

"Whatever you're having."

She grabbed two boxes and popped one in a microwave…and the other in the second microwave. Guess it made sense to have two of everything?

"There's a short answer for the question of why I bought this place and a more involved one. How much time do you have?"

A niggling feeling in the back of my mind let me know this would have been a perfect place to tell her about my practicum. It would have been. But I was riding a high of being privy to knowledge the whole damn town had been desperate for, and I didn't want her to stop talking.

Damn the consequences.

Maybe I don't actually need my master's degree?

"I'm not on a schedule." I'd texted Rachel from the bathroom. She'd told me not to worry about coming back anytime soon.

I want the tea she'd texted.

"Okay. I'll give you the middle ground. After I got fired, which devastated me, by the way. I'd fully planned to work until my pension, and even then I figured I'd still do some sort of public service work. At least I hit my twenty years before they fucked me over. I was forty-two years old when I filed a wrongful termination lawsuit."

"And that was…"

She smirked. "Three years ago. I'd been let go six months before that. Took me a while to see that it was the right thing to do. I come from a cop family. Dad, two brothers, and uncle. They were on my side as much as they could be. Dad supported me filing suit. We talked about it a lot. I showed him case after case of female cops being wrongfully terminated and winning, and my case was even stronger than most. My attorney suggested, and I agreed, that we should seek stupid money."

"The only way to change the system is to make the system hurt," I muttered.

"That's right," she said. "And it's less problematic than saying you want to burn the whole thing to the ground."

I smiled. I so got what she was saying. "Amazing how you have to choose your words carefully around things like that. So you filed the lawsuit, it went to court…did you get stupid money?"

"Ridiculous money. Ludicrous money. And I decided to get the fuck out of Denver. I wanted to go somewhere I was not likely to be known, someplace that was tolerant and diverse and had way better weather than Denver. I sent my attorney on a wild goose chase for a preposterous piece of real estate where I could spread out, have plenty of privacy and space to do whatever the fuck I wanted, and we narrowed it down to five possibilities.

"This was the one that fit all the criteria. Good ole boy Owen was desperate to get out from under this place and accepted an offer that was sizably reduced from his original asking price. My attorney knew this place had been sitting empty for years, and that no one had offered anywhere near enough for him to sell it. It's a ridiculous house, that I bought with ridiculous money, that I received because of a ridiculous situation. I think it's all fitting."

"As long as you're happy," I said, and the moment her eyes shot to mine, I knew I'd pushed it.

"Happy is the lie we tell people who want the simple answer. I'm not looking for happy. I don't know *what* I'm looking for. Appeasement? Acceptance? Acquiescence? Fuck it. At least I'm not angry every minute anymore."

"Not every minute, but still angry?"

She wrinkled her nose and tapped a finger to her cheek. "Maybe once an hour, every forty-five minutes. Like fifteen minutes of every hour? The rest of the time, I've been working on getting this fucking work off the ground, and now that you've gotten me on the right path, I think I can finally make some progress." She took our meals out of the microwaves with hot pads, grabbed some napkins and pointed toward the silverware. "Want to eat in the saloon or out back?"

"Out back sounds good."

"Sweet," she said. "Want to grab drinks? I'll take a Peace Tea."

I opened the fridge door as directed, grabbed her a giant can of sweetened tea and, for myself, an orange-flavored sparkling water. I followed her out onto the back patio, where there was a picnic table. We sat side by side so we could look out over her sprawling piece of land.

"You definitely have one of the most gorgeous views in the county."

She chewed a bite of pasta and nodded. "If this were the good ole days, this would have been an excellent piece of land to fortify because you can see all approaches clearly. No one can sneak up on you with this slight elevation. I love the trees lining the property, they're just tall enough to provide shade but from upstairs, you can see beyond them, where the river runs along the back of the property and then meets up with the lake. You know, I've even got a boat dock out there and Buckley sold me his boats, too. A party boat, and a little fishing boat with a brand-new trolling motor."

"I love those party boats. Papa used to have one when we were kids. I learned how to swim jumping off that boat."

She frowned. "Like, on purpose?"

I shrugged. "Papa was right there. I'd been bugging him to teach me, so once we got out there, I ran past him and jumped in, and he had no choice but to hop in after me. Once was all it took."

She shook her head. "I'm not a strong swimmer. I'd like to be, but I won't be jumping into Frog Lake like a maniac."

"I wasn't a *total* maniac. I was like eight years old. Isn't that typical eight-year-old behavior?"

She closed her eyes, and I laughed at her exasperation.

"Okay, this from the woman who chases kids off with a drone."

"Yeah," she said, taking several pulls on her can. "I'm going to have to come up with something new. They'll tell their little tagger buddies what to expect. I'm thinking of ordering some of those animatronics from the Spirit store. Hide them in the bushes? Maybe those scary zombie babies or the Regan one with the head that spins around. Oh my God, what if she puked pea soup on them?" She cackled, and I almost spit out my pasta.

"How about putting speakers out there and just whispering to them? Uncle Teddy had this thing called an Eviltron that he put in my bedroom when I was a teenager. It would randomly whisper at me, make skittering noises…scared the shit out of me."

"Did you get him back?"

I grinned. "I hid in the backseat of his car at night before he left the shop. He drove home and had just pulled into the driveway when I started talking to him. He almost drove through the garage door! It was great. He checks his backseat every time he gets in the car to this day."

"All right," she said with approval. "You just might make a good accomplice."

We brainstormed other ways to scare off the kids without making Ernie's job harder.

"I probably should quit with the shooting range, get Mr. Tompkins off his back. Maybe I could go to the other side, but then I'm near the winery. They'll probably complain it interferes with their wine tastings or something bougie like that."

I cracked up. "Don't get me wrong, I know the wine industry has done a lot for Calaveras, but I can't tell you how glad I was to get away from all the tourists."

She gave me a serious look and noticed that I'd finished my pasta and was now bending the foil cover into tiny pieces. "That all you wanted to get away from?"

I sighed and slumped a little. "I needed to get out from under the watchful eye of the town. I felt like people were watching me, waiting to see if I would break. Ernie told you that I was home from undergrad when it happened?"

She nodded and then held up a hand. "Wait. Does this story require wine or ice cream?"

I frowned. "Does it require a *choice*?"

She nodded and gestured for me to follow her inside.

"Let's grab both. I'll take you to my favorite room…so far. I still haven't decided."

"Lead the way."

CHAPTER
SIX

"I'M PRETTY SURE, last time I checked, that there was no tropical paradise in Calaveras. No ocean, no sand, and yet…"

There it was. The elusive pool we'd all tried to see all those years. It was incredible. Made to look like an island paradise, there was a whole wall and ceiling of glass, though the glass looking out over her property was frosted for privacy, so even if us bratty little kids would have hopped the fence to come find it, we wouldn't have been able to see anything.

A sound machine gave us the waves and seabirds, and some mellow music wafted out from behind the palm fronds planted around the seating area.

"What is that?"

She stood beside me and looked out into the pool, which had a dark shape in the middle. "What lagoon is complete without its Creature?"

I shook my head. "Of course."

"He's remote control, too. I can make him swim around. It's awesome."

"No doubt."

"This is probably the most ridiculous part of the house, and it's my favorite. I sit here and drink my morning tea, read for a bit, and then a lot of days I end my night here with a drink. It's pretty peaceful, and since it's a saltwater pool, there's no heavy chlorine smell. I'd have hated that, it would permeate the whole damn house."

We sat side by side on lounge chairs facing the pool, which was at least wide enough to do laps, and it had an island in the middle with a movie screen hanging between two palm trees.

"I'm not sure I'd ever leave this room," I said, dropping a foot to the sand and digging my bare toes in. Her eyes tracked my movement as she took another sip of wine from her can.

"That's good. Then we have plenty of time for you to talk." She turned her body sideways to face me, and those giant, intense blue-green eyes focused on me.

I barked out a laugh and nearly spilled my wine. "Is this a new tactic for interrogation? Get the subject liquored up and comfortable?"

"Are you liquored up after a half can of wine? If so, that's sad."

I laughed again but it wasn't free. "I *was* feeling comfortable. I don't like talking about what happened. Not that I can't relay the facts, but it always changes things with people after they hear about it."

"Of course it does—"

I held up a hand. "I'm not sure if it's that people treat me differently after I tell them because they feel sorry for me, or if they just can't relate to someone who's been through something like that. People here stopped really talking to me about more than the weather, or 'how's your grandmother' kind of conversations. At school, I channeled my feelings into rage and I became 'too much' for my friend group." I glanced at her. "No offense, but I'd figure you'd be tired of hearing stories like mine."

"No. Not at all. A good detective learns something from every interview. Plus, I know you crawled your way out of hell and made something of yourself. I admire resilience."

I nodded and took another sip of my wine. I wasn't tipsy at all, but the combination of the beach, the ice cream, and the surreal atmosphere of the day had me ready to open up, despite the fact that I was supposed to be interviewing *her*.

Well, maybe she'd open up if I showed her my underbelly. I hated the transactional aspect of this conversation, but there you go.

"Mom started dating Armando after I left for college. He was a friend of Teddy's from the Marines who was passing through but ended up staying. It got hot and heavy real quick. I guess having the freedom she'd missed out on as a young woman with a kid made her a little wild? He was younger than her, and kind of a dick, but she always had some explanation for his behavior.

"Anyway, when I came home that summer, I stayed with my grandparents. I didn't want to live with a man. Ew. I was pretty anti-men before I went to college, but it became solidified after a few experiences at school. I'd also just broken up with my first girlfriend, who didn't want to be tied down over the summer, and I didn't want be around lovebirds. I hated the way he talked to her." I finished my can and set the empty in the sand.

"I have more behind the bar." She thumbed over her shoulder, and I laughed.

"Instead of how many bathrooms, should I have asked how many bars?"

"Four," she said around a bite of ice cream. "Want more wine?"

I shook my head. "Gives me a headache if I have more than one, thanks."

She gestured for me to continue.

"Yeah. So, we were barely speaking by the time I went back to school. I wasn't going to come home for Thanksgiving, but Ernie asked me to. He was worried about her, said she hadn't been answering his calls. When I got home, she had a black eye. She begged me not to tell Papa, but I did. There was a whole family intervention. Teddy kicked the shit out of Armando. He left. He was back when I came home for Christmas break. I had no idea. Opened the door and he was there. He told me to quit being a bitch and be there for my mother.

"We got into it and he got in my face. Didn't touch me, but it was enough. Mom sent him packing, and I thought it was for good. We had a nice holiday, but before I went back to school, he came over, begging her to take him back. Mom sent me to my room, and I called Ernie, who was home for the weekend from his police job in Stockton.

"I walked out and told Armando to leave, that the cops were coming. He pushed Mom out of the way. She fell and hit her head. He came at me. We were going at it when Ernie got there, the cops right behind him. I didn't care if I got hurt. I knew how to fight, and I wasn't going to just take it from him. Ernie took him down. The cops arrested him. When they searched him, they found brass knuckles and a knife that he wasn't supposed to have. Turned out he was on probation. Got him for probation violation and assault. He went to prison. I thought that was the end of it. Mom spent the next year going to counseling and traveling. Things were going great."

"Until they weren't?"

"Until they weren't. I was home for summer break between junior and senior year, and Mom and I were getting along better than ever. She was talking about coming to stay with me in San Leandro for a little while. She was working from home by that point and thought it would be fun. We even made plans to go to Europe together after I graduated.

"But one night, about three weeks before I had to go back to school, I woke up to her crying. I ran into the living room and found Armando holding her by the hair as she pleaded with him. He threw her down and came at me with a knife. I fought back," I said, pointing at the backs of my forearms, which had several deep scars, "but he stabbed me in the thigh and I fell. Couldn't get back up. He told her if he couldn't have her heart, no one could…and he stabbed her in the chest. He kept yelling at her that this didn't have to happen, if she would've just listened, and then he ran out the door. I called 9-1-1 and crawled across the room to her. I held her until I passed out, and when I woke up in the hospital, they told me she was gone."

I'd told the story so many times, including in depositions, in court, then in victim support groups and counseling. I eventually realized that telling the story let me share how strong my mom was. It was my way of keeping her alive and healing myself. And it was my way of helping others.

"The cops handled everything exactly right, which may or may not have been because they knew my family. I know a lot of victims aren't given that courtesy. But the court system failed. Armando had been let out of prison early due to the COVID release program. He'd only been charged with the probation violation, not the assault, so they let him out, not even considering the fact that he wasn't done with my mom. They didn't even tell her that he was out. Ernie still blames himself. Thought he should have known. It was part of why he decided to come back home instead of staying with Stockton PD."

"There needs to be a better way to track intimate partner violence complaints and convictions. That's a completely different set of details and concerns than a probation violation. The only way to fix it is to change legislation and work with the district attorneys on making the charges stick. I'm tempted to make that part of my post-wrongful-termination mission."

Inspiration hit, and I turned my body to face hers. "That would be huge. Are you really thinking about it?"

She sighed. "I am. Although I'm not sure I'm ready to play nice with politicians. I have before. I'm in this weird place where I have all these ideas of how to be helpful, you know, give back, but I'm also pissed as hell at 'The Man' for everything that happened."

Another opening. This time…fuck it. I went for it.

"Are you familiar with the three female archetypes?"

She frowned and looked out at the water. "You mean, like mythology? Cultural anthropology? Shit like that?"

Shit. *Great.* "The societal expectations of women at the three seasons of their lives: The maiden, the mother, and the crone?"

She rubbed her feet together on the lounge chair. I noticed that her feet had faint tan lines from flip-flops, her toenails had clear polish and were perfectly manicured. Her arches were high and the bottoms of her feet were much lighter than the bronzed skin on top.

"You mean, like, the societal expectations that girls are virgins, mothers are only good for taking care of people, and if you're not married or a mom and you're of a certain age, you're useless or you're a washed-up old hag who eats children in the woods?"

I bent in half, curling forward on the chair with the force of my laughter.

"Well, that's one way to obliterate my entire graduate practicum, but yeah, I suppose that's it."

"I just think it's bullshit, is all. It's based on a heteronormative view of society and it keeps the fucking patriarchy in place."

I fell a little bit in love with her right then.

"Are you willing to go on record with those thoughts?"

She frowned at me. "On record?"

"I have to complete one last practicum for my master's degree. I'm supposed to be studying the female archetypes and—"

"So what am I, the Crone in this scenario?" She shook her head and finished off her wine. "*That's* some bullshit. I'm only forty-five."

"And that's why I wanted to talk to you for my project. You're the antithesis of the traditional view of the Crone. You're beautiful." The wine must have given me courage. Her eyes widened as I continued, her lips playing with a smile. "You're vibrant, energetic, and passionate, and while you *do* fit the archetype in that you're reluctant to help, it's not because you don't want to, but more because society has wronged you and you've learned to be cautious." I shut up when her expression hardened.

"They took *everything* from me." Her voice cracked, and I noticed the slightest tremble in her chin. "My colleagues all turned their backs on me, they wouldn't respond to my calls for backup. I got jumped, did you know that?"

"No, God. I'm sorry." My heart was pounding as I thought about how scared she must have been, but she'd been unable to show it. I knew from speaking with law enforcement folks that they held in their fear and, for many, it led to self-destructive habits.

"Sometimes I wish I *was* an old hag, with poisoned apples or evil spells. I wanted to lay waste to my department after everything happened. In addition to losing my career, I lost my friends. My fiancé disappeared, too."

"*What*? She left?"

She shrugged and looked away again. "I don't know. There were no signs of a struggle at our place, and though she took money out of her bank account, she hardly took any of her belongings with her. Part of my motivation to set all this up," she said, gesturing in the direction of the command center, "is to find her. But the longer I look, the more I think she doesn't want to be found. I know she's alive, but none of her friends and family will talk to me. I've got a couple of private investigators looking...I don't know. At some point I'll let it go. I just need to know if she left on her own or if someone threatened her."

"Do you think? I can't imagine she'd leave you in the middle of everything."

"She didn't want me to go through with the lawsuit. She wanted me to just move on, for us to start over somewhere else."

"Was she a cop?"

She shook her head. "Crime scene tech. She worked in a different department. When we got engaged and moved in together, she transferred over to Denver. I needed to be close to the department, and she didn't want to commute anymore. I think she wanted me to transfer, but that wasn't going to happen. There weren't any positions in her department, and I would have lost my seniority and had to retest for detective."

"Did she support you coming forward?"

She shrugged. "She was supportive to a point. She thought we'd had a hard enough time being accepted as a couple, and she didn't want to be in the spotlight at all. No one bothered me when she transferred, but I guess she got some grief from the techs. I also didn't give a shit, while she was more conscious of appearances.

"The case was fucking awful, and our officers did a shit job. They didn't follow procedure. The kid was being bullied and the parents had made several attempts to get help from the school and from us. Cops in my own fucking department told the kid not to press charges because the bullying would only get worse. That they needed to let it go. The kid was beaten up on his way home from school three times, the last time severely enough to go to the hospital. The kid wouldn't identify their attackers. They were too afraid.

"I tried to get involved with the investigation and when I started digging, I found out who the bullies were. I was told to drop it, that I would be reprimanded if I contacted the family. I did anyway. Still couldn't get the victim to identify their attackers even though a witness had given me their names, but I figured out why they wouldn't talk when I discovered that the suspects were related to cops in the department. I went to my captain, got disciplined, went to IA, they dropped the ball. I went to the deputy chief, and got fired. God, I'm still pissed talking about it. The kid committed suicide."

I put my hands over my mouth. "Roz..."

"I know. My attorney encouraged the parents to sue the department, but they were heartbroken and didn't want to go through with it. I donated a huge chunk of my money to the Trevor Project. I set up a scholarship for his younger brother...but fuck, I felt so goddamned helpless. After my case went to court, after I won the settlement and got paid, I got the fuck out of there. Took a while to find this place, during which time I stayed with a cousin in Sacramento. I got to thinking, there's more I can do in my current situation than I could have done in one police department. Let's hope I can make it happen." She turned and wiggled her eyebrows at me. "How's that for a crone?"

"Completely bucks the archetype."

She raised an eyebrow. "Not completely."

She hesitated one second before hopping up from her chair, tearing off her clothes and running into the water. She disappeared around the island, and I was about to investigate when she surfaced and shouted, the sound echoing off the walls of the pool room. I heard her splashing, and then she came around the opposite side of the island.

"Sorry, had to wash off the heavy stuff. You should join me."

A swim did sound good, but I was still in shock from seeing her. *Naked*. I'd known this woman less than a day and she'd turned my world upside down. We'd shared our wounds and we'd laughed. One thing I knew for certain: she shouldn't be by herself here in this big house doing such a big, important, heartbreaking job. Alone. She deserved better.

I peeled off my leggings and pulled my top over my head, along with the bralette I'd worn underneath. It was quite intimidating strolling casually toward her, knowing her body was in tip-top physical condition and I...well, I could have used a bit more time in the gym, but I'd never let my insecurities keep me from expressing my sexuality.

The water was absolutely perfect. It felt wonderful on my skin. Saltwater pools really were superior in many ways.

I swam toward her slowly, taking my time, and giving *her* time to decide whether this was simply skinny-dipping or the beginning of something more. I stopped about three feet away.

"We got a little heavy. I'm sorry, but I'm not sorry."

Her big blue-green eyes were trained on me, and with her hair wet and slicked to her scalp, they seemed even more intense.

"Same. Although, I should be very clear. As much as I find you attractive and would love to fuck you, I can't."

"Okay." Her blunt admission turned my crank.

A crease appeared on her forehead, and she sighed. "Not until I know... I need to know what happened to Michelle, whether she's okay, before I can move on. If I thought she wasn't, and I..."

"I totally get it. And I'm flattered." I offered her a small smile, and she seemed to relax. "But I think you shouldn't be here alone. Doing all of this. You need help. Holding on to all of these stories as one person is too much. Let someone else bear it with you."

She swirled her arms around her a few times, staring at me. "Bear it with me," she finally said, her voice low. "Help me."

"*Me?*" I hadn't considered myself in that scenario. Everything she'd shared with me had me thinking she was onto something so important. There were myriad possibilities for making a difference. But did I have what it took to be useful to her? To this important mission?

What if this was the type of work that would have the biggest impact rather than working with undergrads?

"Yeah! I know you have school, but you're finishing this term, right? Come back. Help me. Do this work with me. Think about how many people we can help with my contacts and your computer magic. And maybe we can make something of that thesis project of yours, make it palatable for law enforcement to get onboard."

My heart soared at the thought, but I squinted at her. "How do you know I'd even be helpful? I might drive you crazy. I could be a total flake."

She rolled her eyes and splashed me. "You forget I know your uncle."

"Then I'm sure he told you I was a pain in the ass."

"And I'm not? Look. Help me this week. I'll let you interview me about your dumb archetypes, and you can help me organize all these cases. Then you go back to school, do your thing, and we talk when you graduate. Deal?"

I think I'd already convinced myself I wouldn't be taking that position in the fall. This scenario sounded way better. Plus, I'd be close to my family, and I'd finally learn the secrets about the Buckley house.

I took her hand. "Deal— *What the!?*"

The Creature had made his way between my ankles and scared the shit out of me.

Roz cracked up. "He likes you."

"I think you do, too." If we were going to do this, we needed to be honest.

"I do. You won't take my shit, I can tell. Or at the very least, you'll give it back."

"You know it." I put on my poker face. "The first priority should be finding Michelle."

She nodded, her smile gone. "Yeah. I won't be able to move on until I do…and I want to. Move on."

I grinned. "Good."

CHAPTER
SEVEN

ROZ and I got to work the next day, and for the rest of the week, I spent days with Rachel and the kids, afternoons napping, and evenings with Roz.

Rachel and I talked about the expectations of mothers, and how she'd gotten a lot of flak from her college friends when she chose to stay home with the kids instead of going to law school like she'd originally planned. She loved being a mother and saw her role as crucial to developing well-rounded community members. She was also the first one to support her friends who chose not to have children, and she loathed that our society makes women choose and, if they try to do both, makes them suffer for it.

I saw her in a new light after our conversations. I still wasn't ready to have kids, figured I never would, but I appreciated her sacrifices even more. I threatened Teddy within an inch of his life that he'd better take good care of his family.

"Be easier if you came back and helped."

I'd rolled my eyes at him, but he was right. It did take a village, and I missed mine.

Roz and I worked into the wee hours Monday and Tuesday before she brought me home. Wednesday, I convinced her to take a break and come play poker at Ernie's. She kicked everyone's ass. I might have let her kick mine. I hoped that if she felt comfortable with the guys, they'd be a good connection to the outside world for her after I went back to school.

I was becoming very protective of her.

And very attracted to her.

We hadn't had any more skinny-dipping excursions, but every time we touched in passing as we worked, it sent a zing to my heart like an urgent transmission from my brain saying *yes, this is where you belong, she's where you belong.*

"You weren't kidding, they do suck," she'd said on the way to drop me at my aunt's place. Teddy was staying the night so he and Ernie could go fishing early in the morning.

"But they're hilarious."

She agreed. "And damn, Angel can cook. How is it that people learn to *like* to cook? It's always felt like such a waste of time."

"Says someone who's spent years grabbing food on the go, I'll bet."

"Guilty."

"I love cooking." I smiled at her. "I'll cook for you."

So I did. Actually, we cooked together Thursday and Friday, packing up food and freezing it so she'd have some other options than her meal plan.

"You are really good at this," she said Friday, the night before I needed to return to San Leandro. I'd planned to pack up, hug the kids, and leave in the morning. I thought I'd be anxious to head home by now. The opposite was true.

We'd accomplished quite a bit over the week. I'd finished Notion templates for all of the cases she had. There were fifty-seven, from all across the country, some murder cold cases, some missing persons. She'd managed to make connection with law enforcement in several big cities and they were all chomping at the bit to get her to consult on their cases. I increased her security to keep her from getting hacked and losing vital information that needed to remain secure.

"Thanks. I'm glad you like it. If I end up sucking at this job, at least I could keep you well fed." I held up a spoon for her to taste the pasta sauce I'd made that afternoon. She backed me into the counter and closed her mouth over the end of the spoon.

She moaned and licked her lips, the movement making me shudder.

"That's incredible. Where did you learn to cook like this?"

"Abuela Bonita, Mom...I had a roommate for a while who was really good, and she showed me a few things."

She leaned forward to take another bit of sauce and pressed her body to mine. It was such a natural move after spending the past week together, and I wanted it, wanted *her*. She noticed the hitch in my breath and gave me that serious gaze of hers, the one I'd seen less of as we got to know each other.

I set down the spoon and pulled her into an embrace. She held on tightly letting me know she needed the closeness too. I buried my face in her neck and breathed her in.

"Thank you, Elia," she whispered, kissing my temple. "Thank you. You don't know how close I'd been to quitting this ridiculous idea before you got here. How close I'd been to shutting up the house and moving on. But now I have hope. I have direction."

"I'm sorry I have to leave," I said, and I was. I believed in this mission of hers so strongly, I was nearly ready to throw my stupid degree out the window.

"No, don't be sorry. Finish your degree. Enjoy the end of school. Then we'll talk."

"We'll talk before then. I'm gonna be checking on you. I don't like leaving you alone with all of this. And you need to get out more. Or... you know what? You should throw a big party. Let the town get to know you. What about something for Pride?"

She raised her eyebrows. "You mean, let everyone and their little monsters infest my safe space? That's...oh, I don't think I could do that."

"You could. And it would be great. I want you to fall in love with Calaveras. Have a real fresh start here."

She grinned. "Now who's the nurturing one? The maiden is supposed to be looking out for herself."

"And you, the crone. You are helping and nurturing too. We're both bucking the archetype, huh?"

She took my hands. "I told myself I was just going to let you go and let you make up your mind about whether to come back, but think about what we could accomplish together."

"I can't *stop* thinking about it."

She pressed her lips together. "Nope. I'm not going to say anything more. Let's get you home."

CHAPTER
EIGHT

ON THE DRIVE back to San Leandro, I dictated my thoughts about the archetypes and how it would serve all of society to do away with those long-held beliefs about what women should be, or what their value is. They'd only succeeded in keeping women oppressed for generations. The archetypes feed into gender roles that harm young women, making them think they have to meet expectations to have worth. I was thrilled with my thought patterns. I wrote the first draft of the paper on Sunday.

I texted Roz to let her know I made it home and that the paper was done.

I want to read it.

I was hesitant, but we'd shared so much over the week. I felt as though, during our time apart, we should continue getting to know each other. You know, in case we worked together.

Work. I started making a list of what I would need. Roz had told me to come up with a proposal, and I'd agreed, but it felt weird.

Whatever you want, whatever you need, Elia. The sky's the limit. Remember, I'm loaded, and once we get this business off the ground, there will be people willing to pay a lot of money for our services, enough so we can take on all the pro bono cases we want.

It wasn't like a faculty position would have me rolling in dough, but it was time to think about benefits and retirement, shit like that. I would be leaving maidenhood, and I'd have only myself to look after me. No husband, or even a partner, even though I believed Roz and I both were interested in that outcome.

At least I'd thought so.

Three weeks after I returned home, Roz called me on a Friday night.

"Can you talk?"

"Yeah, what's up?" I'd just gotten home from the gym and had blocked the weekend out to work on my practicum.

"I found her."

Background thoughts and noise faded. "Michelle?"

"One of the PIs I hired made contact with her, told her I wanted to talk."

"That's...she's okay?"

"I guess I'm going to find out. I'm flying to Miami to go see her. So we can talk."

I plopped down on the couch. Her halting way of speaking made her sound...thrown. Like she'd never actually expected to hear from her ex and didn't quite know how to handle it.

"That's good. You can get a sense of her...position."

"Yeah. I hadn't really thought of what I'd say to her, you know? At first, I wanted to find her and bring her home."

No, I hadn't known. Roz hadn't been real clear about whether she saw a future for them. She hadn't spoken past finding her and discerning whether she was safe. Could she be thinking of...taking her back? Was that what she wanted?

"And now you're wondering whether she might still want the future you'd planned."

"Right. No. I don't know."

She sounded distracted. I heard banging and hoped she hadn't broken any of the computer equipment.

She sucked in a breath. "Shit! That's hot."

"What are you doing?"

She was quiet for a minute. "Heating up the sauce you made. I cooked a chicken—don't get excited. I finally tried out the rotisserie oven and it's hella easy to use. Why hadn't I done it sooner?"

The thought of her eating the sauce I made…her lips on the spoon, our bodies pressed together.

I hadn't even been able to kiss her. Maybe I should have insisted. Then she would have known what she was missing. She could have made an informed decision as to whether she wanted her fiancé back or…

A twenty-five-year-old woman. With nothing to offer except mediocre cooking and passable tech skills.

"Roz?"

"Yeah?" She sounded more focused now. "Elia, I don't know. I don't know what she'll say, I can't even begin to imagine what reason she could have for being in Florida, of all places. And I'm not sure if any reason she can give is forgivable after the state she left me in."

My heart sank. They had shared history. They'd been together for six years. What if Roz decided she wanted that part of her life back after she'd lost so much?

"You have to go. You need to know what happened." I had to take myself—and my desires—out of the situation.

"Right." She was quiet, and I realized that up to this point, we hadn't really had pauses in our conversations. Once we'd climbed out of her pool that night, got dried off and dressed, we hadn't stopped talking. She was the first person outside my family that I hadn't had awkward silences with.

"Right. When do you leave?"

"Tomorrow. Ernie's driving me to Sacramento to catch my flight. I told him not to be ridiculous—"

"He cares about you." *I do too.*

"I know. Look, Elia. I don't know what's going to happen—"

"I hope you get the answers you're looking for. She owes you that."

"Right."

More silence.

"Have a safe flight."

"Right. Okay. I'll call you."

We hung up. Like strangers.

. . .

I hadn't spoken to Kimbra since I'd been back. She'd emailed me to see how my practicum went so I told her I'd come to office hours.

She had tea waiting for me.

"This one I'm not sure I like. Taste it. Tell me what you think."

I could tell by the aroma that I wasn't going to love it, but I sipped anyway. And tried unsuccessfully not to make a face.

"That bad?"

I wrinkled my nose and set the cup down. "Not my favorite."

She laughed and took a drink of hers. She *did* make a face. "So how did it go with The Crone?"

Rather than tell her I was pretty sure I was in love with her, and that she was potentially getting back together with her fiancé, I stuck to the facts.

"My platform is that we need to do more to destroy the archetypes in our thinking because they've harmed women for generations. And men, to be honest."

She sat back and folded her hands on her belly...which, if I wasn't mistaken, looked a little swollen. Could she be...?

"I love it. I can't wait to read it. You can test out your theories in your discussion section in the fall."

"About that," I said, letting my mouth take over before my brain could figure out that we were making a rash, slightly formed decision. "I am going to respectfully decline the position."

I'd expected her to be disappointed, but she just looked sad. "I thought you might."

"You did?"

"You were already wavering, and it's obvious that you had a life-changing experience over break. I can see the fire in you that's been missing since you lost your grandmother last year."

Abuela Bonita had hung in there after my mom was killed, but her heart had been broken. The stress was too much. Without Papa to hold her when she cried, she passed soon after he died. I'd felt terrible that Teddy and Rachel's kids would miss out on having their grandparents.

And I knew right then, even though I was being impulsive, it was important that I go home.

"Being home made me realize how much I'm needed there, not only for my family but for my whole community. Whether I go into law enforcement like my brother, or I get involved with another advocacy program, I think I need to have more experiences before I'll be the best teacher I can be."

She smiled. "I'm going to miss you, but I'm glad for you. I know you'll do great things."

I thanked her, but as I walked out to my car I thought...*what a dumbass*. I'd just given up a sure thing for a maybe. Wasn't there a golden rule about not quitting a job before you had something else lined up?

Did Roz's gig count?

Would I want to be a part of it if Michelle was back in the picture? What possible excuse could that woman have for abandoning her partner at the most critical time in her career? In her life? To not stand by her as she did the right thing?

Who would Roz be if she took her back?

Then I realized, did I really know who *Roz* was? I'd thought I had a good read on her, but maybe...I'd been looking for something that wasn't actually there.

When I didn't hear from Roz the rest of the week, my heart sank. Had she taken her back already?

But then I worried...what if it had been a trap, and the people who thought Roz had wronged them were lying in wait?

Monday came and still no word. I called Ernie.

"Have you heard from Roz?"

"Yeah, she canceled her flight home from Florida. She decided to buy a new car and drive back. She didn't really say much, just said she had some stops to make."

"Okay." Odd, but then what business was it, really, of mine? "So, I gave up the faculty position. Thought I should tell you."

Ernie whooped on the other end of the phone, making a very un-Uncle-Ernie-like sound.

"Are you all right?" I asked with mock concern.

"You're coming home then?" The excitement in his voice cemented the deal.

I sighed. "I am. I'm not sure what I'm doing just yet, so don't plan my life out for me. Roz asked me to work with her—"

"Yeah, she told me. Sounds like a good deal."

I waited a few beats for my voice to be strong and not shaky. "I'm not sure, though. Can you let me know what opportunities I might have with the department?"

"Are you sure? She sounded really excited at the possibility of working with you—"

"You know why she went to Miami, right?"

"Sure. A lead on her ex-fiancé. Wait—is there more going on with you two?"

"Do you really want to know?"

"No," he scoffed. "But I want you to be okay."

"There was potential, but if she's getting back with her ex...I don't know if our plans would be a good idea."

"Say no more," he said. "You gotta do what you think is best. I'll support you no matter what. Now, you hurry up and finish. Teddy's already making plans how to embarrass you at graduation."

"I bet he is."

The rest of the term flew by in a maelstrom of papers, presentations, and forms to fill out. Then it was done. Teddy and Ernie came for my graduation and helped me pack up my apartment.

Roz and I had texted, but it had mostly been questions she had about how to use the functions of her templates, all business. She hadn't said another word about her trip or Michelle. I didn't ask. I didn't want to know. I didn't need the distraction.

We got into town late on a Saturday evening, and I'd only had enough energy to drag my meager possessions into Ernie's garage. He'd asked me if I wanted to move in with him, and Rachel was okay with it as long as I came to dinner every weekend. I promised I'd be over to help her with the kids all summer, and told her she should start making plans with her girlfriends. Maybe even look into law school online. Her eyes had flared at that. She hadn't said no.

Sunday morning, Ernie was up early, banging around in the kitchen of his three-bedroom, two-bath house. I realized there would be no sleeping in on his days off if he was going to be so loud.

"Hey, get up, sleepyhead. It's Pride today."

"Pride? What are you talking about. Calaveras doesn't do Pride." A fact that galled me.

"They do now, and it's today, so get up, get dressed in your best rainbow gear, and let's go. I'm not on duty, but I promised I'd help."

"Fine." I groaned as I climbed out of bed.

"Come on. You complained for years that Calaveras should have a parade or at least a festival. You can't be a fair-weather Pridester."

Ernie didn't talk to me about his love life, but I was pretty sure he was bisexual. We'd been out more than once when I'd seen him talking to women but watching men. I hoped he'd find someone. Being a cop alone in a small town was a recipe for loneliness unless romance novels were to be believed, and then at any moment, the right unattached person would show up. Maybe he'd thought Roz would be that for him…at least until they became friends.

There wasn't a large queer community in Calaveras, but there were a few of us, and more in the nearby towns. At least I wouldn't have dating as a distraction as I figured out my life.

I put on a pair of black shorts and a white tank from the Human Rights Campaign with a rainbow and "everyone" printed below it. I pulled my hair up into a ponytail and wore pink sparkly flip-flops. It was already sweltering at nine in the morning. I'd certainly appreciated the lower temps in San Leandro. The heat was one of the tough parts about Calaveras, but it was so beautiful in my hometown, and I was still riding the high of not being in school and not having anyplace I was required to be.

Except, apparently, at Pride with Uncle Ernie.

We hopped into his Ford pickup and when he passed by Mark Twain Park, I turned to frown at him.

He grinned. "Roz took your advice."

"My what?"

And then I remembered. I'd suggested she throw a Pride celebration party. My stomach dropped, but I recovered pretty quickly. At least my reunion with her would be surrounded by lots of other folks I knew, and if Michelle was there, I could meet her, be civil, and then I could get drunk with Ernie before signing up to join the police academy.

As we pulled onto her road, there were cars lining both sides of the asphalt.

"Looks like a good turnout," I said.

"What better way to get people to come to Pride than to offer tours of the famous Buckley house."

I stared at him wide-eyed. Man, she was really going for it.

Good for her. I was glad. I hated thinking of her alone out here when she had such a big personality and so much to offer. I cursed her former department and Michelle again for how awful they'd treated her.

The gates to the Buckley property—Roz had yet to rename the place—were flung open and there was a giant rainbow made of flowers in front of the house. She'd definitely had someone in to work on the yard, which was full of color and well-manicured. There were flags representing all of the iterations of the queer spectrum lining the driveway and before we even parked, I could hear music blaring from the backyard.

"Did she hire a band?"

"Uh-huh. A couple local bands. And she got some DJ, I think…"

I had the door to the truck open before he'd turned off the engine. I was so happy to see so many folks from town out and enjoying the festival. She had a couple of food trucks parked out back, and through the back doors, I saw the saloon was full of folks. Past the patio in back, there was a large stage set up, and I recognized a band of Teddy's pals who called themselves For The Birds setting up to play.

"How did she do all of this?"

Ernie stood next to me. "She had help." He grinned and pointed to Rachel, who was wrangling the line of kids waiting to have Teddy do their face painting.

This was good. Good for Roz. Good for the town. I wanted to tell her how happy I was.

The band started to play and people mosied over to the stage area to dance and cheer them on. Ernie and I went inside the saloon to find Angel playing bartender, along with two of his brothers.

"Hey, graduate!"

I stood on the bottom rail of the bar and leaned over to kiss his cheek.

"Hey…barkeep? This a new gig for you?"

He grinned. "Roz is keeping me out of trouble. Keeping me busy." He handed us two sodas.

I raised my eyebrows and stepped down. "Is she?"

His gaze flicked outside, and I turned to see Roz taking the stage to huge applause.

Ernie gestured with his head, and we took our drinks outside.

"Thank you, everyone. Thank you for coming! Welcome to…well, y'all know it as the Buckley House, but I want to share with you the new name in just a minute. I'm so glad you could join me to celebrate Pride. Part of the reason I chose Calaveras to be my new home was because y'all have a reputation for being welcoming, and I've definitely felt that vibe since I've been here, so thank you."

She stared right at a couple of boys, who giggled and waved.

"Some of you may know that I bought this house with money I received in a lawsuit. At the root of that lawsuit was a case involving a young man in Denver. He was bullied at school, and unfortunately, the justice system failed him. His name was Ben Aronson. I want to dedicate the work I do for missing persons and victims of crime to his memory, so from now on, I'd love it if you'd join me in calling this place The Aronson House."

There was applause all around that lasted as long as Roz took to collect herself. She looked even more beautiful after the two months we'd been apart. Her hair was a little longer, fuller. She'd definitely spent time in the sun, and she looked…excited to let these folks in.

"Thank you," she said finally, smiling at the crowd. "I also plan to make the house available for local events and fundraising activities. We're going to have a website—that is, if my helper is still available—

and all of the information will be posted there. Keep your eyes on the local paper and the Calaveras website and social media pages. We'll start tours in a little bit, if you've always wanted to see the wild and wacky things the previous owner left behind. I'm going to be auctioning off a lot of stuff to raise money for The Aronson Project, so also keep your eyes peeled for that. Special thanks to Angel Guillam, Tony Barnes, and the Muse family for their help getting this event set up. Enjoy yourselves!"

There was more applause, and as she waved at the crowd, she spotted me standing with Ernie and made her way toward us.

"Great turnout," Ernie said, bending to kiss her cheek.

"Thanks to all of you guys," she said, giving him a pointed look. Then she turned toward me and held out a hand. "Come with me?"

I glanced at Ernie, who was already walking away, and I took her hand. She led me into the house, through the saloon, through the honky-tonk living room, and then to a door down the next hallway that I hadn't seen before. She turned to face me and looked to make sure we were alone.

"Hi." She bounced on her toes and squeezed my hand.

"Hi yourself, Mz. Pride. You decided to do it, huh?"

"What do you think?"

"I think you're holding my hand."

She looked down at our hands and squeezed mine again.

"I wanted to show you what I've been up to...and explain some things. Can I? Can I have a minute?"

I nodded. "Of course."

She could have anything she wanted. I just didn't know *what* she wanted.

She opened the door to a large room that now housed all of her computer equipment she'd purchased for her investigations work. She had basically moved out of the control room and created an actual workspace in what must have been a large family room or ballroom type space. There were bulletin boards all around the walls, long tables in a U-shape, two desks set up with additional computers.

"It's great! This feels way more workable than the control room. You were a little tight for space in there."

"You like it?"

I glanced at her and realized she was waiting intently for my reaction.

"Yeah, Roz. I think you'll do great things here."

She linked our fingers together and took my other hand. "Or *we* can do great things here?"

My smile fell. "Roz..."

"Hear me out?" She let go of my hands and walked over to the desks. I stepped farther into the room and closed the door behind me.

"Okay."

"I kept communication to a minimum while you were at school for several reasons. One, I needed to get my head on straight after meeting with Michelle. Two, I wanted you to be able to focus on finishing your degree. Three, I wanted you to decide whether to come back on your own, without my persuasion. And four, I was working on a proposal for you. I know I asked you to make one, but I thought it only fair that I share with you what I was hoping your position would be."

"So you did meet with her."

"I did. She was living with college friends I'd never met, working under the table, doing everything she knew to do to cover her trail so I wouldn't find her. Me, nor any of the press who had hounded her after I got fired. She confirmed she left me of her own volition because she didn't want to be in the spotlight."

My shoulders fell a little. How sad for Roz. "I'm sorry."

She shook her head. "Don't be. Better to find out before we got married, right?"

"I suppose..."

"Anyway, she said she'd had a change of heart after talking to the PI and wanted to try again. I told her I was glad she was safe and hadn't been harmed—and that I never wanted to speak to her again. I got the closure I wanted and needed. So I could move on."

The corner of my lip curled up. "That's good."

"It *is* good, but I want to be clear with you, I needed the closure, but I'd moved on when I moved here. I don't want you to think I expected you would want to dive right in, you know? I just didn't want you to decide whether to come home or not based on whether or not we'd be anything more than potentially co-workers."

"I appreciate that."

She exhaled and swallowed. "Having said that...I really missed you."

I rolled my eyes. "I missed you too."

"Good. Now, I know you just graduated, like, yesterday...but here. This is the proposal I came up with. Look at it, take time to decide."

I walked over and took the papers from her and set them down without looking at them. I rested my hips on the edge of the desk, invading her space a bit. "I will."

I could tell by the way she was wringing her hands that she was nervous about seeing me. Seeing as I no longer considered myself the chaste maiden who kept her sexuality under wraps to remain innocent, I crossed my ankles and watched as her gaze traveled up my legs, over my shorts, across my ample cleavage on display, and my bare shoulders before resting on my lips.

"Elia, look. I'm trying to do the right thing here. You have your whole life ahead of you."

I nodded. "Mhm. I do."

She blinked. "And I'm the crone, you said it yourself."

"We both said the archetypes were bullshit."

"I...I want to earn it. I want to deserve a shot with you."

"Good."

She sputtered. "Elia!"

"Look, you said you needed closure with Michelle. You got it. You said we'd talk after I graduated. We are. But now? I just want to—"

She grabbed my face with both hands and kissed me like I was the cool sip of water she needed on the hottest day of her life. She sucked in a breath, and she moaned when she kissed me for the second time. She stepped over my crossed ankles and pressed her body against mine, her high, small breasts brushing against my larger ones. I grabbed her hips and pulled her in tight, ready to show her she'd already earned it. I wanted to give it. Wanted to take it.

"Oh my God. Girl, you can kiss," she whispered, licking my lips. "What the fuck am I supposed to do with all these people outside? I gotta give tours and shit and all I want to do right now is get down on my knees for you."

I let my hands slide around to her ass and grinned. "Plenty of time for that later. You heard I moved back, right? That I'm not going anywhere? Is that good enough for you?"

"God, yes. Come here." She ran her hands over my breasts and sighed as she kissed me again, this time tasting every inch of my mouth until I was the one who wanted to get down for *her*. She nudged my thighs apart and pressed hers into my core, making me gasp. We were going to have each other's clothes off any second.

"God, we have to stop. You're so fucking hot, Elia."

"Happy Pride," I said in a singsong voice, and then chuckled as I kissed her one last time. "You can have whatever you want. Later."

"Good. I know just the room we should christen. I had the movie room furniture reupholstered. I didn't want to think about what that cowpoke got up to in there."

"You mean, you had an idea of what *you* wanted to get up to in there."

"Fuck yeah. Wait till you see it."

"I can't wait."

ABOUT R.L. MERRILL

If you liked "The Maiden and the Crone," check out more of Ro's books at www.rlmerrillauthor.com. You'll find more FF, MM, FFM, and MF stories with a little hope, love, and rock 'n' roll.

Stay Tuned for More…

THE REUNION

SOPHIA SOAMES

Editing by Debbie McGowan

Proofreading by Suki Fleet

ABOUT THE REUNION

The Reunion is a childhood, friends-to-lovers short story.

AUTHOR'S NOTE

This story is written and edited in British English.
No triggerwarnings.

CHAPTER
ONE

ASHTON

The Goose looked the same as always. The bar was stocked with the usual snack packets and signs, the same old brands of beer on tap and wonky paper coasters scattered randomly along the wooden counter where people stood chatting. Nothing new.

A lively atmosphere, the tagline would have said. I could see it in my head—seems I couldn't even turn up at a pub without producing a catchy header for an imaginary advert.

I wasn't here for work, though. Nor was I here for a relaxing pint.

The Goose. Fuck me.

You would have thought they'd choose a classier venue for the school reunion of the decade. Well. *Step back in time for the event you won't want to miss! Ten years ago, we graduated!* That's what the subject line of the email had screamed out. I could think of a hundred snazzier openers. It had been followed by a long line of recipients with names that brought back a mixed bag of weird emotions. Because school...

I shuddered in my fancy jacket and thin shirt, despite it being summer. I was dressed for the office, not for a night out, but these things were hard to read, and I hadn't been fully on board with coming until I'd actually set off.

Friday night. The long drive hadn't helped. My head was sloshed from a full week's worth of meetings and deadlines and finicky pixel work that had all been a waste of time in the end. You win some, you lose some.

Same with people from school. Kirby Grammar. Just thinking the words made the smell drift back to my nostrils. Dusty old corridors. The wooden benches. Dirty windows. Musty curtains in colour schemes so outdated they might once again be all the rage, though I doubted it.

As much as I doubted myself standing here ten years later.

I wondered if anyone would remember me. Or had I become one of those people who faded into lost memories? The one they would point to in the class photograph someone had taped to the bar and say, "That dude? Who was he again?"

Well, he was obviously me. Ash Wallace. The guy with the bad haircuts who rarely opened his mouth and did his best to blend into the background. Even in the photograph, half my face was covered by someone else's head, although truth be told, their hair was better than mine—marginally.

A bunch of ugly kids in badly fitting uniforms. Even worse skin. *Terrible* hairdos. I hoped the handful of people I still had on my social media would at least speak to me. At least Trish would come, because she'd messaged me. I liked her. Always had.

I swallowed. Straightened my jacket. Tried to plaster an open smile on my face. It felt more like a grimace, but Daisy Jo Pickford was coming my way.

"Marcus Matthews!" she shouted, holding out her arms as she advanced on me.

"Hi, Daisy Jo. Ugh." She embraced me in a cloud of perfume. Funny how I remembered her name. I tried not to be insulted that she'd forgotten mine. "I'm not Marcus," I politely reminded her. I looked nothing like him. For a start, Marcus had aged better than me, and he worked in finance. I knew because we still touched base occasionally.

"Oh! Sorry, er…" Clearly, she had no clue. She still smiled, though, which was a win in my book.

"Ash?" I offered, hoping for a light-bulb moment and instead was left standing there looking stupid, my hand raised in a pointless gesture of…well, I didn't know what.

I should have stayed at home.

"Ash, mate!"

Big Don to the rescue. Thank God for that.

"Trish was just saying you were coming. Have you got a drink? Let's get you a pint."

"Thanks." I was grateful he'd saved me from Daisy Jo's clutches. The discomfort was still there, but I was sure I could swallow down some of the horror of this evening with a few more beers.

Big Don. Two resits. Years older than the rest of us, but he was a nice guy. And here was Trish. And Josef and…what was his name again?

"Freddie," he reminded me.

"Freddie. Of course!" Yeah, I'd never have recognised him with hair down to his elbows and a beard that definitely needed trimming.

"Good to see you, man!" he said.

I wondered if it was.

There was the usual chit-chat, the words flowing easier with the aid of pre-set phrases. I listened and nodded along, happy to take an interest in everyone else's lives as they answered one another's questions. Jobs. Partners. Children. Someone's caravan in Dorset. All those things that were personal yet not.

"Didn't you and Daisy Jo hook up for a while?" That one was directed at me, and I dismissed it with a smile. No. We hadn't. I'd gone out with Rosie Quinn for a bit, then snogged Emmeline Kovics at a school disco and had very awkward sex with Peter Lovett. My first time, not his. I looked around with unease.

"Peter couldn't make it," Trish whispered in my ear. "He lives up in Scotland now. Runs his own company."

Good old Trish, still the same. Short, smiley, reliable…also never got picked in PE. The two of us had shared plenty of awkward eye rolls in school, and we'd talked a few times since. She worked in retail, had an on/off girlfriend in the army, and I had…

I had nothing. Well, apart from a good job, an ill-fitting suit and about a gallon of sweat pouring from my armpits. I wondered if the shop on the corner sold T-shirts or if I could get away with a quick wash in the loos.

I'd been the same at school, sweating uncontrollably at any sign of awkward attention. I'd hated talking in front of people. Hated interaction. Group projects? Not a chance. I'd hidden away from anything that required me to speak out loud.

University had changed all that. I could now stand up in front of an entire room full of people and keep them entertained. I held seminars and wined and dined clients like I'd never done anything else. Clients were different, though. Colleagues were just what they were. But these people, right here?

Once, they had seemed like the most important people in the world. The future leaders of industry. I'd been convinced that Patrick Bruce would be the next prime minister. It turned out he worked in construction. He told me when I briefly shook his hand outside the gents'…before I cleaned myself up, rescued my shirt and exited with my jacket hanging over my arm like a twat, but whatever. I had a fresh pint in my hand, and life seemed a little better. The first two had gone down a treat, which made my conversation flow smoother and pushed my angst back a little.

And now I had Daisy Jo on my arm again.

"Archie," she slurred.

"Ash," I reminded her. "Ashton Wallace?"

She grinned. "Of course. I'm a little drunk. You're really handsome. Always were, and you've aged well. Like a fine wine. Buy me another white wine spritzer, will you?"

She pouted at me, and I swiftly offloaded her onto a bar stool next to a girl I recognised but didn't really know, who gave me a grateful grin and tried to get Daisy Jo to let go of her phone.

"Archie!" she shouted as I tried to leave. "Archie, get back here! I need to tell you something!"

I wasn't sure I wanted to hear, but the other girl now had Daisy Jo's phone, and it made me smile. This was a major déjà-vu moment. Ten years ago, this girl, whatever her name was, had called Daisy Jo's brother to come and take her home so she wouldn't get in trouble with their dad, and it was funny finding out that Daisy Jo was still exactly the same.

"Did you know Holland Snow is here?" Daisy Jo breathed fumes into my face. "I just spotted him outside on the veranda."

I swallowed. "Holland Snow, eh?" I said dismissively. *Idiot*. I wasn't even fooling a very drunk Daisy Jo.

Holland Snow had been the most popular guy not only in our year but in our entire school, because every school had a golden boy, and Holland was ours. Sporty, smart, incredibly tall, handsome AF, skipping through life trailing broken hearts behind him. Girls. Always more girls. I'd hated him back then.

"You used to be friends," Daisy Jo said, poking an overly manicured fingernail into my chest.

"We *all* used to be friends," I pointed out. She probably didn't remember in her drunken state, but Daisy Jo and I had attended the same nursery school, and inconceivable as it seemed now, Holland Snow had gone there too. His family had lived in the road behind mine, and we'd played together as kids. 'The boy at the back' my mum had called him. His dad had built him a little platform so we could talk over the fence.

The innocence of childhood.

I hadn't seen Holland in years. Not talked to him since we'd become...who we were. When the teenage years had turned everything awkward and grey.

"I used to be so in love with him," Daisy Jo mused as her friend handed her a glass of water. She spilled most of it down her dress. Another massive hit of déjà vu.

"You go have fun," the friend said to me, rolling her eyes at Daisy Jo. "Gonna get this one home."

The evening hadn't even started, but yes. Ten years later, we hadn't changed, and I wondered what the whole point of this reunion was anyway. Were people really, honestly, having fun? Was I?

My feet took me outside, pint still in hand. The evening sun was warm against my skin as I exchanged casual hellos with others I knew by sight but couldn't have put a name to. I wasn't looking around. I definitely wasn't looking for him.

Daisy Jo must have been drunker than I'd thought because I couldn't spot anyone who looked remotely like Holland Snow.

The fresh air was good, though, and I was enjoying my beer. I leaned against the railing, sipping and watching the world go by below me. The high street was busy with people on nights out, couples strolling arm in arm, children playing in the small water fountain on the square. I'd played there as a child, every weekend during my parents' shopping trips, followed by an obligatory drink at The Goose. A small gin and tonic for my mum, a pint of bitter for my dad, a glass of pop for me.

There was no water in the fountain anymore. Council cutbacks. Times had changed and mostly not for the better.

I could see the whole town from here, the primary school at the top of the hill, Kirby Grammar right behind it. The big discount supermarket where the library used to be, and behind that houses. Rows and rows of them against the backdrop of the hills in the distance glowing orange in the setting sun. The only thing blocking my view was the old church tower to my left.

Ah, Kirby. Once an elegant and vibrant English town, now in its inevitable death throes—another tagline forming in my head. Half the shops were boarded up these days and even the once majestic church had been converted into flats. Life still went on, from one day to the next. Just as it did down in London.

I hadn't been back to Kirby for a good while. I saw my parents from time to time, usually for birthdays and the like, and I still came home for the holidays, but apart from that, I had a good life in London. I worked and went to the gym and on occasion socialised with friends. There was nothing whatsoever I missed about Kirby.

I drained the last of my pint and rolled my shoulders. Why had I even RSPV'd to this shitshow? If I'd wanted to see people up here, I could have texted Trish and met up for a curry or something.

This event was nothing special. Nothing had changed. Absolutely nothing. The cool girls were still draped over the table in the corner. The popular guys stood in a loud huddle at the bar. Us nerds were in a corner where no one would find us, and Daisy Jo Pickford was still drunk on a chair.

We might as well still be kids at school. It didn't matter how many fancy degrees I had, or that I'd won Advertiser of the Year two years ago, or that I pocketed a more than decent salary and drove a BMW. I was still *just Ash*, the invisible, ridiculous idiot with a pint in his hand. Nothing ever changed.

"Ash," a voice behind me said.

The hairs on the back of my neck prickled. I had no idea why.

"Hey."

That voice again. Now by my side. Maybe the beer was getting to me. Or perhaps the evening had suddenly turned chilly, though I was still sweating profusely.

My hand automatically went to my collar, fumbling awkwardly to loosen a button.

"Holl," I said.

Fuck.

"I was hoping you were still here. Saw Trish earlier but I couldn't find you."

"Still here."

My heart was beating too fast, but somehow, I managed to turn around and face him. Look at him.

Still the same thick blonde hair. Chiselled jaw. Strong shoulders and, yes, evolution was truly cruel because where I had stayed exactly the same—dark, slim and ordinary—Holland Snow had become one of those fine specimens of manhood that put everyone else to shame.

"Ashton Wallace." He smiled. I smiled back. It felt forced in a way I couldn't explain.

"How are your parents?" I asked too politely. "Still living round the back?"

"You know they do." A small smile lingered on his perfect lips. "Your mum chats to my mum over the fence. She always asks about me. My mum gives her all the gossip."

Yeah. He was absolutely right. My mum took great delight in keeping me updated on all things related to the Snows' *lovely boy*. He was a vet in London, very successful. Had a great apartment. Central location. Kept a dog. And a cat.

"What's your dog called again?" I asked.

His smile widened. "Bruce."

"Bruce." I nodded. "After *Die Hard*?"

"Yup. Mum is very specific in her gossip, isn't she? Very thorough."

"Yes." I cringed. "And your cat is called…Willis?"

He laughed. God. That laugh. "No. She's called Fifi. But you knew that as well. Didn't you?"

I didn't laugh back. I swallowed, tried to loosen my collar again.

"I also know you're still with that ad agency, doing very well," he continued. "Project managing some great campaigns. I do keep track, Ash."

I didn't know what to say to that. I hadn't seen him in ten years, at least. Every time I visited my parents' house, I could see the window to his old room, but the lights were never on. I'd sometimes wished they were.

I sometimes wished I could be a child again. When things were easy and exciting, and the most beautiful boy in the world was my best friend.

"I sometimes go look at the fence," I blurted out. It wouldn't have been my first choice if my brain had been working, but I had to add something to this conversation and stop behaving like a total numpty.

"I remember it like yesterday," he said. "Standing there, talking to you. You told the best jokes. And then I would go get biscuits and pass them through that little gap in the fence panels, pretending I was a zookeeper and you were my—"

"Pet monkey!" I laughed. Good times.

"It's really nice to see you again," he said like he meant it. I didn't know if he did.

"You too," I murmured. I felt all warm inside. He did that. Looked at you and made you feel like you were basking in the sweetest, warmest sunshine.

"Want another drink?" he offered.

"Yeah…I guess?"

Already, he had me so enthralled I would have done whatever he'd asked. Suddenly ten years seemed like nothing because he'd always done this. One smile and I believed his world revolved around me, and me only.

But I was a child then, and I'd been stung before. Holland Snow was *not* exactly who I wanted him to be. I knew that. I think he knew it too, but he still walked me back to the bar, ordered me a pint and tapped his card in payment. Then someone grabbed his arm and pulled him away, and once again I was standing on my own with a pint in my hand that I couldn't drink. I didn't want it. I wanted nothing to do with anything related to Holland Snow.

Other people filled the space where he had been, but I could still hear his laughter, see his sunshine smile in my mind's eye, and I wanted to cry because I wasn't five years old anymore. But I felt like it.

CHAPTER
TWO

HOLLAND

I hated shaking hands with people, but it was still the done thing up here. Everyone in the pub seemed to have morphed into their father, even the ladies, as Trish Hollingsworth shook my hand with a very firm, businesslike grip.

"Holland Snow," she said, leaning suggestively against the bar. Not in a sexual way, I might add. That wasn't Trish's style. She was farm folk, a solid woman with acres of land. Even at school, she'd always smelled slightly of cattle.

The memory made me smile, and at first I wasn't sure why, but then I figured it out. She smelled like home. Yes, that was it. I always liked coming home. Our small bungalow overlooked Trish's farm, and home had always smelled like this.

I didn't have much time for parental visits these days, running a partnership of a twenty-four-seven vet clinic in North London. We were busy, always, and maybe I worked a little too much. Thank goodness for the apartment above the clinic, the place I called home these days, but it was nothing like coming home for real to this small town and its fresh country air.

Not that it was helping me much right now, because I'd lost him again. My fault entirely, having been lured off by yet more people with their handshakes and chatter. I'd tried to be polite, but by the time I'd excused myself, he was gone. Again.

"Don't suppose you've seen Ash?" I asked Trish casually.

"He's around," she said. She took a gulp of her freshly poured pint and tapped her phone against the barman's card reader. "Still so handsome. Can't believe that nobody's snapped that boy up."

I grinned and almost said something inappropriate before remembering where I was. I was out. Proud. A very much settled gay man in my late twenties, yet here I was, swallowing my tongue. These were people who...well, they gossiped.

"Still gay?" Trish asked with a cheeky smile.

Oh. Well. Whatever.

"Very much so." I laughed, and she high-fived me.

"Not much action for us queers round these parts," she mused, taking another sip of her beer. "But I tell you this. Inside tip." She leaned closer. "The TomCat at Horley, Friday nights. Seriously. I gave up my Friday night action for this?" She gave me an overdramatic eye roll, and I squeezed her arm in solidarity. I knew what she meant, even if I wasn't missing out on something better for this crappy school reunion.

I'd come for one thing only, and it wasn't the beer, however inviting the pint in my hand looked.

"Go find him," Trish said quietly. "You know you want to."

God. Why had I been worried about being out up here? I was as obvious as always. Well, to everyone except Ash, it seemed.

I left Trish to her pint and made my way back out onto the veranda. The evening light was fading fast, and the twinkling fairy lights hung all around the railings were doing their best, but...well, it wasn't Christmas, was it? I'd have laid good money on the staff saying, "They'll look great in the summer," and leaving them only because they couldn't be bothered to take them down.

But it wasn't the out-of-season fairy lights that had me catching my breath. It was Ashton Wallace's back, at the other end of the square, his jacket slung over his shoulder as he disappeared from view.

Fuck.

He was leaving. And I was still here in this stupid pub with my stupid pint in my stupid hand.

I dumped my glass on the nearest table, mumbling an apology at the people I almost took out in my haste as I headed for the door.

Someone called my name as I set off across the square. I was no runner, especially in the fancy shoes I'd put on for tonight, along with dress slacks and a good shirt. I'd drawn the line at a tie. I wasn't really a tie person. I was way more comfortable in scrubs and trainers, but this was an event for actual grown-ups.

I didn't feel much of a grown-up running down the high street trying to spot that light-blue shirt and mop of wavy brown hair.

Hair that curled just so at the nape of his neck.

Damn, he was a fast walker. Or maybe he'd gone in for a pint at The Haystack. Fuck. No. Please don't make me show my face in that dive.

I had a quick snoop through the door and backed out in relief. Not there.

I charged up the hill and onto the main road but had to stop to heave in a breath.

"Ash!" I hollered.

He had to have heard me, yet he kept walking. This wasn't London, the air was still, and the one car passing us slowly wasn't going to hamper his hearing.

"Ash!"

I set off again.

"ASHTON!"

He stopped. Thank God for that. I had zero breath for shouting a fourth time.

He turned around and stared at me, his jacket hanging slack at his side as he waited for me to catch up. It took a while. As I said, I was no runner.

"Ash," I wheezed out, stumbling to a stop and doubling over, hands on my knees.

He said nothing.

"You left," I pushed out.

"Yeah?"

I glanced up at him. God, he was still gorgeous. Big blue eyes. That sweet kink to his nose. The strand of hair that fell over his face. Small dimples when he smiled. Except he wasn't smiling.

"It looks like rain." *OMG, Holland Snow.* What on earth was I on about? I'd been on a roll earlier—chatted a bit, bought him a pint. The plan had been to find somewhere comfortable we could sit and talk, not to hijack him on the corner of Cornwall Road and waffle about the weather.

"Dad said so too," he replied flatly. "You know what he's like. Has, like, five weather apps on his phone."

Despite my shameful attempt at small talk, I had to laugh because my dad was the same. Retired life was obviously thrilling.

"Ash." I metaphorically grabbed myself by the collar and gave myself a good shake.

"Walk?" he suggested.

The mental map was clear in my head. Cornwall Road, up to the next junction, left, down the alleyway, right at Devon Close. I'd walked this way every day for years. Back and forth. Always keeping an eye on Ash. I could probably still describe his backpack in full detail. The badges. Pen marks. The way his left strap had frayed…

"Yes. Good thinking."

We set off, and I put my hands in my pockets, then took them out again. I'd probably trip over my feet in a minute and fall flat on my face. It would serve me right.

"Holl, what happened?" he asked out of nowhere. "We were best friends, and then we weren't. Once we hit Year Six, you just…we just…"

"I know," I said. "Awkward and weird. Everything…" I paused to put it into words. "I hated everything for a while, but I think that's normal. When you're a teenager, and you start to figure things out… It took me a long time to figure myself out. Didn't…you know…" I shrugged, not sure what else to say. Mum might gossip, but I very much doubted she discussed my well-being and sexual awakening with Mrs Wallace over the fence.

Ash kept walking, taking the corner with that elegant gait he'd always possessed. Where I bumbled through life, Ash's feet barely touched the ground.

"You know, when we moved to senior school…" His voice was strong, firm, a reminder that we weren't kids anymore. And up close, he had stubble. Gorgeous darkness on his smooth skin.

"Yup," I said absentmindedly.

"You blanked me. For all of it. Never spoke to me again. So, Holland Snow. What the hell is this? Are we friends again now?"

His venom didn't surprise me. I'd expected it, not like the subtle kindness he'd shown me earlier, when he'd let me buy him a pint.

He smacked his fist into a wall we passed. "You're a dick, shouting my name all over the high street and following me. For what? To walk me home?"

"Yes." I was trying to gather my thoughts, get myself back on track. "As I said, there are things I need to tell you."

He stopped, which was good. We were still between high garden walls and secluded from view.

"Ash, I know we haven't spoken for a long time, but there was…I mean, you know as well as I do that Kirby Grammar…it was—"

"In the distant past," he interrupted. "I graduated. In one piece. Then I went to uni, got a degree, a career, found my place in the world. I don't really want to go back and dwell over the shittiest years of my life."

"They were shitty," I agreed.

"Says the Prom King who shagged his way through the entire year *and* the year below. It must've been really shitty for you, getting those scholarships. And then you just pissed off!"

"I know. I—"

"No goodbyes. My parents sent you flowers for graduation, and you never even came round to say thank you."

"Couldn't."

He shook his head. "That it? No explanation?"

I'd never seen him this angry before, and I couldn't blame him. Admittedly, my one-word answer didn't explain my weird and wild straight youth, but it was the truth.

"Like I said, you're a dick."

"Well, Ash. I could hardly go round your house and say thanks for the freaking flowers, could I?"

"Why not?"

"Because you'd be there, all right? Because I didn't want to face you. Because...I couldn't." I dragged in breaths, deep, big, horrible ones, while he just snarled at me.

"Again, why the hell not? It wasn't like *we'd* fallen out. *You* blanked me. For YEARS!"

He was livid, and truth to be told, so was I, but not with him. Something familiar was building in my chest that I'd struggled to suppress for so long, and now it wanted out.

"Because I fancied you, okay?"

Not the words I'd have chosen if I'd actually planned a sweeping, romantic declaration of love instead of blurting out the first thing that came into my head. I stared at the ground, crestfallen. I'd missed my opportunity.

"Bullshit!" he countered.

Or maybe I hadn't because his rebuttal somehow gave me strength.

"No," I said and took a step closer to him. *Well, that worked brilliantly, didn't it, Holland?* Because now he was backed up against the garden wall, right underneath the one handy streetlight lighting up the entire alleyway. And in case he didn't feel trapped enough, my arm was blocking his escape, my hand resting on the wall next to his head. Cold, prickly stone dug into my palm. I pressed a bit harder, the sensations helping me focus. *Talk, Holland. Talk.*

"Listen, I..."

"What?" he asked coolly, but at least he was looking at me. Those mesmerising blue eyes, staring right into my soul, sucking the life out of me. Yes, I was being overdramatic, but my chest hurt from gulping air like I was new to this whole breathing thing. I took a minute, inhaled, exhaled, in, out, in, out, nice and steady.

"You want to know why I stopped talking to you?" Better. I was back in control of my body. Mostly. "Why I couldn't even walk home with you after school? You want to know why?"

"Yes?" His smile was all sarcasm. "An explanation would be nice, Holland."

Bloody Holland. I'd hated my name all my life. Who the hell names their kid that? My parents apparently.

"Because just looking at you gave me a boner. And when you're thirteen, it makes things awkward as hell."

Great stuff. I mean, it wasn't a lie. He only had to walk past and teenage me sprang a boner, but it was so much more than that, and… Oh, good. Now he was going to punch me.

Or not.

He lowered his arm, said nothing.

So I went on.

"This isn't some scripted confession I planned on making tonight. Or ever. But then I saw you, and it was still there. Not the boner…well, maybe a bit of one. The thing is, Ash, what I'm trying to say is I spent all our time at Kirby Grammar being stupidly in love with you. It was only ever you. Even with all the girls and stuff I got up to, it always ended up with me sat there in class, staring at you, hoping you would look up and see me."

Now I was on a roll. Good. Get it out. Over and done with. Go home. Move on.

"I don't believe you," he said.

Oh, Ash. Even using that incredibly stern tone and the seriousness of his expression, he was still beautiful.

"You sometimes did," I argued. "Sometimes you looked back. Yeah, I'll admit I acted like I didn't notice, because when you did look at me, it made my insides burn. That's how it felt. It physically hurt me to ignore you, but I could never have told you, not back then. I still hadn't figured it out, what I was feeling, and even if I had, being out was not an option."

"Nope."

It was a relief to hear him agreeing with me. I was still half expecting a punch in the face, but he was calming down. And he was talking to me.

Breathing was getting easier too, though my heart was fluttering with him so close. I wanted reach out, stroke his cheek, touch his lips with my fingertips, see if they were as warm and soft as they looked.

"Ash, I…I've done a lot of things in my life. Fucked a lot of people.

But you know, things like that don't matter when you get to where we are now. We have good jobs, homes, lives, and mine is so bloody empty, and I only realised tonight it was because when I was eighteen, I left this place behind, and you were still here. But then I came back and you'd left too. It was like the whole town had died."

"Overdramatic much?" He smiled. I did too.

"You know me far too well."

"Head boy. Prom King. Drama queen."

I laughed. That had been me in a nutshell, and it was very him to put it like that. He'd won awards for his taglines. I'd seen it on LinkedIn. I followed him. Everywhere. Like I was still the teenage stalker who...was I really going to tell him?

"I used to look through the fence if you were in the garden." Apparently I was. "Just so I could see you." God, my face was burning.

"I know," he said. "It drove my dad mad. He used to call you out on it too, stalker boy."

"Ugh." I laughed.

"And look how far you've come. Holding me prisoner against a garden wall in Sussex Alley."

"Idiot." I grinned. "I'm not holding you...prisoner...or whatever.

"Then what do you want? I mean, so you had a crush. It got a little bit out of hand and weird, but it was ten years ago."

That was one of the things I loved about him. He was sensible. Level-headed.

I was not.

"Because I got to talk to you today, and nothing had changed. You still do crazy things to my insides, and I smiled at you, and you looked back. I couldn't read things like that when we were younger. I don't think anyone can, you know? See the signals when someone is flirting with them? And I couldn't spot another gay boy to save my life."

He spluttered a little—with laughter, not anger, I hoped.

"And how exactly do you spot another gay boy?" He rolled his eyes. Ha! And he called *me* a drama queen! "It's not like people have rainbows tattooed on their heads."

"No," I said seriously, reining this in. "But there's a certain way someone looks at you. His eyes focusing on your lips, like he's asking permission. You know? An invitation searching for an answer."

Like I was doing right now. Tentatively, I reached for him, put my hand on his neck. Well, just two fingers, the tiniest of strokes against his warm skin, my eyes on his lips. My stomach felt like it was on bloody fire.

"Really?" he said, still acting pissed off, but his voice cracked, and his eyes flickered a little, down to my lips, back to my eyes. My lips again. Then he closed his eyes, swallowed as I moved my hand slowly, trailing my fingers over the soft skin of his neck and throat.

He was beautiful. So bloody beautiful.

"I didn't lie about having been with other people," I murmured. "I have, just as you have, I'm guessing. But this was always here, wasn't it?"

"No. I don't...I..."

"Is there someone in your life? If there is, I'll back off. But...I hope there isn't."

Bossy much? Well. Holland Snow might be a softy in the office, all about the small, cuddly animals and warm smiles, but that wasn't always me.

"No," he said quietly. He opened his eyes and looked up at me. Truly looked at me. "No. I'm not doing this. Not with you. Because I have to come up here and see Mum and Dad, and I need to be able to do that without knowing that the guy on the other side of the fence... fuck... Fuck you, Holland." He almost whispered those last words.

"Fuck you too, Ash," I said softly. "It's not just you. It's me too. And I think there's an *us* that is long overdue."

I had his neck in a firm grip now as I closed in, my chest pressing against his, my groin...

Fuck. FUCK.

I was quite assertive when it came to hook-ups. I preferred meeting people in pubs or clubs, literally feeling them out to see if they wanted take things further. A quick mutual grope usually sealed the deal. But Ash was more than a hook-up to me, yet here I was, my nose squashed up against the prettiest nose in the world, and in my hand?

I had a very nice boner.

His boner.

Ash Wallace was hard.

How was he so bloody calm about it, being pushed into a wall like this and being indecently groped?

I panicked, pulled my hand away like I'd been burnt. He caught it and slammed it back in place. My panic dialled up another notch, and so did my dick.

Fuck. Fuck. Fuck.

"Holl." He pushed his palm against my chest. "This is not a good idea."

"Yes, it is," I said, no clue where my ballsy-ness was coming from. Grabbing his wrist, I pinned it to the wall with one hand, my other still on his dick, my chest keeping him in place while my tongue…

God help me. This was out of control.

I licked a line up his cheek. Just the tip of my tongue so I could feel him, taste him. The whimper that came out of his mouth was…insane.

"Holl," he warned. I loved that he was so in control when I clearly wasn't. I trailed my lips over his chin, back towards his ear, and he angled his head, opening himself up to me, shivering as I licked down his neck.

"Ash," I whispered desperately, lacing my fingers with his and scraping my knuckles on the wall.

I was bigger than him, taller, broader, but it didn't matter. He had me. Right there. And I felt like I was having a heart attack.

"We're not doing this here," he whispered, his lips vibrating against my cheek.

"I think we are," my brain replied on my behalf. I grinned hopefully.

"Idiot," he breathed, and there, a soft kiss on my ear. I was so screwed, all pretence of control gone.

I sucked a bruise into his neck, and he moaned, in the very best way. Twisting our joined hands down, I tried to figure out how to bring his body closer to mine without taking my mouth off him. I couldn't get enough of him, dragging my lips over his chin, rubbing my face against his as his heart beat against mine. *Ash. Holl. Ash. Holl.* A rhythm that just made sense.

"I need—" he started, but I shut him up with my lips on his. Everything about him drove me into madness because I agreed wholeheartedly that this was not the place to fuck on a Friday night. Any minute now, someone would turn the corner into the alley and catch me with my hand down Ash's trousers, but there went his button, and his zip, and the sound coming out of his mouth was truly obscene.

He wasn't new to this, not at all, and I matched his obscenity with a raspy groan of my own as he expertly popped the button on my slacks and, with an oh-so-elegant shove, slid them down to my knees, followed by my briefs, and wrapped his hand around my dick. My legs almost gave out, and I fell forward, my head landing hard on his shoulder, my nose grazing the brick wall.

"Thick," he whispered into my neck and bit down into the tender skin. I didn't care. Fingers. Hand. Warmth. And then it was gone as cool air surrounded my poor manhood and my hand jerked away from the wall.

He pushed me backwards, making sure I was watching him, his eyes boring into mine as he licked his palm.

Ash Wallace.

Fuck me.

He shoved me across the narrow alleyway, so my back bounced into the opposite wall, and smashed his mouth on mine, thrusting his tongue in so deep I could feel him at the back of my throat. His fingers gripped my face while his spit-lubed hand worked my dick, frantic movements that made me want to cry, howl, roar, tell him to go the fuck faster.

I couldn't, though. We were in public. The soft music coming from somewhere reminded me as he kicked my feet further apart and I sank down. I was going to end up flat on my arse if I wasn't careful, but he was kissing me again and any lingering worries I had about someone coming around the corner were lost, as was I.

I needed to touch him too and grabbed his dick, pumping it hard, matching his rhythm as I tangled the fingers of my other hand in the curls at his nape, tugging, forcing him closer. His cock was a perfect fit in my grasp, and those curls...it was like they were made for me to pull. He had a lot of hair, I'd noticed. On his head, on his thighs, surrounding that perfect dick of his... Fuck manscaping. He was perfect just as he was.

His breaths were shallow, rapid hot pants against my ear.

"Come," I demanded, scraping my teeth over his coarse stubble before biting his pillowy lower lip. I was so fucked. Ash the boy had been the bane of my life. Ash the man would be the death of me.

"Harder," he rasped out, then he gripped my chin and held it firm, made me look at him as I jerked uncontrollably in his grasp the same way he was trembling in mine.

"Holl," he said. "Holland...fucking...Snow."

That's what he said as he completely lost control of his limbs, to the point that I struggled to get traction against the asphalt. Bloody trousers around my ankles.

It was dark, and the streetlight put his face in the shadows, but I knew he was coming. His orgasm made every muscle in his body twitch, my hand pumping all that pleasure out of him as I tried to hold him up. I was slowly but surely losing the fight with gravity.

"Ash," I whimpered as I fell, my bare arse hitting the ground with a soundless but painful thud. All that gravel. There was probably broken glass and all sorts, and I swear I'd impaled myself on a bloody thistle.

And what was my Ash doing? He was laughing. Sparkling rays of sunshine in the dark of night.

Well, dark other than the streetlight shining down on us—our very own spotlight.

I had to laugh too at the absurdity of him fastening his trousers like he was getting dressed for an ordinary day in the office.

"Help?" I said, reaching for his hand. He grinned down at me.

"The great Holland Snow, stuck on the ground with his pants around his ankles. What a sight."

"Ash," I warned. This wasn't funny. And my legs were at a really uncomfortable angle. "Are you going to just leave me here?"

"Would I ever?" He got down on his haunches and studied me, helpless and half naked. And my dick, that treacherous little bastard...

Ash only needed to look at me and my dick jumped with joy.

Nothing new there.

What was new was that Ash went down on his knees and leaned

in, angling his face. Then he kissed me, hard, his fingers tilting my chin so he could devour my mouth.

I was usually the one in control. I made the rules. I set the scene. This side of him was so unexpected. Made me do things.

The number of times I'd fantasised about ravaging Ashton Wallace…never him ravaging me! To be honest, jerking him off down Sussex Alley had never featured in my teenaged pornographic scenarios either, but him on his knees, kissing me and unbuttoning my shirt as I jerked myself off with unsteady fingers…

A kiss on my naked collarbone, the shirt shoved off my shoulder. A wet mouth on my pec. A soft lick over my nipple. Instinctively, I craned my neck, only realising when my head whacked the wall. I'd have bruises everywhere tomorrow. Grazed elbows and arse. And my wrist was about to give out.

Any minute now, someone would walk up on us and my life would be completely…

Fuck.

Fuck.

I roared into the air, temporarily blinded by the streetlight and the orgasm that ripped through me, my bare back scraping the wall as Ash clamped his teeth around my nipple, hard. Somehow, he knew how to set me off, and I had a thing for…

Shit.

Ashton Wallace. His face, his hair, his mouth, the way he did things to me. All of him.

It took a while to come down from that. The orgasm had completely destroyed me, the realisation of what it meant even more so. The way he'd run from me, refused to believe how I felt about him and then torn my breath away with that little show. Yet he was still here, gently stroking the hair off my forehead while I lay in a heap in Sussex Alley.

There were people coming. I could hear them.

"Come on," he said.

I nodded, didn't move. Wasn't sure I knew how. My head was completely obliterated.

"Get up, you tosspot. Time to go." Grabbing my hand, he dragged me off the ground with no help from me whatsoever and buttoned up my shirt while I clumsily tried to fix my trousers. There was wet stuff down my leg, and it was starting to rain, at first a gentle, soothing patter, followed by a huge droplet that splatted on my nose. I didn't care.

"Your dad was right about the rain," he said. He picked his jacket up off the ground, shook it out with a small smile. "Come on. Let's go before we get drenched."

I don't know how I got my legs to move, but I did. And then I followed him, like I always had.

CHAPTER
THREE

ASHTON

I could have slept until lunchtime, but my parents didn't let me. The usual hoovering started up just after nine, accompanied by the radio blaring out the local news and songs nobody wanted to hear at any time of day.

At least they made me a cup of tea. As Dad shoved it into my hand, I silently praised myself for the genius idea of sleeping in my hoodie, blaming it on all that rain last night and having caught a bit of a chill on the walk back.

Yes, this wasn't my first rodeo, and I had memories. Specific ones relating to the real possibility of Holland Snow having inflicted visible damage to my neck. Damage no parent should ever have to see.

We'd stopped there. Well. It wasn't like I could have dragged him into my childhood bed and had my way with him. Nor would his parents have been pleased with me turning up at their breakfast table.

Not the done thing. This was Kirby, after all. The neighbourhood was no doubt already scandalised by some ruckus going on in the alleyway last night. So what was new? Daisy Jo had apparently lost her virginity there in Year Eight, if you believed the rumours. I didn't for a second. But whatever.

He'd kissed me by his front door. Held my face in his hands and claimed my mouth under cover of the porch. We'd been quiet. Not said a word.

I could still feel him. Taste him on my furry tongue.

Holland Snow.

Ashton Wallace-Snow.

Ashton Snow.

Fuck thirteen-year-old me and my stupid notebook full of lovey-dovey drawings. I probably still had it somewhere, hidden inside my childhood storybooks.

Before I was tempted to go looking for it, I shrugged off the stupid teenage me who'd somehow crept back under my skin while I wasn't looking and joined my parents at the kitchen table to gossip about people I no longer knew. This person's new boyfriend, that person's divorce, the new family who'd moved in at number twelve and so on. Nothing too heavy…until they turned the question on me.

I was not the kind of guy who felt the need to tell my parents who I had sexual contact with, and a boyfriend was not on the cards. Never had been. Nor a girlfriend for that matter, although I preferred men. No, last night was a hook-up, nothing more, and I was no stranger to those. The ease of brief encounters. No clingy aftercare required.

Which was a brand-new pang of complicated emotions that snuck up on me and winded me like a kick to the chest.

With the excuse that I was still hungover, I left my parents to their magazines and crosswords and headed out into the garden, stroking the leaves as I passed my dad's prized plants, colourful displays wherever I turned. I reached the far end of the lawn and sat on a chair, pulled my hood right up and wondered where I went from here.

I wanted to know what he looked like naked. I wanted to see his face again when he came. I wanted to be the one who made him come. In so many different ways. Wanted to use my fingers on him. My mouth.

Which brought me back to the worst thought of them all. I wanted to see him again.

No. Nope. Ashton Wallace, back away now. Get in that car of yours and drive as far away from here as possible. But where the hell was I supposed to go? I lived and worked in London. The same place where one particular vet had a practice of his own.

Yeah.

"Psst."

I didn't need to turn around to know who was trying to get my attention, but I did anyway.

When we were kids, that platform meant he could just get his head over the top of the fence. Now he was way too big for it and looked ridiculous, hanging halfway into our garden in his T-shirt and joggers —I could even see his waistband.

Any minute now, that fence would give way, Holland Snow would crash into my dad's prize-winning dahlias and my life would be over.

Honestly, my dad loved those dahlias more than he loved me.

"Get down before you hurt yourself," I hissed, carefully negotiating the precious plants so I could get right up to that fence.

"My knight my knight, will you rescue me?" he mocked, winking at me and sipping the cup of tea in his hand. Stupid twat.

"Did I not rescue you enough last night?" I huffed, a little bit in annoyance.

"You did." The fence creaked dangerously.

"Seriously, Holl, get off the fence."

"Can I come round?" he asked like we were still eight and needed permission for a playdate. And he was serious.

"No," I said firmly. "Anyway, I need to go. I'm back at work Monday, and I want to spend some time with my folks, having come all this way, you know."

It sounded grown up, and it was the sensible thing to do—put a little bit of distance between us—but all I wanted to do was scream.

"No problem," he said. "I need to leave too in, like, half an hour. I'm working tonight." And there he went, completely shattering my world. Again.

"Oh," I managed to squeeze out. I hated it, having him this close and knowing he was leaving.

"Yes," he said, his voice soft like a caress. "But that doesn't mean anything. You know? In the grand scale of *us*."

"Us," I repeated, still doubting every word that came out of that mouth of his. God. His mouth. His skin. Against mine. Even now, I could barely breathe and he was only talking to me.

The attraction had always been there, but could I forgive him for ignoring me for ten years? It still hurt, despite everything he'd said last night. Our friendship, past and present, was so sweepingly beautiful in all its complexity, the idea of him just walking away again was so unbearably painful I felt sick. He did that to me. I wasn't forgiving shit.

"They've made a WhatsApp group this morning," he continued, undaunted. "Well, Lesley-Anne set it up, naturally. Still thinks she's head girl. So anyway, thanks to her, I have your number."

"Oh." Great, Ash. Good conversation.

"And you have mine. So will you promise me something?"

I took it back. All was forgiven. Because he was stretching right over the fence, his hand on my skin again, and fool that I was, I leaned into it, craving every millimetre of his touch.

"Friday evening after work, are you free? Could you come to mine? Stay the weekend. Just...see where we go."

It was too soon, no time even to come up with a feasible excuse or get my head straight.

"Yeah," I said, surprising myself. Turning my head, I kissed his palm.

"Good," he murmured. "I wish I could kiss you properly right now. That's why I wanted to come round."

"Just to kiss?"

"Yep."

"Liar." I grinned, and he laughed.

"Can't wait to touch you again. But next time, I want you stark naked in my bed. And I...I don't care. I want to fuck you so badly."

"Your arse is mine," I said firmly. "Princess."

"Yeah. Right." His cheeks flushed like he was embarrassed. "I thought I was the drama queen—doesn't that make you the princess?"

"Definitely not." Although he was actually quite a built prince. I could see the outline of his defined pecs under his T-shirt and his nipples poking at the fabric. No doubt he had a boner brewing too. I know I did.

"Go," I said. "Save that kiss for Friday, yeah?"

"Friday," he said.

Then he was gone.

I spent the rest of the day doing...well, not a whole lot. I'd thought, with a firm arrangement to see each other again, it wouldn't hurt so much, but it did. Every part of my body ached worse the more physical distance he put between us, like we'd bonded and now he was stretching those strings.

"Ashton, darling, stop fretting," my mum said when I messed around with the dinner on my plate that evening. She leaned sideways and looked sternly at my leg jiggling under the table. "What's up with you?"

"Must have been something I ate last night," I lied. "Those nibbles they had, you know. Sat out all evening."

Dad nodded knowingly. Mum just sighed.

"You spoke to Holland, then?" Dad said.

"Yes. We had a nice chat." I needed to go to bed. Sleep this stupidity off.

"Good. He's a nice boy. Very successful."

I grimaced.

Mum reached over and stroked down my arm. "He lives down in London. You could meet up. Have a drink sometime. Friends do that."

"He's a gay, you know," Dad added. Like this was essential information.

"Ashton knows that," Mum huffed at him and then to me, "Of course you know that."

"Yes. Of course," I parroted, slightly weirded out by this conversation.

"Valerie's very proud of him. Says he always asks about you. You were always close, the two of you. Wherever you were, he was usually just a few steps behind you."

"We weren't that close," I argued and shrank in my chair. I should have done what Holl had done and pissed off back to London.

"Oh, he loves you, that boy." Dad laughed. "He always did. Even this morning, he was up and down that fence, looking for you like he did when you were boys. I remember one time you were ill, and he stood on that fence waiting for you all day. Didn't matter how often I told him you were unwell and asleep, he wouldn't come down. Kept saying he'd wait to make sure you got better."

Mum laughed. "I remember that."

My father wiped his eyes. "Ah, happy days. Holland Snow and Ash—"

"Dad," I warned. *Enough.*

"All I'm saying is you should cherish the people who love you."

"Funny thing, isn't it?" Mum winked. "You're still both single, and Holland still waits at that back fence for you."

"I'm done," I said, pushing my barely touched plate away. I got up and walked out, letting the kitchen door slam on my laughing parents. I wasn't amused.

***

I drove back home on the Sunday, doing well over the speed limit. I had so much aggression in my veins, and I took it all out on the traffic, swearing loudly at random motorists until I ran out of steam and had to stop at the services for fuel and a cry. Sometimes I did that.

Holland had texted me—only a short message to wish me a safe drive home and to say he couldn't wait to see me on Friday, plus his address.

I'd needed a good cry to get all those confusing emotions out of my system. By the time I'd put myself back together enough to leave the car, my eyes were red and I was a bit of a mess, but so what? I was allowed to be a mess because this weekend had been weird as hell and I couldn't handle it.

I also needed to reply to him.

But I couldn't make myself do it.

Back in the car again, I drove fast and little bit dangerously with the windows down, letting the noise of the asphalt calm my nerves, the rhythm soothing as the tyres sped from concrete block to concrete block, carrying me home. *Ash, Holl, Ash, Holl. Ash, Holl.*

I sorted my emails when I got in. Got out my clothes for work tomorrow. Checked my schedules. Made something to eat.

I couldn't eat.

I went to bed. Well, that wasn't going to work either because I kept staring at his messages and at his profile photo on WhatsApp. God, he was so…him.

My stomach was whirring again, and I was winding myself up into a state where I knew I'd never be able to sleep. So I did what I had to do to end this mess.

He picked up straight away, and there I was, all tucked up in bed, staring at a man in scrubs holding a very tiny kitten.

"Just born!" He pulled down his face mask, revealing a huge grin. "Emergency c-section—mum and the other babies are doing okay, but I'm trying to hold on to this one. She's the runt of the litter and far too small, but let's see if I can get some extra milk down her. Not easy with a tiny, wriggly kitten and a slippery syringe."

Looked easy enough to me, since he'd propped the phone up against something so I had a perfect view.

"You got home okay then?" He glanced up at me and smiled. God. Why did he do this to me?

"Yes. A couple of hours ago. It was…you know. Nice to see everyone?"

He nodded. "Drives me mad being at home. I can manage the first night with my folks. Day two is usually kind of ropey. By Sunday? That's when I start going a little bit crazy. Too many questions and enough tea to sink a cruise liner. I was glad I had to come back yesterday."

I smiled. Yes. I knew it all well. "I'm with you on the questions." I folded my pillow, raising my head. Stared at the small kitten in his big hands.

"I'm really happy we…did what we did," he said softly.

"Mmm." Okay. "Me too."

"Us—it's going to be a good thing, Ash. I promise. We can do this. I mean, it's…"

"Us."

"Us. I mean it. You and me. We're good together. Really good. And I can't stop thinking about you, and what we said and—"

"How's your back?"

"Bloody scratches all down my arse. Sussex Alley surely left its mark on me."

"Speaking of leaving marks..." I turned my head so the dark bruise on my neck filled the screen.

He looked proud. "Ash, you're amazing. I...I'm really glad we caught up."

"Took us long enough. And yeah, it was...good," I admitted.

"Listen, I have my nurse here—"

"Oops."

He chuckled. "It's fine, but mamma cat's owners will be in in a tick, so I need to go. I just wanted to say..."

"Yes?"

"Ring me. Anytime. Text. Talk to me. This week's going to be hard, and I can't wait to see you. You're still coming on Friday, aren't you?"

"'Course! Shall I bring something? Wine?"

God, this was becoming awfully civilised.

He looked around the room and walked over to something that looked like a fridge. Did he have wine in there? No, it turned out, as he grabbed another syringe and closed the door. I was getting motion sickness watching him move around, the tiny kitten still balanced in the crook of his arm.

"Ash, bring lube, condoms and whatever else you...enjoy."

"Wait—is your nurse still there?"

He laughed. "No, he's gone." Still, he lowered his voice to a sexy murmur. "We have a whole weekend to...indulge."

God. This man.

"Indulge?" I grinned into the screen.

He grinned back. "Us," he said.

"Us," I repeated.

Everything suddenly felt...like butterflies and snowflakes, a soft fluttering sensation settling in my stomach. Despite the air being terribly cool, I was snug and cosy. Like I had felt on Friday. Because it wasn't about what we were doing or where we were. It was about...us. I didn't know if I was terrified or excited. Horrified or calm.

But I slept.

CHAPTER
FOUR

HOLLAND

By the time Friday came around, I was a bit of a wreck. Mostly because I was over-hyped and over-caffeinated and one hundred per cent overthinking everything. There were not enough cups of coffee in the world to keep me going.

I worked all day. Ran a full clinic as well as surgery on a dog's fractured leg over lunch, followed by an emergency visit from an impressive python. I didn't mind the smaller reptiles but a huge, grumpy one, today of all days? I handed off that delight to my colleague so I could go sit down for a minute and breathe before I continued with my afternoon appointments.

Grabbing a glass of water, I sat in the office and scrolled up and down the week's text convo with Ash, smiling to myself as the small snippets of our lives rolled past me. Only a few more hours before I'd get to see him again.

A loud, familiar mewling from the waiting room announced the arrival of my next patient—the mamma cat from last Sunday in for a wound check. I put away my phone and downed another espresso from our rather snazzy coffee machine on my way back to my consulting room.

I was lucky. I'd met my partners at college, all of us sharing the same vision for the kind of place we wanted to work. So we'd done our research, found a location in North London and opened up a few years back. Twenty-four-hour vet care between the four of us and a few locum vets. We were expanding again, but the small extension being added at the back was only a part of why I was excited about my life.

I was going to have Ash here. My Ash.

Ashton.

I said it out loud. Whispered it gently.

My clinic finished half an hour late, which normally wouldn't have bothered me, but I ended up taking Bruce for a very short, stressful walk around the block instead of his usual run in the park. I was a bad human today, and despite my many apologies, poor Bruce still refused to perform. No doubt I'd have to clean up his mess at some point—not his fault. He was an old dog, a rescue with as many issues as I had.

I threw myself in the shower, cleaned myself thoroughly, hoping It didn't look like I was trying too hard. Who was I kidding? I'd known Ash all my life. He'd seen me at my best. Also—from a distance—at my worst. When I'd been so confused about what I wanted from life. When I'd struggled to figure everything out. He'd heard me cry in the garden many times, I was sure of it. You could hear everything through that wooden fence, and I'd always known when he was on the other side of it.

I'd seen him a week ago. I hadn't been a mess then, had I? Was my hair too long? Did I need to shave? Was this aftershave too much?

Which boxers should I wear? Or should I go without? Would he want to have sex? Like straight away? Or would we...?

Ugh. Overthinking much, Holland?

He texted when he rolled into the car park, and I gave him directions how to get upstairs but still ended up running down and holding the door open for him.

Ash. Standing there like he'd never belonged anywhere else.

I'd never seen him down here. Why? Sure, London's a big city, so I wasn't expecting to just bump into him in the pub or anything, but I could've called him to arrange something. Thing was, I'd been so terrified, thinking he'd laugh in my face and reject me. Not even when I'd known he'd been home at Christmas had I dared to pop over. I could've dropped in a card for the parents—the perfect excuse—but no.

I don't know why all these thoughts were rumbling through my head right now, but when I finally gestured for him to come in, he folded himself into my arms and hugged me, his nose buried in my shoulder, mine buried in his hair.

"Hi," he murmured softly.

"Hi."

I had to spin us around so I could close the door, the two of us dancing on tiptoes in the small hallway before he let go of me and headed up the stairs. I followed, my heart doing somersaults all the way.

I gave him a brief tour. The sitting room, the bedroom next door, the kitchen and... I grimaced. The bathroom. God, the state of it.

"Holl, I have no expectations. You don't have to...you know."

I did know. We didn't have to spell anything out here, but I sometimes wished we would for my own peace of mind.

"I just worry," I admitted. "Are you hungry? Want a drink? Or should we head down the pub?" I was trying to be hospitable, offering up the delights of North London.

"There was a nice-looking Indian on the corner?" he said with a wink.

Fuck.

There would be no eating going on here if he kept looking at me like that. His shirt was unbuttoned just enough to show off his chest hair. I wanted to tangle my fingers in all that dark goodness.

"Or Thai?" I croaked out. "The one across the road keeps winning awards. Or so their leaflet says."

"Okay?" He rocked on his heels like he was trying to decide whether to take his shoes off or keep them on. To take a seat on my crappy sofa or not.

"This is Bruce." I nodded to the dog, who had traipsed out of the bedroom to join us, completely cool with life. "He's the worst guard dog. Doesn't even bark at the postman. Would probably give a potential robber a sniff and go back to bed."

"Hey, Bruce." Ash reached down and gave the dog a gentle head rub. As expected, Bruce went over to the sofa and went back to sleep.

"Useless dog," I muttered. "I was hoping he'd charm you and you'd want to stay here forever."

"Holl…" He sighed.

"And Fifi's behind the fridge. You won't see her at all. Hates people. Most of all, she hates me. Doesn't even eat the food I put out for her. Goes down to the clinic and demands food from reception. Rude and entitled."

"That's cats for you." His hand gripped my arm reassuringly. I got the impression there were things he wanted to say, but he was waiting for me to give up on all this stupid nonsense talk first.

"Holl," he said again and took hold of my other arm, pulling me closer. Too close. My breath hitched.

"You know what you do to me when you look at me like that," I whispered. I was losing it. Fast.

"We don't have to do anything," he said quietly, staring at my mouth.

"Okay." I stared back.

He licked his bottom lip.

My dick pulsed.

"The scar on your chin. Year Nine. School ski trip."

I nodded. "You were on the lift ahead of me. I was staring at you instead of looking where I was going. Fell over. Flat on my face."

"I remember." His breaths were hot against my face, and my head was swimming as I struggled to find words for…something.

Then he went for me, his arms tightening around me, hands at the back of my neck, pulling me in as he smashed his lips on mine, our teeth clacking together and his tongue down my throat. I grabbed his arse and lifted him up, laughing against his mouth as his legs wrapped around my waist.

Stumbling a few steps forward, I pushed him up against the wall and kissed a trail down his neck. His feet back on the floor, he ripped his shirt open, like he wanted me exactly where I was desperate to be.

I shoved his shirt back over his shoulders and buried my nose in his chest hair, inhaling the scent of him, the strongest I'd ever smelled. Like concentrated Ash. God, what he did to me.

He was way ahead of me, stepping out of his trousers and tugging my jumper over my head with ease, his lips on my shoulder, my chest, my mouth again as I half carried him to my bed.

Boxers. Off.

And here he was. Stark naked and splayed out like a vision of wonder against my white sheets, masses of dark hair in all the right places, pecs to die for. A feast, right there.

I wanted everything. Absolutely everything.

The last of my clothes gone, I lowered myself on top of him, my nose settling gently against his, our dicks fighting for space between us, both of us stupidly erect.

This felt like a dream. He was here with me, at last.

"What do you need?" I could barely get my voice to sound, too emotional to function.

"I..." He paused, shuffled his hips, moving me with him as he once again wrapped his legs around my waist. My cock was in a new place, warm, inviting. I rocked gently, welcoming the friction as the head brushed against his opening. I was on the edge. How he knew, I had no idea. I'd thought I'd be the one with more experience, but he knew exactly what he was doing, as his hands moved down my back onto my arse, holding, controlling my movements.

"I really...really want to fuck you, Holl. I love all this. The teasing. The kisses." His mouth found mine again, too much tongue as usual. I wasn't complaining. "But I want to be inside you."

"You're vers?" Wow. Expectations were a thing. Setting boundaries. "I'm not...really?"

"Yeah." Okay? "But you know what? After all those years, I think I have a right to, you know, show you a good time. Truly destroy that arse of yours."

"You did a good job of that last weekend, and I have the marks to prove it."

"Still?" He flipped me over and straddled me with his arms either side of my head. "You're going to work hard to pay me back. Give me what I want."

His hair fell in front of his eyes. I reached out and twirled a curl around my finger.

"Yeah," I answered. I wasn't even sure there'd been a question.

"Gonna do what I like. Get you all worked up for me. That good for you?"

I nodded.

"A little hurt. A little rough. That okay?"

"Who the hell is this Ash Wallace and what have you done to the guy from Kirby?"

"Oh, princess. That boy left Kirby a long time ago. Got himself some skills."

I laughed. "Again with the princess?"

He bit down on my bottom lip, tugged a little at the skin, released and looked me in the eye again.

"You'll always be my princess, sitting on top of that fence like it's your castle, waiting for me to rescue you."

"You never did."

"You grew up. Got too big and tall. I would have done some serious damage to my dad's dahlias if I'd tried to get you over that fence. Which brings me back to where we are now. It would be a massive shame to waste your boner. You have a very, very nice cock. I mean, I knew you had a sizeable package…"

"Not that sizeable." I was blushing a little. *Ash!!!* "To be fair, every time I saw you, I had a massive boner, so yeah."

God. I loved hearing him laugh.

"So, Holl, d'you mind if I use my mouth on you, give you some head? Eat you out while I loosen you up a bit?"

Head side to side. Mouth too dry to speak.

"Legs up. Hold yourself open for me when I tell you to, yeah?"

Gulp. God help me.

"Ash?" There was no fear in my voice. Zero. He could have brandished a giant dildo at me at this point or said he was going to fist the hell out of my poor bottom. I should have sorted an enema, cleaned myself out properly. I'd just assumed. Because Ash? He was so surprising.

"Honestly. Don't worry. I have no issues with your arse." He prattled on, his hands seemingly everywhere at once. "I figured out I was mostly gay when I was super young. As in when I was still reading fairy tales, because the literal princess in the tower was no princess to me. No, he was a handsome boy with the most ridiculous name. I mean, how many people do you know who are named after a country."

I laughed. "Let me guess…Belgium? Germany? Not that boy called France?"

"Holland," he said, his voice full of smiles. "It was always you, Holl. You know that."

"Yeah," I whispered, suddenly too full of emotions to keep up the joking around. "It was, wasn't it? Always us. You and me."

"Us," he repeated softly, and then he was hoicking my leg over his shoulder and kissing his way down, bending me into impossible positions, a tongue on my nipple, his fingers on my arse. He licked a circle and then bit, softly at first, then harder, sending zings through my body like he'd electrocuted me. Down, down he went, until his hot breath huffed over my dick, followed by soft, wet lips.

"God, Ash. Just—"

"Shush," he said, his mouth full of cock. I was so hard I thought it would explode. "Behave. You'll get everything you deserve. Trust me."

"Sadist," I muttered.

"Nope. Just…" A lick down my shaft. "I love this. Having you…" A tug on my foreskin. "Being with you. I…" A sweet kiss on the tip. "Can't believe I'm actually here."

"Oh, just shut up and suck my dick."

He laughed. I did too. Stupid, spluttered laughter that stopped when my body jerked involuntarily as his tongue lapped over my arse. Oh, hell.

Rimming. Not my favourite thing to do. But having it done to me by him… I threw my hands back towards the headboard because I couldn't trust myself not to grab my cock, which would no doubt have meant me coming right there and then.

Fuck. Fuck. Fuck.

He pushed his fingers into me. Fucking two! Because apparently,

Ash didn't do slow and steady, but he'd brought some top-end lube, which he was generously destroying my sheets with.

Rough, he'd said. I'd give him rough.

"You're trashing my sheets."

"Shush." He pushed deeper and made small movements that made my insides sing.

"Aww, fuck!" I roared. My dick was pulsing and neither of us was touching it. A squirt of white landing on my stomach.

"That's it, baby. Just let your body do its thing."

Like I could stop it with his fingers massaging my prostate with precision and his mouth on my balls.

"Let's get you fucked then. Get you really screaming for me."

Who was this guy? Whoever he was, he was mine. Mine. Mine. Mine.

I almost screamed at the loss of those fingers, but there went my other leg, over his other shoulder. The snap of a condom, more squelching sounds of lube, then his cock was against my opening and I was roaring again as he pressed inside me. After that, I lost all coherent thought, floating in some kind of weird haze as I came in seemingly never-ending waves of painful pleasure. It was the longest, most intense orgasm of my life. Insanely long, like I couldn't stop coming, still twitching and kicking at him as he finally screamed my name amid a wild symphony of swearwords while I panted and stared up at him.

Ash. Ash. Ash.

He landed hard on my chest, my useless legs flopping to the sides, his arms around me, my lips in his hair.

Ash. Ash. Ash.

Cold, wet condom against my leg.

"You're beautiful," I said. I couldn't find any other words.

He gave a small snort. "Holl?"

"Yeah?" I couldn't open my eyes. I was utterly blissed out.

"Your dog is watching us. Is that normal? He's wagging his tail."

"Bruce," I said sternly.

Bruce barked in return. Yeah. Thanks, mate.

"He probably needs to go outside. He's old."

"Okay?"

"It's—"

"Holl." Leaning his chin against my chest, he peered up at me. He looked so alive. The glow-up? He was happy, full of laughter lines, biting his bottom lip in mischief.

"Ash?"

"Is this how it's going to be from now on? Our weekends spent like this. Fucking and starving to death while the dog watches us?"

"Did you think I was going to feed you? Like take you out and wine you and dine you?"

He laughed. My sarcasm was obviously on point.

"I had my lunch at midday. It's almost eight."

"Is it?" No wonder Bruce was getting twitchy.

"And...Holl?"

"Yes, Ashton?" He was such a little shit. I might have been the bigger of the two of us, but he was always the one who got us into trouble.

He leaned in. Kissed me softly.

"Let's walk your dog. Get some grub. Bring it back here and just veg out. Because that? That was so good, I think we need to refuel and do it again. What do you think?"

I kissed him back, tangled my fingers in his hair.

"I think that sounds like a plan."

EPILOGUE

ASHTON

A Year Later

The Goose hadn't changed at all. It was just one of those places. Like when they'd tried to paint the outside a different shade of grey, there had been an absolute outcry from the locals.

The building was still grey, but the sky was blue, and I was sitting in the sun on the veranda, a pint in my hand, my fingers greasy from the packet of crisps we'd shared.

It had been a long drive. Holl had slept most of the way, having come straight off a callout on his night shift.

Holl. And me.

I smiled, remembering that first weekend with him. I'd tried to leave on Sunday night but had stayed until Tuesday in the end. Already out of excuses for why I couldn't stay longer, I'd headed home and washed my clothes, gone to work, then driven that extra half an hour after work on Wednesday back to his place.

He'd laughed when I'd turned up. Then he'd dragged me inside, pulled my trousers down and sucked my dick until I'd screamed.

After that, I'd never really left. There was no point leaving when that was where I wanted to be. So I'd slowly moved my stuff over, and he'd quietly made space for me. Bruce wagged his tail when I walked through the door. Fifi still spent most of her time behind the fridge. She seemed to like me, but she hated Holl. She hissed at him if he ever tried to go near her but would sometimes happily sit on my lap and let me stroke her.

"Here, Bruce," I said quietly, sneaking the last crisp to him. We always brought him with us now because he was too old and frail to deal with being in the kennels. And he liked the car. Liked being with us.

"Don't feed him crisps, Ash," Holl complained, coming back from the loos. "The grease is really bad for him."

"I know." Guilty as charged. "But he loves them."

"Bruce doesn't know what's good for him."

"Neither do you." I laughed, seeing he'd grabbed a menu from the bar. The Goose didn't serve anything remotely healthy. Everything here came with chips, and I, for one, I was having them. All the chips. And those sausages with onion gravy and some crispy bacon strips on the side.

Let our chefs slowly destroy your insides with our range of greasy processed delights!

My taglines were frighteningly on point. Good thing I wasn't handling any pub accounts. My latest venture was a supermarket Christmas advert. I'd been driving Holl crazy with festive jingles for weeks, singing loudly in the shower until he banged on the door.

"Sausages even your dog will eat," Holl teased. "Wasn't that your tagline-of-the-day last time we were here? I want the gammon today. With a fried egg."

"Healthy." I nodded.

We did this now. Drove up here and stayed in the rooms over The Goose so we could visit our parents from a more civilised distance. It was less hassle and gave us more time to relax.

We were having lunch at my parents' house tomorrow, then Sunday roast at Holl's before we drove back home. My parents were coming over too.

They referred to us as *their boys* now, like we'd morphed into two instead of the unit we'd always been.

Us. We were an us. It was still astounding how happy that made me.

"You okay?" Holl stroked his fingers down my arm. "You drifted off there for a moment."

"Yeah." I smiled. "Reminiscing. I really don't want to go to any more school reunions."

His laughter was my favourite thing in the world.

"The WhatsApp group is still going strong. They're talking about a late summer meet-up."

"No." I grinned. "Absolutely not. I only went to that damn thing for you."

"Same. I drove past your house and saw your car there."

"Stalker boy."

"Nah. Never stalked you. Just kept an eye on you, made sure you were safe. I was just…you know. I needed this."

"Yeah. Me too."

"You make me happy," he said, looking straight at me. He still made me quiver deep in my bones. "I can't remember anymore what my life was like before I got you back. There was always this big Ash-shaped hole."

"You like my hole." I winked. He laughed.

"I wish you'd let me top you more." He knew exactly what he was doing. If we weren't careful, we'd end up going for a fuck and our food would go cold. It wouldn't be the first time. He also knew full well that I would be the one fucking him.

"But you like bottoming too much," I pointed out.

He was…*a very enthusiastic sexual partner*, my advertising voice narrated in my head. Holland Snow. God. He drove me crazy. A year back, my sexual appetite had been rather restrained. These days, I had to grab my junk, take a deep breath, calm myself down.

We were having so much fun. Every single day. Sex with Holland was wonderful. Mind-blowingly so.

"I bought you another…surprise for later," he said, a small blush creeping over his face.

"Did you now." My face was probably pink too. Naughty. God. The things he made me feel.

"And extra lube." He grinned. "You're so pretty when you blush, Ash."

"Shut up. We'll scandalise the locals."

"Only us staying tonight. I checked. So we'll both be walking funny for lunch tomorrow."

"Well, my mother was asking about that muscle you pulled in your leg last time. She was going to recommend a good chiropractor."

"It's very slow to heal." He giggled, taking a cheeky sip of his pint. "And you know what these steep stairs at The Goose are like. Really aggravates that old injury."

"At least let me be able to sit down properly." I pretend winced. "Last time…"

"That dildo was fantastic."

Now it was me spluttering my drink.

"Holl," I warned. "There are other people on this veranda. I think we should be discussing more appropriate things."

"Oh? Like what?"

"Like—"

"I love you."

He said it all the time. We both did. But it still gave me butterflies.

"I love you too, Holl. Always and forever." No words truer than those.

"Us." He smiled, clinked his pint glass against mine.

"It was always us."

"Ready to order? Want another pint?"

He knew I did. And the sun was shining as I picked up his hand, pressed his fingers to my lips. Smiled as the breeze lifted his fringe from his face before he got up and disappeared towards the bar.

Him and me.

Us.

Right where we were meant to be.

ABOUT SOPHIA SOAMES

Sophia Soames is a Scandinavian author residing in the UK. She writes contemporary MM romance, always with messy difficult men finding their imperfectly perfect HEA.

Discover more stories from Sophia Soames at:
    https://www.sophiasoames.com
    Social media links: https://linktr.ee/sophiasoames

PIPE DREAMS

LEE BLAIR

Editing by Abbie Nicole

Proofreading by Lori Parks

Sensitivity read by Brennon Lane

ABOUT PIPE DREAMS

It was supposed to be a normal D&D night with my friends, but a plumbing emergency has my bestie convincing me to swipe on a dating app in search of someone to clean my pipes. The literal ones, unfortunately.

Among a sea of unsolicited dick pics, SumsOfAnarchy (a.k.a. Brandon) answers my distress call. My friends are pushing me at the gorgeous and charming guy who showed up with a smile and a toolbox. But I know as much about flirting as I do about plumbing, so as a thank you, I give Brandon some cookies. Just the cookies. No phone number, no IG handle, nothing. Did I mention I was bad at flirting?

Luckily, I see him again. Joke's on me though, because plumbing isn't Brandon's day job, and he witnesses my internet-viral embarrassing moment up close and in person. Good thing he's got a great sense of humor and a soft spot for geeks whose only "game" involves dice.

Pipe Dreams is a low-angst MM novella with a gaggle of queerdo geeks, environmental activism, and finding love how you least expect it.

CHAPTER
ONE

MYLES

"I'm going to seduce the guard with a limerick about my sexual prowess." My best friend in the world, Sami, wiggled her eyebrows suggestively. For game night, she'd drawn freckles across her olive-toned nose and curled her hot-pink mullet. Sami's *Today I'm* pronoun pin, which resembled a danger meter with an adjustable arrow, pointed to she/her.

Jay, the resident pale-skinned elfish goth in our merry band of D&D-loving misfits, shook his head, which made the faux-ruby jewel hanging from his headpiece bounce. "Do you have to try and seduce *everyone?*"

Sami narrowed her eyes. "I haven't tried seducing your dad yet."

Christian, our eternally patient dungeon master, leaned back in his chair. He steepled his hands in front of him, which combined with his sparkly crown, completed his DM vibe. That was my cue to grab the second bowl of guacamole. Tempers always flared on game night when the first bowl ran out. The second bowl always fixed all.

"We're preparing to face a dragon and you want to fuck *another* guard. We're never going to fight at this rate." Jay frowned as he scraped the last guac from the bowl.

"You two talk it out. I need a bathroom break." Christian rose from the table.

I loved hosting our weekly game night. Since moving into this cute bungalow in Dahlia Springs, it made sense for me to become the permanent host. I had the best parking and was the only group member who didn't share a wall with anyone. Game night could get...loud.

I hadn't always loved this geeky part of myself. It was bad enough getting teased mercilessly as a kid for being a geek, but the only Black kid in school who played D&D? It had made me an easy target. My friends were the only thing that got me through. *Look at us now.* Two of my oldest friends were busy arguing over how much sex a bard needed.

I chuckled to myself as I pulled the backup guac from the fridge. High school me would've never imagined an adulthood full of even more geekiness. I'd kept expecting I'd have to change—to leave the fun behind in my childhood. Now, a decade later, I had adult money to spend on my interests. Like the new custom Funko Pops I'd ordered last week to represent characters from my favorite K-drama. My built-in shelves in the living room were full of figurines with teetering stacks of games on the floor. Being a geeky adult was way more fun than I could've ever imagined.

As I set the bowl on the small counter, I spotted about an inch of water sitting in the sink. Weird.

"Uh, Myles?"

I turned toward Christian, who'd stepped into the kitchen.

"Yeah?"

"The bathroom sink is draining really slow."

My stomach dropped to the floor. "Uh-oh. I'll take a look." Not that I'd know what to search for. I dropped the guac at the table before trudging toward the bathroom. Water was now sitting in the bathroom sink and tub. *This can't be good.*

"What's up, buttercup? Christian said there are plumbing issues?" Sami dropped her chin on my shoulder.

"Yeah, in the kitchen too."

Sami sucked air between her teeth. "Looks like you should call your landlord."

I groaned. My landlord was unreliable on the best of days. Whenever I actually could get a hold of him, he acted supremely inconvenienced.

I checked under the sink, and fortunately, there weren't any leaks. I didn't want to flush the toilet in case it overflowed. Maybe I could get everyone to stop drinking anything to delay bathroom needs until my landlord showed up. *If* he showed up. I could call a plumber, but my landlord would never reimburse me for an expense he didn't authorize. Not to mention, I was tight on funds after my Funko Pop order and all the avocados for game night.

"Do you know how to fix this?"

Sami snorted and straightened. "You think *I* know how to fix plumbing issues? The person who managed to catch our hot pot on fire when I tried to boil water in our dorm? Babe, the only plumbing I understand is cleaning my pipe. Or swallowing them." She winked.

I laughed. Sami could always cheer me up, and on her femme days, she was extra snarky.

"I'd better call my landlord."

"Too bad Heather is out of town."

The masc lesbian of our group could fix anything. "Yeah, she'd know what to do."

I opened my contacts to find my landlord's number.

"Myles, your washing machine is leaking!"

I rushed to the laundry nook next to the back door to find a pool of water slowly spreading from underneath the washer and dryer.

"Towels! I need towels." I spun in a circle like they'd magically appear. I wasn't great in a crisis.

"Where are they?" Christian asked.

I blinked. "Closet next to the bathroom."

Christian rushed away and returned moments later with a stack of towels in his arms. We placed them around the machines to soak up the water.

"I googled how to turn off water to your washing machine," Jay said.

Duh. I should've done that first. Good thing I wasn't alone when this happened, or I'd be adding tears to the growing puddle, waiting for my landlord to call back. "Brilliant idea. How do we do it?"

"Have you called your landlord yet?" Sami asked while trying and failing to tilt the washing machine back to slide a towel underneath it.

"Was I supposed to have done that in the seconds it took me to run awkwardly from my bathroom here?" I asked in a high-pitched voice.

"Fair point. Call him. We'll work on the washing machine."

"Don't break anything," I said as I stepped into the kitchen to call my landlord. It went to voicemail. *Son of a sea hag!*

"Hi, this is Myles in the cottage on Walnut Street. I'm calling because something's going on with my plumbing. The sinks are backing up and the washing machine is leaking. I don't know what to do. Can you call me back, please? Thank you." A pulsing ache pounded against my temples as I ended the call.

What in the world was I supposed to do now?

Text. I could text. I sent a quick message in case he saw that first.

"You okay?" Sami put her arm around my shoulders.

"When I get nervous, I have to pee, but I can't pee because the plumbing isn't working and my nosy neighbor would probably catch me peeing outside!" I begged my bladder to hold on for a little while. Surely, my landlord would call soon. It was a plumbing emergency, for crying out loud.

"Let's eat some guacamole. It'll calm your nerves."

I followed Sami to the living room, where Jay and Christian were shoving guac-covered chips into their mouths. "Did you guys get the water turned off?"

"We did. We could play until your landlord calls. That'll keep your mind off it." Christian always had a positive outlook.

"Okay, but I want to check the sinks first to make sure the water isn't filling any faster."

Fortunately, the water didn't look any deeper. Maybe it was a backup but not a leak? I didn't know anything about plumbing. Hopefully, it would be an easy fix.

I returned to the living room, but instead of playing, everyone was sharing horror stories about plumbing and other reasons they'd had to call their landlords.

A half-hour and some truly traumatizing stories later, my landlord still hadn't called. I'd dang-near chewed a hole in my bottom lip.

"Do any of you know a plumber?"

They all shook their heads.

"I've got an idea."

It never boded well when Sami said that. The rest of us groaned.

She stuck her bottom lip out in a pout. "Okay, rude. I haven't even said what it is yet. I saw a plumber on Findr once."

"Super helpful. Thanks." My voice dripped with sarcasm.

Sami rolled her eyes. "*What I mean is,* maybe we can find him if we start swiping or find a different one."

"You sure he was a real plumber and not someone making pipe-laying jokes?" Jay asked.

"All I know is he handled my pipe like a pro." Sami winked.

"God, you're, like, perpetually horny." Jay's long, black hair swayed as he shook his head. "We could always Google local plumbers and call someone."

"I don't want to spend the money on an emergency call. My landlord probably wouldn't reimburse me if he didn't pre-approve it."

"Myles, your landlord sucks," Sami said. "Which makes hopping on a dating app to find a plumber the perfect solution.

"You're suggesting I flip through a digital deck of random, horny strangers on an app in hopes of finding someone who mentions in their profile that they're a plumber so they can come to fix my literal pipes?"

"I'm absolutely certain there are dozens of guys who would happily fix your pipes." Sami booped my nose.

I stared suspiciously at my phone. "The odds of finding someone before I hear from my landlord are slim."

"You could swipe while we play. It couldn't hurt," Christian suggested, always reasonable.

I sighed and opened the app I'd sworn off months ago. I was growing increasingly desperate as each minute passed without my landlord calling and didn't even want to think about being unable to shower before work tomorrow. I should've joined that fancy gym with the huge showers.

"You should add to your profile that you're looking for a plumber," Jay said.

"A real plumber," Christian added. "Weed out the creeps."

"Say that you can't clean your cute, wittle hole without working plumbing," Sami said in a creepy baby voice.

I blushed so hard that I got lightheaded from the blood rush. But they made good points, so I quickly added a note to my profile about needing real plumbing help.

"You gotta swipe yes on everyone so they can send you a message if they're a plumber. That's the only way this will work," Jay said as he adjusted his ornate headpiece.

"That makes sense." My stomach tightened at the prospect of swiping yes on a bunch of people, even if it was fake. What if no one swiped back? I wouldn't be able to wallow in that knowledge in private with an audience of my nosy friends. The apps were brutal in the best of circumstances.

Within minutes, I got my first message.

9inDomTop: [photo: poorly lit penis from a weird angle]

"Ugh. Dick pic."

"Eyyy! Let the fun begin!" Sami held up her hand for a high five.

The "fun" kept coming. I received varied peen pictures in every shape, size, color, and...texture. Not to mention the other messages that showed they clearly hadn't read my profile.

MarkJohnson1962: show me ur hole
@$$e@ter69: hey. U top?
QuTee: [photo: closeup of a hairless butthole]
10inchPDXBear: into?
10inchPDXBear: [photo: a huge penis with a watermark across the picture listing the source as an adult stock photography website]
10inchPDXBear: can u fit that in your mouth? Show me ur hole

As another message came through, I sighed, expecting another dick. Couldn't the guys put a bit of work into making their dicks appear desirable if they were going to send them unsolicited? Decent lighting or at least flushing before taking a dick pic over the toilet. *Gross.*

> SumsOfAnarchy: Hey. Do you really need a plumber, or is this a coy way of asking for pipe puns?

My mouth twitched at the message.

> Frogtastic: I really need a plumber. My sinks are clogged and the washing machine is leaking, and my landlord isn't calling me back. Desperate times. But I also have a healthy admiration for puns, as any civilized adult should.

"You're smiling. Did you get a bite?" Sami tried peeking over my shoulder.

I angled my phone away. "Uh, maybe. Not sure yet."

> SumsOfAnarchy: Only the best people enjoy puns. I can help with a plumbing emergency. It looks like you're in Dahlia Springs? I live here too.

I checked out his profile. There wasn't much beyond a photo showing fairly defined abs on a white guy and another of a silhouette of someone in front of a sunrise. His bio talked about hiking and enjoying football. I was instantly on guard. Those were usually indicators of the kind of guys who never wanted to waste their time with me.

> Frogtastic: I am. Are you a plumber? I have some friends over for game night, and I can't get a hold of my landlord to get it fixed before we need flotation devices.
> SumsOfAnarchy: I've cleaned a lot of clogs. I could at least check it out.

"Don't give him your address yet. Make him prove he's really a plumber so we know he's not catfishing you," Jay said.

"Catfishing me with his ab photo?"

"Wait, he's got an ab photo? Lemme see." Sami tried to grab my phone, but I dodged her.

"I just want to see if it's a real ab photo. AI can be quite deceptive these days."

> Frogtastic: That would be really nice of you. I have a feeling I won't hear from my landlord tonight.
> SumsOfAnarchy: I've got nothing going on now. I can head over.
> Frogtastic: Seriously, thank you!
> SumsOfAnarchy: It's no problem. What's your address?

"You should ask him to take a picture of him giving a thumbs-up with his plumbing tools in the picture," Sami said.

"That seems unnecessary. Do you really think a creep would respond to a request for plumbing?" I grimaced at their deadpan expressions. "Yeah, you're right. I'll ask." I sent him the request.

The app went silent, as did my friends, while we waited for SumsOfAnarchy to reply.

"He probably unmatched me." I wouldn't blame him. Though, for some silly reason, that prospect bummed me out. It'd been the first quasi-normal conversation I'd had on the app in ages.

After a few minutes, the dots bounced, and I let out a unified sigh of relief.

> SumsOfAnarchy: I added a newspaper to prove it's a photo from today. Yes, I still read paper newspapers. Don't judge me. [photo: an open toolbox with a newspaper dated today folded on top]

I laughed. "Those tools look legit, right?"

"Better than some of the other 'tool' pics you've gotten tonight.

He's got big hands. Look at the circumference of his thumb," Sami purred.

Frogtastic: Thanks for indulging my request. If you can spare some time to help me, I can compensate you with homemade guacamole and cookies.
SumsOfAnarchy: You had me at homemade guac.

I bit the inside of my cheek as I sent him my address.

SumsOfAnarchy: I'll be there in ten minutes.

"We have ten minutes to come up with a game plan." Sami beamed. "Look at me talking sporty!"
"Game plan?" I glanced around the table at my friends.
"With abs like that? We're gonna get you a date with a plumber." Sami grinned.

CHAPTER
TWO

BRANDON

I maneuvered my trusty Camry into a space in front of a rhododendron shrub with buds waiting to bloom once the spring warmth arrived.

What the hell am I doing here? I'd been perfectly content vegging on my couch for the evening and binging a favorite British mystery show for the umpteenth time. When I'd hopped on Findr, I'd expected to waste some time before it was a reasonable hour to head to bed. If I got lucky, maybe a little sexting. I sure as hell hadn't expected to bring my plumbing tools to a stranger's house without even sneaking a bottle of lube and a condom inside.

I glanced at my phone and then the house numbers on the cottage with flaking beige paint to make sure I had the right place. Despite looking slightly weathered, it was a cute place with the tiniest strip of grass in front.

I retrieved my tools from the trunk. As I walked up to the house, I reminded myself that, at the very least, this would make a funny story.

When I knocked, there was a muffled yelp then a thud. The door opened slowly to reveal the cutest, adorable guy. The first thing I noticed was the bright-red glasses accentuating his big brown eyes. His tightly coiled, shiny black hair—no longer than a few inches—radiated from his head like a halo. He was at least a half-foot shorter than me, with a petite frame. I was surprised by the pointy ears he wore that were the color of brown terra cotta. They matched his skin tone but were clearly fake.

Oh! He'd mentioned game night, but my brain had gone to board games, not the kind that required elfish accessories.

He looked tongue-tied, and my first thought was wanting to untie his tongue with mine. *This isn't a real Findr hookup. Chill.* The whole geek-chic thing really worked for me though.

"Frogtastic?"

The guy nervously glanced at his friends. "Yeah. Myles, actually. Um, I really like frogs. Hence the username." His friends chuckled.

"Yeah? That's cool. I don't know much about frogs, but they seem really awesome. I like your ears, by the way. They're cute." I smiled sincerely. I wanted to ask him to tell me about frogs, but I was here on a mission. A plumbing mission, which was probably the least sexy way to meet someone my dick was perking up for.

Myles blinked wide-eyed at me. "Thank you."

I shifted the toolbox to my left hand and held out my right. "Brandon. Nice to meet you." His soft hand fit perfectly in mine, and his shy smile twisted something in my gut.

"Let the guy in. Jeez. We want to take a look at him."

Three others crowded around the doorway, each wearing a costume piece of some sort. They stared at me like I was a circus animal with a performance trick of unclogging drains.

Myles introduced each of them. I liked Sami's pronoun pin.

They reminded me of a group of kids at my high school who I always imagined had intelligent conversations while playing games in the library, understood Shakespeare, could curse people out in several languages, recited *Monty Python* in their sleep, and got high under the bleachers behind the track. Those kids had always seemed intriguing and fun. Very different from my football team buddies, who mostly cared about parties, getting laid, and playing the latest *Madden* game. I'd enjoyed that stuff too, but I'd always felt something was missing.

Seeing this group of friends having a fun game night together reminded me of that.

"Want to show me the issue?" Hopefully, it was an easy fix because I didn't have much equipment.

"Of course. Thank you so much for helping us." Myles's smile revealed a dimple in one cheek.

"My pleasure. You rescued me from watching too much TV." I followed him inside once his friends stepped back.

"What were you watching?" Myles asked.

"A British murder mystery." Myles's kitchen was small and clean. There was enough room for me and him in the narrow space, but it grew tight when his friends joined us.

Myles's eyes lit up. "*Midsomer Murders* or *Agatha Raisin*?"

My eyebrows jumped. "You watch those too? It was Midsomer. The most murderous small town in the world."

"Such a good show." Myles adjusted his glasses.

"One of my favorites too." We smiled at each other for a moment before Myles looked away.

He gestured to his sink, which had a couple of inches of murky water in the basin. "This is where I first noticed it."

My mind was already running through possibilities. "You mentioned issues elsewhere?"

"Bathroom and laundry. I'll show you."

I followed him through a tidy home full of clutter. Not in a bad way, but the type of clutter that showed Myles had interests and wasn't afraid of displaying them. It was comfortable and preferrable to the borderline bachelor-bare aesthetic of my place.

The more I watched him, the more intrigued I was by his mannerisms. Like the careful way he gripped the side of his glasses to adjust them and how he nibbled his bottom lip.

As he completed the tour of the laundry area, I was already mentally troubleshooting. It was an issue I'd handled plenty of times before. "This shouldn't be a problem to fix, but if I notice any major issues, I'll let you know because that should probably go through your landlord." I was interested in helping out a cute guy, not getting him in trouble.

"Really?" Myles's hopeful voice was too cute.

"Yup. Feel free to get back to your game. I'll let you know when I'm done." Part of me wanted to prolong what would likely be a quick fix so I could stay longer and watch game night, but I didn't want to impose. Myles reminded me of one of my coworkers who got nervous around new people, and I didn't want to cause any distress.

"Are you sure you're okay doing this?"

I employed the smile that usually got me a guy's phone number. "Always happy to rescue a cute guy's game night."

There went the lip nibbling again. "Oh. Um. Thank you. I'll be over there. Grab me if you need anything."

I set my toolbox on the dryer and tried to ignore the whispering as I got to work. Within a few minutes, they seemed to have resumed their game since they were talking about a dragon at a louder volume. I didn't quite follow, but it sounded interesting. I wished I knew how to play.

"I'd like to enhance my dick size."

Several people groaned.

"You've got to be kidding me."

I peeked around the corner and saw Sami throw her hands up.

"What's wrong with that? I'm the one who found an amulet with the power to grant me an enhancement, so I get to choose what to enhance. And I want to enhance my dick."

Jay, if I'd caught his name correctly, crossed his arms over his chest. "We're about to face a fucking dragon, and you only care about your dick. Peak bard behavior. Trying to fuck everything."

"*Exactly.* I can seduce the dragon with my huge dick!"

Myles pinched the bridge of his nose. "If you enhance your charisma, you could increase your performance. Then no one will care how big your dick is. It'll increase your deception too, and you could deceive anyone into thinking it's bigger than it is."

"Thank you. Finally, some logic here." Jay gestured to Myles. "If you cared about the rest of us, you'd consider using the amulet to enhance your dexterity. A higher dex would increase your acrobatics for whatever weird dragon fucking you have planned, but also your stealth. Which, you know, would *actually* be useful."

"You're such a cockblock." Sami huffed. "But you've given me a lot to think about." She turned to Christian, who had a folio standing in front of him at one end of the table. "Before I decide what to enhance, I'd like to roll for dick size. I need to know my baseline."

I snorted and got back to work. Never in a million years would I have guessed that this type of gaming involved discussions of dick size and monster fucking.

It only took a few minutes to fix the issue, and then I went around to all the faucets and ran the water to ensure things were draining properly. After letting Myles's washing machine run for a few minutes while listening to them describe how they were approaching the drag-on's cave, I figured I'd stalled long enough.

I packed my tools, then wandered over to their table, where a couple of books, stacks of paper, and figurines were placed on a map.

"What are you playing?"

"Oh, just a tabletop role-play game called Dungeons and Dragons," Myles said almost dismissively.

"I've always been curious how that was played. It sounds interesting."

Sami beamed at me, and I could've sworn she was swatting Myles's leg under the table.

"It is interesting," Myles said more confidently. "Is everything working, or is it a bigger issue?"

"Got it all fixed up, but I recommend your landlord have someone check it out. It could be a sign of a bigger issue closer to the septic."

"Thank you so much for your help. I had no idea what to do." Myles's sincerity made my chest swell.

"Glad I could be of service."

"Want some guac? Myles makes the best. Tons of cilantro." Jay held out the guacamole bowl while Christian passed over the chips.

I'd already washed my hands, and the guac did look good. "Thanks." Myles had no way of knowing I was a slut for cilantro, but if I wasn't already digging the guy, he'd have scored major brownie points with this. I popped the chip in my mouth and my tastebuds did a happy dance at the strong, fresh, herb-forward flavor of cilantro. "Delicious." Myles's friends smiled smugly like I'd passed a test.

I scooped a couple more chips while listening to the group talk about their favorite variations of Myles's guacamole.

"You're welcome to stay and help us finish it," Sami said before glancing at Myles, who avoided eye contact with me.

I didn't want to make him uncomfortable, and my gut said overstaying my welcome would do exactly that. I'd rather leave early and make a good impression, so Myles might be more inclined to message me later. I wanted to learn more about the beguiling geek.

"Though I am curious whether you'll fuck the dragon, I should probably get home and get stuff ready for work tomorrow."

Myles stood. "Let me at least send you home with some cookies. I'm so grateful you came to our rescue."

"I'll never turn down cookies." I followed him to the kitchen after saying goodbye to his friends.

He moistened his lips as he carefully wrapped a half-dozen cookies in a bed of paper towels. He went to hand it to me, then stopped. "You need a free hand for your keys." He rummaged under his sink, giving me a great view of his pert ass, and grabbed a plastic grocery bag. After placing the cookies in the bag, he held the handles out to me. "The least I can do. Seriously, thank you. My landlord still hasn't called me back, but now I know I can shower before work in the morning."

With that picture in my head, I shifted my toolbox in front of me. "Glad I could help. You made my evening much more interesting."

His dimple deepened with his smile as he led me to the door and opened it.

After walking through, I turned back to him. "You should message me on the app sometime. For plumbing needs or, you know, anything else." I winked before leaving Myles staring after me with his mouth open.

CHAPTER
THREE

MYLES

"Onesies? I thought we were doing T-shirts." I picked up the olive-green garment and studied the spots Sami had painted on them.

Sami clucked his tongue. "T-shirts don't make enough of a statement. If we're going to sway the city council, we need to make a splash. Pun intended."

"I gotta say, you did a good job of making it look like a spotted frog." Heather said. The five of us were all crowded in Sami's cramped bedroom, trying to look in his mirrored closet doors while holding our onesies up.

I couldn't believe my friends had insisted on supporting me by going to the Dahlia Springs City Council meeting tonight and speaking alongside me to try and save one of the only local habitats for the Oregon Spotted Frog. They were the absolute best.

They knew how important the wetland on the east edge of Dahlia Springs was to me. It had been my special place since I'd learned about it in college. When I'd mentioned offhand at a recent game night that a developer had submitted a permit application to build homes around the wetland, they'd developed a full tactical strike within minutes. Costumes, talking points, poster messaging, chants, and even bribes. I'd had to threaten no more guac to pull them back from their most extreme ideas, but unfortunately, I'd failed to convince them that dressing up as frogs for the meeting was among the extreme ideas.

Maybe it would work. Crazier things had happened. Sometimes, I wished I didn't care so much, but if that were the case, I wouldn't have become an ecologist.

"She's right. You did a great job." I caught Sami's eyes in the mirror and smiled. The costuming skills he'd picked up at the community center were really getting a workout.

"My makeup friend from the theater will be here any minute to help us with the face paint," Sami said after glancing at his phone.

Makeup too? Jeez. At least the onesies had hoods and the face paint would hide my identity. The anonymity was the push I needed to get myself up to the podium. Public speaking and I were enemies at best. I'd fainted in college when my professor gave me and my rugby player opponent the debate topic of whether student-athletes should be paid at the collegiate level. It had been a living nightmare.

At least tonight, there was no live debate on a topic I was ill-suited to discuss. There were only my carefully written and rehearsed remarks.

About an hour later, I put my glasses back on after Sami's friend finished painting my face dark green with spots.

"Hey, did you ever talk to that plumber again? He was hot," Christian asked as he took a selfie while giving a peace sign.

I ignored Sami's side-eye. I'd heard enough from him on the topic. "No, I haven't been on the app since." But I'd opened it nearly every night over the past two weeks. Brandon had seemed like a nice guy, but I'd thought that before and had been burned. He'd likely simply been polite until he could get out of there and away from our weird game.

"I did some swiping but never came across him," Jay said.

I clenched my jaw. "Shame."

Jay and Christian smirked at each other, while I could feel Sami telepathically telling me I was ridiculous for not messaging him. Brandon was a hot, athletic guy with great abs and a disarmingly attractive smile. There was no way he'd ever be interested in me.

"We should head to city hall," I said.

We piled into two cars and drove the few minutes to downtown Dahlia Springs.

My shoulders hiked toward my ears as we walked to city hall with our poster boards in tow. *I can do this. It's for a good cause.* At least I wouldn't know anyone other than my costumed besties.

We got more than a few startled looks and chuckles as we made our way through the public entrance to the city council meeting room. My heart rate climbed as we signed in for public comment, then claimed the second row of chairs facing a half-circle table with spaced-out microphones and name placards. I kept my attention on a framed award across the room while taking steadying breaths.

Sami squeezed my bouncing leg. "This'll be great, I promise."

I smiled at his reassurance, then tuned out the chatter around me as more people filled the room. My friends knew me well enough to give me time to process my anxiety. I ran through my speech again in my head. I'd practiced it enough that at my last rehearsal, I'd almost had myself convinced that I sounded confident and knowledgeable. Knowledgeable, absolutely. Confident? Not so much.

A few people entered from a door at a far corner of the room opposite where we had. It must be for city staff. I vaguely noticed them walking over to tables set up at one end of the council-member seats.

My brain caught bits and pieces of my friends whispering to each other.

"Whoa! It's him."

"…that plumber."

"He looks hot in a button-down. I'd let him…"

"Now I get the hype."

Sami elbowed me in the side.

What the? Brandon stood behind one of the tables. He wore form-fitting khakis that hugged his thick thighs and a green button-down not too far off from the shade of my face.

Oh gods, I'm wearing green face paint and a onesie with frog ears attached to the hood. No. Nope. This isn't happening. There's no way the universe would be so cruel.

"Look who it is!"

"I see who it is," I hissed at Sami. "Don't draw his attention over here."

"Babe, pretty sure our costumes already did that for us."

I dropped my head forward until my chin hit my chest and let out a quiet whine. As soon as I mustered the courage to look up, my attention landed right on Brandon.

Correction: Brandon's eyes. Staring back at me.

His head tilted to the side as he studied me, hand suspended several inches above the table, grasping a notebook.

I waited, heart in my throat, for the judgment to cross his face. His eyebrows jumped, and then he did the most miraculous thing. He smiled widely, then waved. He started toward us, but someone tapped his shoulder, and he turned away. It couldn't have been longer than a moment, but long enough to turn my hair gray.

I was confused. Wasn't he a plumber? But then the councillors entered and took their seats, and Brandon took his own at an official-looking table with official-looking people. Why would a plumber need to sit at a city council meeting like he was part of it?

The meeting soon started, and Brandon spoke during the financial report. Did he work for the city? Maybe he did freelance plumbing on the side. I'd forgotten how sexy his deep voice was. He was even more attractive than I remembered. With the ball cap he'd worn that night, I hadn't seen his hair beyond the peek of dirty-blond. It was short on the sides with longer strands on top that were styled back.

I was so distracted by trying not to look at Brandon too much and failing that I momentarily forgot that I had to speak.

In front of people.

In front of *Brandon*.

And then Sami whispered, "Public comment time."

Okay, Oregon Spotted Frog in the sky, you can beam me away now.

One of the councillors explained the public comment process while my heart rate elevated. "The first person signed up to provide public comment is Myles Johnson. Myles, please approach the microphone. You have three minutes."

I swallowed and stood, bumping knees as I passed my friends.

"Myles, your sign," Christian whispered urgently.

Wincing, I turned back and grabbed it before walking to the podium and making a fool out of myself in front of one of the hottest guys I'd ever seen.

CHAPTER
FOUR

BRANDON

I bit back a smile as Myles approached the mic. I couldn't help it. He looked ridiculous in the most endearing way. He wore a green onesie with darker green spots, a hood over his head with exaggerated eyes mounted on the sides, and his face was painted green. All his friends were dressed to match.

I'd seen a lot at city council meetings over the years. Childish arguments, conspiracy theories, and blatant bribery attempts, but costumes outside of Halloween were new.

Myles set his poster in front of the podium that read *Frogs deserve homes too*! in big, block letters. His hands shook as he straightened his notecards. Even dressed as a frog, he was so damn cute. I hadn't recognized him until I'd clocked his bright-red glasses. They were a dead giveaway.

Seeing Myles sent the butterflies in my stomach fluttering into overdrive. Even weeks later, I had to admit I was bummed that Myles had never messaged me after that night, but I wasn't surprised. He'd been clear that he had a plumbing need and hadn't hinted at a possibility of more. I could've sworn there'd been a vibe, though, and I'd tried to indicate I was interested in talking again. I had to accept that he wasn't interested.

I'd be lying if I said that Myles hadn't popped into my mind, like when I'd lingered at the grocery store hoping to run into him. I figured since we both lived in town and there was only one place to buy groceries, the odds were decent that I would.

Myles's voice was unsteady as he spoke. "Good evening. My name's Myles, and I'm an ecologist. As a citizen of Dahlia Springs, I'm here to share my concern over the proposed development of the wetlands." He took a shaky breath. "Everyone deserves to have a home, including animals. Humans can make homes anywhere, but most animals don't have that freedom. The Oregon Spotted Frog is one species simply trying to live their lives like the rest of us. The species is listed as threatened within the federal Endangered Species Act, and we should do all we can to protect its habitat. The wetland up for proposed development is one of the few remaining homes of this fascinating species. What is so important about this housing development that it needs to destroy ecosystems critical to many animals?"

Myles paused and glanced up, our gazes locking. I gave him an encouraging smile. He swallowed before continuing to talk about why that land was so important to the Oregon Spotted Frog and other species. *He really does love frogs. So cute.*

"I know people need homes too, but there must be other land that would work. Enjoying places like this wetland was among the highlights of my childhood. I'd hate to see this land closed off and developed where countless kids in future generations can't experience it. People deserve the opportunity to explore the environment around us, and the living creatures deserve to keep their homes."

"I hope you'll consider the severe damage this development would have on numerous species we teach our kids about. Reading about important ecosystems in school is important, but nothing makes more of an impact than having a place to take kids to so they see it in action. Thank you for your time."

I wanted to give him a standing ovation, which was the more polite O I'd wanted to provide since he answered his door that night. Myles's brain was as sexy as the rest of him. I'd always been a sucker for smart men.

Despite Myles basically being a stranger, I was proud of him. He clearly wasn't comfortable speaking in front of crowds, but he'd done it anyway. I admired that courage.

I willed him to look at me once more before going back to his seat, and when he did, I winked. It was the most subtle form of a thumbs-up I could offer while working. Myles's painted face shifted into a small smile I greedily seized as a win.

My attention kept wandering to him as his friends got up one by one and gave their remarks. Myles beamed like a proud parent at his kids' first tee-ball game, which made my heart sink. Realistically, the odds of him getting his way were slim. Many people in Dahlia Springs were counting on the development project.

"I mean, how can you *not* veto this project? The Oregon Spotted Frog is named after our beloved state. Do you want to be known as the unpatriotic city council that destroyed the state's namesake frog? Our state might not have an official frog, but I postulate that if Oregon did, it would be this. In conclusion, we should treat the Oregon Spotted Frog with the reverence it deserves. Your honors, I rest." Sami nodded solemnly. I couldn't get a close enough look to read where they'd set their pronoun pin today, but I liked how they'd slicked-back their mullet.

Myles was the only one in his group who'd expressed a personal or professional interest in the matter, so I figured they were doing it to support him. What incredible friends to have. I sure as hell couldn't imagine any of mine doing that. My friends were more the "get together for pizza" type, not the "go in full costume to give public comment at a city council meeting for each other's strongly held beliefs" type.

The remaining agenda crawled. I wanted to talk to Myles, but the universe made me wait, so I marked each agenda item with a heavy checkmark as a countdown until I could talk to him. I had a feeling that if he ran out of here right after the meeting, I wouldn't get another chance. I didn't want to pressure him, but I felt compelled to tell him he'd done a good job. I wanted to make him smile.

When the meeting adjourned, people immediately rose and began spilling out. I glanced at Myles as I hurried to gather my things, avoiding eye contact with others so I didn't get pulled into a conversation by one of the chatty councillors. Instead of his friends following the crowd out, they remained seated with Myles trapped in the middle as he squirmed in his seat.

I mentally thanked his friends for doing me a solid as I beelined to them.

"Hey, good to see you all again." I smiled at each of them but focused most of my attention on Myles.

"Hey, big guy. Surprised to see you here." Sami's pin pointed to he/him. He smiled knowingly when he glanced at Myles.

"The feeling is mutual." I looked at Myles. "A good surprise."

His lips curved into a sweet, nervous smile .

"I've got to go to the restroom."

"Yeah, me too."

"Um, smoke break?"

"You don't smoke. Ow! Oh, right, uh, yeah, smoke break."

His friends scattered, leaving us alone. Myles squeezed his eyes closed and looked like he wanted to disappear. What was it about this guy that had me in knots?

I dropped into the seat in front of him. "Surprisingly, the costumes aren't the least subtle thing about your friends."

Myles let out a startled laugh as his shoulders relaxed. "So embarrassing, but they mean well."

It was cute that his crew seemed to be playing Cupid. "I wish I had friends like that."

Myles stared at me with surprise.

"Want to start walking out?" I didn't need an audience of my colleagues watching my rusty attempts at flirting.

"Okay." He grabbed his sign and followed me out.

"You did an amazing job," I said as we entered the hallway outside the council chambers and after making sure no one I knew was within earshot. "If I were a councillor, you'd have me convinced to turn down this permit request."

"Thanks. I'm not sure it helped, but at least I tried." His fingers tightened around the edge of his sign. "So, you do budget stuff for the town? And plumbing?"

I rubbed the back of my neck as we paused at an alcove in the hallway. "Not exactly."

Myles's eyes widened.

"My dad's a plumber, and I worked for him in high school and college. I never did an official apprenticeship or got my license, but Dad made sure I knew the basics so I wouldn't need to call someone unless it was a big issue." I winced. "Sorry for misleading you that it's my actual job. I really do know how to fix the basics. If your issue had been above my skillset, I promise I wouldn't have messed with it and risked causing more issues."

Myles's smile eased my worry. "I believe you. You fixed it, and I haven't had an issue since."

"That's great. You're an ecologist at an environmental consulting agency? That sounds so cool."

Myles stood straighter and his eyes brightened. "I am! I specialize in conservation biology and wetlands ecology."

"I'd love to learn more about your work. Maybe we could talk again?" I braced myself for the rejection. Trying to insert myself into his life was a long shot, but I felt an intense urge to get to know him.

Myles glanced at his friends, who shamelessly watched us through the wall of windows facing the parking lot. His dimple appeared with his smile, though I saw hesitance in his eyes. "I'm still at the same username."

"Perfect. I'll message you, Frogtastic." I trailed my fingers down his arm, offered a smile I hoped came off as flirty instead of leering, and then left before I did something to mess it up. It took all my self-control not to skip away while whistling.

CHAPTER
FIVE

MYLES

I'd been staring at my bedroom ceiling in the dim lamplight for so long that I was seeing shapes in the popcorn texture. Sleep eluded me with the emotional roller coaster from the city council meeting. My body wasn't built to sustain those kinds of adrenaline rushes.

Of all the possible places to run into Brandon, it had to be while I was wearing a onesie and face paint? Not somewhere normal like the grocery store or A Whole Latte Love while grabbing a coffee. I'd bought a lot more coffee than usual the past two weeks, hoping to run into him in the wild and gauge his reaction. Would he be flirty? Polite but distant? I'd second-guessed any cues that he'd seemed interested that night and needed more data.

It would've been easy to message him, but I'd been the nerdy guy who couldn't get a clue one too many times to put myself out there again.

I couldn't believe Brandon not only approached me but asked if he could message. My goofy grin after we parted had led to a lot of teasing as my friends and I debriefed at Sami's place. They'd serenaded me with an out of tune, *"Brandon and Myles sitting in a tree, K-I-S-S-I-N-G."*

I smiled, biting my cheek as I rolled onto my side. I kept thinking Brandon was simply being nice to me because he was working, but Sami's words kept running through my head.

"Babe, if he was simply being polite, he wouldn't have asked to message you. He could've asked if your plumbing was still good and made a quick escape. Or not even come over at all and busied himself chatting with a coworker until we left. Myles, the man rushed over to you like you were the scoop of guac."

I had to trust Sami's words. It was hard to argue with his logic, but why would Brandon be interested in talking with me? *Me.* I was a dorky game lover who cared more about the environment and its creatures than I did for most people.

Now, I would be a nervous wreck until Brandon messaged or until enough days passed for me to convince myself he wouldn't so I could move on. I wasn't sure which possibility worried me more.

Huffing out a breath, I rolled to my other side. Maybe a podcast would help distract my brain enough to fall asleep. When I grabbed my phone, I saw a notification from Findr. Crap. I'd forgotten that I'd silenced them on the app ages ago after too many creepy messages. The night I'd met Brandon, I hadn't noticed because I'd kept the app open.

Brandon had messaged an hour ago. *Oh my gods.* I eagerly tapped the notification, which launched our chat.

SumsOfAnarchy: [GIF of a frog wearing a top hat]

SumsOfAnarchy: Did the face paint stain your skin?

Giddiness raced through me. He'd messaged! Feeling an unusual surge of boldness, I snapped a selfie with the flash on but second-guessed myself when I attached it to my message. My 'fro was slightly flattened from the hood and my skin still had a faint sickly green hue. Screw it. I pressed send.

I navigated the settings to turn notifications back on. My phone immediately buzzed.

SumsOfAnarchy: You got more off than I expected. I figured you'd be cosplaying the Wicked Witch of the West for a few days.

Frogtastic: Ha! I think the green is faint enough that I might be able to convince my coworkers I'm sick tomorrow.

SumsOfAnarchy: Lol, brilliant. What's your work look like day-to-day? I've never met an ecologist before.

Frogtastic: It's a lot of report writing, research, meetings, and trying not to think about the collapse of civilization from climate change.

SumsOfAnarchy: Yikes. I hadn't thought about the heaviness of that kind of work. Do you get to be outside a lot? You must be really outdoorsy.

Frogtastic: Hardly lol. I get by. Your profile says you enjoy hiking?

SumsOfAnarchy: I do solo hikes to clear my head.

Frogtastic: That's always a nice go-to to have. What's your job like?

SumsOfAnarchy: Endless spreadsheets and numbers. I basically spend my days trying to figure out where to find money we don't have and do a bunch of bureaucratic I-dotting and T-crossing. Good thing I enjoy solving puzzles.

Frogtastic: Ohhh! Now I get your username. Sums. Ha! That's pretty good. I like puzzles too.

SumsOfAnarchy: As a kid, whenever my family would go camping, I got to buy one puzzle magazine in the grocery store. Now that I think about it, it's sort of weird I never asked for them at home.

Frogtastic: I totally get it. There's something different about vacations. It's the only time I enjoy shellfish. Vacation Myles can't get enough of it. Home Myles? Nasty.

SumsOfAnarchy: [laugh-cry emoji] Glad I'm not the only weirdo [smile emoji]

Frogtastic: Oh, I'm far weirder than you.

SumsOfAnarchy: Prove it. [wink emoji]

Frogtastic: Did you not notice my collections? Funkos, board games, nerdy friends.

SumsOfAnarchy: I think those things are cool, not weird.

Frogtastic: You do?

SumsOfAnarchy: Confession? I've always been intrigued by games. The analog kind. There were some kids in my math class in high school who always talked about their D&D games. It seemed so much fun. Love board games too, but my siblings stopped playing with me when I got too competitive.

Frogtastic: D&D is super fun! My friends and I have had a campaign going for almost five years.

SumsOfAnarchy: I'm not sure I fully know what that means, but it seems impressive.

Frogtastic: It's like a serialized game that doesn't end. We just keep playing the same story with more quests without starting over.

SumsOfAnarchy: Wow. I can't imagine the detail that goes into something like that.

My stomach fluttered as I smiled at my phone. I wasn't sure if Brandon was just saying things he thought I wanted to hear, but he seemed genuine.

Frogtastic: It's pretty comprehensive, which is part of the fun. We have a great dungeon master. What kind of board games do you like?

SumsOfAnarchy: I used to love Monopoly. The strategy, the money, and I like that it takes a long time. But most of my friends never had that kind of attention span. If we played anything, it was poker, black-jack, or some sort of card-based drinking game.

Frogtastic: I've never played poker before. [grimace emoji]

SumsOfAnarchy: It can be fun. The best kind is strip poker. [wink emoji]

Frogtastic: Oh god, that sounds so stressful.

SumsOfAnarchy: But fun?

Frogtastic: Maybe a little. [blush emoji]

SumsOfAnarchy: I've got an idea, but you can totally say no.

My heart thudded against my chest as my fingers fumbled to reply. I couldn't believe I admitted I'd never played poker, let alone strip poker.

Frogtastic: Okay…

SumsOfAnarchy: How about a game night?

My gut sank. It would be cool to have Brandon as a friend, but was it ridiculous to hope he might be interested in more?

Frogtastic: Totally. You're absolutely welcome to come to our game night anytime. We do it every Thursday. We can teach you how to play.

SumsOfAnarchy: I was thinking just the two of us... Is that okay? Maybe we could teach each other some games?

My ears rang as I reread his message several times.

Frogtastic: Yes! That sounds great. I've already got plans with my friends this weekend. How about next Saturday?

I worried my lip. Spending so much time with my friends had always been a touchy point with guys.

SumsOfAnarchy: It's a date. [smile emoji] I'd better get some sleep. Maybe now I actually can. [wink emoji]

Frogtastic: [blush emoji] Me too. Night, Brandon.

SumsOfAnarchy: Goodnight, Frogtastic. Talk to you soon.

I put my phone back on my nightstand and fell asleep smiling.

CHAPTER
SIX

MYLES

"I can't believe you're going on a date with him." Sami's voice rang through my speakerphone as I stood in front of the mirror, debating between two shirts.

"Me neither." I still couldn't wrap my head around why Brandon was interested in me.

"Hey," Sami said in their I-mean-business voice. "I'm not saying that because I don't think he has a reason to want to go out with you. I'm saying it because I'm surprised you agreed to it."

Sami knew me too well.

"Don't do anything to sabotage this," Sami warned.

I pulled off my *Gamers Do it Better* shirt and grabbed the burgundy button-down Sami said looked good on me. I wasn't sure how nice I should dress for a date at my house.

As if reading my mind, Sami chuckled. "Are you having the date at your place so you're close to a bed?" Their voice dripped with suggestion.

I snorted. "Yeah, you know me. Destination Pound Town on all my first dates."

"Please, god, never say 'Pound Town' again."

A part of me—okay, most of me—still wasn't convinced Brandon was into me that way. Sure, he'd said it was a date in a text, but people often casually threw that word around.

"Anyway, it's not going to go there. This is probably just a friend hang."

"I love you, but you're delusional. That man wants to lick you like a lollipop. You should spend less time convincing yourself people aren't into you and more time preparing yourself to get railed."

My cheeks burned. I hoped Sami was right, but I'd had decades of primary data to tell me that the social hierarchy didn't operate like that. Guys who looked like him didn't date geeky guys who looked like me. He reminded me of the jocks who used to hide my clothes after gym class.

"We're doing the date at my place because we're playing games. I picked out a few easy two-person tabletop RPGs to try."

The sound Sami emitted was high-pitched enough to summon dogs.

"He wants to learn how to game?"

"He says he does."

"You could've taken him to The Dice Den."

I'd considered it. I loved that Dahlia Springs now had a pub catered to people who enjoyed various tabletop games, but I'd decided against it.

"This is his first time attempting any tabletop RPG, and I thought the pub might be too distracting."

"Sure, Jan."

There was a knock at my door. "Shit, he's here."

"Okay, take a deep breath. You're gonna do great. I know it's been a while since you've gotten laid, but I'm sure you touch yourself enough to remember what it's like. Handling a dick is like riding a bike. You'll find your groove."

"*Goodbye.*" I hung up on Sami's laughter.

As I walked to the door, I gave my home another anxious glance to make sure it was fit for company. As if it wasn't already in pristine condition after my hours of cleaning this week.

I'd surprised myself when I'd invited him to my place. I wasn't usually open to having someone over in a one-on-one situation so soon after meeting, but oddly enough, I felt comfortable with Brandon. It helped that we'd kept our text conversation going pretty much non-stop all week. Surely, that level of talking equaled a date or two in terms of familiarity. Brandon had put in far more effort to get to know me than any man I'd dated.

My hand shook as I reached for the door handle. I opened it to reveal a smiling Brandon looking divine in a forest-green Henley. The shirt's trim cut accentuated every plane and curve of muscle.

"Hey. You look really nice." Brandon leisurely perused my body, making every part of me twitch from my toes to my hair follicles.

"Thanks. You too. Um, green is a great color on you."

Brandon reached into the reusable grocery bag he held—*sustainability is sexy*—and pulled out a small white box wrapped with a green ribbon.

"I thought you might enjoy this more than flowers."

He'd considered bringing me flowers? I accepted his gift and stood back to let him inside. "Thank you."

"Don't thank me until you open it. I might've gotten the wrong thing." The crease in his forehead seemed out of place from his usually confident demeanor.

"You didn't have to bring me a gift." A wide smile tugged at my cheeks.

"I know, but I wanted to."

His words made my belly warm.

While removing the ribbon, I absently noticed him closing the door. I lifted the lid and revealed a set of milky, jade-green resin dice with gold printing.

"They're as close to the color of your painted face as I could find."

I didn't know what to do with something so thoughtful. The simple gesture short-circuited my brain.

Instead of finding words, my body took over and reacted. I stepped into his space, stood on my tiptoes, and pressed my lips to his. At contact, my brain came back online, screaming, *Abort! What the hell are you doing?*

Brandon made a surprised sound, but before I could pull back and profusely apologize for my uncharacteristic impulsiveness, he wrapped his arm around my waist and pressed our bodies together. He tilted his head, slotting our lips with better contact. Despite my brain calculating all the ways this could go wrong, my body purred under his touch.

He pulled back and rested his forehead against mine as his lips curved into a smile. "With a response like that, I'll keep bringing you gifts."

Brandon's arm provided a comforting pressure around my waist, like a weighted blanket preventing my anxiety from spiking too high. I managed another moment of indulgence before mortification flooded my system.

I covered my face with my hands. "I'm so sorry I accosted you. I'm not usually like this, I swear."

Brandon's warm laugh had me peeking through my fingers.

"I'm glad you did. Now I finally know what you feel like in my arms, and it broke the ice, right? Instead of spending the rest of our date wondering whether we'll kiss and who will make the first move, we can relax."

"Now I finally know what you feel like in my arms." Whoa.

I couldn't help but smile at his sound logic. He was right. Half my mind would've been distracted by that all evening.

"Though I'm bummed you're not in costume this time." He tightened his grip on my waist. I allowed my senses to overtake my brain. He smelled like the forest after a fresh rain—one of my favorite scents. "But I have to say, my favorite Myles is you as you are."

I leaned toward him. Whether it was because I was about to faceplant in a swoon or he had magnets in his pockets pulling me in, I wasn't sure. One thing was for certain—frankly, the only rational explanation—I'd somehow *Weird Science*'d Brandon into existence. A small, reckless part of me was already getting attached.

"Thank you for such a thoughtful gift. I'm excited to use them at my next game night." My lips still tingled from our brief kiss as I stepped back.

"You're welcome."

We stood there for a moment in the entryway next to my kitchen. I wasn't sure what to do next. "Oh. Um, I put together some finger foods for dinner. I thought that would be easiest to eat while we played." I walked into the kitchen.

"It's perfect." His reassuring smile hit differently now that I knew the feel of his lips.

"Do you want to start with the game you brought or mine?" I busied myself gathering the simple appetizers.

"Yours. I'm ready to learn something new." There was an eagerness to Brandon's voice that made me even more excited to teach him something. Though I was curious what game was hiding in his grocery bag.

While we filled our plates, I talked Brandon through the game options I'd agonized over all week. I hadn't been on a lot of dates, but the little experience I did have involved sitting across the table from a relative stranger at a bar or restaurant with forced small talk while we waited for our food. Talking TTRPGs was my comfort zone.

"Some are easier, some are quicker, but they're all good beginner options." I set my plate on the expandable dining table I used for games. Usually, I had all the inserts in for games, but tonight, I'd kept it small for two. Intimate.

"I'm in no hurry. The detective duo game sounds fun."

I grinned at him. "It does. I haven't played that one yet, but it's supposed to be entertaining." I liked that we were going to play something new to me too.

Brandon swiped a carrot stick through a pile of hummus while I unpacked the box. "When did you start playing games?"

I watched his lips close around the carrot and shook my head to clear the dirty thoughts creeping in.

"In high school. My friends and I got really into Dungeons and Dragons."

"Did a lot of people at your school play?"

I snorted and focused on sorting through the game pieces. "Hardly. I stood out. Not only for being one of the only Black kids at my school, but for my geekier interests." That was the nicest way to gloss over being a target of school bullies without trauma dumping on a first date. "Most of my friend group went to college together. Our group grew and we continued playing D&D regularly. Most of us stayed in the area after we graduated from college, so we've kept our game nights going."

Brandon's lips curved into an almost hesitant smile. He didn't strike me as a shy person, but what did I truly know about him? Maybe I'd been too hasty with my assumptions.

"I was always envious of people in high school who played those games. After football practice, I passed the library on the way to my car, where a group of kids hunched over tables played something that might've been D&D. Though I never heard them talk about rolling for dick size."

I shook my head as Brandon chuckled.

"It always looked like fun." His smile turned rueful. "The closest I got to gaming with my buddies was playing *Madden* on the PlayStation."

I leaned my elbow on the table and dropped my chin in my hand. I barely held back a contented sigh over the fact that he wasn't immediately judgmental about high school me.

"*Madden*? I have no idea what that is."

He smiled. "You're adorable."

How was he so easy with his affection? I wasn't used to that from men.

"It's a football video game. Silly, right? Playing real football then spending my time playing electronic football."

I frowned. "It's not silly at all. If you like football, you should enjoy it in whatever way you want. There should be games for everyone."

There was something in his eyes that had me catching my breath. "I agree," he said softly before clearing his throat and looking at the stack of game boxes on the table. "So, how do we play?"

"We have to choose who's going to be the straight-shooter detective and who's going to be the wildcard detective."

"Like a fun version of good cop/bad cop?"

"Exactly! Then we each create three characters who will end up being the witnesses and the criminal."

As I explained the game and rules, I was impressed by Brandon's patience and attentiveness. He asked thoughtful questions, and when it was time to create our characters, he filled out the character sheets at lightning speed, grinning to himself. I got the feeling he'd enjoy more complicated games than this one, and I wanted to teach them all to him. Having his full and focused attention was dangerous because nothing hurt worse than wanting someone who didn't return the feeling.

"I'm sorry, Detective, but I didn't see anything. I was too busy crocheting." Brandon spoke with an older woman's voice as he played one of our witnesses.

"What were you crocheting, ma'am?" I asked while playing the straight-shooter detective.

"Keychains to hold ChapStick. My granddaughter is always losing hers." Brandon mimed holding it up.

"Wow. That's, um, realistic. I've never seen a penis-shaped Chap-Stick holder before. Do you crochet phallic things often?"

Brandon's eyes twinkled at my improv volley. "You should see my collection of cock cacti!" He grinned.

I tilted my head back and laughed. Brandon had gone all-in without a hint of embarrassment, which wasn't always the case with newbies. I'd played with plenty of people over the years who thought they'd love role-playing games but quickly learned they were too uncomfortable acting silly. It took a certain amount of nerve to put yourself out there in this way.

The game flew by, and I was having a blast. Surprisingly, I was getting to know things about Brandon I wouldn't have if we were slogging through the usual first-date conversations. Seeing how he approached a new challenge, experiencing his improvisational skills, and watching his brain puzzle through things was fascinating. In moments where he could easily get frustrated, he went with the flow.

As Brandon wiped the tears from his eyes while laughing at my side character, who only spoke in Pig Latin, I realized I hadn't been holding back. I'd thrown myself into the game like I did with my friends.

A while later, we solved the crime. Brandon's bright-blue eyes sparkled as he collapsed against the chair and laughed.

"That was so much fun! It's different than I expected. It requires a lot more creative thinking than I realized."

"It's improv, *dahling*," I said with a nasal voice. "I'm glad you enjoyed it. I had fun too." I looked down at my empty plate and smiled as I realized I was having the best first date of my life and it wasn't even over yet. "What are we playing next?" I asked as I looked back up at him.

His thick lips curved into a heated grin. "I think it's time you learned how to play poker."

My stomach fluttered like a herd of pegasi had flown through it. He hadn't said strip poker, but I couldn't help but imagine him sitting across from me sans clothing. Thank the gods for the table over my lap.

CHAPTER
SEVEN

BRANDON

Myles's lips parted, and I couldn't help but hope that his thoughts went where my own had. Some of my most memorable nights in college began with a round of poker and a few beers that ended with strip poker and body shots.

All those young-adult hormones had nothing on the way my body responded to Myles's shy smile and how he held eye contact for longer periods as the evening went on. Or how he openly laughed and his dimple popped out before he got that proud little smile after he said something funny during the game.

Myles nibbled on his lip and glanced away. "Um…the regular kind or the strip kind?"

I wanted to cup his chin and gently turn his face toward me but stopped myself from acting too intimate on a first date. But then I remembered we'd already kissed. I didn't need to play coy.

I stood and leaned across the table. Myles turned toward me, and I gently pressed my lips to his. He sighed into the kiss, leaning forward like he'd fall into my lap if there wasn't a table between us. The wanton sound made my blood run south.

"We should start with a regular game so you can learn how to play." I brushed my lips against his once more before sitting back down. "That way, it's fair when clothes are on the line."

Myles hummed. "Good point. It wouldn't be fair for you to lose yours right away. You probably need to refresh your skills before the stakes are raised." A teasing grin broke through as he straightened and squared his shoulders.

Myles's game face was sexy as hell. If he kept distracting me, he might win after all. This side of him was as intoxicating as the shy Myles I'd initially met before he began letting me in.

"What makes you think I'll lose?" I quirked my eyebrow.

"I'm a quick study." He adjusted his glasses, which sent my pulse skyrocketing. I was growing addicted to that movement.

"I bet you are." His natural competitiveness was working for me, as was his patience as a teacher. I had to admit, I'd been nervous about learning how to play a tabletop RPG. I'd feared he would get frustrated with me, or I'd get frustrated with myself for not catching on right away, but he'd made it easy to try. I wanted to learn more from him.

Hell, I just wanted to play more. A part of me had craved this kind of gaming for years, but until I'd met Myles, I'd never considered trying it.

I retrieved the deck of cards and poker chips from my bag, then quickly explained the difference between Five-Card Draw and Texas Hold'em. I told him we'd start with the former. Within minutes, I dealt our first hand.

Myles cracked his knuckles. "Let's do this."

After several hands, Myles won. He looked pleased with himself as he wiggled in his chair after slamming his winning cards on the table.

"Someone caught on quickly."

"I guess I did." He smirked.

"Does that mean you're ready for strip poker?"

Uncertainty flashed in his eyes, but I could see him working to maintain the confidence that had become more consistent throughout our date.

Jesus, I was already completely gone for the man. I liked everything about him so far. His earnestness, his passion for things he believed in, the effort he put into his friendships, the confidence he exhibited when doing something he enjoyed, and how he'd given me the gift of slowly letting me in as we'd gotten to know each other throughout the week.

"I was born ready." He chugged the rest of his water.

"Let's play it the easy way. The loser of each hand picks a piece of clothing to remove."

Myles's Adam's apple bobbed as he swallowed. "Okay."

I couldn't wait to see what was under Myles's clothes. Within minutes, I got my wish as I won the first hand. The air whooshed from Myles's lungs when he saw my cards.

I reached out and covered his hand. "Hey, we don't have to do this." His comfort was all that mattered.

Myles licked his lips. "It's okay. I'm good." He smiled sincerely. "Just hate losing." A calculating glint flashed in his eyes as he reached under the table and, moments later, came back waving a sock, looking smug as hell.

I laughed loudly. "Good strategy."

"Thank you," he said, all prim and proper.

I lost the next hand and pulled off my shirt. I loved the way Myles's eyes bugged out as he took in my torso. His attention snagged on my tattoo exactly as I'd hoped it would.

"Why'd you take off your shirt?" He hadn't looked away yet.

I chuckled. "I've got my own strategy."

Myles dragged his attention up to my face and his mouth formed an *O* before he narrowed his eyes. "You're trying to distract me!" He sat straighter and collected the cards, shuffling with more force than necessary as he looked everywhere but my bare chest.

"Gotta do what I can to combat your beginner's luck."

"Beginner's luck, my butt," he mumbled while he dealt the cards.

When it was my turn to shuffle the next round, I might've added some unnecessary flexing to capture his attention. His eyes widened behind his thick glasses as he tracked my arms. Eventually, his attention returned to my tattoo as I dealt the cards.

"I saw a TikTok video of a tattoo artist listing tattoos white guys get that are red flags." His tone was way too casual.

"Yeah? What were the tattoos?"

"Lions, barbed wire, and tribal tattoos on someone without tribal or indigenous connections."

I hummed, waiting for what had his lips twitching. "Makes sense. Anything else?"

"Half-sleeves with trees." He pinched his lips to the side like he was trying to bite back a laugh.

I looked down at the forest scene covering my upper arm, shoulder, and part of my chest, then made my pecs bounce. A silly trick I'd learned back in college. "Good thing mine's not a half-sleeve."

"Guess it's a green flag then. Does it mean something?" Myles's inquisitive expression was so cute.

"My family and I did a lot of camping at a lake near Mount Hood when I was growing up. This is my favorite view of the place." I traced the edge of the lake above my nipple. My dick perked up at Myles's quick intake of breath.

While we played a few more hands, we chatted about childhood vacations, which shifted into the basics about our families. Soon, we were both down to our underwear, and I couldn't take my eyes off the constellation of freckles sprawling across Myles's shoulders. His long, shaking fingers unbuttoning his shirt had been delicious torture, but he'd managed to shed his pants under the table without showing me anything. Tease.

I'd been far more brazen and basically given him a strip tease. His mouth had fallen open wide enough to give me some very dirty thoughts, which had quickly become apparent through the thin material of my boxer briefs.

Myles barely had any chest hair. He was lean with light muscle definition and smooth skin that deserved to be kissed.

"Last hand." I waggled my eyebrows as I dealt our cards. I had no expectations that anything would happen when the game ended, but damn, I hoped it would. I wanted to touch him.

I studied my three jacks. Not a terrible hand, but I'd been beaten by a higher three-of-a-kind plenty of times. I discarded my other two cards and pulled in an ace and a nine. Three-of-a-kind with an ace high wasn't bad.

Myles discarded three cards and began nibbling his lip as he rearranged the cards in his hand. I smiled triumphantly at his tell. When he looked at me and nodded, he squared his shoulders as he'd done each time he'd lost.

Feeling confident, I stood, leaned across the table, and pulled his bottom lip free with a kiss.

"Three jacks," I whispered against his lips.

Myles's smile grew. "Full house." He slapped his cards on the table. I stared down at his pair of eights and three tens.

"But you bit your lip!"

He sported a shit-eating grin. "Did I?" He batted his eyelashes.

"You sneaky devil."

Myles grinned. "I told you I love to play games. All kinds." He glanced down as though he also wished for x-ray vision and cleared his throat.

"Guess it's time to ditch the underwear, huh?" I winked, then straightened as anticipation raced beneath my skin like a current. Emboldened by his eye contact, I hooked my thumbs into the waistband and slowly pulled them down, pausing when the top of my trimmed pubic hair became visible.

Myles swallowed, which made me even more eager. When he licked his lips, I pushed my underwear down until I could kick them off. My half-hard dick jerked under Myles's stare.

He opened and closed his mouth a couple of times, so I stood there and waited him out. That was something I'd figured out tonight. While texting, he had all the time he needed to reply, but in person, it was different. Sometimes, he needed a moment to gather his thoughts.

Despite playing strip poker, I had no expectations that anything physical would happen between us. Did I want something to happen? Of course. I wanted to show Myles how much I desired him.

He turned his face back to me and squared his shoulders in the same confident way he'd done while playing. "May I touch you?"

"Baby, you can do anything you'd like." I walked around the table, grabbed Myles's hand, and pulled him over to the couch. I'd hoped that might make him feel more comfortable than me towering him.

I had no shame about sitting wide-legged on his couch with my arm over the back of it. I wanted to pull him onto my lap and feel his smaller body against mine, but my gut said to go slow.

Despite keeping my hands to myself, I couldn't contain a proud grin at the bulge in Myles's Pokémon boxers. I wanted to eat him up, adorable silly boxers and all.

"Pokémon, huh?"

"*Gotta catch 'em all*?" He nibbled on his bottom lip as he shifted next to me. "I didn't expect you'd see my underwear."

"What would you have picked out if you had?" I watched Myles's fingers inch along his thigh toward me. I doubted he realized he was doing it.

"Um, something normal? Like a solid color?"

I laughed and glanced down at my boring, solid green pair. I preferred his Pokémon ones. "Whatever you wear is normal because it's normal for *you*. And I like you as you are."

Myles turned his head to me. "You do?"

"A lot." Falling so fast scared the hell out of me.

Myles's fingertips pressed into my knee as I leaned in and caught his lips in a kiss. As our tongues danced, he gripped my thigh. Good. His hand moved farther up as our kiss deepened. I shifted toward him, wrapping my arm around his shoulder as his fingertips brushed against the head of my dick. I sucked in a breath at the contact, then moaned as his touch grew in confidence. Nothing made me feel sexier than watching Myles become comfortable with me.

I settled deeper into the couch as he wrapped his fingers around my cock, which was hard enough to pound nails. Myles moved to his knees and pressed against me, swallowing my sounds of pleasure with his kisses as he stroked me firmly.

"Feels so good." I tilted my head back as he kissed and nipped along my jaw. I slid my hand down his back until I reached his ass and cupped his cheek.

Myles pressed into my hand as he kissed a path down my chest, teasing a nipple for the briefest moment before bending over my lap. He paused and adjusted his glasses as he looked up at me. "Can I?"

"Please."

I felt his warm breath pass over my cock before his tongue darted out, placing kitten licks on my cockhead, driving me fucking wild. Having someone's mouth on me always felt good, but Myles's mouth was like a bullet train to orgasm station. Better than the first time I'd tried a vibrating plug.

I slid my fingers into his coarse curls as he dragged his sloppy, wet tongue around my shaft. He might not give the most practiced head, but his enthusiasm was significantly more pleasurable than any skill.

Jesus, my balls were already tightening with the tingles racing along my lower back.

"Gonna come," I warned as I worked my fingers toward his crack. Myles gave me a thumbs-up without taking his mouth off me. Why was that so cute?

Goddamn, I wanted to play with his hole. Get my tongue as sloppy as his and eat him out until he was screaming my name, bent over his gaming table. That fantasy pushed me to the point of no return. The muscles in my stomach tensed and my hole clenched as I shot into his mouth. He swallowed everything I gave him while moaning.

My body grew so relaxed I melted into the couch. "Mmm. That was amazing."

Myles wiped the corner of his mouth as he sat up. "Yeah?"

The uncertainty in his voice twisted something in me. "Pretty sure I haven't come that fast since I discovered my prostate."

A playful grin replaced his hesitant smile.

"Can I play?"

He nodded eagerly. "Yes."

I pushed him back on the couch.

He bounced against the gray material and giggled. "Taking turns is an important component of gameplay."

I grinned. "So is competition. Bet I can make you come faster than I did."

Myles's eyes flashed eagerly. "Oh yeah? Let's see what you got." He tucked his hands behind his head, but his shallow breaths gave away his excitement.

I kissed my way up his legs as I tugged down his boxers, then nuzzled his groin before sucking one of his balls into my mouth, which pulled a delicious gasp from him. I had a competition to win and no time to waste.

"You taste so good."

Myles's legs fell open wider at my words, and I squeezed in between them. I kept kissing around his cock without touching it. It was about the size of my favorite dildo but more curved. He squirmed, letting out frustrated growls. When he clenched his fist, I took the cue and swallowed him to the root.

Myles curled up and groaned as I took my time working my way back up his shaft, tonguing all the skin I could reach. I lapped his glans, learning how his body reacted to the various sensations. When I gripped his waist and pressed him down, he let out a dirty sound that would feature in my dreams for months to come. Keeping my hold firm, I focused on sucking him off, pulling out every trick I could think of until he warned me.

I employed my last move—pressing the skin behind his balls—until Myles came, moaning my name. I licked every drop until he pushed at my shoulder.

I stretched alongside him, squeezing between him and the back of the couch. His dazed, happy expression made me smile. "I think I won."

"Hmm?" He curled toward me, and I wrapped my arm around his waist, pulling him close. Then, my words seemed to sink in. He stared up at me with narrowed eyes. "No way."

"Pretty sure I did."

He nipped at my collarbone. "Impossible to determine a winner since we didn't time it."

"Guess we'll have to next time."

I felt his lips shift into a grin against my chest. "Guess we will. You, um, don't need to leave?"

"It's Saturday night, and I've got nowhere else I want to be. After some cuddling, want to play the detective game again?"

He wrapped his arms tightly around me. "I get to be the wildcard this time."

CHAPTER
EIGHT

MYLES

I floated into work with a wide smile. Certainly, the most chipper I'd ever been on a Monday. How could I not be after an incredible third date with Brandon last night? He'd cooked a delicious steak dinner before I taught him another game, and then we'd ended the night with BJs, cuddling, and *Midsomer Murders.* The perfect night.

It had been a while since I'd reached three dates with someone. I was more used to getting ghosted by now.

I cheerfully greeted our front desk person before heading to the hallway that led to our cubicles. There was a mischievous glint to her smile. Maybe she'd had a great date over the weekend too.

My brain kept warning me to rein it in before I got my heart crushed. It was too easy to get caught up in the statistics. It'd never worked with anyone, so why would Brandon be interested in more? Sure, we never had trouble finding things to talk about and he treated me like I was fascinating instead of someone to tolerate. But that would fade. Right?

Or maybe I'd just needed to kiss a few frogs to find my prince. But I really wanted that to be Brandon. There was something special about him and how he made me feel, and I wanted to hold on to that.

My pace slowed as I took in the new additions to the hallway walls. Speaking of frogs, there were at least a dozen printed pictures of them between framed photos from the company's successful projects over the years. I quickly recognized the Oregon Spotted Frog.

Maybe there'd been some movement on its endangered status. I tried to keep an eye on developments, but I'd been distracted since meeting Brandon. I could've missed something.

When I reached my cubicle, I was greeted by more printed photos of the frogs mixed with photos of...oh gods. No. *No way.* Screenshots from the footage of my friends and I speaking at the city council meeting. How had they found it? No one at work had been there, so they shouldn't have found out what we'd done.

Heads popped above the cubicle walls like meerkats. My colleagues sported a mix of proud grins and apologetic smiles. I locked eyes with my closest friend at work, Lori, and raised my eyebrows.

"How did you find these?" I asked no one in particular. I thought we'd escaped attention since nothing had shown up in the local paper after the meeting.

Heads dropped out of sight.

"Cowards." Lori approached and hooked her arm through mine. "Come on, I'll treat you to coffee."

"It's free."

"Even better." Her nose scrunched under her hot-pink glasses as she smiled.

"So, how'd they find it?" I asked as we walked to the break room.

"Someone saw it in a Facebook group for people monitoring threatened species. You and your buds are heroes, according to them."

My chest swelled. "Oh. That's nice. I suppose I should be glad it wasn't from one of those accounts that shares ridiculous clips from public meetings as a big joke."

Lori patted my shoulder before dumping the coffee dregs from the nearly empty pot into the sink. "I'm sure that's coming soon."

"That's reassuring," I muttered.

"Hey, you're the one who dressed up like a frog and spoke at a city council meeting." While she filled the pot with fresh water, I added grounds to the machine.

"If I thought people would actually *see* the recording, I wouldn't have done it. Who watches those anyway? City council meetings are the most boring meetings on the planet."

She grinned. "Not when adults dress up like animals. Don't worry, no one will recognize you. Well, outside of us. Lucky for me, someone spotted you." She winked.

"Yeah, yeah." I grabbed our mugs from the shelf. Hers was from her last trip to Disneyland and mine was shaped like an owl. Though I had a feeling my office Secret Santa this year might get me a mug with one of those screenshots on it.

"Nice of your friends to go all out and support you." Lori gave me a calculating smile. "Still not hooking up with any of them? They're so adorable!"

I scrunched my nose. "Ew. No. That would be like dating a sibling."

She dumped creamer into her mug. "You know, my neighbor is still single. You two would be so cute together. He's tall and strong. So hot. Let me set you up on a coffee date. Low commitment. I really think the two of you would hit it off." She leaned toward me and lowered her voice. "Plus, I bet he's strong enough to have some fun with a petite person like you." She sighed longingly. "I'm still waiting to meet my lumbersnack king with the strength to haul my plump ass around."

My cheeks burned as I remembered the dream I'd had the other night where Brandon used his strength to pin me against the wall. I'd wrapped my legs around his waist but woke up before I got to the good part. Time to reroute that train of thought before things got awkward at work.

I'd turned Lori's offer down several times because her description of her neighbor had been closer to triggering than enticing, but since meeting Brandon, I'd been thinking a lot about my own assumptions and biases. The things I'd put in place to protect myself, which probably wasn't fair to others. People made judgments about me for being a small, Black, queer nerd my entire life. It wasn't right of me to do the same thing to others by dismissing them based on their physical char-acteristics.

Now, I had a different reason to turn her down.

"He sounds great, but I'm sort of seeing someone?"

Her eyebrows shot above her glasses frames. "Is that a question? Sort of seeing someone?"

"I'm dating someone," I said more firmly, then grimaced at her ear-piercing squeak.

"Tell. Me. Everything!" She dumped the coffee from the partially filled pot into my cup, then put it back to resume filling.

I wasn't sure how much I wanted to share since it still felt too soon, but it might be nice to talk to someone who wasn't already mentally planning our wedding like Sami. They were too invested to be an objective party.

"Myles, do you have a minute? I want to talk to you about that assessment you've got scheduled tomorrow," our boss said from the doorway.

"Of course. Be right there." I smiled before turning back to Lori and gesturing to her with my full mug.

"Saved by the boss. I've got to run some errands at lunch today, but tomorrow, you're spilling." She squeezed my shoulder. "I'm glad you found someone, Myles. You deserve to be treated like a king by your own lumbersnack."

I clinked my mug against hers. "To lumbersnacks." I smiled, then turned toward the door.

Fortunately, it was a quick meeting to go over a project plan. As soon as I was back at my desk, my attention was shot. Despite trying to finish a report I could do in a couple of hours with proper focus, my mind kept wandering to Brandon and our lunch plans.

My phone buzzed on my desk.

Brandon: Miss you. [kiss emoji] Still on for lunch?

A wide smile took over my face. He'd been thinking of me too? I rubbed my chest. I was more familiar with unrequited crushes.

Myles: Yes! I can't wait. Miss you too. [kiss emoji]

Brandon: I'll pick up sandwiches. What do you like?

I sent him my sandwich order, and he said he'd love to see where I worked. I did my best to read the words on my screen, but now I couldn't focus for a different reason. Brandon was coming to my work. Where my coworkers were.

My attention slid to one of the photos from the city council meeting. I hadn't taken them down yet because it made me feel good to be included, and I wanted to encourage it. If that meant photos of my ridiculous attempt to save an Oregon Spotted Frog habitat hovered in my peripheral vision for a few days, so be it.

In my first job out of school, most of my coworkers had gotten birthday cakes and balloons, whereas mine was always forgotten. Getting teased by my coworkers like this made me feel special, as ridiculous as it was. And now I had a guy to come visit me at work.

I watched the clock on my computer monitor drag with each passing minute.

At noon on the dot, Brandon texted that he'd parked and was heading inside. I excitedly rushed to the front to meet him. He looked hot in his khakis and blue button-down. His smile was as wide as mine felt. Brandon wrapped me up in a hug and planted a quick kiss on my cheek.

"Hi." He said it almost breathily, as though he hadn't seen me in weeks instead of a day. I could've sworn I heard the front desk person let out a romantic sigh.

"Hi. Do you want a quick tour of the place? You might find my cubicle interesting." Was I trying to show him off? Definitely.

"I'd love to see where you work." He was as enthusiastic as a Golden Retriever.

It was difficult not to take his hand as I gave him a quick tour of the hallway. *Gods, what am I doing?* I'd spent last night lying awake in bed, second-guessing everything and worrying that Brandon would lose interest. But a little pep talk from Lori and a *miss you* text from Brandon had me discovering my newfound confidence.

He was also my first visitor at work, and that felt special. I'd had friends pick me up when my car was in the shop or drop food off for me, but I'd never brought someone back to the cubicles before. Several of my coworkers were visited regularly by their partners, and now I was a part of the club. Even if it was too early to call Brandon a partner.

When we reached my desk, I gestured to it with a flourish. Brandon's attention bounced around the pictures before he tilted his head back and laughed.

"This is amazing. I like your coworkers."

Lori popped up from her cubicle. "Brandon? What are you doing here?"

Brandon looked between her and me as a crease formed on his forehead. "*This* is where you work?" He turned back to me as something like awe dawned on his face, as though I was the latest video game console he'd just opened on Christmas morning.

Lori hurried over to us. "How do you know each other? This is the *neighbor* I've been telling you about."

My mouth fell open. "You've got to be kidding me. This is the hot jock?" I slapped my hand over my mouth.

Brandon's eyes twinkled. "You might need to change my name to that in your phone." He shook his head. "What a small world."

"I told you so," she said in a sing-song voice. She pointed at me. "Lunch. Tomorrow. Details." She winked at Brandon before returning to her desk, singing a tune about being the best matchmaker in the world.

"She's going to be insufferable." I groaned.

He knocked his shoulder against mine. "Worth it."

My smile widened. Yup. I'd definitely *Weird Science*'d him. "It is. Ready for lunch? There's somewhere special I want to take you."

CHAPTER
NINE

BRANDON

I couldn't stop smiling as I followed Myles down the narrow dirt path from the street near the edge of the wetland. He was a man on a mission, happily chatting about this special place.

"There's a volunteer work party each month where we come here to pull invasive weeds, plant native plants, pick up trash, mulching, and other things to help with conservation. I've been volunteering here since I did a college research project on the Oregon Spotted Frog. Did you know invasive weeds are one of the biggest threats to native plants?"

Myles talked about the various species of plants and animals as we passed them. I could listen to him talk all day about his favorite topics. His passionate eagerness was captivating.

"Where do the Oregon Spotted Frogs live?"

Myles shot me a wide smile over his shoulder before he launched into an engaging description of their habitat.

"I was thinking we could eat here." Myles stopped next to a weathered bench by a creek dotted with wide, flat rocks. The area was mostly shaded by the thick trees lining the creek, but the sun peeked through the gaps to add a glittery quality to the slow-moving water. It was incredibly serene.

I sat beside him on the bench and placed the sandwich bag on my lap, then rummaged through to pull out our food and napkins.

"It's hard to imagine this place not existing as it is but instead becoming a backyard view for a handful of people in another development full of cookie-cutter houses close enough to hear your neighbors fart inside their home."

I snorted as I unwrapped my sandwich. "Vivid description."

He shrugged while chewing. His tongue darted out to clear the bread crumbs from his lip.

"I hadn't thought of it that way." In the short time I'd known Myles, I'd grown more philosophical and noticed a renewed interest in my work. Myles helped me think beyond the numbers on my spreadsheets to try and understand the impact they had on people, our environment, and our community. "Thank you for showing this place to me. It's clear why you and your friends are fighting to save it."

Myles knocked his shoulder against mine. "It's pretty special."

"I realized I haven't asked how you got into this line of work? Were you a kid going to school board meetings and advocating for the rights of children to have more recess time?" I pictured a little Myles pushing glasses up his nose, loose clothes covering his small body, pulling out a stack of papers from his backpack, and shaking as he courageously read them aloud to a room full of people.

He chuckled. "I wasn't that brave. I spent a lot of my childhood escaping outside. My dad worked long hours at a tech company, and when he was home, my parents fought all the time."

I squeezed his thigh. I hated imagining a young Myles in pain.

"I always had a fascination for the animals I encountered and spent as much time as possible outside with them. I used to get in trouble for trying to bring all sorts of insects and outdoor critters inside the house, but I got pretty good at knowing how to hide the jars of caterpillars and frogs." He tilted his head, which put part of his Afro in the path of a sunbeam, making it extra shiny. "Which, thinking back now, I wasn't doing them any favors."

"At least you're making up for it now." I grinned.

Myles held my gaze and smiled before he turned back to the creek. "I'm glad I've been able to make a career out of it, but I still struggle when people don't see these places like I do. The people who'd buy homes here would probably lose interest and not see the creek as anything more than a hazard for small children. Then they'd likely want to drain it, arguing that it draws mosquitoes."

I sat with his words for a moment. Damn, it'd been a long time since I'd dated someone who made me want to sit and have deep conversations. I wanted that with Myles. To uncover what else was hanging around in his head. He made me want to chew on difficult topics, to figure out how I felt about things, to talk for hours about our environment before playing a silly game to unwind from the deep talk.

"I love that you were able to fulfill a childhood dream with your career. I never dreamed about town budgeting as a kid. I like my job well enough, but it's exactly that—a job, not a passion. Sometimes, I wish I had more of what you have, but I think I need to find my passion elsewhere. You make me want more substance in my life." More of him in my life.

Myles smiled before taking another bite.

"I wish there was something I could do to help save this place."

He hummed. "I appreciate that, but you listening to me talk about it is more than enough."

"I chatted with a couple of the councillors when they stopped by city hall this week, but I didn't learn anything."

Myles's eyes widened as he turned to me. "I don't want you to get in trouble. You don't need to do that."

His concern made me fall even harder for him. "Don't worry, I didn't do anything inappropriate. I asked a couple of general questions that any constituent would. They didn't say much, but that's not unusual. They're often hesitant to be open about where they're leaning before a possible vote."

"Is there going be a vote?" Myles's wide eyes stared at me from under his glasses.

"I got the impression there will be a vote to rezone the wetland. Likely in the next month or two. I'll keep an eye on the agenda draft when it goes around."

"Thanks, Brandon."

I squeezed his thigh. "I really hope this place can be saved." It had already mattered to me because it did to him, but now that we'd shared time together here, it was even more special. Especially since Myles had shown me an important part of himself by bringing me here.

He made a noncommittal sound that broke my heart. I wanted him to get everything he desired. It should scare me how hard and fast I was already falling for him.

Myles carefully folded the sandwich paper with his napkin inside and kept folding and folding as he nibbled his lip. I waited him out.

"So, I was wondering if you'd be interested in going to The Dice Den with me and one or two of my friends as an, um, practice round of game night."

I couldn't help my giddy smile. Jesus. He made me feel so special. I caught his chin and turned his head to face me, then kissed him with the eagerness I felt at his invitation. When I pulled back, Myles sat in a daze with his mouth slightly ajar.

"I'd love to."

Myles smiled softly as he opened his eyes. "Saturday?"

"I can't wait."

CHAPTER
TEN

MYLES

"What are your intentions with Myles?" Sami asked Brandon as soon as we settled at our table. He stared Brandon down with his hands steepled on the tall bar table between us.

My mouth dropped open in horror. We'd *just* arrived at The Dice Den for an evening of drinks and games—hadn't even ordered drinks yet—and he had to start an inquisition immediately? Good gods. What in the world was he thinking? Did he want this to crash and burn? He'd been so excited for me to be dating someone, but it wouldn't last long if my friends came at Brandon this hard. There had been a contentious relationship between my friends and each guy I'd dated— the few times it had gotten far enough for me to introduce them.

Heather pushed Sami's shoulder hard enough that he nearly fell off his bistro chair.

I dropped my face in my palm and groaned. "You promised you'd be chill."

"Honey, do you know me?"

I peeked at Brandon, my stomach twisting at what I might see on his face. The last thing I expected was a wide grin.

"I'd say my intentions are purely noble, but that's a lie. He's adorable." He kissed my cheek.

The crease in Sami's forehead smoothed as his mouth curved into a huge smile. "Perfect answer. First round is on me."

"I'll help you carry," I said sternly. "Sorry," I mouthed to Brandon. He gave my arm a reassuring squeeze as I climbed off the tall chair. At least Heather would be on good behavior while I lectured Sami at the bar.

I tromped behind Sami. He aimed a flirty grin at the bartender and ordered a pitcher of the local Tap That Brewery's pale ale.

"What the heck was that about? Are you *trying* to scare him away?"

Sami rested his elbow on the bar and turned toward me. "If that scares him away, he'll never survive your friend group. That was simply me helping you relax."

I frowned. "How in the world does that help me relax? You made my blood pressure spike so high I was about to look for an AED."

He squeezed my shoulder. "I wanted you to see that Brandon can handle us—especially me—just fine. He's not going to run, Myles. You've been a nervous wreck all week about tonight. Trust that he's in this. Remember how you first met? He already knows what he's getting into with you and the rest of us. Give him a chance."

I was stunned silent as Sami's words sank in. Had I been standing in my own way? So focused on reasons someone wouldn't stay that I risked pushing people away? I'd been half-prepared for Brandon to use a familiar refrain and tell me my friends were too weird or I spent too much time with them.

Gods, if I pushed Brandon away, I'd never forgive myself. We'd only been dating for a couple of weeks, but they were easily two of the best weeks of my life. For the first time, I was living every part of my life as *me*.

"Being a know-it-all isn't attractive."

Sami smirked as he passed his debit card to the bartender. "On me it is. Grab the glasses?" He picked up the pitcher.

I nodded as I grabbed the stack of glasses and turned to follow Sami.

"Thanks," I said before we reached the table.

He paused and turned to me. "Anytime, babe. I just want you happy, and Brandon is making that happen. Now let's teach your boyfriend some games and make sure he's got the chops for game night."

Boyfriend? Whoa. Was he? Did Brandon think of me in that way? I didn't even know where to begin with a conversation about that.

I set the glasses on the table and hopped onto the chair. Brandon caught my eye and gave me a look that asked if I was okay. I nodded and smiled, noting Brandon's relaxed shoulders. I glanced at Heather and settled with her encouraging smile.

Brandon pointed at a game in the middle of the table. "Heather and I picked out a game. Is this one okay?"

Sami cheered. "Love that one! You're on my team, newbie."

I sent a thankful smile to Sami as Brandon squeezed my leg under the table.

The evening passed in an endless stream of laughs and games. It didn't take long before I'd completely forgotten it was Brandon's first time hanging with my friends. I wasn't reminded until we went to the bar to cash out, and I heard Sami warn Brandon that Jay was a "Puritan prude who gets off on cockblocking sexual exploration in games." I couldn't help the laugh that bubbled up.

"Plus, Jay uses his phone during trivia," Sami said with judgment dripping from his words.

"It was *one time*, and he was ordering food for us," Heather said while rolling her eyes.

Sami lifted his chin. "Spin and mistruths."

While Brandon and Sami briefed each other on their best trivia topics, Heather moved closer to me. "He's great, Myles. Like really great. If you dump him, I'm sure one of the other guys will try to snap him up. Now I'm extra sad I missed your epic first meeting. I bet you were absolutely freaking out." She grinned.

There was no better ringing endorsement than that. "I have no plans of dumping him."

Brandon's attention was on Sami as he talked about how we were robbed at the *Lord of the Rings* trivia championship last year, but I could tell Brandon was biting back a smile.

Oops. I must've said that louder than I thought.

After settling the bill, we exited the pub. Brandon placed his hand on the small of my back as we walked, which made me feel possessed in all the right ways.

"Thanks for a great evening. I'm stoked for game night next week and the one-off—wait, no, one-shot?—campaign you're teaching me." The sincerity in Brandon's voice triggered a lump in my throat.

"It's no hardship. You're pretty to look at." Sami winked at Brandon before pulling him into a hug. Sami only hugged people he'd accepted into the circle. My eyes stung. Sami turned to Heather. "Ready to drive me home?"

Heather pulled her keys from her pocket. "One of these days, you'll need to get your license."

"Not when I've got such good friends to drive me around." Sami batted his eyelashes before turning to me and pulling me in for a hug.

"He's a keeper. You deserve a good one like him." He kissed my cheek, then bounced over to Heather's car.

I turned to Brandon. Instead of being anxious that the happy smile would fall from his face as he told me how weird my friends—and, by extension, me—were, I was excited to debrief the night with him.

He hooked his finger in my front pocket and pulled me close. "Your place or mine?"

I kissed him. "Mine? No shared walls."

His warm laughter chased away the chill from the late hour as we headed home.

CHAPTER
ELEVEN

BRANDON

"Where are we going?" The eager curve of Myles's lips gave me all the validation I needed that keeping my plans for our Saturday brunch date a surprise had been the right move. It killed me not to tell him the news last night at dinner with Lori, but I had a plan and wanted to follow through.

"I'm sure you'll figure it out soon." I tossed him a teasing grin.

Though we'd only been dating for about a month, it felt like he'd been a part of my life for years. We clicked on every level. Even with the things we didn't have in common, we were excited to learn from each other. When we disagreed on something, we heard the other out. Even among my better relationships, the connection had never felt as natural as it did with Myles. Every decision I'd made in my life had led me to him. It was way too early to be thinking that, but I couldn't help it. He made me so damn happy.

Not only Myles, but his friends too. That queerdo gaggle of geeks had welcomed me with open arms and pointed ears, encouraging me to let my inner geek shine. And, boy, had I. I'd embraced every game they taught me like I'd been starving for it. Though, considering how badly I'd wanted to join the geeks in high school as they played games, I supposed I had been. Myles even got me my own set of dice. He said the blue matched my eyes.

Myles gasped when we turned on the road to the wetland. He squeezed my thigh. "You're taking me on a date to our spot? What's the special occasion?"

My heart melted at "our spot."

I took my eyes off the road for a moment to soak up his smile. "I wanted to do something nice for you." And share some great news. The wetland was no better place.

I pulled the picnic basket I'd borrowed from Lori from my trunk. The savory scent from the brunch I'd grabbed at Inkwell Bistro on my way to pick up Myles hit my nose, making me salivate.

Myles practically bounced down the path to the bench, eagerly naming the species of the birds flying by. I wanted to travel the world with him so he could do that everywhere.

Once we reached the bench, I set the basket on the ground and turned to Myles, grabbing his hands. "I've got some good news for you."

Myles's eyes widened. "What kind of good news? Did you get a promotion?" His face scrunched adorably. "Is that jerk Jerry finally retiring?"

I tilted my head back and laughed. It was adorable that he got so indignant on my behalf when I complained about a coworker being a know-it-all dickhead. "I wish, but it's not that." I squeezed his hands. "I know you don't love that the video of you and your friends went viral."

Myles squeezed his eyes closed and gave his head a couple of quick shakes. He'd been a good sport, but he'd struggled when it spread from the niche animal-conservation circles to viral status. Fortunately, only a few people had identified him.

"But I hope this makes you feel better about it. The developer pulled back their permit request and is exploring other locations. The video brought too much attention to the project, and they didn't want the bad PR. Your adorable stunt saved this place."

Myles's wide eyes filled with tears. "No way."

"Yes, way." I kissed away the tear that fell. "I found out at work yesterday when they sent a revised agenda for the next council meeting. When I noticed that item had been removed, I asked, and that's what I was told. The council didn't want the attention either. You won."

Myles wrapped his arms around my neck and jumped, hooking his legs around my waist. Laughing, I stumbled forward until I rested his cute little butt on the back of the bench. I claimed Myles's mouth, humming happily as he melted into me.

I trailed my fingers down his back as I deepened the kiss, forming plans for how I could get him off in his favorite place. Crouching as I sucked him off or pulling him onto my lap as I stroked him to bliss. Before I made my move, voices sounded in the distance. I was startled when Myles squeaked into my mouth.

I pulled back and pressed my forehead against his. "I guess my plans will have to wait."

"What plans?" he asked breathily.

I squeezed his upper thigh as close to my prize as I could get.

He groaned, then hopped down as I stepped back. "I want those plans now." He glanced in the direction of the voices, then huffed.

"Let me distract you with food."

"Inkwell Bistro?" His hopeful tone made me smile.

"Only the best for my boyfriend." I removed warm containers from the picnic basket. I'd wrapped them in a towel and stuck a hot water bottle in the bottom to hold in as much heat as possible.

I handed the eggs benedict order to Myles and froze when I saw him staring at me with his mouth hanging open. "What?"

"Boyfriend?"

I thought back over what I'd said. "Oh. Uh." I panicked. I probably shouldn't have blurted that out.

"It's okay. No rush." He smiled valiantly even though hurt lingered in his eyes. "Yum. This smells delicious."

I barely restrained a facepalm. "No! 'Oh,' meaning I can't believe I said it without talking to you first. I assumed you were at the same place as me, and that's not fai—"

Myles shut me up with a kiss so tender it made me feel like I was floating.

"I want to be your boyfriend. I wanted to bring it up but got nervous."

I grabbed his free hand. "You can talk to me about anything. Let's promise to talk about stuff instead of worrying about it?"

He snorted.

"Bad choice of words. Let's talk about stuff to try to minimize the inevitable worry."

"That sounds great." He grinned. "Boyfriend."

We'd talked a lot about his anxious points, and it was helpful to try and understand that part of him so I could do my best to minimize what might add unnecessary stress. But, obviously, I was still learning since I hadn't anticipated this.

He dug into his food and wiggled his shoulders in his little happy food dance I adored.

"I've been thinking about something else."

His hand paused with his fork halfway to his mouth. "Okay…"

"It's nothing bad. Well, I don't think so."

"Not helping."

I smiled apologetically. "How do you feel about meeting my family? My mom's birthday is coming up, and I'd love to bring you to our family dinner."

His owlish eyes blinked at me underneath his glasses. "You want to take me to a special family event? Are you sure?"

I scooted closer to him on the bench. "As my boyfriend, I'm hoping you'll be my date to a lot of family events."

Myles's eyes lit up. "I can't wait to meet your family. What kind of flowers does your mom like?" He dug into his food with relaxed shoulders and an easy smile.

"She loves carnations because they last a long time." I hoped Myles and I lasted a long time too. I couldn't wait to bring him into another part of my life. God, it was difficult to imagine any part of my life without him.

I adopted a serious expression. "But be forewarned, my parents aren't gifted in the art of seasoning food. Salt and pepper rule the roost."

Myles's shoulders shook with laughter. "I'll sneak some spices in my pocket."

I grinned.

"Thank you for bringing me here to share the news."

I kissed his temple. "Thank you for bringing me into your world."

As he rested his head on my shoulder, I sent my dad a silent thank you for teaching me basic plumbing skills all those years ago. I never thought being able to clear a pipe would lead me to the man of my dreams.

EPILOGUE

Six months later

I giddily traipsed along the mossy path behind Brandon through the Hoh Rainforest. We had to be over two, maybe three, miles from the visitor center. Brandon's day pack bounced with his long stride. It was adorable watching him hike ahead, suddenly remember I had short legs, and then slow himself before shooting a sheepish smile over his shoulder.

I wanted a slower stroll to enjoy all the life around me. Brandon did enjoy intense hikes, but he was happy to compromise with me this weekend. The Olympic Peninsula, or Oly Pen as I'd lovingly nick-named it when I'd first visited many years ago, was an ecologist's wet dream. Brandon whisking me away to spend a few days together in Oly Pen was the best thing ever.

"Did you know there are three distinct ecosystems here? This corner of Washington is amazing, with temperate forests, coastline, and glaciated mountains. The diversity of flora and fauna is astounding." I cooed as I passed the cutest little fern.

"That's so cool," Brandon said with an impressive amount of enthusiasm, like he could listen to me blab all day. Actually, he had because I'd waxed poetic about the Olympic National Park on the over six-hour drive up here yesterday, and he was still happy to let me geek out.

The past six months with him had been a dream. The kind that leaves you smiling while sleeping and never wanting to wake up. Six months wasn't *that* long, but it was almost impossible to remember my life before Brandon was a part of it. He'd fit in seamlessly.

And, shockingly, I'd fit in perfectly with his family. We'd discovered his dad used to play D&D in high school—a fact that Brandon was delighted to learn—and there'd been talks of trying an easy campaign with his family.

Brandon already had practice being a dungeon master from a one-shot campaign he'd run with my—*our*, swoon—friends. They'd frothed for him when he showed up with his stack of papers and competent organization and earnestly handled Sami's and Jay's squabbles.

Gods, I loved him.

"I love you."

Brandon stumbled. I realized what I'd blurted and froze. Brandon stilled for a moment, and my life flashed before my eyes as I braced for his response. I didn't expect him to be upset—the man thought the world of me, and I'd finally learned to accept that. But that anxious part of me hadn't wanted to be the first to say it. He might not be there yet, and that was okay.

I caught my bottom lip with my teeth and scanned his face as he turned. I took in the soft surprise of his warm smile, the familiar cocky curve of his lips, and love shining in his eyes. Of course he loved me. We might not have said the words, but as I thought about it, he'd been showing me his feelings for ages.

In a few quick steps, he closed the distance between us and pulled me into his arms. He tilted down as I rose on my tiptoes to meet his eager lips. I melted into him as he showed me his love with a kiss that left me breathless. His possessive hold around my back, the warmth of him, the cedar body wash he kept using after I mentioned I thought the sample smelled delicious on him ignited my senses.

I was so grateful to my finicky plumbing and scattered landlord for bringing Brandon into my life.

"You love me?" Grinning, he gripped my hips and pulled me close.

I swallowed. "I do."

His smile grew impossibly wider as his baby blues sparkled. "I love you so much, baby."

Ungh. I needed a fainting couch to appear nearby every time he called me that.

"If I'd have let Lori set us up, we could've met earlier." I pouted.

He kissed my pouty lip. "At least it happened, and now Lori gets to gloat that the universe wanted us together, and she was the first to spot it."

I sighed happily. "Destined to be."

"Rainforests make you romantic." Brandon kissed the spot beneath my ear that always made my toes curl.

I giggled at the tickle of his scruff against my sensitive skin. "And a little horny." But that was all him.

"When you see what I brought you here for, you're really going to love me."

I stared up at him as my eyebrows shot up. "What you brought me here for? More than taking me to one of my favorite places in the world?"

Brandon grabbed my hand and pulled me to the boardwalk. "We're almost there."

What special thing could there be to show me in the middle of a temperate rainforest?

The wooden planks rattled under our steps as we crossed the boardwalk.

"We need to go through that." He pointed to a tall split in the base of a tree, oddly large enough to walk through.

"Through it?" The trail wasn't as pronounced through the tree, but it was the obvious choice given the undisturbed foliage on each side of it.

Brandon seemed to know where he was going, so I followed him along a barely there path over downed trees and muddy patches. He stopped next to one of them and turned toward me.

"Notice anything?"

I glanced around. "It's gorgeous. I could spend hours poking around and looking at everything. Is that what the surprise is? Setting a timer and asking me how many species I can identify before it goes off?" Or maybe it was a sexy surprise. I'd never had sex outside until Brandon and I christened our spot at the wetland. The idea was kind of thrilling.

"No, but that's a fun idea. What do you hear?" He stared at me intently. Clearly, there was something I was supposed to get.

I let the sounds settle so I could pick them apart. Persistent trills of several birds, the Hoh River rushing through the forest, raindrops finding their way through the tree canopy, and wind whistling through the trees. There might've been small animals rustling around. It was the kind of audible immersive experience I wished I could get at the wetland, but it was too close to urban life for that. I relaxed at the natural sounds.

"It's the One Square Inch."

"The what?" I tilted my head.

He pulled a tumbled red stone from his pocket and then pointed to a similar stone on the downed tree next to us that I hadn't noticed. He handed me the one that had been sitting there, then placed his in its spot.

"This is supposed to be one of the quietest spaces in the country because it's so far removed from human noise pollution, aside from the planes that fly overhead periodically. The guy who initially wrote about it started a tradition of marking the spot with a red stone and encouraging others to bring their own red stone to swap. It's supposed to be great for acoustic ecology, and I thought you might like it."

Welp. Official ruling in. Rainforests and thoughtful boyfriends made me horny.

"Sorry, I need a moment. I think my brain rebooted at you talking about acoustic ecology."

Brandon's warm laughter was the best sound of all. "I thought it would be a great place to tell you that I love you."

"Oops. Sorry I beat you to it."

"Never be sorry for telling me that. You've changed my life in ways I could have never imagined." He twined his fingers with mine. "What do you think about moving in together? I'd love to build a dice collection with you."

This man had stolen my heart, slotted into my life, and understood me better than anyone else. I was so glad I'd gotten over my fear of letting him in because Brandon was the best thing that ever happened to me.

"I'd love to. Your place or mine?"

"Your lack of shared walls is a definite perk."

We stood, wrapped in each other's arms, enjoying the One Square Inch. I couldn't wait for—hopefully—a lifetime of experiences like this with him.

ACKNOWLEDGMENTS

Thank you to Xio and Susan for organizing this fabulous anthology. It's an enormous project, and I'm so grateful for all you do! I'm thrilled to get to participate.

Also, thank you so much to the amazing people who helped me with this story: Abbie, Beck, Bix, Brennon, and Lori. I couldn't have finished this story without you!

ABOUT LEE BLAIR

Lee Blair is a queer author and screenwriter from Oregon who writes low angst queer contemporary romance full of sweet, steam, fun, and laughs. She's constantly amused by the antics of her two ginger cats, spends too much time daydreaming about her next trip to Scotland, and considers starting hobbies its own hobby. Much like buying books and reading books are separate hobbies.

Learn more about Lee and her books at LeeBlairBooks.com.
Lee also hosts a podcast for readers of low angst queer romance called the Low Angst Library.

OUR NEXT CHAPTER

A.D. ELLIS

ABOUT OUR NEXT CHAPTER

Widowed librarian Darren is at peace with his job and cat. A caretaker at heart, he can't help but worry about the guy with the backpack who has been frequenting the library.

Brady wasn't surprised when his parents kicked him out. He just needs enough of a reprieve to get settled with a place to live and a job.

When Darren offers Brady a place to stay, both men take a leap of faith and hold on tight. Will they crash and burn? Or will they write the next chapter of their story together?

Our Next Chapter is a 13,000+ word low-angst, M/M age-gap love story.

CHAPTER
ONE

DARREN SINCLAIR

The kid had been hanging around the library for nearly two weeks. And not just like he'd been there studying, using the internet, or making copies. I'd been the head librarian at the small-town library for six years, and assistant librarian for almost ten years before that. I recognized faces. I knew names. And I also had no trouble piecing together clues and noticing patterns.

He'd shown up two weeks ago with a ratty old backpack. His clothes didn't vary beyond rotating flannels every other day. His shoes had seen better days, his jeans needed a wash, and he used the flannel to cover up the holes in his black t-shirt.

I had no doubt he was unhoused and using the library to help meet his basic needs. I'd taken to watching him like a hawk. My late husband, Kevin, was likely chuckling in his grave, laughing at how I couldn't help but take in strays. The kid was about twenty-five. He was educated and enjoyed reading based on the books he'd take from the shelves and devour while he cuddled against the wall in a far corner and charged his phone.

When he wasn't reading, he was using a computer. So what if I stole quick glances at the screen every time he vacated the workstation as closing time approached? He mostly searched for jobs, but occasionally he also looked for places to rent.

Do it. You know you want to. You know you're going to do it. Might as well do it sooner rather than later. The voice was Kevin's and the teasing grin was obvious.

Backpack Boy as I'd taken to calling him in my head—okay, he wasn't a boy, but at forty years old, twenty-five definitely qualified as an age gap. Anyway, he'd gotten into a routine, and I found myself rushing to work each morning battling a weird combination of feeling bad for him, wanting to help him, and just wanting to watch him go about his day.

He'd get to the library right as the doors opened. We weren't one of the biggest libraries in the area, but we weren't the smallest either. And our building was the newest in the county—remodeled just a few years ago. Which meant we had newly updated restrooms. No doubt, the kid was making use of the one larger, accessible stall in the men's restroom which contained a baby changing table, a sink, a mirror, and a hand dryer.

He walked in every morning wearing the flannel from the day before and made straight for the restroom. Twenty minutes later, he'd emerge with damp hair, his other flannel, a hint of mint following him, and sometimes he had even shaved.

He had two water bottles he filled up at the fountain first thing every morning. Then he'd go to the little café cart and order the smallest, cheapest coffee, and a protein bar. He wasn't scrawny, but if he kept existing on coffee and protein bars, he wasn't going to last for long.

This went on day after day for two weeks. I came up with a variety of plans. I'd leave him a change of clothes in the bathroom stall. I'd pretend someone left their coffee and breakfast sandwich at the circulation counter and ask him if he wanted it. I'd tell the café cart clerk to offer him a huge discount on the little breakfast combo and then I'd cover the difference later. I'd drop a roll of quarters into his backpack along with the address for the local laundromat.

But all the plans had sticking points that made me hold off.

I found myself worrying over Backpack Boy from the moment the library closed until the doors opened the next day. Where was he sleeping? Where was he getting food? He couldn't survive on water, coffee, and one protein bar a day.

I mean, he could, but I didn't like thinking about him being hungry.

The fact he read book after book yet never checked anything out made me think he wasn't from the area, and getting a library card would cost money as a non-resident. The annual fee wasn't exorbitant, but the kid was clearly on a very tight budget.

"If that vagrant doesn't vacate the premises within the next few days, I will be calling the police." Judy's rheumy glare squinted through her bifocals.

Catching where she was focusing her haughty anger, I fought panic swirling in my gut. Judy was the former head librarian. She'd retired six years ago, and I'd been promoted. Recently, our amazing assistant librarian took family medical leave and Judy agreed to return for a few shifts a week until I got a part-time spot filled.

She'd been back about a week, and she'd changed a bit in six years. Judy wasn't as punctual as she'd once been. She forgot things a lot more than she used to. And she moved much slower.

However, her patience and empathy hadn't improved in the slightest; I was pretty sure it was worse.

Much worse.

Backpack Boy wasn't hurting anyone. He wasn't doing anything illegal. But if Judy called the cops, he'd be told to go to a shelter if he needed to clean up. They couldn't kick him out of the library completely, but if he didn't have a library card, they could suggest he find somewhere else to hang out. In short, a call to the police would put him on their radar, and he didn't need that.

Shit.

The kid was just trying to get by.

I spent that night dreaming of his messy curls, scruffy jawline, and big blue eyes. He was the definition of boy-next-door attractive, but more than that, he just screamed take care of me. The next day, I went through about a hundred new plans. Ways to keep Judy from calling the cops. Ideas to persuade the cops to just let him be; I could tell them I'd vouch for him. Could I get him to stay hidden, so Judy didn't see him; maybe skip the library on the days she had a shift?

Damn it.

It was useless.

Do it. There's no reason not to. He's clearly not dangerous. You've got that big ol' house. And you haven't had anyone to take care of since I died.

Plus, he's cute.

I scoffed. I often heard my late husband's voice, but he'd never taken to encouraging me to take in cute, young guys.

A stray cat, sure.

Donating to a good cause, definitely.

But asking a kid nearly half my age to come home with me wasn't something I'd ever considered, and I never would have thought Kevin would be cheering me on.

"It could be a disaster. He might think I'm some creepy old man."

Great. Now I was talking to myself.

You're like fifteen years older. First, you're not old. Second, he needs some help. Offer him a place to stay.

"There is a part-time job at the library," I mused, rubbing my hand over Cher's head as she purred one morning before I left for work. She was a tortoiseshell who'd shown up at my door shortly after I lost Kevin. He'd been allergic so we'd never had a cat, but no one had claimed her despite the signs I posted. The vet said since she wasn't chipped and I'd searched for her owner, I was fine to keep her.

Cher had been by my side ever since.

"So, what? I just put him up and boom I've got a second companion?" I muttered.

He's cute. He's on his own and struggling. Plus, you promised.

"Yeah, sure, let me just go up to him and be like, 'Come home with me. If you're down, we can have a little fun.' Ewww, Kev, that's just not right."

No one said you had to proposition him. Just offer him shelter and a job. See where things go from there.

I sighed and ran my hands over my face.

Do.

It.

I couldn't help but roll my eyes and smirk. It wasn't as if I thought Kev's ghost was actually talking to me, but after knowing the man for so many years, I could imagine every single word he'd say down to the last syllable.

Kevin and I had been together since college. He was my best friend and closest confidant. We knew each other better than we knew ourselves. When he got sick, I vowed I'd take care of him until the end. That day came much quicker than I wanted it to, but Kevin had been ready for the pain to end. I'd held him and told him it was okay to let go. He'd pressed a kiss to the back of my hand and made me promise I wouldn't be sad.

"You can be sad, but not too sad. We had so many wonderful years. Don't waste the rest of your life mourning me. Meet people, live your life, be happy. Fall in love again. That's all I want for you."

My eyes stung at the words I knew would be in my heart forever. The love we'd shared had been special, but neither of us thought it was the only love we could ever experience. I would go on and live my life. I would be happy.

I just hadn't taken that step yet.

I got to the library super early that morning and made a list of things for Judy to do in hopes she wouldn't have time to focus on Backpack Boy.

Unfortunately, by lunchtime, she'd declared herself finished with all the busywork—her words, not mine—and plopped herself down with a crossword puzzle.

He'd mostly stayed out of sight all day—coincidence or he had a sixth sense—but Judy had locked in on her target about an hour before closing time. She'd huffed and every minute or so she shot murderous looks toward the corner where Backpack Boy dozed with a book in his lap.

"He's not bothering anyone," I hedged. As head librarian, I was in charge, but Judy was definitely the type to cause a fuss.

"He's clearly homeless, a vagrant. We aren't a shelter. He can check out books, use our internet, or pay for copies. If he's not here to do that, he needs to move on."

"He uses the internet."

"He uses us like a shelter. Washing up. Charging his phone. Taking naps." Judy put fists on her hips.

"The library is open to the public," I argued.

"And as a member of the public, I have the right to ask the police to look into someone suspicious," she shot back.

It was useless.

I glanced at the clock. It was under an hour until closing time. I was off the next day which meant I wouldn't be able to keep Judy in check.

Grabbing my sweater and bag, I slid my phone into my pocket. "I need to take off a bit early today. Can you handle the last hour?"

Judy harrumphed. "Ran this place by myself for years before they opted to hire an assistant. I could do it with my eyes closed."

"Great, thanks." I gestured toward the stacks. "Might want to check the poetry section. I saw a young giggly couple head that way a while ago and they haven't returned. Who knows what kind of inappropriateness they might find surrounded by Blake, Wordsworth, and Shelley."

"And Coleridge," she muttered. Judy grunted and grabbed a yardstick. "Young people these days don't even appreciate the romance of such great poets." She waddled her way toward the poetry section.

I didn't have long. There'd been no young couple. I just needed her away from the circulation desk long enough for me to make my move.

Thrusting my arms into my sweater and shouldering my backpack, I turned toward the back corner.

Backpack Boy was gone.

CHAPTER
TWO

BRADY TURNER

The guy in charge was kind, I had no doubt about that. No one wore cardigans and had the softest gray eyes without being sweet, good, and caring down to their damn core. I knew he'd clocked me within the first couple days, but he and I both knew I wasn't breaking any laws by hanging out in a public place all day.

Professor Cardigan—what? He reminded me of a sexy professor, and no one had the right to make a damn sweater look so fucking delicious. Hell, he even made the chinos stretched over his well-defined ass look good. Anyway, Professor Cardigan watched me, but he let me be.

The old hag, on the other hand, had quickly become a problem.

It wasn't like I planned to live at the library forever. I just needed a job and a place to stay. Luckily, it was early summer in the Midwest, so sleeping on a soft patch of grass just beyond the edge of the woods behind the library wasn't terribly uncomfortable. The library allowed me to stay relatively clean and safe throughout the day as I searched for jobs and a room to rent. My sleeping arrangements weren't five-star, but it was temporary.

If the old lady with the beady eyes and hateful sneer would just go back to wherever she came from, maybe I'd be able to stretch my situation out a week or so more.

I'd been preparing for my parents to kick me out since I was about sixteen. The moment I finally accepted I had a thing for dick, I knew there was no way they'd ever be okay with a gay son. Somehow, I made it through high school and college without them finding out. Don't get me wrong, it wasn't just luck. I worked hard to keep the real me hidden at home during all those years. My parents were so proud of me for focusing on my classes and laying the foundation for a successful future. Dad would have preferred I'd followed him into the ministry, but he and Mom both agreed that social work was a worthy career for a minister's son. They had no problem telling their friends, family, and congregation their son was going into social work.

No problem at all. Honestly, they made it sound like I'd been instructed by the big guy himself to become a social worker and minister the good word just like dear ol' Dad, only in a slightly different setting.

It was annoying as hell because I had no intention of attempting to convert people, but at least they'd stopped pushing for me to enter the ministry.

That problem had resolved itself fairly easily.

The real problem was my affinity for cock.

Not for me. I had no issues with being gay.

But my parents definitely would.

My days at home were numbered from the moment I returned from earning my bachelor's degree in social work. The plan was to live at home for a bit as I saved up money and took classes toward my master's degree. Dad also demanded I help at the church. He was never one to miss out on free labor in the Lord's name.

So, I worked, stashed away money like a squirrel preparing for winter, and helped at the church while counting down the days until I could tell my parents my truth and walk away without an ounce of regret. I had quite a bit of money saved. I just needed a job and a place to stay wherever I ended up when I left. Online classes would start in the fall, and I already had scholarships to cover the first two semesters.

I didn't want to get kicked out of my home, but I knew it was coming.

Best case scenario, I could make it through the summer.

However, I'd gotten sloppy living at college. I wasn't super out on campus, but it was easy to mess around with guys in private and not worry about my parents. Back home, though, there were a lot more prying eyes and gossips.

I messed up and got hot and heavy with the song minister's son, Evan. It wasn't like we even liked each other. He was snooty, judgmental, and not even that attractive. But he sucked dick like a pro. Unfortunately, when his mom happened to get home early from Bible study and heard two distinctly masculine voices behind Evan's closed door —and we definitely weren't memorizing Bible verses—she flipped her shit. While I was sneaking out Evan's window as per usual, Mommy dearest was on the phone with Daddy.

By that evening, after Dad's slap across the face, Mom's tears, and plenty of threats, I was on my own.

But now I was far enough away from my hometown so as not to be recognized. If I continued living frugally on my savings for a while longer, surely I'd land a barista position or something. I thought about looking for a job using my degree in social work, but I thought it would be easier to keep up with my master's degree if I was working something like a coffee shop or similar.

The shelter had a waitlist a mile long—and I felt bad taking a spot when I wasn't in a bad place; seemed there were people worse off than me who could use the shelter space a lot more.

Although, I would have done some sketchy shit for a real shower.

I'd seen a few rooms for rent, but one wanted a female, one was definitely a homophobe, and the third room seriously looked like it had barely survived a zombie apocalypse.

When Professor Cardigan slipped his arms into his sweater and shouldered his bag, I knew I had to make a move.

Hateful Hattie wasn't going to let me hang out until closing time. And if I'd pegged his schedule correctly after two weeks, my cardigan-and-chino-loving hottie would be off the next day.

I needed to make myself scarce until he was back.

Actually, I needed the hateful hag to disappear. She didn't work daily, but I hadn't been able to find a pattern in her schedule.

If she stuck around, I'd need to be moving on. The last thing I needed was to get on the local police department's radar. Not because my parents were worried and wanted me found safe and sound.

No.

They'd made it very clear they'd find me and deliver me to conversion camp.

Obviously, I had no intention of ever seeing them again. Plus, I was twenty-five and couldn't be dropped off at conversion camp without my consent—although, I had a feeling Dad wouldn't care much about consent.

My phone was mostly charged. Maybe this was the day I went to the all-night diner and didn't leave until I'd exhausted every possible job and room opportunity I could find. I'd order an actual meal and keep myself going with copious amounts of coffee.

As a challenge to myself, I decided if I could find a job and a room, I'd buy a change of clothes and take my old stuff to the laundromat.

While Professor Cardigan pointed toward the shelves, Hateful Hattie huffed and grabbed a yardstick.

That was my chance. I'd be gone and she wouldn't have a single thing to tell the cops. Law enforcement couldn't kick me out of a public place for making use of their services as intended. But they could ask for my ID; question why I didn't get a library card; ask me where I lived; tell me to go to a shelter. All of that would make me more visible in the small Midwestern town than I wanted to be.

I had no clue if my parents had told their friends at sister churches to keep an eye out for me. Who knew what kind of terrible stories they'd told about me. His last words after threatening me with conversion camp were about reporting me as a pedophile.

So, yeah, I definitely didn't need to get on the police department's radar.

Something weird caught in my chest as I realized I'd miss seeing hot-guy-in-charge every day, but I needed a job and a room before I could give any real thought to a hookup.

I chuckled to myself as I made my way out into the bright

sunshine. Professor Cardigan didn't look even slightly like the type of man who did hookups. In fact, he looked like a guy with a husband, two-point-five children, a dog, and a white picket fence. Had I not caught him ogling my ass, I may have doubted his sexuality—okay, the little rainbow watchband helped too—but he definitely wasn't going out and picking up random guys on the weekends or arranging sex on dating apps.

And I had to leave.

Bummer.

Maybe I'd come back when things were working out better for me.

I knew I'd miss those soft gray eyes and that smile.

And the cardigans.

CHAPTER
THREE

DARREN

For a moment, the bright sun blinding me, I feared I'd lost him. Shielding my eyes, I turned in a circle. I caught the tail of his flannel just as he disappeared around the corner of the brick building.

As I made my way toward the bench where he'd settled, I gave one last thought to the ridiculous idea.

Was it stupid? Yes.

Well thought out? Not even slightly.

Impulsive? Not really; I'd been thinking on it for nearly two weeks.

Did I have answers to anything he might ask? No.

Did I have a timeline for how long he could stay? Also, no.

Was I worried he'd think I was some creepy, old man? Hell, yes.

None of that stopped my feet from moving me to the bench and sitting down.

He looked up, surprise in his big blue eyes. "Professor—" He clamped his mouth shut.

I quirked a brow, but let it go. "My name is Darren Sinclair. I'm the head librarian. This is possibly going to sound somewhat unhinged, but there's a part-time job at the library." I cleared my throat. "And I have a spare room."

His eyes got even bigger. "You're offering me a job and a room? What's the catch?"

"No catch. I'm sure it sounds weird." I splayed my hands in front of me, palms up. "Hell, I feel kinda weird. But it seems like you need a place. The job doesn't pay a lot, but you'd be eligible for raises every six months."

"How much is the room?"

"What? Oh, no. I didn't mean you had to pay for it."

He scowled. "You're going to take a complete stranger into your home and let them stay for free? Again, what's the catch?"

I shook my head. "How about we discuss payment once you've gotten a few paychecks under your belt."

"What kinda of payment?"

"What?" This wasn't going well.

At all.

The kid narrowed his eyes. "Don't get me wrong, you're hot and I'd gladly get a little dirty for room and board, but you can't just invite strangers into your home."

My cheeks burned. "What? No. God, no. That's not what I mean. I've never offered anyone a room. Like ever. Aside from dinner parties Kevin and I used to have, I don't think I've ever really had visitors."

Oh, god. Now I sounded lame as shit.

"And I'd never...you wouldn't have to...oh, god...no...thank you for the compliment, but I'd never ask you to..."

I wasn't sure if I was more flustered by the you're hot, I'd get a little dirty, or the fact he thought I was offering...what? To be his sugar daddy?

What did he mean by get a little dirty? My dick had ideas, but I needed to stop thinking about all of that. Immediately.

He chuckled. "It's all good, Professor. I can see you've never propositioned anyone." He turned to face me, tucking a leg under his body. "So, you'd get me a job and give me a place to stay. What's in it for you?"

"Honestly? I don't have a fucking clue."

Backpack Boy threw his head back and laughed. "I knew I liked you. My name is Brady, by the way. Brady Turner."

I stuck out my hand and shook. "Nice to meet you. I'm sorry if I've fucked this all up. My husband, Kevin—he died a while back—always said I was a caregiver, a nurturer. I saw you and figured out you were struggling. It makes no sense to me, but I wanted to help. I've always thought if more people helped when they were able, fewer people would struggle." A warm breeze ruffled Brady's curls, and I realized our hands were still connected. I liked the feel of his skin against mine.

A lot.

"So, you're just helping? Not scheming up some elaborate plan to get me on my knees?" Brady cocked his head, his thumb brushing over my knuckles. "My slutty era is behind me I think, but I'm pretty much a sure thing if you buy me dinner and tell me I'm pretty." He batted stupidly long lashes.

I choked on a bubble of laughter.

Brady put his hand on my knee. "I'm joking." He winked. "Mostly."

"No, this isn't an elaborate plan to have sex with you," I said. "I have a job and a room. End of story."

Brady bit his bottom lip. "And sex is out of the question?"

Fuck.

Clearing my throat, I tried to answer without my voice quivering. "Let's take care of the job and the room first. I'm pretty much stuck in my spinster widower era, so I may need a few dinners and getting to know each other first."

"So, you're saying I have a chance?" Brady asked, his voice husky and flirty.

"I'm saying never say never."

Brady slapped my knee. "Well then, take me home, Professor. I think I have a room to see."

CHAPTER
FOUR

BRADY

I couldn't decide if I'd lost my fucking mind or if I was the luckiest bastard on the planet. Maybe a little bit of both.

As I followed Professor Cardigan—Darren—to his car, I recapped the last thirty minutes of my life.

Hateful Hattie had it out for me.

I needed to avoid getting noticed by law enforcement.

I was sad to walk away from Professor Cardigan.

Sexy Mr. Cardigan offered me a place to stay.

And a job.

I flirted, offered to suck him off, and watched him blush and stumble over his words all in one conversation.

And now I was going to a virtual stranger's house to…well, hopefully, to look at a room and not get chopped into little pieces or have my skin made into lampshades.

"What are you thinking?" Darren asked as he pulled his little blue Prius onto the road. Of course, he drove a Prius.

"Huh?" I pulled myself from my thoughts.

"Just wondering if this is as crazy for you as it is for me."

I shook my head. "Nah, I go home with strangers all the time. Get a real thrill from the unknown. I get off on putting myself in dangerous situations."

Darren stared at me, soft gray eyes unblinking, until the car behind him honked when the light turned green. "Really?"

I chuckled. "Professor, you're going to have to get used to my sarcasm and sense of humor. For real though, I'm thinking that if you say this room is in the basement, I'm out. I have no desire to become the next headliner. Young Gay Man Found in Local Librarian's Basement; Held Captive for Years as Sex Slave."

A laugh bubbled between Darren's lips. "Oh god, you don't really think I'd do that, do you?"

I patted his chino-covered leg. "Not in the slightest. I watched you for nearly two weeks. You're a good guy. I've hooked up with some strangers before but never trusted any of them enough to go to their house. But you don't give off any red flags."

"I swear, I'm not trying to hurt you or use you for anything. The room is attached to mine by a bathroom, but both of your doors have locks."

"It's all good. I appreciate your help." Honestly, I'd been looking for a room before Darren offered; I would have been living with a stranger either way. Instead of looking at it as weird, I decided right then and there to count my blessings. A room and a job all in one day.

The fact my boss and landlord was fucking gorgeous was icing on the cake.

I was a positive person by nature, and I knew things were going to start looking up for me if I just gave it enough time.

Getting away from my parents for college had given me a glimpse into what life could be like for me. Being smart enough to save up money and bide my time until I found my way again was a wise decision. While I'd never really been one to trust in fate to get me through life, I was taking this situation and throwing up a huge thank you to the universe.

"Why do you call me Professor?" Darren asked as he turned onto a quiet, well-kept little street.

For a moment, I couldn't help but stare in awe at the beautiful houses as my cheeks pinked and I tried to think of an explanation. Finally, with Darren giving me an adorable, cocked brow, I shrugged. "I started thinking of you as Professor Cardigan because no one has ever made sweaters look so sexy, and you remind me of a professor."

It was Darren's turn to blush—something I wanted to make him do over and over—and I couldn't help but wonder if that delicious flush spread out over his chest. Was the hint of silver at his temples evident in the hair on his chest? God, I wanted to nibble on his collarbone, press kisses along his jawline, and whisper dirty words in his ear as I straddled him.

Never had I been so quickly and utterly attracted to a man before, but Darren did it for me. I had to play my cards right—couldn't give up the chance at a job and a place to stay—but I had every intention of getting in that man's bed if he showed me even the slightest bit of interest.

"Guess that's fair," Darren said, "I'd dubbed you Backpack Boy."

"Because no one had ever made a backpack look so sexy?" I teased.

"Pretty sure you make everything look sexy," Darren said in a rush.

And there it was. That blush, his pulse pounding in his neck, the way he gripped the steering wheel. Darren maybe wasn't up on his flirting game, and I had a feeling it had been a very long time since he stretched those sex muscles, but he had at least an inkling of a thing for me.

It was the sweetest thing I'd ever seen.

Was this why I was twenty-five with no real relationship to speak of in my past? Because I took the hookups I could get rather than worrying about a man's personality? I'd never fucked around with a guy who wasn't right around my age. Was Darren's sweetness, his maturity, that caring vibe…were all those things because of his years of experience?

If so, hello Daddy. I'd gladly wave goodbye to the guys my age if it meant getting to spend time with a man who could not only get my dick interested but could also offer substance.

Darren pulled his little car into the garage and closed the door. The interior light of the car lit the way to the side door, and we walked out into the sunshine.

The little patio area was well-kept and decorated with colorful flowers and whimsical insects on garden signs, windchimes, and pinwheels. "This is cute," I said.

Darren smiled. "I like it out here. A fire in the pit, some music, a drink, it's relaxing."

"Sounds nice." I hefted my backpack and followed him up the back steps.

"Oh shit, what about cats? Are you allergic?"

I shook my head. "I love cats." Smiling at his sigh of relief, I waited as he fumbled with the door.

Darren slipped his key in the lock and gripped the doorknob, but I put my hand over his. He looked at me in confusion. "What's wrong?"

"Nothing is wrong," I said quietly, moving slightly to put myself between him and the door, my backpack lodged against the house. With my hand pressed gently against Darren's chest, I stared into those soft gray eyes. "Thank you so much for taking me in and the possibility of a job. I know you aren't expecting anything from me, and that's not what this is, but the whole time I watched you at the library, I couldn't help but imagine what type of guy you were. What it might be like to catch your eye and get involved." I chuckled, my hand moving up to cup his jaw as his eyes bore into mine. "It was wishful thinking, imagining you asking me out, us enjoying dinner dates, movies on the couch, simple stuff." Swallowing, I took the plunge. "But then you did notice me, and maybe I'm way off, but I think there might be some sort of spark—at least, there is on my end..." I let my words trail off and gave Darren the chance to tell me I was totally off-base.

"There is," he choked out. "A spark. I'm way too old and I have no clue how to do this anymore, but you're not wrong."

"Then let's give things a chance," I whispered, leaning in, and brushing my lips over his, allowing Darren a moment to decide if he wanted the kiss.

He closed the distance between our mouths, sealing my lips with his in the most breathtaking kiss of my life. Warm and comforting; exciting and full of promise. Darren brought a hand up to cup the back of my neck, angling his head to deepen the kiss.

One of us moaned and the keys jingled, just enough of an interruption to bring us back to ourselves.

"Sorry." Darren's words were ragged. "I shouldn't have—"

"Shhh, don't apologize." I ran a thumb over his lips. "This is a new situation for both of us—and we definitely need to keep the lines of communication and honesty wide open—but we're consenting adults who can make our own decisions about what we want. Maybe we'll find out later on down the road that we're not meant for forever, but that doesn't mean we can't have for now."

Darren's eyes locked on mine, and he pressed a chaste kiss to my lips. "I like that. How about we chat over dinner?"

I nodded. "Throw in a nice, long shower, and you're on."

Darren's eyes went wide.

"Just me. I haven't had a real shower since I left home."

Understanding and concern filled his eyes. "I've got a great water heater." He brushed my cheek with his knuckles before walking into his gorgeous home.

I followed.

Maybe what I felt for Darren was much too quick and much too insane, but I couldn't help it. I'd known he was different from the moment I caught him watching me in the library, and there was no way to explain the trust and attraction I had for him.

I knew we weren't promised forever, but I was going to enjoy every single second of whatever time we'd been given.

For the time being, I was home.

CHAPTER
FIVE

DARREN

Dinner with Brady was simple and easy.

The shower put a bit more pep in his step, and he smelled like heaven when he found me in the kitchen with damp curls and flushed cheeks.

"I kept myself washed thanks to the sink, but I hadn't realized how badly I'd missed a shower." His bare feet on the tile floor sent a jolt of awareness straight to my balls. "What can I do?"

Cher peeked her head around the corner, eyeing the new person.

"Well, first, you'll need to meet Cher," I said.

Brady's brows climbed his forehead. "Meet Cher? Um…"

I motioned toward where my cat had hedged her way toward his feet.

"Oh my god," Brady said, dropping to his knees. "Hello, pretty kitty."

And just like that, Cher—and me, if I was being honest—was a fan for life.

Brady settled in on the floor and cuddled with Cher while she preened and purred and showed her belly.

"Okay, miss," I said to my spoiled cat, "it's time for dinner. He's staying, so you can have him to yourself later." I reached out my hand and pulled Brady to standing while Cher gave me an annoyed look and sauntered away.

We worked together seamlessly to make a salad, grilled chicken, and baked potatoes. Our conversation never faltered. I laughed more than I had in years. And the delicious sexual tension bubbling through the evening had my heart pounding wildly.

By the time we had the dishes cleaned up, I was torn between bringing Brady to my bed and locking his door to keep me away from him.

What was I even doing? Was I taking advantage of Brady needing a place to stay and a job? Everything between us was new and exciting, but it also felt as if I'd known him forever. How were we so settled and relaxed with each other so quickly? Even with Kevin, things had taken longer.

Was I setting myself up for heartache when Brady realized playing house with an older guy wasn't as fun as he'd hoped?

I thought of the promise I'd made to Kevin about moving on and loving again. Could I love Brady? I thought of his blue eyes and sandy curls. Those warm lips against mine, how good it had felt to kiss another man again. I didn't know him, but I liked him. Liked how he'd used his resources to survive. Liked how he spoke up for what he wanted. Liked how things felt exciting and full of promise with him.

Maybe I was getting in way too deep, way too fast, but if I went in with my eyes wide open, I could enjoy whatever Brady and I had for as long as it lasted.

Right?

"Are you tired?" I asked. "I'm off tomorrow, but I'll pull up the application and you can get it filled out so we can get things set up with the job."

"I'm tired," Brady said. "Hadn't realized how stressed and exhausted I was these last couple weeks." He ran a hand over his face. "But not really sleepy yet, if that makes sense."

I nodded. "It does." I edged closer to him. "If you want to head to bed…"

Brady shook his head. "Not yet. I need a bit of time to wind down."

"Wine? Coffee? You can tell me what happened—if you want. No pressure."

His eyes shone with mischief. "Wine is a very bad idea if we're pretending we aren't both wanting to fall into bed."

Oh, god.

I cleared my throat. "It's not that I don't want that..." Swallowing thickly, I attempted to gather my thoughts—which had run straight into the thick of things with images of what Brady would look like naked, what his warm strength would feel like pressed against me. "It's just, as much as I'm drawn to you, it feels better to wait. Like taking you to bed your first night here would be wrong in some way."

Brady bit his lip and stepped forward, so close his bare toes brushed my socked feet, our breaths feeding on the same air. "I can respect that. Honestly, I'd be worthless in bed tonight anyway. Maybe we give ourselves at least a couple days to settle into this whole thing? You may decide I'm a terrible housemate and be ready to toss me on my ass before next week."

Chuckling, not really thinking about what my hand was doing, I reached out and stroked a finger down his arm. Gently grasping his wrist, then trailing my fingers down to tangle with his.

Brady's breath caught as the warmth of our skin seeped together, his big blue eyes meeting mine.

"This evening has already been the most enjoyable I've had since Kevin died. I like talking to you—even more than I liked watching you at the library."

His eyes flitted from mine to my mouth and back. "Do you think that's why it feels like we know each other? Because we had so long to watch?"

I thought about his words. They made sense. "Could be. I knew you were smart and resourceful just by watching. You were careful to clean up after yourself. You always took care to stay out of the way. Always polite to workers and other patrons. I didn't know your name or your story, but I knew without a doubt you were a good person." Frowning, I went on. "I couldn't explain it then and I can't really explain it now, but I knew just from watching you that I wanted to know you."

"Don't forget about how sexy I looked in my backpack," Brady teased.

"That too."

"But I get what you're saying," Brady said. "That first day, I'd been struggling to find a place, and I saw you the moment I walked in. Something about you caught my eye and I felt safe with you around. Aside from how hot you looked in your chinos and cardigan, I knew you were one of the good ones." He scowled. "Unlike Hateful Hattie."

"Who?"

"The old biddy who kills me with her beady eyes every time she's there."

"Oh, Judy. Yeah, she was going to be a problem pretty soon." I dreaded the reaction when she found out Brady would be taking the part-time position. I had no doubt she'd cause a ruckus over me hiring the kid she'd been determined to get kicked out. Especially since Brady taking the job would mean Judy would no longer be needed.

"Great," Brady muttered. "I'm sure my new coworker will be lovely to work with."

"Actually," I hedged.

Brady's eyes went wide. "What?"

"Hiring you will mean she won't need to come in anymore."

He thought that over. "So, we won't be working together, but she'll likely still have it out for me?"

I sighed. "Yeah, probably. But the director and I are friends. She knows how Judy is—we were all thrilled when she retired—so my decision to hire you won't be questioned." Worrying my lip between my teeth, I said, "But that doesn't mean I think Judy will go quietly and let it go. She's got it in her mind that you're a grifter and a vagrant."

"If I get the job, and now I've got an actual address, she won't really have anything to complain about."

I blinked at him. "You clearly haven't ever met the woman."

"If it's going to cause trouble to give me the job, I can just take the place to stay and look for a job somewhere else," Brady offered.

"And make me have to keep Judy filling in?" I pretended to shudder. "No, we'll get through it."

A weird little thrill zinged through me at that thought.

We'll get through it.

Like Brady and I were a team. This man I'd just met was on my side and I was on his. Supporting each other, standing by the other's side.

"I like that," Brady whispered, leaning in close enough his lips brushed my ear. "Like we're a team. Brady and Darren take on the world."

"Or at least Judy," I teased, turning to feather my lips over his cheek.

Without warning, Brady wrapped his arms around my neck, pulling me into a tight hug. "Thank you. I was making it on my own, but it wasn't sustainable. Coming here today. The shower, the thought of a bed, eating an actual dinner...I'm realizing just how hard things had been." He shook his head, his face cuddled against my neck. "Like, I was doing fine, and I had it better than so many, but it was getting to me."

He was warm and solid in my arms. The press of another body against mine was something I'd missed since Kevin died. "You're welcome. I'm glad I could help. Not going to lie, I've been lonely for a long time. Having you here, even just having you at work, will be good for me."

"We can be good for each other then because I was getting hella lonely," Brady said. "Now, unless we're going to go back on the deal to hold off on sex stuff, we need to grab some herbal tea and head to the living room, or I won't be able to keep my hands off you."

As much as part of me wanted to see where sex stuff might go, I knew we were better off giving things a bit of time. We made mugs of tea sweetened with honey and moved to the living room. Brady sat close to me on the couch and gave me an unsure glance.

"This okay?" he asked as Cher walked along the cushions, butted her head into Brady's arm, and plopped down plastered next to him.

As if it were the most natural thing in the world, I stretched my arm along the back of the couch and let him scoot a little closer. "It's fine. Whatever you're comfortable with." I eyed the cat. "And clearly, she has no boundaries."

Brady smiled and ran his hand over Cher's pretty head.

We sipped our tea for a few easy, quiet moments.

Then Brady cleared his throat. "I guess you should know all this, just in case anything comes from it."

"You can tell me as much or as little as you want."

"So," he paused to take a sip of tea, "I've known I was gay for a long time. I didn't really act on it much during high school—I mean, I did, but it was tame compared to when I got to college. Mostly because there were eyes and ears all over my town and I had no clue how to go about finding other gay guys. A few sought me out, but mostly, I held out for getting away to school. Being away from home was great. My parents didn't love that I didn't follow in my dad's footsteps..." He paused when I cocked my head in question, shifting slightly closer to me. "Dad's a minister. They wanted me to go to Bible college and go into ministry like him."

"You didn't want to?"

"Hell, no. Growing up in the church, I saw it for what it really was and wanted nothing to do with the hypocrites and bigots. I convinced them I'd still be helping others by being a social worker." He shrugged. "If they chose to believe I'd be sharing the Word with those I came in contact with through that job, that's their own fault."

He was quiet for a moment while he drank his tea.

"Anyway, college was great. Definitely my slut era and it was the happiest I'd ever been. But as the years of school went on, I recognized sleeping around was getting a little old. Plus, it was exhausting. But when I went home after graduation, it was hard to curtail the hookup lifestyle just because I was back under their roof. I wasn't ready to settle down yet—and I knew I needed to save up money to be on my own because once I told them my truth, they'd kick me out in a heartbeat."

My chest ached for the kid. I knew what it felt like to have an unsupportive family. It was one of the things Kevin and I had bonded over when we first met.

"So, I worked and helped at Dad's church while saving money for grad school. The song minister's son at church came on to me in the sound booth one Sunday. He wasn't my type at all, but being away from school had me taking what I could get." Brady shook his head. "I don't think I'd act on it now if I had the chance to go back, but at that point, it was kinda thrilling, ya know?"

I nodded, my fingers brushing over his shoulder.

"So, Evan and I got together a few times. The last time was the nail in my coffin. His mom came home early. I snuck out the window before she walked in, but Evan threw me under the bus, said I seduced him into doing things he didn't want to do. His parents called my parents. I could have lied, but by that point, I'd known my time there was ending—plus, I was tired of lying. Being mostly out at college had shown me what it could be like to live authentically, and I wanted that more than anything." He nestled into my side. "So, I told them I was gay."

I moved my arm to hold him close.

"Mom cried and worried about her Bible study ladies finding out. Dad went ballistic. They told me they'd send me to conversion camp. When I said those places killed, Dad said—" He broke off, clearing his throat. "He said he'd rather I died from trying to cleanse my soul than living in sin."

"No," I growled, hugging him with both arms and kissing the top of his head. "You are perfect the way you are. I'm sorry they couldn't see that. Nothing about you needs to change and it's their loss."

Brady shuddered in my arms, sniffling. "You're the only person I've ever told that to."

"You left and made your way here? No friends to couch surf with?"

He shook his head. "Since graduation, most of my college friends had spread out all over the country. I figured if I got a few towns away, I could blend in, get a job, keep saving up money for school, and start over. Just didn't count on it being so hard to find a cheap place to stay." Brady took a deep breath. "Thanks for listening. I don't think I'd realized how much all of that was weighing on me."

"It's good to talk things out sometimes," I said.

"Like, they weren't great parents. The fact I always knew they'd pick the church and their religion over me—that they'd rather I die than be gay—is enough to prove that. But having it actually happen, knowing I can't ever go home, that's finally sinking in and it sucks."

I kissed the top of his head again. "I get that. My parents gave me an ultimatum when I came out to them. I could say it was all a lie and still call their house my home, or I could say I was gay and be on my own."

"You left?"

I nodded. "Yep. I lucked out that I had a full scholarship to school with room and board. So, I moved to campus and never looked back. Met Kevin our freshman year. He had the same type of situation as me and we became friends quickly."

"If you want to tell me about him, I'm a pretty good listener," Brady said, his words soft against my chest. "Just know that I'm not sure what route my parents opted to take—pretend I'm dead, report me missing, accuse me of being a pedophile, coming after me to take me to conversion camp. There are a million possibilities."

"You're an adult. They can't make you go to conversion camp. The rest of it, we'll cross that bridge if we get to it." Refusing to question it, I tipped Brady's chin up and brushed my lips over his. Loving the tiny gasp of surprised pleasure that escaped him, I deepened the kiss slightly. Pulling away before we could get ourselves in trouble, I nuzzled his nose. "We're a team now, remember? I gotchu."

The way Brady melted into me stabbed at my heart, but also reminded me how badly I'd missed having someone to do life with. And something told me this man was the first page of my next chapter.

CHAPTER
SIX

BRADY

I'd never felt as comfortable and safe with someone as I did with Darren.

I knew some people would say I was coming off a traumatic experience and likely wasn't thinking clearly—taking the first nice person to show me some attention and thinking it meant more than it did—and maybe there was some truth to that.

But I wasn't the type of person to fall headfirst into something without thinking it through. I had maybe just met Darren, but those weeks of watching him hadn't garnered a single red flag about the man.

He was a caring person by nature.

He knew what it was like to have an unsupportive family.

It wasn't like he was after me for money. All I brought to the table was a shitty estranged family who might cause problems.

And maybe it sounded weird, but we just clicked. From the moment we officially met and even before when we'd danced in each other's orbits at the library, there was just something about him. Like my soul recognized him; like I knew I could breathe easy by Darren's side.

I'd arrived in town just hoping to survive until I got my feet underneath me, but meeting Darren had given me a spark of hope that maybe fate had brought us together.

I wasn't against the universe or God or whatever guiding me toward something good. And right into Darren's arms seemed like a soft place to land.

"How did you and Kevin meet?" I asked, loving the feel of Cher's purring under my hand as I stroked her gorgeous fur.

For the next several minutes, Darren's love for his late husband held me captive. My eyes stung to hear of Kevin's illness, the pain he went through, the couple's loss of what they thought would be forever.

Through it all, I saw what an amazing person Darren was. I wouldn't have wished Kevin away. Never would have wanted either man to suffer through sickness and death. But for some reason we likely wouldn't ever understand, Kevin was no longer with us and the spark between Darren and me grew with each passing moment.

"He was lucky to have you," I whispered, still cuddled against his side with the cat glued to my thigh.

"I think we both had it pretty good." Darren's words were soft, his chin resting gently on my head. "Thank you for listening. The two disastrous dates I attempted—way too soon after he died—were totally turned off by me talking about my dead husband. I think it freaked one guy out to have to think of our mortality. The other guy seemed jealous—like he thought he was competing with a ghost." He pressed a kiss to my temple—something that was quickly becoming my favorite thing. "It was good to talk about him."

"He sounds like a good guy. Don't ever feel like you can't talk to me about him."

Darren tightened his hold around me. "Thanks. He would have liked you." He sighed. "We had lots of time to talk and prepare before he died—it was hard watching him suffer and we both hated knowing how things would end, but having time to get ready for it helped… some—and he used to tell me I could be sad that he died, but not too sad. He made me promise I'd move on and be happy." His words caught. "We had so much love and so many good times. Neither of us thought we were destined for only one great love. We both wanted happiness for each other if we couldn't be together."

Later, I wasn't sure how long we'd dozed on the couch, Darren gently shook me awake. "Let's get you to bed. You've got a job to apply for tomorrow."

He walked me to my room, his arm wrapped protectively around me.

"Can I sleep with you?" The words were out before my sleepy brain could even process them. I should have taken them back. Should have ducked into my room and pretended the awkward situation hadn't happened. Instead, I turned in his arms and snaked my arms around his waist. "Just sleep. I promise."

Darren leaned in and kissed me. His tongue hot and promising, making me want to take back the just sleep deal. One of us groaned and he pulled away, pressing his forehead to mine. "Just sleep," he murmured, shifting to brush a kiss to the spot between my brows. "For now."

I couldn't help the heat in my belly and the sleepy smile as we made our way a bit farther down the hall and Darren pushed the door to his bedroom open.

"Will it be strange to share a bed with me after Kevin?" I asked while he stripped down to boxers.

"No, this wasn't our bed. I missed him so much after he was gone, I got a whole new bedroom suite after a while," Darren said, pulling down the blankets. "It hurt to move on, but it helped dull the pain of sleeping here night after night without him."

I crawled into the big bed. "Which side?"

Darren slipped in behind me and nudged me toward the middle. "This works."

We were quiet for a moment until the door creaked open.

"She sometimes likes to sleep in here," Darren said as Cher meowed and jumped up on the bed. "Since you're in here, I'm not surprised she found her way."

The cat cuddled by my legs as Darren pressed against my back.

"Where did you sleep?" he asked just as I touched the edge of sleep.

"Behind the library at the edge of the woods," I mumbled. "There was a nice soft patch of grass. The nights weren't too cold."

Darren gave me a squeeze, tucking the blankets around me tightly. "You're safe now."

Just as sleep began to creep over me, a thought struck. "You took care of him, but who took care of you?" I asked.

"Hmmm?"

"Who takes care of you?" My words slurred with exhaustion.

"I'm good, sleep." Darren kissed my shoulder.

"I can take care of you." It was a sleepy-time promise, but I meant to keep it.

CHAPTER
SEVEN

DARREN

I wasn't sure what Brady and I had done to deserve such a break, but we got a huge one. Over the first week of Brady living with me, we got him some clothes, refreshed his toiletry supplies, and started him at his new job in the library.

And Judy was home sick the whole time. When I'd called her to let her know I'd filled the position, she was relieved to know she didn't have to drag her "tired, old ass" in to work.

Brady and I had entire days at work without Judy sticking her nose where it didn't belong. Time at home to talk and get to know each other. Laughing over dinner, nights spent wrapped in a blanket on the patio, walks on our days off. Cher had officially adopted Brady as her own, and I wondered if she'd smother me in my sleep if I ever let him get away.

Things would change a bit when Brady started school, and I'd miss having him all to myself at home and work, but I couldn't help looking forward to watching him take his next steps toward what he really wanted to do in life.

When he'd officially been hired and gotten started at the library, I introduced Brady to the director, and later blushed my way through her not-so-subtle questions about what he was to me.

"Darren, I'm not going to make a big deal of it. I just noticed he has the same address as you." My friend had smiled and touched my arm gently. "Not to mention the looks you give each other nearly had the stacks engulfed in flames. You deserve to be happy." She'd been there when Kevin got sick. Been there when he passed away. It was good knowing she was on my side.

"He's good for me," I said, glancing over to where Brady reshelved books. When his eyes caught mine and he gave me that adorable little grin, I couldn't help the flare of desire in my gut. But it was more than just physical longing. Brady meant something to me, and I planned to keep him by my side for as long as he'd have me.

"Well, you two go on being good for each other," Donna said. "Judy's doctor has advised she not work any longer, even just short shifts, so you won't have to worry about her." She let her gaze linger on Brady for a moment. "Whatever she thought she had against him there in the beginning must have cleared up for her. I've talked to her at least once a day in the last three days and she hasn't once brought him up." Donna huffed and rolled her eyes. "Which is a huge improvement from the two phone calls a day I was getting from her to voice her complaints about him being in the library, and the increase to four a day about him being hired by you. Dear Lord, the woman was relentless."

I frowned. "But she hasn't said anything in the last couple days?"

"Not a word."

It was good news, but I also didn't trust Judy much farther than I could throw her.

Now, a month since he moved in, Brady and I worked together to finish up before closing. We had the next two days off thanks to a federal holiday and creative scheduling on my part.

I had every intention to make the most of our time.

By the time we got home, the sexual tension between us crackled. We'd been talking a lot, learning each other, and leading up to giving in to what we both wanted.

"I'm going to take a shower," Brady said, biting his lip.

"Go ahead. I'll run to the grocery and grab things for dinner. Don't use all the water," I teased.

I knew Brady planned to prep for whatever our night might bring, but I also knew he'd hinted at wanting me to bottom.

God.

I hadn't bottomed in years. Not since before Kevin.

Lube. Definitely needed lube from the store.

We'd spent an evening cuddled naked in bed as we discussed being on PrEP, getting tested, and whether we wanted to use condoms or not.

Tests had been negative.

No partners for a while for Brady.

What seemed like a lifetime for me.

We'd opted out of condoms.

When I got home from the store with groceries to last the next couple days, and a new bottle of lube, Brady met me at the door smelling of sage and sandalwood soap, and citrus mint shampoo.

He took the bags from me. Put away anything cold. Grabbed the lube. And pulled me to the living room. Kissing me, our tongues meeting in a dance we'd both come to savor, he worked my shirt over my head. "Gonna suck you off," he whispered against my lips. "Then you can shower."

Brady's long, slim fingers made quick work of my button and zipper, and soon I was naked on the couch with a gorgeous man between my legs. His mouth was sweet heat engulfing me. Fingers toying with my nipples, tongue teasing my slit, and hollowed-out cheeks as those damn mesmerizing eyes stared up at me.

The orgasm came too quickly, but we had time.

The rest of our lives if I got my way.

Brady stripped for me, his long, hard cock slim and beautiful like the rest of him.

"Sit on the back of the couch," I demanded.

Cher moseyed into the room, gave me the stink eye, and left with her tail high as I knelt between Brady's knees and spread his legs. The weight of his cock on my tongue, the flavor of his precum, had me gripping his thighs and bobbing my head. I groaned when Brady fisted my hair, loving the way he bucked his hips.

His release came hard and fast. We both needed to take the edge off if we were going to last longer than five minutes once I got him in bed.

Brady wrapped his legs around my torso, pulling me close, my chest smearing his cum against his belly. Our kiss was sloppy, but so damn good.

"Go shower," Brady said. "I'll clean up in the other one."

An hour and a half later, I walked into our bedroom and dropped my towel over the rocking chair. Brady, stretched out on our bed, stroking his half-hard cock, was the most gorgeous thing I'd ever seen. "Come here," he demanded.

When I neared the bed, he gripped my ass and brought me close, taking my dick between his pretty lips. "Fuck, Brady."

Not wanting to come that way, at least not right then, I pulled from his mouth and joined him on the bed. Kissing him, exploring him with hands and lips, I learned each inch of his body.

"Fuck," Brady panted as I sucked on his nipple and rocked our cocks together. "Do you only like to top?"

I shook my head. "Kevin was a strict bottom, so I always topped."

"But you like to bottom?"

Nodding, I bit my lip. "But I like topping too."

Brady gripped my chin. "Right here, right now, what do you want, Darren?"

Lava shot to my balls. "I want you to fuck me," I whispered, desperation lacing each word.

"Anything you don't like?" Brady asked and I loved how his open communication eased any uncertainty.

"Um, rimming."

"Giving, receiving, or both?"

"Giving? Never tried it, really. Or receiving."

Brady reached for the lube, worked two fingers into his hole as he straddled my waist, and tossed the bottle aside. "Hold your cock for me," he ordered, and I complied, in awe of how good it felt to be told what to do.

Brady lowered himself down my cock, tiny whimpers of pleasure

escaping him with each inch. "Needed to feel this gorgeous dick in me first," he panted, rocking his hips. "But here's what we're gonna do." He leaned forward, gripping my chest as he rolled his hips. "I'm gonna eat your ass and work you open until you're begging for my cock. Then I'm gonna slide into that pretty hole and fuck you until we can't walk. Sound good?"

My hands found his thighs and my fingers dug into his flesh. "Oh god, Brady. Fuck. Yes, fuck, so good."

When he slipped off my cock, we both groaned, but Brady made quick work of shoving a pillow under my ass. Spreading my legs and draping them over his shoulders, Brady buried his face in my ass and tongued my hole.

"Fuuuuck," I moaned. I'd respected that Kevin wasn't into rimming and never pushed him for it, but damn, it was easily going to be a top-ten favorite with Brady. He worked me open with his tongue and fingers, telling me how pretty I looked opening up for him. "Oh, fuck, Brady, I'm gonna come." I fisted my cock to stave off my release.

"Not yet. Wanna feel you come with my cock in your ass." He kissed his way up my body, our mouths meeting for a hungry kiss. The taste of myself on his tongue was new and exciting and had me wondering about what he'd taste like on mine.

"Brady, please," I begged. "Fuck, baby, please."

Brady growled into the kiss and rocked our cocks together. "Mmmm, like when you call me baby." He moved to kneel between my spread legs. "You wanna ride me so you can control it this first time?"

I shook my head. "No, I want you like this."

He leaned in to kiss me again, his slick tongue offering promises of what was to come. When he straightened, Brady grabbed the lube and slicked himself. Then he pressed his cockhead against my tight pucker and pushed. Slowly and gently he worked himself past the ring of muscle, my body screaming at the intrusion, the sting stealing my breath. When his balls pressed against me, Brady paused to press kisses to the inside of my knees. "You good?" he asked.

I nodded. "Good. Make me come," I pleaded.

Brady fucked into me with long, slow thrusts. "So gorgeous. You look so pretty opened up and stretching for my cock." He held my legs so the backs of my thighs pressed against his torso. "Stroke yourself. Wanna feel you on my cock when you come."

Taking my cock in hand, I jerked off, my eyes never leaving Brady's as he fucked into me over and over. "Oh, fuck, Brady. Baby. Fuck." My words turned into a chant of Brady, baby, Brady, baby until my balls drew tight and I exploded all over my chest.

"Oh, fuck," Brady grunted. "God, baby, so good. So tight on my cock."

"Come in me," I begged.

Brady's orgasm erupted, heat flooding my ass as he groaned and held my legs tight.

Letting my legs fall open, he collapsed onto me, his chest smearing my cooling cum. "Oh my god," he mumbled against my neck.

"Was it okay?" I asked, caressing my hand from his shoulder to his ass and back again.

"Well, you've ruined me for anyone else now. So, I guess you're stuck with me."

My heart fluttered.

That didn't seem like a bad thing.

CHAPTER
EIGHT

BRADY

Shit.

I hadn't come to town looking for anything serious.

Hell, I hadn't even come to town looking for anything with anyone.

But it seemed as if a higher power had different plans because I'd met Darren, moved in, and gone right ahead and fallen head over heels in love with him.

"Ruined, huh?" he asked, his hand sending shivers up and down my spine. "I think I'd be okay with that."

Fuck.

Good thing because I was totally gone for this man.

I slipped from his body and rolled from bed to grab his damp towel. Once we were clean, I let him play big spoon. We'd need to eat later, but for the time being, all I wanted to do was sleep.

"Thank you," he whispered, his warm breath tickling my ear.

"That doesn't ever need a thank you, it was my pleasure."

"For taking care of me. For putting me first. For worrying about me. I love caring for others, but sometimes I forget that I need to let others care for me."

I rolled in his arms and kissed him. "I will always take care of you. I love knowing I'm safe and sound with you, but that doesn't mean you have to always be the one taking care of me. I like what we have." I took his lip between my teeth and sucked. "And if you're okay with it, I'd like to keep it going."

"Yeah?" Darren asked, his eyes bright and happy.

I nodded before tucking my head to his chest and giving myself over to sleep.

Cher jumping off the bed woke me sometime later. We'd shifted positions and my hips pressed against Darren's delicious backside. My own ass clenched at the memory of how good it felt to take him deep and ride his cock—definitely something we'd be doing later—but the thought of sliding into Darren's body, slick with cum and lube from earlier, had me hard and ready.

I kissed his neck, his shoulder, his back. When he rocked his ass into me, I gripped his chest, thumbing over a nipple. "You awake?"

Darren mumbled. "Enough."

I chuckled. Stroking down his torso, I took him in hand and ran my thumb through the precum leaking from his slit. "This okay?"

"Fuck, baby, yes."

I jerked him gently, loving the little noises he made. "You too sore to go again?"

Darren groaned. "Sore, but not too bad. Just go slow."

Moving to grab the lube, I worked a dollop into him and smeared my cock. Shifting his top leg to bend against the mattress, I pressed my cock to his entrance and inched my way inside. Tight heat engulfed me, and I moaned Darren's name.

With gentle thrusts in and out, I reached for his cock again. Stroking him as I owned his ass, whispering sweet dirty words in his ear, losing myself to this man. When Darren's body tensed and his cock throbbed his release over my fist, I savored every bit of it.

Knowing he was too sensitive from earlier to go as hard as I longed to, I pulled from his body and rolled him to his back. Straddling him, I fisted my slick cock. Jerking off with his cock pressed between my ass cheeks, his fingers digging into my flesh, those soft gray eyes staring up at me, I let the orgasm wash over me. I grunted with each pulse of my cock, painting him with my load.

The shower a few minutes later was soft and slow. Easy kisses, gentle hands, whispered words. When we stripped the sheets and collapsed onto the blanket, Darren took me in his arms and held me tight.

"I wasn't against this," he said a few moments later. "Just never saw it coming. Didn't think I'd ever find this connection with someone else."

"I left home because I wasn't wanted," I started, closing my eyes against the onslaught of feelings when Darren squeezed me tight and kissed my temple. "Every step, every bus ride, every rideshare that took me away from people who were supposed to love me and protect me—" I cleared my throat, fighting against the emotions. "All I had on my mind was finding a safe place to land. Just a room and a job, and I'd pull myself through." Kissing his chin, I smiled. "And then I saw you in the library. I didn't know why at the time, but there was something about you. Now I know," I paused to nuzzle my nose to his, "you're my safe place. The room, the job…"

Darren carded his fingers through the hair at the back of my head and pressed his forehead to mine.

"And maybe even the forever," I whispered. Terrified I'd said too much, but unable to hold back how I felt, I opened my eyes and stared into Darren's soft gray gaze.

"I've got no problem with forever," Darren said.

"Yeah?"

He nodded. "It's different because you're different, we're different, but I've only felt this way one other time in my life."

"What way?"

Darren's lips met mine, the kiss slow and sweet. "I love you, Brady."

With my heart in my throat, I kissed him back. "I love you."

Safe in his arms, I let myself trust as we looked forward to our next chapter.

Together.

CHAPTER
NINE

DARREN

Six Months Later

"Hey, babe," Brady said when I climbed into the car after work. "We've got just enough time to run to the store, jump into the shower, and have dinner ready by the time Scott and Nick get to the house."

Brady still worked at the library a few shifts a week, but his main hours were spent working toward his Master of Social Work degree. His first semester was going very well, and I knew he'd be an amazing social worker when he finally finished with school.

The fact Brady had so much energy after a full day at school and I was a wilted leaf after a shift was proof positive of how much older I was. But it also warmed my heart at how this gorgeous, caring, driven young man kept me going, lit a fire under my ass, and made me want to take better care of myself.

I had never felt better in my life, and I swore having Brady by my side was a key component. The very active sex life, renewed interest in fitness, and getting creative with healthy meals as we cooked side-by-side didn't hurt either.

"Oh my god, did I tell you that Scott texted me that he was maybe bringing his grandmother?" Brady asked as he turned into the grocery store parking lot.

"What?" I squeaked.

Scott was Judy's grandson. The fact we were friends with him and his boyfriend was one of those truth is stranger than fiction type stories.

"Luckily, he was joking," Brady said. "I guess she's not as bad as I used to think she was, but I didn't want to spend the evening with Hateful Hattie."

"One of these days, you're going to forget and call her Hattie instead of Judy," I teased.

Not long after I'd gotten Brady the job at the library, Judy had shown up at our door. Pinched face, arms crossed, foot tapping, she'd demanded I let her in.

She'd bustled into our kitchen and told me, "Get the boy in here, he needs to hear this."

Brady had reluctantly come to stand by my side as Judy told us a story.

"I'm going to keep this as brief as possible," she'd started. "I'd like to first and foremost say I'm sorry. I'll explain more, but I was wrong about you, young man."

Brady had shifted next to me, but quickly melted into my side with relief.

"I didn't like you hanging around the library. Made me suspicious." She grunted. "My family says it's a trait that doesn't show my best side. Anyway, when you got hired on and had the same address as Darren—" She paused when my brows shot up. "I know the computer system, it wasn't hard to get his information. Like I said, I was suspicious and that made me even more so. I had my grandson help me look up your former address."

A shiver traveled through Brady and his breath caught.

"That's one of the things I need to apologize for. Shouldn't have stuck my nose where it didn't belong," Judy said. "I went to meet your parents. Long story short, I'm sorry for what you grew up with. I didn't stick around there long once I figured out the type of people they are." She sniffed. "No one deserves to be treated poorly for who they are."

Brady scoffed and I gave Judy a look.

She waved us off. "Yeah, yeah, I know. I need to take my own damn advice. But my youngest grandson is like you, and I wouldn't wish that type of hate on anyone."

When an incredulous giggle escaped Brady's lips, Judy at least looked contrite.

"I am working on it, I promise. I'm better in some areas than others." She pursed her lips. "I truly am sorry for any trouble I caused. If it's any help, I can tell you your parents have told everyone in town that you moved for grad school and took a job elsewhere. Seem to be spinning it that you've turned your back on family, town, church, but I think they plan on leaving you alone."

It had been a strange interaction, but overall, a good one.

Brady had been a mix of sad and relieved to know his parents had basically written him off, but knowing they weren't going to come after him or cause him trouble seemed to ease the pain at least a little.

Judy and Brady had a bit of a truce. She was kind to him when she came in to check out books. Brady, Scott, Nick, and I had hit it off as friends, and the four of us had quickly moved into hanging out as couples. Judy adored her grandson and his boyfriend, and we saw a different side of her from time to time when she was around Scott.

"Before bed," Brady said as we stepped into the shower after we'd put away the groceries. "We're starting that new book we got."

A new chapter had become our motto over the past six months. We were each taking steps into our new story, individually and together. So, we'd decided to start reading books together.

We took turns picking the titles. Sometimes we cuddled on the couch to read, sometimes we settled into bed with Cher curled on Brady's legs. But it was our thing and I loved every minute of it.

"Deal," I said, pushing his wet curls from his forehead and leaning in to kiss him. "Maybe tonight I can stay awake longer than one chapter."

"And maybe I can keep my horny ass focused on the book rather than my gorgeous boyfriend," Brady said with a huge grin as his hands traveled up and down my back.

"Mmmm, I don't think your boyfriend minds." I reached for the soap and lathered my hands.

"I'm lucky he loves me," Brady said, dropping his head back to expose his neck to my mouth as my slick hands took hold of his dick.

"He loves you very much," I whispered, sucking a tiny spot just under his collarbone.

"Well, I love him right back."

ABOUT A.D. ELLIS

Want longer, more in-depth stories?
    Love those addictive, sexy, emotional M/M romances?
    Check out A.D. Ellis's <u>website</u> for all the book info!

THE EXCEPTION

SKYLAR M. CATES

The Exception

ACKNOWLEDGEMENTS

Thank you to Xio and Susan for all your hard work. Also, thanks One Love Editing who did a terrific job on the story's content. Thanks to the readers out there too. I hope you enjoy the story!

ABOUT THE EXCEPTION

Tenderhearted Sam's entire life changes when he becomes blind. Despite a falling out years ago, it is up to his childhood friend Nick to help him. Nick is able to aid Sam with his guide dog, but will he be able to earn a second chance at love?

One day might decide.

CHAPTER ONE

ONE DAY WAS ALL it took for me to leave town. One day to say goodbye to anyone who'd mattered. The list had been short: only Sam.

Sam had been my first friend, my best friend, the only part of my past I'd grieved leaving. Every memory I had of home was also tied to a memory of Sam. If only all those memories didn't also remind me of heartbreak.

I knocked on his assigned apartment and swallowed hard, my palms sweaty as I waited. Ten long years. Would I still feel that spark between us?

We'd kept in touch over the years, with exchanges through texts and social media, but each year our exchanges got shorter until our real lives had nothing to do with each other. How weird that the one person I'd lived for as a kid had become a near stranger to me. Weirder still was how our paths would cross again after so much time had passed.

I was glad that Sam wouldn't see my face, which might show all the longing I'd bottled up as a teenager... then felt guilty as fuck for thinking that.

Blind.

Sam Harris, the boy with the most beautiful hazel eyes in the world, was blind. Blinded in a firecracker accident helping some stupid kids on the Fourth of July. Sam, who'd loved the beautiful colors of the deep browns and greens of the woods. As kids, we'd lie under a tree for hours, just talking about nothing and cloud-gazing. Sam would peel the bark off the tree with his fingers, a relaxed smile on his face, his gaze locked on the blue sky, mine locked on him.

Briefly I had been there to welcome him when he'd arrived at the foundation, an on-campus service animal training facility, a few days ago, but there had been too many other people around. My job was dog trainer for PSTD clients, whereas Patti handled dogs for the visually impaired and therefore assigned to Sam. It was crucial that Sam be with her and meet his dog as soon as possible. Patti had met with him earlier, and I'd offered to stop in to follow up tonight, since tomorrow was the only day of the week he could simply relax with his dog. All the rest of his time, Patti was assessing and working with them.

I heard a dog's low bark inside Sam's apartment and listened for a response to the dog, but there was only silence. I shifted the grocery bag to my other hand, then decided to set it on the ground. The foundation offered temporary apartments during the time our clients worked with our dogs for several reasons. It helped promote the client's independence, for one thing, away from protective family members, and it also developed the dog-and-owner relationship at a faster pace. I heard the dog again and then a muffled reply. Too soft for me to really hear Sam's voice.

Just when I was considering knocking again, Sam opened the door, his brand-new guide dog at his side.

"Hey, Sam."

"Hiya, Nicky, come on in."

My heart jerked in my chest. He was the only one to ever call me Nicky.

"And this must be Teddy?"

"Yep, that's him. Seems like a good guy so far." Sam shifted slightly. "But until we are an approved match, I don't want to get too attached."

"I get it." I bent to rub the top of Teddy's head. He was a gorgeous yellow Lab, with dark kind eyes and a goofy grin. The type of dog that instantly loved you and everyone else. Teddy wagged his tail like a maniac, and his butt wiggled with glee at my arrival. He stayed, however, right with Sam.

I straightened to shake Sam's hand, our fingers briefly clasping, palms grazing. Except for the dark sunglasses covering his eyes, Sam was still the same. He was taller than me still, broad-shouldered and gorgeous, with the same dark hair, high cheekbones, and firm jawline.

Fuck. I'd left my boyhood crush behind, but I was just as attracted to the man. Back in our hometown, Sam had been the popular one, the athlete at school, whereas I was the skinny wise-ass with a mouth full of braces. If we hadn't been next-door neighbors, I doubt we'd have become best friends. I ran my tongue over my teeth as if the metal of my braces might still be there.

"How's your mom?"

"She's good. Working too hard."

"So like always, then?"

"Yeah," Sam laughed, but with a thread of sadness. "Wish I could do more for her."

That was the boy I remembered. Sam always wanted to help everybody, his mom most of all.

I put my hand on his shoulder. I was never the touchy-feely one in the past. My family were pretty miserable people, more interested in wounding each other with their words than offering comfort. I'd spent years struggling to accept that I would just not be close to the people who were supposed to love me but didn't even love themselves. Sam was always the exception to my rules, and seeing the melancholy in his smile, I couldn't resist touching him.

He stiffened at the shoulder squeeze and took a visible breath as if forcing himself to relax; it was such a role reversal from the easy affectionate boy I'd known. The first real sign that he'd changed in more ways than his lack of sight.

"She's sorry she had to turn right around and go to work when she dropped me off. She would've loved to catch up with you."

"I'll be sure to meet with her when she returns." I picked up my bag of groceries and followed him.

What I didn't say was that Sam's mom had been the one to call me after so many years. After Sam's accident, she was the one to reach out.

"Nick, Sam is in trouble." And those simple words had knocked me sideways. I had wanted to drop everything and rush back to Mulberry Creek, but Mrs. Harris told me Sam needed time. She knew I worked for the guide dog foundation and that the waiting list was long, and as soon as I ended the call, I spoke with my supervisors about him and added Sam's name to the list.

He'd always been super close with his mom. Mrs. Harris had to work two jobs to support them after Sam's dad had died. She sliced deli meat at Foodland and was a nurse's aide. She'd urge Sam to have me over so she wouldn't have to worry about him at night. Many times, Sam and I could have the run of the place until she arrived home way past midnight. We'd play endless battles of Nintendo, and Sam liked to make us dinner, mostly macaroni and cheese with bits of hot dog or waffles and runny eggs. He was an enthusiastic if not excellent cook. We'd binge on his desserts, though, because Sam knew how to cook all kinds of things with chocolate chips. His specialty? Wrapping chocolate chips in Wonder Bread and frying it with lots of butter. Delicious. But I couldn't live with them full-time. I knew how much Mrs. Harris had struggled to provide enough for Sam. Besides, it had become difficult enough to keep doing sleepovers with Sam once I hit puberty and realized my feelings were more intense than normal.

"I've got pizza dough, sauce, and cheese. How does pizza and music grab ya? Unless you changed your mind and want to go out?" I asked.

"No, I'd really rather be someplace we can talk."

I winced, wondering if Sam would want to discuss my abrupt departure from Mulberry Creek or all the years I'd barely answered his texts or messages, but said nothing. Back then, I was a pretty loud-mouthed, scared kid, who'd failed miserably with talking about real feelings. Maybe that was why I got involved with animal rescue and eventually got certified to train dogs. People required talk and explanations; dogs just required love.

I began to unpack the ingredients I'd brought, canned sauce and a whole assortment of cheese. I knew Sam didn't like toppings like anchovies or pineapple on his pizza. We used to argue about that. He was more a sausage guy, so I'd brought a big link of it.

"Did you bring any mushrooms or red peppers?"

"What? Since when do you like veggie pizza?"

"Some of my tastes have changed. Including my taste buds as an adult."

"So no longer a fan of Gatorade with extra sugar and syrup?" I teased. "You swore by that pregame crap."

"Oh, God! I thought it was delicious, and now it might make me puke. I drank my body weight in sugar back then."

"Claimed it made you faster," I chuckled.

"Well, now it would only make me sick. Like I said, I'm not the same as I was."

He most likely had given up making Wonder Bread chocolate chip melts too. I scuffed the toe of my sneaker along the floor like I could uncover the old days there, hidden at my feet.

"I could run out to the store again and get some veggies?" I offered.

"Nah, it's fine. Sausage is still king of the pizza."

"No, mozzarella is the king. A pizza without enough gooey cheese is just a pathetic wasteland."

I'd brought some rolling pins since the apartment only stocked the basics and began to work on the dough. The foundation provided a small kitchen for the clients, but also had a big dining hall for those not ready to cook.

"Can I help?"

"I got it handled. You can just relax. And maybe check out this playlist I made on my Spotify." I was going to put on the music when Sam's expression stopped me. "What's wrong?"

"Nothing... I just, I used to cook for you all the time when you slept over my house, and now I'm just standing here letting you do it all."

"And you were good at it too."

"Since the accident, Mom's been doing all the cooking, but I thought— Never mind, it's a bad idea."

"This time is all about risk and change. There are no bad ideas. I get it's much harder now to cook and do other tasks, but given practice, you'll get back to cooking full meals again."

"What if I can't do it without burning myself or worse, starting a fire?"

"You aren't incapable of learning new things."

"Yeah, well…" He raked a hand through his hair. "Maybe I am?"

"You aren't." My voice was thick with emotions that felt strange to me, hard to let find voice.

I put a rolling pin in his hand. He gripped it, flexing his long fingers around it. I could still see the athlete in him the way he grabbed the rolling pin like a bat. We'd been on the baseball team together, and Sam had also played soccer and run cross-country.

"Okay, here goes nothing. Let's make some pizza, Nicky."

As we began to roll the dough, I just prayed we could help Sam get his life back on track. The foundation had a high success rate partly due to its rigorous adoption process. Not every person was a match, but once a person was accepted, we had a two- to three-week training program and on-campus accommodations for the guests that usually led to positive results. The dog had to match the person's mobility requirements, personality, and lifestyle, so we often worked to cross-train the dogs before their match arrived.

U2 began to play in the background, and Sam tapped his foot along with the song "With or Without You."

"They're still great," Sam said. He paused a beat before adding, "But not in the same class as Led Zeppelin or Pink Floyd."

"Led Zeppelin," I groaned, falling right back into one of our familiar arguments. "Why not go back to Elvis? You weren't born in time for any of them."

"Classic rock never should die. And have you heard the crap on the radio today?"

"Oh, Jesus," I chuckled. "You sound like your mom."

"Who do you think introduced me to all the great music? And what's wrong with liking the same music as your mom?"

"Everything, man. Look, your mom's amazing, but that's just pathetic. Didn't anybody ever tell you that a kid's job is to rebel against his parent? 'Course, I rebelled against mine enough for the both of us."

"You ever talk to your folks?" he asked softly.

"Only on special occasions. I don't interact with them if I can avoid it." I shrugged. "You must remember how much fun holidays at my house were."

The cursing, the slamming doors, punches in the walls…

The endless hatred of anybody different… like me.

I swallowed hard, bile rising to my mouth. What lasts? Except the good and bad of childhood? I stared at Sam, who was all the good. "Anyhow, they don't approve of me much these days. We all agree to keep our contact limited."

Sam hesitated. We'd been friends since before we could walk. Yet there were some subjects we'd avoided. Having been so loved, he'd always struggled with what to do or say about my folks. And honestly, I never told him or anybody the worst of their behavior. He only knew they yelled a lot, not what they had yelled at me or how often. I'm not certain he knew just how unsafe I'd felt.

"I'm sorry."

"Don't be. I got over them long ago," I answered, but my voice caught. I hated hearing the weakness in my tone.

"Anyhow…" Sam cleared his throat. "There are just no decent bands around."

"Untrue! And I'll fucking prove it to you when my hands aren't full of sticky dough."

"Big promises. But I'll be convinced when I hear it, and I heard a lot of current crap in the bar. Most of which I hated, with a few exceptions. I've heard the DJ play a few good singers at work. Not bands—they all suck—but a couple decent singers do exist."

"You're still such a music snob! But I'm going to put on my diva hit list later and blow you away."

"Diva hit list? It'll be like being back at work."

Sam had been a bartender in a club before his accident and hadn't adjusted enough to return to that job. Since he'd been blind for only a year and a half, this was understandable. But with Teddy it might be possible to try again or he might explore other choices. Right now, the most important decision he could make was with Teddy and if he wanted him.

"It is round?" Sam asked, gesturing to his slightly misshaped dough, changing the subject.

"Like my belly will be after I eat all this," I drawled, and was rewarded with a smile.

No matter how awkward some things were between us, just seeing Sam smile brightened my day. The early tightness from discussing my parents vanished with his smile. Being around Sam had always been my refuge. And although I no longer needed saving from my actual home life, being near him again immediately made me feel safe to be my old self, to let my guard down just enough, to play again.

"I'm going to flip my pizza dough like they do in the restaurants."

"Bragger." Sam had already poured the sauce mixture over his dough, but I was still fussing with mine. I pounded it a little more, then smacked it between my palms. It was flatter, but not as good as I wanted.

"Always." I stuck out my tongue before remembering Sam couldn't see me.

Not wanting to think about that fact, I busied myself with tossing the pizza dough above my head. My nostrils flared as I concentrated on catching the dough.

"I did it."

"Once."

"I can do it again."

Sam frowned. "Why do you need to repeat the trick?"

"'Cause it's fun?"

And because I needed a distraction.

I had missed all these years with Sam. We could have spent time together, done things that now would be a challenge for him. He could have seen me stick out my tongue, or wink at him, or a million other gestures that he'd *never* see now. I could fucking bawl for all the time I'd wasted without my best friend.

And why? Because I'd run. I had tried to kiss him that one day, and when he drew back, looking as if he'd been stung by a bee, his lips swollen, eyes wide, I'd run.

I'd always planned to leave my toxic parents as soon as possible, but the day I kissed Sam, weeks shy of our high school graduation, I'd left in a hurry, packing my shit with angry tears, instead of staying for the summer, or saying a proper goodbye, or keeping him in my life for real.

Aggravated, I tossed the dough higher in the air. For one shining moment, I thought this would be the greatest pizza toss on the planet. Awards should be given out for this toss. But the dough didn't come down this time to me. Instead, it hit Sam, who jerked hard in surprise and knocked against a kitchen chair. Dough struck the top of his head and then flopped onto the floor as Sam stumbled.

"Oh, hell!" I went to grab him, but Sam turned sharply away.

Shamefaced, I retrieved the dough instead, feeling like an idiot for showing off.

The dough was ruined of course; I had no choice but to throw it out and begin again. Teddy sniffed at it before I grabbed the dirty dough and carried it to the nearby garbage, Teddy at my heels.

"Eh, sorry, man. I'm too cocky, just like all those times in our baseball games when I tried to catch a pop-up one handed. Remember? I shouldn't have gone for another one then or now. I should've known that I'm still a crappy athlete, and that first pizza toss was dumb luck."

I swung away from the garbage, only to see Sam was on his knees in the tiny kitchen, his hands spread out in front of him waving in a frantic motion.

"Where are they?" he hissed.

"What?"

"My glasses."

Teddy would soon be taught to fetch many items on a simple command, but right now, he didn't know what Sam needed, only that he was hurting. He lay down at his side, his head cocked, trying to figure his human out.

My mind was screaming at me to do something fast, but my body was slow as glue to react. Crazy-guilty feelings flooded me. Like, if only I'd been with him when Sam lit those fireworks. I could have stopped it. If only falling for him as a messed-up teenager hadn't felt like being shoved off a cliff, I would have stayed longer and kept in touch better. And maybe, somehow, prevented all the shit that he had gone through without me.

Illogical. Stupid as fuck thoughts. But I couldn't control those feelings with logic.

Sam made a choking sound of distress, and my body finally jump-started into action. I found his glasses quickly and wiped them clean on my shirt. Not wasting a second more, I thrust them into Sam's desperate hands.

"It's all right. Here you go, Sam. Your glasses."

He looked up at me, and I smothered a gasp. His eye area was shredded. Like it had been put through a grinder and only a mass of horrible scars, angry and raised and purple were left. Nothing else. I'd been prepared for scars, sure, but not for the empty sockets where Sam's beautiful eyes used to be.

His beautiful eyes.

"Thanks," Sam grunted, jamming the glasses on. Putting one hand on Teddy's back for support, he slowly rose to his feet. He wrapped his elbows over his middle and turned his head. His shoulders and neck were stiff, as he purposefully expected a blow. I used to stand that way with my folks. Like me, Sam was proud.

He was also suffering. It broke my heart that we had been estranged for so long and that he was hurting so much. I wanted to fix it all for him. Or at least, say the right thing at this moment.

"Listen, it doesn't matter that—"

"Please Nicky, *don't*. Don't say anything. Let's just finish the pizza."

My teeth sank into my lower lip. I should get him to talk about the accident and reassure him that his lack of sight didn't matter to me. That Sam was still the only one to reach the tightly locked parts of my heart. Sure, I'd dated since I'd fled Mulberry Creek. I'd flung myself into a gay culture denied to me for years, but I'd never fallen in love in all the time I'd been away.

Had Sam? In the years since I left, I kept waiting for that wedding invitation or something. Girls had always buzzed around him, and Sam would briefly look back. He was always so damn nice that most of the girls stayed friends with him too. But he had no wife, no kids. It'd puzzled me since from the time we were little Sam had spoken of having those things.

It was too soon to question him, this being our first full night together in years, and I wanted Sam smiling again, so I went back to the pizzas. Maybe I was an idiot not to say more, but I didn't want to pressure him.

I snuck Teddy a little handful of cheese despite knowing better. His brown eyes looked so hopeful, and I could make Teddy happy much easier than Sam or myself. The void in our friendship was going to take work to fill. So I kept my big mouth shut, afraid of hurting him more than helping.

When we were kids, Sam had liked my mouthy quality, my constantly chattering on about various topics or bragging about what I'd do in the future. He'd liked my animated bravado since Sam tended to be more steadfast and quiet. Physically, Sam had been the big presence between us, large shoulders, strong and muscled physique.

I looked at him now. He was still tall and built, but fragile. I pressed my lips into a flat line, holding back my words. All the talking I usually did was a combination of jokes or smart remarks, not honest feeling. I ached to help, but what if I said the wrong thing?

As we finished cooking, I vowed to tell Patti that Teddy should learn words like "glasses" right away in order to fetch them for Sam. Hell, I might teach it to him myself before the night's end.

Less than an hour later, we sat on Sam's couch, sipping beer out of frosty mugs and listening to more music. It helped. The intensity in the air eased a little with each new song. I was just so glad to be here with Sam. If the night hadn't gone perfectly, it didn't matter.

He was looking more relaxed, that was what counted. And was I looking at him too much? Fuck, I was, and with every song, I scooted closer to his end of the couch too. But he was so beautiful. His skin like cream, his dark hair so thick and rich with different shades of brown, and his lips so full. I felt guilty for looking. Confused. There was no need to hurry—I kept reminding myself of this since hurrying was usually my go-to mode. Whatever was meant to happen, would.

I took a calming inhale through my nose and let it out through my mouth. When I'd left home, I'd been pretty messed up, and the two things that saved me were therapy and dogs. Meeting brave men and women suffering from PSTD and training dogs for their special requirements, I'd slowly realized my own trauma and sought out help for my past.

"This is the playlist I put on the most," I said, switching off the classic rock to the diva songs. Feeling better, I took another breath. My goal wasn't to sleep with Sam. My goal was to renew our friendship, to be lifelong friends again. Sam was the person I needed in my life, even if he couldn't be all I needed.

"It's all female singers?" Sam asked, his deep voice breaking my thoughts and making me jump.

"Nope. I got some males in there. Is it mostly Cher, Mariah, and Janet? Hell yes. But I got some Sam Smith, Bowie, Elton, and Bruno. 'Cause those guys are divas to me."

"You do realize some of them are as old as the bands I like? At least Elton and Bowie are."

"Yeah, we have liking older music in common." I shrugged. "I just like giving you shit about it."

Janet Jackson's "Nasty" began on my Spotify.

"I saw her in concert. Amazing. And before you say it—I know Janet is getting up there too. But she's not ready for a rocking chair in a retirement home just yet. And she's still fierce as fuck."

"If you say so."

"I do."

I left out the story of my date to the concert. He'd "forgotten" his wallet, which was bad enough, but halfway through the concert he ended up running into some ex and left me waiting in our seats. At least Janet hadn't disappointed.

"You go to a lot of concerts?"

"Some." I fiddled with the tiny threads on my jeans. "You?"

"In Mulberry Creek? Yeah, sure, I went to all the giant names who passed through town."

I giggled. "'Member when we learned Principal Clarke sang the National Anthem?"

"Who could forget? You called him Lady Liberty to his face all week. And his singing was atrocious. Sometimes, I'd think he went to all the games just to let people hear him sing."

"And on those morning announcements? He got so into our mascot's cheer. Attention, Mulberry Creek Eagles, one, two, three—"

"Soar!" Sam finished with glee. But after we'd had a laugh together, his expression sobered. "I always knew you'd leave someday. Mulberry Creek couldn't hold on to a force of nature like you."

I grimaced. "I was more like major asshole than force of nature. Principal Clarke was good to me despite all the crap I pulled. He tried to talk to me a couple of times and reach out to my parents even, not that they ever responded much. But no matter what he did, I was such a little shit. To him and everyone else..."

"I never thought that," Sam said slowly. "You simply called people on their bullshit. Or asked questions that nobody else dared to in school. I only thought you were meant for greater things. Amazing things."

So much for regaining my calm. My heart tightened like a vise had seized it. If it were any other guy, I'd say he might be flirting a little? But this was Sam. I waited, holding my breath, to see what might come next.

But he said nothing else, just absently giving Teddy's head a scratch behind his ear. We munched on our pizza, and I drank some more beer.

The night was overwhelming. I thought I'd show up with music and pizza and everything would work itself out. But I was kidding myself. I couldn't keep ignoring that friendship was only part of what I wanted. What was I going to do? How could I rid myself of all the yearning? A bead of sweat formed at my forehead and trickled down my neck.

"Are you hot in here?" I swiped a hand over my eyebrows. "I guessed I drank too much beer or something."

"No, I'm comfortable. I can turn down the air conditioner though?"

"Nah, I'm good."

"Sure?" he asked with gentle concern. "If you're not, I can make it better?"

I ignored how, like an idiot, my pulse sped up a little. "Just need a bottle of water or something."

Getting a water for me and one for Sam, I regrouped a little. Everyone always said that I plowed through life at breakneck speed. Sam needed me to just be here, be a friend, to listen to him and spend time with him, not get all hot and bothered at every innocent touch. Christ, I'd have to go to yoga or something in the morning. Anything to let go of these old feelings.

Setting the waters on the coffee table, I sat back down near Sam, just as the final section of my Spotify mix began to play. And I closed my eyes, listening to the music and trying to steady my pulse. I could control the way I felt. I wasn't some overly sensitive kid anymore, steps away from begging.

I pretended to be lost in the music, keeping my eyes shut still and humming a little. I could feel Sam turning my way a few times as if he might speak, but nothing came of it. Was this how he felt with no visual cues? Because closing my eyes—really to not stare at Sam's chiseled cheekbones or strong jaw—wasn't really helping me much. I could still sense the heat from his body and hear his soft breathing.

Sam hadn't been impressed with most of my diva hit list so far, but he lit up at Lady Gaga, who ended my playlist.

"God, I love the hell out of her," Sam declared. "She's the one I was thinking of earlier when you mentioned having a diva hit list. I listened to her stuff every weekend in the bar, and I never got tired of it."

I opened my eyes and grinned. "Me too."

"If you tell me your favorite Gaga song, I'll let you eat the last slice of pizza."

"Unfair to make me choose! But, you know how much I like pizza." I snatched on the slice.

"And your favorite song?"

"'Always Remember Us This Way' from *A Star is Born*. I know the other song 'Shallow' is a bigger hit, but the lyrics in that one just get to me."

I blushed, glad Sam wouldn't know it. The lyrics were over-the-top romantic, and when I first heard it, I'd thought of him.

"I haven't seen it," Sam admitted. He touched his glasses and added wryly, "Or rather heard it."

I was relieved that he could joke a little. I'd been worried that I'd ruined things before in the kitchen, but Sam had recovered from the dough incident. He was stronger than he thought, always had been. He'd be all right, I knew it in my gut, even if Sam still had doubts.

"I bought the movie on Amazon Prime, so I could log in to my account and we could watch—er, listen. The music is awesome, and we can turn on audio description."

"I'd like that."

"You got it." I reached for the remote. Soon the movie credits began, and Sam and I got wrapped up in the film, laughing at Lady Gaga's antics and sighing over the songs. We sat with our arms and thighs pressed close. So close, I felt my arm hairs standing on end, and my whole body was tingling. My heart rate quickened. And as Sam swayed a little with the soundtrack, his head bopped near mine, and I caught a whiff of his scent, some kind of citrusy aftershave and something all Sam, manly yet sweet. All my nerve endings went into high alert, so I pulled away.

With measured movements, I kicked off my sneakers and placed a throw pillow on the opposite side of the couch, giving much-needed space between us. Over time, I could stop the hot thrill of attraction. I was going to conquer these feelings, just not tonight.

I finished my beer, and somewhere during the middle of the movie, I must have dozed off on the pillow. The next thing I knew, Sam was gently shaking me.

"Oh, hell. Sorry."

"No problem, although you were snoring through your favorite song."

"Story of my life. Fuck me, I do love that song."

"We can rewind it."

I yawned and stretched my hands over my head. "Yeah, let's. Nothing makes this gay boy happier than more Gaga."

I froze, realizing what I'd brought to attention. I hadn't hidden being gay or anything—from our social media exchanges Sam must have known that, and from the way my parents had treated me—but bringing up my sexuality did bring up the unwanted kiss—the rejection and my running away.

"I'm glad we have the chance to be friends again," I said quickly, wanting to be clear that I wasn't expecting anything else. "I've missed you. As a friend," I stressed again.

"I've missed you too, Nicky." Sam's hands balled into fists. "How I wish…"

"What?"

"I wish I could *see* you at this moment." Sam's expression became agitated. "It's important."

I took his hands and placed them on my face. I wasn't sure what had upset him, but this much I could do. "You *can* see me, Sam. Look at me."

Sam gave a jerky nod of understanding. He slowly trailed his fingers over my features. "Is your hair still as blond?"

"A shade darker."

"And is this a stud?" He touched my earlobe.

"Hmmm, I got some piercings." I chewed my lip as Sam's fingers grazed the shape of my ear.

His thumbs next traced the shape of my forehead and eyelids, and the bump in my nose.

"I remember when you broke it," he laughed suddenly.

"Yeah, me trying to be all daredevil on that mountain bike was a dumb move."

"Not as dumb as letting fireworks explode in your face."

I inhaled sharply. "It was an accident. Sometimes, with an accident you're dumb but lucky, like me on that bike only getting a broken nose. But other times, you're unlucky, that's all it is." I wanted to add that none of this was his fault. But my saying the words wouldn't make him believe them.

"People at home—they all know what happened—but I've been stopped a few times here, walking with Patti and Teddy. And the other day some guy asked if I'd served our country… and I felt so fucking stupid, that the reason for my blindness wasn't that or anything good or noble, it was just… not paying enough attention." He covered his mouth with his hand and shuddered.

"That's bull. I'm not just saying that to be nice—I know it. We get service people in here all the time. Some for physical disabilities, others for emotional needs. I work with some of them, and I can tell you, they don't feel noble either. They all just wish it could be yesterday. That they could do it over and be fine and nothing bad would have happened to change the whole course of their lives."

Sam sighed. "Thanks for saying all that."

"It's the truth," I insisted.

"With my mom, I try to act like I'm fine. You know? She's already taking care of me like I'm a kid again when I should be the one taking care of *her*. It sucks that just when she should get to slow down and relax, she had all this to deal with. Me to deal with. So I don't tell her how much I miss seeing, especially certain things and colors."

"Seeing what, exactly? Tell me what you miss." I took his hand in mine and squeezed it.

He squeezed back.

"I miss seeing deer in my yard early in the morning. Or the birds flying overhead. Or the sun golden in the sky. Stuff like that is hard to not see anymore."

I searched for words—something healing. Sam spoke without bitterness, being so much better about the loss of his vision than I would be. It sucked so badly for him, for anyone. I might not be blind, but if Sam hadn't shown me those things, I wouldn't have ever looked. He was the one who had a sense of the world and its beauty, not me. He shouldn't have been the one to have that taken away.

Sam shifted in his seat. "But the music tonight reminded me of how many sounds I love. Like I can't see the birds, but I can still hear them, or the sound of a river rushing."

"Like Mulberry Creek?" I quipped, knowing full well our town's namesake barely rippled much less rushed.

"Not exactly. Although we sure had good times there, didn't we?"

"Yeah, we sure did." I blinked away some tears. My only good time had been with him. And now I had my friend back in my life and was never going to lose him again. Even if I could never let myself fall in love with him. I never felt as if I belonged in Mulberry Creek, but I'd always felt that I belonged with Sam.

I took a giant breath. "Sam, I never did apologize for the way I left town like that. For ignoring your calls. Sorry for doing that to you. To us. I never should have grabbed you and given you that unwanted kiss."

There. I had finally acknowledged the massive elephant in the room. It hurt already, but I wasn't going to let Sam repeat the rejection of that kiss. I searched his face, wishing like hell I could lock eyes with him. We just had to get past this moment, no matter how much it fucking stung, and then we could be in the friend zone for good.

"Don't. God, Nicky, I'm the one who—the kiss wasn't unwanted."

"What?" I shook my head, dazed, certain I misunderstood. "But... you pulled away in disgust."

Sam laid a hand on my knee. "No, in denial. I tried so hard back then to be perfect. I wanted to be everything for my mom, including being the perfect son who liked girls and would give her grandchildren someday. She never pressured me to be anything but myself, but it was me piling on all these expectations of what I should be—what normal should be. I wanted to just be a regular, normal guy. Joke's on me now, huh?" Sam's mouth twisted. "I pushed away the boy I was in love with to go after some image of myself that was destroyed anyhow. I'm the one who owes you an apology, not the other way around."

My mouth gaped, and heat rose to my cheeks. "Oh my God." My mouth opened and closed like a stunned fish as I struggled to process what Sam was telling me. He'd been in love with me? He'd wanted my kiss?

"Fuck, if only I'd have stayed and really talked to you." I buried my face in my hands.

Sam shifted, and I felt a light touch at the top of my head. "We were both so young and immature. I could have ran after you and told you how I felt, but I was scared of it. And now, it's too late."

I raised my head, swiping some tears away. "Why is it too late?"

"Because..." Sam gestured to his glasses. "Why would you want to take on this mess?"

I thought of Sam's warm hazel eyes. The color hadn't been what made them special, not to me. It was the way Sam had gazed out of his eyes, his tenderness and patience. And he hadn't lost that. I could find it in the curve of his mouth, the gentle way he had touched my hair. His worry still about how I felt or his mom felt above himself.

"You're perfect to me. For me," I replied, and meant it. "I don't want it to be too late. I want a second chance. We can take it slowly. We can talk about everything you want to talk about. But first tell me the truth: do you want a second chance with me?"

My heart dropped to my stomach in that silence.

"If not, it's okay. I'll still be here for you. I'll be just a friend."

"You've always been more than a friend." Sam's voice shook. He removed his glasses and set them aside. Deliberately this time, he let me look at him. Really look. He was so fucking brave. My throat constricted as a lump formed there.

Sam released a nervous sound. "It's ugly, I know it must be. I can consider prosthetic eyes. It's an option for me, but the thought of the cost and more time in a hospital…"

When we met, Sam had been the golden boy, and I was the sad one. The broken one. He took me as I was, became my friend, protected me. Now it was my turn.

I leaned forward and pressed my lips to the empty sockets. With tenderness, I kissed the jagged skin, making Sam quiver at the touch.

He cupped the sides of my face, his thumbs stroking my lower lip before he bent to kiss me back. When he moved toward me, my stomach fluttered. It took everything in me not to jump into a kiss.

"Please," I whispered.

I knew we'd both been damaged in different ways, and that together we simply worked. Our mouths fit, confirming it, softly moving in a rhythm all our own. I never wanted to stop kissing him. To feel the heat of Sam's body, to taste the sweetness of his tongue. The kiss took away any hesitation, any stiffness. It was natural, it was right. At Sam's moan, I relaxed. My brain stopped its fighting that I didn't deserve him, or that I had to fight the attraction to him, and my body took over. Because I could do that much, I could give him a kiss.

With the first stroke of his tongue, I knew I was wrong, that I was "giving" Sam anything. His mouth against mine was an equal exchange. Every sound, every touch, every groan. He gave and he took. Our tongues brushed, lingered, tasted. A sweet pressure was building, and bringing with it a ray of sunshine, a warmth from fucking Heaven. I tilted my head and deepened the kiss, ignoring any need for oxygen, because the only thing that mattered was Sam.

This was what I needed for so long. Sam was what had been missing in my life since I'd left home. We'd both been so afraid of risking our hearts that it had taken a horrible event to push us into action. Sam touched me like I was worth touching, as if we were a part of each other. And we were.

Pulling back, we were panting heavily, both of us were gulping air. And despite the kiss ending, I was still trembling a little, still aware of the adrenaline coursing through me, and how much I desired him, and how everything else had melted away.

We didn't do more than kiss, yet it rocked my entire world. I should tell Sam how I felt right then, but I was a coward.

"Man, that was something." Sam's voice was soft and gentle, as if he sensed how spooked I was. My chest tightened, and it was all I could do to breathe. My need for him was so massive.

"I haven't done too much of this sort of thing. With guys." Sam chewed his lower lip, his cheeks flushed.

"Oh, shit, I'm sorry—"

"No, I wanted to kiss. I want—" He broke off and shifted closer. Sam's finger gently trailed over my neck to my shoulders.

I shuddered, unable to form words, but Sam felt it. To make it totally clear, I arched against him, giving him silent permission to do whatever he wanted with me.

He leaned in and pressed a soft kiss at my collarbone. "I can smell your soap," he laughed, inhaling loudly. "And your scent underneath."

"Good thing I shower regularly these days," I joked weakly.

Sam smiled. He slipped his fingers beneath my shirt, feeling along my pecs to my nipples.

At his simple caresses, heat moved through me, starting low in my belly and unfurling all the way to my toes.

"Can… can I feel you? I've never…"

"I can take my shirt off if you want."

"Please." He swallowed.

I tugged my shirt over my head, and even though he couldn't see me, I felt self-conscious, exposed. But then he reached behind his neck and slipped his own shirt off.

Sam was broader in the shoulders and more muscular, but I had a thicker amount of chest hair than he did.

I guided his hand to me. "Go on," I urged in a hushed tone.

"If you're sure?" Sam stumbled over his words.

I slid my leg over his. "Hell yeah, I'm sure."

Although the idea of Sam touching me more had my nerves jumping.

Sam returned to skimming his fingers along my shoulders, chest, belly, following each brush of his hand with more light kisses. With each touch, Sam gained increasing confidence. And I was shocked by the intensity of my responses. My pulse raced, and it was difficult to control myself. Sam already had me hot and shaking. It took all my willpower to let him lead.

He pinched my nipples, and I ran my tongue along his earlobe. My cock was pulsing for more, but I ignored it. I pulled back and wrapped a hand in Sam's hair, tugging at the silky locks. Sam let out a small grunt.

Sam's hands slid down my back. His fingers were strong as they kneaded my muscles there. I would think about every touch... later... when I was alone again. Sam's palms were warm on my skin. I buried my face in his neck. I felt Sam touching lightly down my spine to my lower back. I made a noise in the back of my throat, and my whole body felt hot and ready, but I just stayed still in his arms.

Although my arousal was sharp, I did no more than mirror his moves. I touched him as Sam touched me, gazing at his smile. He brushed his cheek at mine, his stubble rough, before kissing my lips.

"So beautiful," I panted.

"Yeah, I never imagined being with a man could be beautiful." Sam stomach muscles quivered a little as I circled a finger over his navel. "Until you."

"I meant you. You're so beautiful, Sam." Our breaths mingled near.

He stilled. His expression was a little more guarded, as if he doubted my words. It broke my heart that Sam would ever doubt it.

"I don't lie, do I? I might run when I'm uncomfortable, but I don't lie."

"No, you're blunt as hell." Sam relaxed. He continued his exploration, running his hands over my thighs. I lay back on the couch, giving him all of me.

His hand rested on my calf muscle before gliding higher to my thigh. Having my jeans still on didn't help ease the yearning building inside me for more. I wanted to take his hand to my crotch, wanted to buck my hips. Every caress sent sparks through me. But this moment meant more than some quickie with a stranger could ever be.

This was Sam. And being with him meant so much to me. I let him learn my body as he'd learned my face. As his fingers ran over me, I hoped it gave him comfort and strength. Sam rubbed his fingers over my navel, and I moaned. Who knew I was sensitive there? What guy had ever slowed down enough to find out?

Sam cleared his throat. "Okay?"

"Yeah," I answered. He fidgeted a moment, unsure. So I circled my arm around his shoulders, kneading the flesh there. It helped that we were both nervous.

I was doing my best to give Sam what he needed. But he was equally giving to me. He continued his soft caresses, which thrilled me more than any experience in my memory. Something special, something new, was rising all around us, a promise that I couldn't name. Not just yet.

Sam lowered his body over mine so our cocks touched through our jeans, and we moaned at the same time. He slid his body back and forth against mine. Electric shocks pulsed through me each time Sam would move rhythmically, making me harder than hell. I gave up holding back my noisy moans, and Sam panted heavily in return.

Our mouths joined in another kiss.

Our tongues flicked back and forth, teasing each other. I was aching and heavy in my body and happy in my heart as so many sensation tore through me at once.

And I knew then how much we belonged to each other.

Always had.

"Jesus." Sam trembled against me, breaking the spell of the kiss.

"It's okay."

"Your voice says otherwise," he chuckled.

I put my hand on his leg and used it to push myself back to a seated position. He was right about my voice. It was hoarse as hell. Desire burned through me, and I shifted, adjusting myself, waiting for my breath to even out.

"Sorry, Nicky. I just—" Sam shook his head. "I'm not used to this. And it's going so fast. I'm so sorry."

"Quit it. Nothing to be sorry for."

"Damn, I just shouldn't have… Sorry."

"Stop saying that. I'm good if you're good."

"I'm good."

"Promise?" I asked. The last thing I wanted out of tonight was Sam regretting seeing me or spiraling out of control. The entire point of living at the foundation and working with Teddy was to increase his independence and confidence. If I had done anything to hurt that, I'd never forgive myself.

"I promise, I'm okay." Sam heaved a breath. "Can you give me my shirt?"

"Sure." I scooped our shirts off the floor, and we put them back on in the silence. I wanted to ask him one more time if he was okay. I wanted to hug him.

"Sam… This can go however you want. I can be whatever you want."

"I wish I could see your eyes."

"They're looking right at you," I whispered.

"Aw, Nicky. You make me feel…"

"Like what?"

"Like I'm still *me*. And everything is going to be all right."

"It is."

Sam gave a tiny shake of his head. He reached for me, his hand cupping my jaw. I leaned into his touch, pressing my lips to his hand.

"All this shit you're going through will work out. I know it. You're stronger than you think. And I'm wise as hell, so you need to listen to me."

Sam laughed softly.

He was still the sweetest, best guy in the fucking world. Sam hadn't lost the things that mattered. But he needed time to figure that out for himself.

"It's late." I stated the obvious. "I should go home."

"Yeah, I do need some sleep. Only one of us snoozed on the couch earlier."

"Hey! I'd watched the movie like a bazillion times before."

"Still." Sam shook his head. "Falling asleep with Gaga singing. The shame."

Laughing, I gave him a tight hug. This time I didn't hold the hug back. And it felt good to offer comfort. But if I couldn't hug my oldest friend in the world, who could I hug? I still wanted Sam, but above all I wanted to remain his friend.

Sam hugged me back and kissed lightly at the side of my cheek, making me warm all over.

"God, I was nervous about tonight," Sam confided. "And being with you again."

"Same. I almost turned around a bunch of times before I got enough courage up to knock on your door."

"For me, it was just like before a big game. 'Member how nervous I got? I was shaking and nauseous as if tonight was a tournament."

"If it was, you won."

"We won." Sam laced his fingers in mine.

The simple touch grounded me.

I didn't leave. Instead, we began to reminisce a while, recalling Sam's glory days on the field and some of the silly team pranks. Sam was always the hero, and I was always the troublemaker, but our stories shared a history. The dirt of the same small town was underneath our fingers and buried in our souls. Whether we had loved the town or hated it, the connection was there.

Hours flew by, and pretty soon, we'd talked half the night. It was like one of our old sleepovers. Only I was long past crashing on the floor in a sleeping bag and knew it was long overdue to go home to my bed.

"I should go," I said, not moving. "This time, I mean it."

"Yeah, I suppose…" Sam didn't move either.

"Hell, what's my problem? I keep saying I'm going to go, but I don't."

"That's okay with me." Sam ducked his head. "You could even spend the night."

My heart flip-flopped, beating wildly in my chest. "God, Sam, I wanna do that. I also don't wanna go super-fast with this and screw it all up."

We still had sparks. Hell, we had a whole damn fire between us. But I meant it when I said we could go slowly. I wanted to get to know Sam as an adult and for him to know me.

Sam heaved a deep breath. "You could just sleep with me in my bed. Nothing more has to happen tonight."

"Do you think that's realistic?"

"Maybe not." A wry smile curved his lips. "Hell, I'm less honest than you. You're right it isn't realistic. Truth is that I can't keep my hands off you. It's just that I've already waited so long for this chance. And I want you so badly, that's all."

I wet my lips, my willpower crumbling. I imagined us in Sam's bedroom, our bodies pressed close, Sam entering me for the first time. I made a needy, low sound, still imagining how good it was going to be between us. How I wanted Sam riding my ass until I was sore and— God help me—I couldn't say no.

Luckily, Teddy made a different choice for me, taking that second to lick our joined hands with a wet slobbering stroke of his tongue. Sam startled, jumping away.

"Holy shit. For a crazy second I thought *you* licked my palm."

I would lick his palm and every delicious part of him. All over. But his dog had definitely broken the hot and steamy mood, so I kept that to myself... for now.

I patted Teddy's head, even if he was a canine cock-blocker, still chuckling at his big pink tongue hanging out of his mouth.

"So, I'm really heading out this time."

"Right."

"I am."

"And I believe you," Sam laughed.

Reluctantly, I pushed off the couch to my feet.

He walked me to his front door. "Can we do this again soon? Maybe do a taco night?"

"Sure, with lots of heat and guacamole."

"Jalapenos it is. And I'll be making you one hell of a guacamole, so you better bring some tortilla chips and some kind of dessert."

"Deal." I grinned goofily. And even though he couldn't see it, Sam smiled just as stupidly back.

One day was all it took. I was already lost in Sam's smile.

"Thanks for putting the brakes on things. I do need to gain control in my own life before starting something serious with you. And we should learn all we can about each other again. But Nicky? I am sure of my feelings. And I want to get it right this time."

"Me too."

Sam's smile widened. "Until tomorrow, then?"

"Tomorrow," I agreed. But I was thinking about another word: forever.

Forever could arrive in just one day.

ABOUT SKYLAR M. CATES

THANKS FOR READING!

I hope you enjoyed Sam and Nicky's story. It's my pleasure to interact with my readers. You can find me on social media here:

Facebook: www.facebook.com/skylar.cates

Newsletter signup: http://eepurl.com/cxODzT

Or check out my other books on my Amazon page:

https://www.amazon.com/-/e/B00IY6NTG4

Sincerely,

Skylar

AFTERWORD

Many thanks to all of the authors who participated in this year's anthology. And a special thank you to Susan Scott Shelley for helping me to heard cats for this project.

As the attack on the rights of the LGBTQIA community continues, particularly targeting transgender individuals, I encourage you to find organizations in your own area that are on the front lines. Volunteer, donate, spread awareness, or do whatever you can to ensure the safety and prosperity of the most vulnerable among us.

Happy Pride!

Xio

Milton Keynes UK
Ingram Content Group UK Ltd.
UKHW041133030624
443552UK00001B/67

9 798869 392596